A LOVE WICKED AND BEAUTIFUL

"YOU'RE FORGETTING THAT YOU'RE MY WIFE," HE REMINDED HER. "AND THAT I AM A SOLDIER, RETURNED FROM THE FRONT!"

"I am forgetting nothing! We are bitter enemies, mi-lord, and no matter how I try, you refuse to believe me."

"You speak of war again. You chose to fight this particular battle. Well, I won, madame. You lost. And you are my wife."

"Your despised wife! Eric, for the love of God—"

"For the love of God, lady, no. I will not free you this night. If it is war, madame, than know the truth of it. If the rebels win, then I am a hero. If the king is victorious, then I am a traitor indeed. But this night, lady, I am the conqueror, and the rewards of the conquest are as old as time."

QUANTITY SALES

Most Dell books are available at special quantity discounts when purchased in bulk by corporations, organizations, and special-interest groups. Custom imprinting or excerpting can also be done to fit special needs. For details write: Dell Publishing, 666 Fifth Avenue, New York, NY 10103. Attn.: Special Sales Department.

INDIVIDUAL SALES

Are there any Dell books you want but cannot find in your local stores? If so, you can order them directly from us. You can get any Dell book in print. Simply include the book's title, author, and ISBN number if you have it, along with a check or money order (no cash can be accepted) for the full retail price plus $2.00 to cover shipping and handling. Mail to: Dell Readers Service, P.O. Box 5057, Des Plaines, IL 60017.

LOVE
NOT A
REBEL

*North American
Woman #3*

HEATHER GRAHAM

A DELL BOOK

Published by
Dell Publishing
a division of
Bantam Doubleday Dell
Publishing Group, Inc.
666 Fifth Avenue
New York, New York 10103

ISBN: 0-440-20237-X

Printed in the United States of America

Published simultaneously in Canada

October 1989

10 9 8 7 6 5 4 3 2 1

OPM

Prologue

BETRAY NOT THE HEART!

*Cameron Hall
Tidewater Virginia
June 1776*

"**A**manda!"

The door to the bedroom burst open just as she heard the distant thunder of the cannon upon the sea. Amanda leapt up from her bedcovers and dreams to streak across the polished floor to the full-length windows. There were ships in the harbor. Flying the British colors.

Danielle stood behind her. Another cannon boomed; Amanda saw the explosion of black powder upon the sea.

"It's Lord Dunmore! Aiming at the house!" Amanda gasped. She swung around to see that Danielle was watching her, her dark eyes condemning.

"Aye, 'Highness.' He's come for revenge against Cameron—no matter what service you've offered him."

Amanda's eyes flashed in offense at Danielle's blunt words while fury reigned in her heart. She had fulfilled her part of every bargain she had ever made with the royal governor. And still he was threatening Cameron Hall. After fleeing Williamsburg, he had asserted his royal vengeance from the sea, destroying so much of the coast! And now he was here.

Fear struck her heart. He knew! He knew about the weapons and powder that had been brought to the dock. He knew . . .

But *she* had not told him! She would never have gone so far. There had not been anything left to threaten her with, and she could not have done so . . . not now. Not against . . . Eric.

"Amanda—"

"Shush! I have to act quickly!"

Amanda ran to her wardrobe. "Help me!" she commanded Danielle sharply. She stepped from her nightgown, her fingers trembling as she tried to tie the knots of her corset.

Danielle came at last behind her. "What do you intend to do?"

"Send the slaves and servants and workers into the forest. I'll go out and speak with Dunmore—"

"And if your father is with him? Or Lord Tarryton?"

"God's blood!" she swore in panic, as no lady should. But the events of the last two years of her life had prevented her from being the lady she might have been. She stared hard at Danielle before the woman could offer reproach. "Stop! I cannot think—"

"You should have thought before taking on the role of spy, milady!" Danielle told her woefully.

"Leave off, mam'selle!" Amanda commanded her. She chose a shift and gown and quickly pulled them over her head, then stumbled into her garters and stockings. She gazed across the room to the now-empty bed and shivered in sudden fear of what was to come. What had she done? Should she be praying for British defeat or victory at this moment?

She didn't dare think. "My shoes," she murmured, sliding her feet into a pair of black leather slippers with rhinestone buckles. "Now, Danielle—" she began, but broke off. A British officer was standing in her bedroom doorway. Lord Robert Tarryton. She realized instantly that he had ridden in while the attack had been staged upon the sea.

"Hello, Amanda." He paused for a moment, looking her over from head to toe, then taunted, "Ah, Highness! You are a sight. I feel that I have waited a long time to claim you."

"You cannot *claim* me," she told him flatly, despising him.

She stood warily watching the man. He was handsome, with light hair and light eyes and beautiful lean features. Once she had thought him the most beautiful man she had ever seen. Then she had come to notice that there was a twist to his smile which marred his good looks, for there was a hint of cruelty to it.

Alas, she had discovered the truth of the man too late.

"We've come for you," he said.

Her heart quickened with horror. "I will not go with you."

"What? The Tory princess is suddenly casting her fate with the rebels? Don't be a fool. They say that Cameron knows you alerted us. Take care, lady! My touch would be ever more gentle than his!" Robert spoke swiftly as he moved into the room. He looked from the elegant bed to the wardrobe and the tables and the graceful length of the windows, and his jaw twisted further with some inner rage. The essence of the man who owned the room remained. And something of his power. Perhaps it disturbed Robert, Amanda thought.

It had often disturbed her.

"Eric knows!" She gasped suddenly. "But I did not betray—"

"Lady, you did. We are here. And I *have* come for you!" he told her with sudden fury.

Her mouth went dry as he came toward her. Danielle tried to block his way, and he shoved the Acadian woman to the side. In seconds he was before Amanda. She struggled with him, tearing her fingers down his cheek. He laughed as he caught her fingers, twisting them brutally. "Don't play your games, Highness. You called, and I am here."

"No!" She gasped, horrified. *She* was the one who had been betrayed. She knew that the arms had been stored at the docks, but she was no longer Highness! She had told no one.

She struggled furiously against him but he held her firmly in a viselike grip. Danielle lay on the floor where she had fallen, her eyes closed.

"You've killed her!" Amanda cried, trying to escape him. "God, how I hate you, loathe you—"

"The crone lives," Robert replied. "Let's go! Warn your people to get out. We're firing the house."

"I'll never come with—" Amanda began, then she realized what he'd said. *We're firing the house. Firing the house. Cameron Hall.* "No!" With a rage of energy she flung herself against him, tearing at his flesh again. His cheek bled as she fought for the house, bricks and chimneys and walls that suddenly seemed so desperately dear to her. "No, you can't burn the hall, you can't—"

He caught her fingers, his face white with fury except for the blood-red scratches her nails had left. "I have to fire the house," he said. "But . . ."

"But?" She cast back her head.

"Walk out of here with me. Come aboard the *Lady Jane,* your husband's *seized* ship, of your own free will, and I will see that the fires are set small, and that your people can come back and quickly put them out."

She stared at him in anguish, thinking quickly. She knew that she had little choice. He could drag her away screaming anyway.

"I'll walk," she said, fighting the tears that threatened to fill her eyes. They could not burn the house! They couldn't! She jerked away from him as he pressed a handkerchief to his face and prodded her forward.

The stairway was filled with the servants. Amanda swallowed hard and looked at them all—Pierre, Margaret, Remy, Cassidy. "You all must go outside quickly. They plan to burn the house."

"Look at 'er—the Tory bitch!" Margaret cried out.

Amanda's face went ashen. Robert stepped forward to strike the woman.

"No!" Amanda called.

He turned back to her, smiling, offering her an elbow. "Highness?"

She bit her lip and took his arm. Amanda didn't turn back as he led her down the stairs. Remy spit at her, but she stiffened her shoulders, remaining silent. She was a Tory. That was the truth. But the rest of this was some bitter irony. At the door she pulled away from Robert and turned back to the servants. "Get out. Get out, please! They'll—"

"This is a house of wicked rebellion against God's own anointed King of England! Leave it or die in the flames of hell!" Robert shouted, pulling her along.

But on the porch he paused, conferring with one of his lieutenants. The young man cast her a leering gaze, then nodded to his superior.

"The house, lady, will survive. The docks will not," Robert stated.

She could smell fire. One of the tobacco warehouses was ablaze. When the shed with the powder went, there would be explosions everywhere.

Robert dragged her along to his horse. The sun was shining high overhead and a multitude of birds were singing. The grassy slope had never appeared more green. But the fresh river air was polluted already by the acrid smell of smoke. Amanda could see far down the hill that Lord Dunmore had come in, that his men were rowing from his ships to the *Lady Jane,* at berth on the dock.

"Mount with me, lady. We will ride," Robert whispered in her ear. Her stomach roiled. That she had loved him once she could scarcely believe. She shoved away from him and leapt upon his mottled gray stallion. He followed behind her. In seconds they were racing down to the dock. Her hands were cold, but no colder than her heart. She had gone numb.

They came to a halt. Robert reached for her, lifted her down.

Suddenly a cannon boomed out on the river. The men in British navy uniforms who were milling about the *Lady Jane,* preparing her for sail, twirled around to see the new angle of attack.

"God's blood!" Robert swore. Dazed, Amanda stared out to the river. Ships were appearing. Ships that did not fly the colors of the British Crown.

"He's come!" Amanda gasped. He should have been in New York, or in New Jersey. Far, far away.

"Aye, he's come. And what will he do if he finds you? Hang you? Highness, you'd best pray that we are victorious! Now come!"

Robert set his arm about her, practically lifting her from her feet. Amanda seemed to skim the ground until they reached the *Lady Jane,* ready now to sail. They raced up the gangplank and aboard.

Captain Jannings, one of Lord Dunmore's men, bowed to her regretfully. "Highness! We are under attack. Fear not, I will see you into Lord Dunmore's hands, and then you shall be safely whisked away to England!"

Tears stung her eyes. Once she would have begged to hear those words. Now she had no choice. Her dreams had burned away in the fires that had raged on land.

Cameron Hall would remain standing. Yet from the moment the British had come for the arms stored in warehouses along the docks, she herself had been doomed. The truth would not matter now.

A cannon exploded near the ship. A man screamed as a shard of steel cut into his flesh. Battle was engaged, and they weren't even out into the open water.

The young captain raced to the fore, putting his glass to his eye. "Be damned, but it is *Cameron* riding the ship! Gunners, to your weapons. Sergeant, call the orders to fire!"

Robert grabbed her hand and hurried her toward the aft of the ship where the captain's large cabin commanded a fine view of the sea. He threw open the door and shoved her inside.

Then he followed her, closing the door behind him. His eyes were bright with the excitement of battle, with the pleasure of winning. "He will die, Amanda. I swear it."

She felt as if she would faint. Cannon boomed again, and even as they stood there, the room seemed to fill with the black soot of powder and fire. "You'll never kill him!" she vowed.

"I'll kill him, I swear it." Two steps brought Robert to her. She struggled as he swept her into his arms. "I'll kill him, and I'll have you naked beneath me while the blood still runs warm from his body."

She lashed out at him, and he started to laugh. "Pray to the saints that it is so, lady, for he knows of this treachery, and *he* will kill *you*!"

She shoved her knee into his groin with all of her strength. He staggered back. Amanda gripped the wall, ready to do battle again. But the door was thrown open and a uniformed Highlander stepped in. "Lord Tarryton! You are needed, your Grace. Milady! I am here to die for your protection! Lieutenant Padraic McDougal at your service."

Robert gritted his teeth against the pain and cast her a glance that promised sure revenge. Then he straightened, ever the military man, and exited the cabin. The Highlander nodded to her, closing the door and standing guard beyond it. Amanda clamped her hands over her ears as the cannon boomed again.

They would all die.

She raced to the velvet-draped windows and looked out to the water. A ship called the *Good Earth* was almost upon them, coming about with grappling irons. Men were leaping from the rigging to come aboard the *Lady Jane*.

Eric's ship.

His ship, which the British had taken . . .

And now she was on board. He would never believe her innocent!

With a cry of anguish she rose, determined to have none of it. They could not have traveled too far from shore yet. She needed to reach the deck and be quit of them all. Robert would betray her. He would never take her to Lord Dunmore, never see her safely to England.

And Eric would . . .

Kill her.

She hurried to the cabin door. Beyond it she could hear

the sound of clashing steel. Still she threw the door wide open, but then she halted in horror at all that she saw.

Battle had come hand to hand, and to the death. Even as she stood there, the captain fell dead, skewered by a blade in the hands of a mountain man. Amanda stepped aside as two boys, fighting with ropes and fists, crashed down before her. She nearly slipped in a pool of blood that oozed from the throat of a bearded redcoat. She looked forward, and her heart caught in her throat.

Eric was there.

On the bow of the *Lady Jane,* his rapier drawn, he and Robert were cast heavily into the fray. Both men knew their swordplay, yet no man was so subtle, so swift, as Eric Cameron. He moved forward suddenly, pushing Robert back, his black crackling silver beneath the sun despite the mist and smoke that hung over the deck. He was talented and dramatic, provoking Robert to angry lashes, taunting him then as he flecked his sword against his opponent's chin. His left hand remained behind his back as he moved again with speed and grace, demanding that Lord Tarryton cast down his sword.

"God's blood, someone take this man!" Robert screamed.

Five of Dunmore's finest navy men turned at Tarryton's call for help, daring opponents as they sprang forward.

She heard Eric's reckless laughter. He lived on the edge now, and enjoyed it. He cared nothing for danger for they had attacked his very home. They had attacked her! Amanda thought.

But he would not see it that way.

Her hand fluttered to her throat as she watched him fight. Silently she screamed as men thrust and parried. Not knowing what she did, she dipped low to the deck, grabbing up a sword.

Robert Tarryton had turned. Amanda watched as he leapt to the rigging by the mainmast, then catapulted into the sea.

"So you'd give fight, eh?"

A cheerful young man in West County buckskins and a bloody shoulder stood before her. She looked down at the sword in her arm. It was covered with blood too. She wanted to scream. She wanted to cast the sword down and back away screaming. She'd never seen bloodshed like this before. War had always been distant; battle something one heard of in glorious accounts that didn't mention the cries of the dying. She shook her head, but the lad had grown serious. "Milady, if you must give battle, then I shall engage you so!"

"Highness!" someone yelled out. "The woman must be Highness!"

Amanda held up her weapon in terror. She didn't want to kill the man, nor did she want to die in a pool of blood, there upon the *Lady Jane.* "No, I shall not fight or surrender!" she claimed, thrusting the sword forward in warning so that the lad fell back. Then she turned and raced blindly back toward the captain's cabin. Men streamed after her.

She raced through the door, breathless, slamming it closed behind her. Her Highlander was there, rushing forward to meet the enemy, carrying his loaded Brown Bess. He never lifted the weapon. A sword was thrust through his heart, and he came crashing down at Amanda's feet. "Dear God, no!" she cried, falling to his side, trying to staunch his wound.

It was over, she realized. There was silence on the deck.

But the echo of the shots had barely ceased, the ring of steel had just gone silent, when the door to the captain's cabin burst open, the wood shuddering as if it would splinter into a million fragments. A man stood there, towering in the doorway, framed by the combination of sea mist and black powder that swirled upon the deck. He was exceedingly tall, broad shouldered, lean in the hips, legs firm upon the deck. He stood silent and still, and yet from her distance, Amanda felt the menace of his presence, felt the tension hot upon the air.

Amanda's mouth went dry. She didn't know whether to exult in his surviving, or damn him for not dying.

She did not scream, nor even whisper a word. She looked up quickly from where she knelt at Lieutenant McDougal's side, still trying in vain to staunch the flow of blood that poured forth from his chest. McDougal was dead. There was really no more that she could do for him.

And she had to face the man in the doorway.

Amanda grabbed the lieutenant's Brown Bess, staggering up with the heavy and awkward five-foot gun. McDougal could help her no more, and she had never needed protection so desperately. She stared at the doorway, at the man who had come for her. Although she was determined to fight, still she trembled, for the look in his eyes made her heart shudder, as if a blade had cut cruelly into the very depths of her.

Cameron. Lord Eric Cameron. Or Major General Lord Cameron now, she thought, near hysteria.

"Eric!" she whispered his name.

"Highness," he said. His voice was deep and husky, sending shivers down her spine. Watching her, he removed a handkerchief from his frock coat and wiped clean the blade of his sword. She braced herself as he kept his eyes upon her and sheathed his sword at his side.

"How intriguing to see you," he murmured. "You, milady, should be tending the home fires. And as I am a special adjutant to General Washington, I should be with him. But how could I be when I received an urgent request from Brigadier General Lewis, commander of the Virginia militia, warning me that our arms and my very home were in danger. That we had all been betrayed."

"Eric—"

"Lord Dunmore, Virginia's gallant royal governor—who now decimates her coast—was driven from Williamsburg in the summer of 1775, but as you know so well, Highness, he took to the sea, and from H.M.S. *Fowey,* he descended upon the towns, harrying them in the name of the king. He always seemed to know so much of what was going on! Then on New Year's Day this year he burned Norfolk to the ground with the seventy big guns of his fleet, and he continued to haunt the Tidewater, attacking my very home, milady."

"If you would listen to me—"

"No, Amanda. I listened to you for too long. I kept believing that some sense of honor would keep you silent, even if we did not gain your loyalty. And now, well I know the full truth of it." Eric spoke so softly. Still she felt the sizzling heat and tension behind his words, the energy behind his quiet stance. "Put down the gun," he warned her.

Dread filled her. She had chosen her course. If she was not guilty now of the treachery he suspected, she had still chosen her own side in the conflict. She held her head high, trying not to show her fear. Once it might have been a game. Like chess. Check, and check again. But even when they had played and he had allowed her to seek certain advantages, the warning had been there. Nay, the threat, for he had told her that she would pay if he ever caught her betraying him.

And now that she was innocent at long last, she'd been caught!

He stood there so tall and unyielding. As the powder and mist faded, she saw him so much more clearly. His taut white breeches defined the rugged muscle and sinew of his thighs and the navy frock coat with the epaulets upon the shoulders emphasized the breadth of them. His hands were gloved, but she knew them well. Knew their tenderness, and their strength.

It was the power of his eyes that held her now. Those startling, compelling eyes. Silver and indigo steel, they stared at her with such fury that she nearly forgot that she held the loaded gun. Amanda could barely hold the unwieldy weapon, but she couldn't let him see that. She couldn't falter; she could never surrender.

She wanted to cry out. She wanted desperately to remind him that she had never turned her back on England, that she had always been a loyalist, and could only follow her heart, as he had followed his. But he was not angry because of her beliefs. He was angry because of all that he believed she had done.

"I am innocent of this!" she told him heatedly.

His brow arched with polite interest. "You are innocent —Highness?"

"I tell you—"

"And I tell you, milady, that I know full well you are a British spy and the notorious 'Highness,' for I oft fed you

misinformation that found its way to Dunmore's hands.
You betrayed me—again and again."

She shook her head, swallowing against the fear that
closed about her throat. He spoke with dispassion, but a
fire burning beneath his words brought terror to her
heart. She had never seen him like this. When she had
despised him, he had been determined and patient. When
she had been cold, he had been an inferno. He had been
there for her, always, no matter what scandalous truth he
discerned, he was ever there, a ferocious warrior to wage
her battles. She had known how to take care; she had
feared for her heart should she lose it to him.

And now that she was cast into that desperate swirl of
love and abandon, she was lost indeed. All that was left
was the tenacious grip with which she tried to cling to
some semblance of dignity and pride. She had to be
strong; she needed to remember how to fight.

Yet it was terrible to think that she must find the wit and
reason to battle him now. Never had he seemed more a
pillar of strength, filling the doorway, taller than all other
men in his boots and cockaded hat, striking with his hard
handsome features, his dark hair queued but unpowdered,
his stance so confident yet so fierce. And so determined.

"Give it to me, Amanda," he repeated. Low and husky
and deep, his voice seemed to touch her. To sweep over
her flesh. Assured, commanding, touched by the rawness
of the colonial man, yet with a trace of his Oxford educa-
tion, he was a contradiction. In a land the British often
considered to be peopled by criminals, Eric Cameron was
one of their own, but with all the strengths and rugged
power of the colonial. He knew the strategy of war, and he
knew, too, the skill of hand-to-hand combat. He had
learned how to fight from master generals—and from the
blood-thirsty Iroquois and Shawnee. He was like the country, made of muscle and sinew, wild and untamed, no
matter how civil his manner, no matter that they called
him "lord."

"Amanda!" He moved toward her.

"Get away from me, Eric!" she warned him.

He shook his head, and in his eyes she saw the depth of

his anger. She wanted to throw down the gun, to back away. All was lost this day.

"Now, Amanda! I warn you that my temper is brittle indeed. I almost fear to touch you, lest I strangle the light from those glorious eyes! I'll take the gun."

"No!" Her voice was barely a whisper. "Let me by you. Let me go. I swear that I am innocent—"

"Let 'Highness' go? Why, milady! They would hang me for the very act!"

His words were light; they were followed by a long determined stride in her direction. She backed away as he lunged for her with the finesse of the fencer. "No!" she cried. "I'll shoot you, Eric, I swear it—"

"And I do believe you, milady!" he countered, approaching her nonetheless, a mocking light of challenge in his eyes. "Shoot me, then, if you dare, milady! But take heed that your weapon be loaded!" He moved like lightning, catching the gun by the barrel, sending it flying across the room. The firing mechanism snapped; the gun went off, sending the bullet into the wall.

He stared at her, hard. And then he smiled slowly, bitterly. "It *was* loaded, milady. And aimed upon *my heart.*"

She had never seen his eyes colder. Never seen his lip curl with such disdain.

She faced him, thinking frantically. She needed to turn, to run. There had to be somewhere else to go. If she could reach the door, she could escape the ship. No other man would seek to stop her. She could cast herself into the Chesapeake Bay. Eventually she could reach the shore. Dunmore's ships were lost to her, Robert had kidnapped her just to desert her to her fate, but if she could swim to the shore, she could eventually make it north and find General Howe's troops. If she could just escape Eric this night! He would offer her no mercy, not this time. She knew that as she saw the cold and wary eyes.

"And now, Highness . . ."

"Wait!" Amanda swallowed hard. She feared that she would faint as a rush of memory swept over her, leaving her hot and trembling. She knew so much about him. She knew the searing hellfire of his passion, and she knew the

ice of his fury. Just as she knew the gentle sweep of his
fingers . . . and the relentless power of his will and determination. He could step forward now and break her neck
and be done with it, and by silver-blue rapier blades of his
eyes that struck upon her now, it seemed that that was
what he longed to do.

God! Deliver me from this man I love! she prayed in
silence.

"Wait for what, milady? Salvation? You shall not find
any!"

She stared at the gun, broken upon the floor. He had
seized it with such power that the heavy stock had shattered. She glanced at him one more moment, then she
burst into motion, determined to run, to risk any factor,
just to escape him.

She was not quick enough. His arm grabbed her, his
fingers winding into her hair. She screamed with the pain
of it and panicked as she was brought swirling back into
his arms. She fought his hold, squeezing her arms between
them, pummeling his chest. Tears of desperation stung her
eyes. She tried to kick him and quickly earned his wrath.
He caught her wrists and wrenched them hard behind her
back, and through it all she felt the simmering liquid heat
of his body, bold and vibrant and recalling echoes of the
past. She cried out as he pulled upon her wrists, and went
still at last, pressed against him, tossing back her head to
meet his eyes.

With one hand he held her wrists at the small of her
back while he placed his left palm against her cheek and
slowly stroked it. "So beautiful. So treacherous. But it is
over now. Surrender, milady."

She met his gaze. Something of all that had lain between
them touched her heart and seemed to skyrocket. Just the
touch of his strength against her seemed explosive. Once
love had flamed so fiercely and so strong! But their battles
had been as passionate, and now she did not know what
tempest ruled the blood that flowed within them and the
air that churned about them. Her eyes burned with tears,
but she could not give in now. Be it love, be it hate, what
burned between them demanded that she not falter now.

She shook her head and dared to offer him a rueful, wistful smile. "No surrender, my lord. No retreat, and no surrender."

Footsteps echoed upon a stairway and a second man came to a halt behind him. He was young, barely beginning to grow whiskers, and his eyes widened at the sight of her. "We've found her! Highness! She gave the ship and the intelligence to the British."

"Aye, we've found her," Eric said softly, and still his eyes bored into hers, with what thoughts she could not fathom. She did not look away, even with the young officer watching them. Then Eric muttered an oath and cast her from him. She nearly fell, but caught herself, and stood tall, backed against the paneling. She braced herself with her hands, and thought, How peculiar. The sea was so very calm she could scarcely feel the ship rock, and the room was alive with storms.

The young man suddenly let out a soft whistle as he watched her. "No wonder she played our men so false so easily!" he murmured.

Eric Cameron felt everything inside of him tighten like a vise at the man's words. She was still beautiful. More beautiful than ever. She was flush against the wall, cornered, yet still defiant. She was a perfect picture of femininity, of grace. So delicate and glorious as she stood, her breasts rising from her bodice with each breath, her flesh pale, as perfect as marble. She wore green silk with an overskirt and bodice of golden brocade. Her throat and shoulders were bare, and her hair was worn in soft ringlets that curled just over her shoulders. She was as cool and smooth as alabaster as she returned his stare, her eyes as green as the gown, her hair a startling and beautiful contrast with the shades of the silk and brocade. It was deep, deep red, sometimes sable, sometimes the color of the sunset, depending on the light.

He wanted to wrench her hair from the pins, he wanted to see it tumble down. He did not want to see her so silent, so beautiful, so still, so regal. Damn her. Her eyes defying him, even now.

"Aye," he said quietly. "It was easy for her to play men falsely."

"I wonder if they will hang her," the soldier said. "Would we hang a woman, General?"

Amanda felt a chill of fear sweep over her, and she swallowed hard to keep tears from rising to her eyes. She could see it. She would hear the drums beat. Hanging. It was a just punishment for treason. They would lead her along. They would set the rope around her neck, and she would feel the bristle of the hemp against her flesh.

Dunmore had sworn that he would have Eric hanged, were he ever to get his hands upon him. But Eric had never cared. Amanda wondered what fever it was that could fill a man with such haunting loyalty to a desperate cause. It was a passion that made him turn his back on his estates in England, risk his wealth and title and prestige and even his life. He had everything, and he was willing to cast it aside for this rebel cause of his.

She had risked her life upon occasion for her cause. Indeed, her very life might well stand on the line now.

The young officer stared at her still. He sighed softly again. "Milord, surely you *cannot* have her hanged!"

"Nay, I cannot," Eric agreed ironically, the silver and steel of his eyes upon her, "for she is, you see, my wife."

The man gasped. Eric turned to him impatiently. "Tell Daniel to set a course for Cameron Hall. Have someone come for this lieutenant. The Brits must be buried at sea; our own will find rest at home." He turned back to Amanda. "My love, I shall see you later." He bowed deeply to her, and then he was gone, the young officer on his heels. Two men quickly appeared, nodding her way in silence, and carefully picked up the body of the slain Highland lieutenant.

Then the door closed. Sharply.

He was gone. Eric was gone. The tempest had left the room, and still she was trembling, still she was in fear, and still she didn't know whether to thank God or to damn him. They had been apart so long, and now the war had come to them, and the battle was raging in her very soul.

Amanda cast herself upon the captain's bunk, her heart

racing. Through the sloop's handsome draperies and the
fine paned windows she could see the distant shore, the
land they approached.

Cameron Hall. Rising white and beautiful upon the hill,
the elegant manor house itself seemed to reproach her. It
looked so very peaceful! The British had set their fires, but
Robert had spoken the truth about the blazes. Obviously
those fires had been put out with very little difficulty.

No dark billow of smoke marred the house or the outbuildings. Only the warehouses on the dock seemed to
have burned with a vengeance. They were not so important. It was the house that mattered, she thought. She
loved the house, more than Eric himself did, perhaps. It
had been her haven in need. And in the turbulent months
that had passed, she had strode the portrait gallery, and
she had imagined the lives of those women who had come
before her. She had seen to the polishing of their silver,
she had taken tender care of the bedding and furnishings
they had left behind.

A chill swept through her suddenly.

He wasn't going to hang her. What was he going to do
with her? Could she vow that she would not leave the
house, that she would take no more part in the war? She
could never, never have set fire to the house. But he would
never believe that now.

She closed her eyes and heard the orders to dock. She
imagined the men, pulling in the *Lady Jane*'s sails, furling
them tightly as the ship found her deep-water berth. She
heard the fall of the plank, and the call of victory as men
walked ashore.

The patriots had needed that victory! The British were
heading toward New York, and Washington hadn't enough
troops to meet them properly. The colonials were up
against one of the finest fighting forces in the world.

Oh, couldn't he see! she thought in anguish. The British
would win in the end, and they would hang Eric! They
would hang him and George Washington and Patrick
Henry and the Adamses and Hancock and all those foolish, foolish men!

The door opened again. Amanda sprang up. Her heart

seemed to sink low in her chest. Frederick had come for her, the printer from Boston. Eric had saved his life once, and she knew Frederick would gladly die for him now.

"Where is Eric?" she demanded.

"Your husband will be with you soon enough, milady," Frederick said. "He has asked me to escort you to the house."

"Escort me?"

"Milady, none of us would seek to harm you." He was quiet for a moment. "Even if you are a spy."

"Frederick, please, I—"

His anguished eyes fell upon hers. "Oh, milady! Cameron Hall! How could you have betrayed his very home?"

"I did not, Frederick," she said wearily.

"Then—"

"I have no defense," she told him.

"Milady, I will take your word."

"Thank you." She did not tell him that her husband would not do so. She lowered her eyes quickly, feeling that tears sprang to them. If he had condemned her, if he had spoken with fury or wrath, it would have been easier.

"Come now," he said.

"Where are you taking me?" she asked him.

"Nowhere but to your own home, milady."

Amanda nodded to Frederick and swept through the cabin's narrow doorway. She climbed the ladder to the deck. As she came topside to the early-evening air, the chatter of the men died down, and one and all, they stared at her. They paused in their motions of cleaning the *Lady Jane*'s guns or in tying her sails. They were not navy but a ragtag outfit of militia men. She knew the men from the western counties by their buckskin fringed jackets, and she knew some of the old soldiers by the blue coats they wore, leftovers of the French and Indian Wars. Still others were clad differently, and she knew that they were the uniforms of the counties they had come from. Some were friends, and others were strangers.

She tried to steady herself to walk before them, and yet it did not seem that they condemned her too harshly. Someone began to whistle an old Scottish ballad. Then one by one they all began to bow to her. Confused, she nodded her head in turn as Frederick led her from the ship. She walked the plank to the dock.

The small coach awaited them. Pierre was driving. He did not look her way. Amanda walked to the coach and hoisted herself up, Frederick close behind her. She looked back to the ship. The old captain in a green rifleman's outfit saluted her.

She glanced quickly to Frederick. "I don't understand," she murmured.

Seating himself beside her, Frederick smiled. "All men salute a brave enemy in defeat."

"But they must hate me."

"Yes, some of them. But most men respect a fallen enemy who fights true to his or her heart. And those who do know the secret of 'Highness' might well wish that you had chosen your husband's side."

"I cannot help where my heart lies!"

"Neither can any man, milady," Frederick said. He was silent then. Pierre cracked the whip over the horse's head, and the wheels jolted over the rough path.

Amanda pulled back the curtain and stared up the expanse of verdant sloping ground to the mansion.

From the large paned windows to the broad porches, the house exuded the charm of the Tidewater. Amanda loved it; she had loved it from the moment she had first seen it. From the sweeping, polished mahogany stairway to the gallery with its fascinating portraits of the Camerons, she loved every brick and stone within the place.

The coach came to an abrupt halt. Pierre opened the door, still refusing to look at her. She wanted to strike him. She wanted to scream that none of it had been her fault.

He would not understand. She had left with Robert.

Amanda leapt from the carriage and started for the house, ignoring the servant. Frederick was quickly beside her, walking with her up the steps. He wasn't merely delivering her to the front door, she realized.

Frederick cleared his throat. "Lord Cameron will come to his chambers, milady."

Amanda looked at him and nodded. She thought about attempting to fly past him, to race into the woods that fringed the fields. She would never make it, she knew. Some of these people might still believe in her, and some of them loved her. But they loved her husband more.

And their cause was the cause of liberty, and not her own.

"Thank you, Frederick," she said, sweeping up her skirts and heading for the stairway. As she walked she heard his footsteps behind her.

She looked down and saw that the silk was stained with the Highland lieutenant's blood. She smelled of cannon fire and black powder.

She passed by the portraits in the gallery and felt as if they all, the Camerons who had come before her, stared down at her with damning reproach. *I did not do this thing!* she longed to cry out. But it was senseless. She was damned. She saw her own portrait and wondered if Eric would not quickly strike it from the wall. What other Cameron bride had ever betrayed her own house?

Finally Amanda stepped into the master chamber. Frederick closed the doors, and she was alone.

A rise of panic swelled within her breast. It hadn't been long ago that she had lain in the bed, dreaming. Spinning fantasies of the time when her husband would return.

Now she knew that he would return very soon, and she hadn't a fantasy left to believe in.

A soft cry of misery escaped her. She couldn't bear waiting for him, not here. Too many memories rested here. Memories of storms and fire and passionate upheaval, memories of laughter.

She had come here, determined to despise him. But from the first, her eyes had fallen upon his every movement. In the deepest anger she had watched him rise, watched him dress, or stand bare-chested before the windows, and even then, in the very beginning, some sweet secret thrill had touched her heart when she looked upon him, for he had been so fiercely fine, and he had wanted her with such blind, near-ruthless determination. He had wanted her so . . .

Once upon a time.

But now . . .

Her gaze fell upon the handsome bed that sat atop a dais. Beautifully carved of dark wood, draped in silk and brocade, it had always seemed a place of the greatest intimacy and privacy. She drew her eyes from the bed and looked up at the Queen Anne clock upon her dressing table. Nearly six. Night was coming at last.

But not Eric.

Amanda began to pace the room, too nervous to dwell on the future, too frightened to recall the past.

Darkness came.

Cassidy, Eric's ebony-black valet, came to the room, knocking before entering. He looked at her sadly.

"What? Have you come to hang me too, Cassidy?"

He shook his head. "No, Lady Cameron. Perhaps there was more than the eyes could see." He was her friend—but Eric's first.

Still, she smiled. "Thank you."

"I've brought wine and roasted wild turkey," he told her. He moved back into the hallway and returned, bearing with him a heavy silver tray. "And Cato and Jack are bringing up water for the hip bath."

"Thank you, Cassidy," she told him. She smiled awkwardly at him. His accent was wonderful, with traces of Eric's own enunciation, as acquired at Oxford. He was in white and black, very much a lord's gentleman. He was born a slave and had become a free man here.

She was no longer free, she realized.

She was a prisoner in her own room in her own house. More than any slave the Camerons had ever owned, she was a prisoner here. The slaves were allowed to earn their freedom if they chose. She would not have that luxury.

Cassidy said no more to her, but set the tray down upon the table. Jack and Cato, in the red, white, and green Cameron livery, came with water, and the bath was dragged out. She waited until the hip bath was halfway filled with the steaming water and then thanked the men. Her fight was not with them. Margaret might well call her a Tory bitch, but perhaps the others understood that life was far more complex than any neat little label.

"Where is Lord Cameron?" she asked Cassidy.

"Involved with affairs, milady. They plan to follow on the heels of Lord Dunmore and see that he is pushed from our coast once and for all."

Affairs . . . so he might not come back to her at all. She might spend day after day in this room, awaiting her sentence. She cleared her throat. "Is he . . . is he coming back, do you know? Or am I perhaps to be turned over to some Continental official?"

"Oh, no. Lord Cameron will come."

His words were not reassuring.

She wished that she *had* been dragged before some Continental court. Any man would deal with her more gently than her husband, she thought.

"May I see Danielle?"

"I am sorry, milady."

"Is she all right?"

"Yes, she is well."

Cassidy bowed to her and left with the others. The door closed. She heard a key twist, locking her in, and she sank down at the table and tried to eat. The food was delicious but she had no appetite so she sipped wine and stared at the darkness beyond the windows.

At length she realized that the bath water was growing cold and that the charred smell of her clothing and hair was distasteful. Glancing at the door, she felt her numbness leaving her as she wondered if her husband would return.

He could be gone for days, she reminded herself.

She finished the wine for courage, then shed her rich gown, hose, corset, and petticoats and stepped into the water. The warmth was delicious. She sank beneath the water to soak her hair, and scrubbed it thoroughly, as she scrubbed her flesh.

She could not wash away her fear or her thoughts. What would Eric think if he knew that she had bargained with Robert Tarryton to save the house? He would not believe it, or worse. He would think that she had sought to leave with Tarryton.

The evening was cool. Rising from the tub, Amanda folded a huge linen towel about herself and shivered, wishing that she had asked Cassidy for a fire. She walked to the window and pulled back the drapes. Down the slope by the docks she could see tremendous activity. Half the militia was camped out on their property, so it seemed.

God, give me courage! she prayed. And if you cannot, please let me disappear into the floorboards.

God did not answer her prayer.

She started, hearing a sound, and whirled around. Eric was there. He had come, opening the door in silence, standing there now in silence, watching her. Their eyes met. He turned and closed and locked the door, then leaned against it, his eyes fixed on hers once again. His tone was soft, its menace unmistakable.

"Well, Highness, it has come. Our time of reckoning."

Amanda's heart slammed against her breast. She wanted to speak but words failed her.

He awaited her reply, and when there was none, a crooked mocking smile curled his lip, and he walked toward her, dark, towering, and determined.

"Aye, milady, our time of reckoning at last."

A time of reckoning.

It had been coming a long while. A long, long while. Ever since he had first set eyes upon her that long-ago night in the city of Boston.

It had all begun then. The tempest of war.

And the tempest that lay between them. . . .

Part I

Tempest in a Teapot

I 🍁

"**W**hiskey, Eric?" Sir Thomas suggested.

Eric Cameron stood by the den window in Sir Thomas Mabry's handsome town house. Something had drawn him there as soon as the contracts had been signed. He stared out at the night. An occasional coach clattered by on the cobbled streets, but for the most part, the night was very quiet. The steeples of the old churches shone beneath the moonlight, and from his vantage point, high atop a hill, Eric could see down to the common. The expanse of green was dark with night, cast in the shadow of the street lamps, and as peaceful as all else seemed.

Yet there seemed to be a tension about the city. Some restlessness. Eric couldn't quite describe it, not even to himself, but he felt it.

"Eric?"

"Oh, sorry." He turned to his host, accepting the glass that was offered to him. "Thank you, Thomas."

Thomas Mabry clicked his glass to Eric's. "Milord Cameron! A toast to you, sir. And to our joint venture with your *Bonnie Sue*. May she sail to distant shores—and make us both rich."

"To the *Bonnie Sue!*" Eric agreed, and swallowed the whiskey. He and Sir Thomas had just invested in a new ship to sail to far-distant ports. Eric's stores of tobacco and cotton went straight to England, but with some of the recent trouble and his own feelings regarding a number of the taxes, he had wanted to experiment and send his own ships to southern Europe and even to the Pacific to acquire tea and some of the luxuries he had once imported from London.

"Interesting night," Thomas said, looking to the window as Eric had done. "They say that there's to be a mass meeting of citizens. Seven thousand, or so they say."

"But why?"

"This tea thing," Thomas said irritably. "And I tell you, Parliament couldn't be behaving more stupidly over this than if foolishness had been a requisite for representatives!"

Amused and interested, Eric swallowed most of his drink. "You're on the side of the rebels?"

"Me? Well, that hints of treason, eh?" He made a snorting sound, then laughed. "I tell you this. No good will come of it all. The British government gave the British East India Company a substantial rebate on tea shipped here. It's consigned to certain individuals—which will shove any good number of local merchants right out of business. Something will happen. In this city! With agitators like the Adamses and that John Hancock . . . well, trouble is due, that it is!"

"This makes our private venture all the more interesting," Eric pointed out.

"That it does!" Thomas agreed, laughing. "Well, we shall get rich or hang together then, my friend, and that is a fact."

"Perhaps." Eric grinned.

"Well, now that we've discussed business and the state of the colony," Sir Thomas said, "perhaps we should rejoin the party in the ballroom. Anne Marie will be quite heart-broken if you do not share a dance."

"Ah, Sir Thomas, I would not think to break the lady's heart," Eric said. He had promised his old friend's daughter that they would not tarry on business all night, that he would come back to the ballroom and join her. "Of course, her dance card is always filled so quickly."

Sir Thomas laughed and clapped him on the shoulder. "But she has eyes only for you, my friend."

Eric smiled politely, disagreeing. Anne Marie had eyes that danced along with her feet. She was ambitious, and a flirt, but a sweet and honest one. Eric was wryly aware of his worth on the marriage mart. His vast wealth would have made him highly eligible even if he had been eighty, his family pedigree would have stood him well had he rickets, black teeth, and a balding pate. He was not yet thirty, he had all his teeth, and his legs were strong and very straight.

Perhaps Anne Marie would catch him one day. He simply was not of a mind to be caught at the moment.

A tapping on the door was quickly followed by an appearance by the lady herself. Anne Marie was a soft blonde with huge blue eyes and a coquette's way with a fan. She smiled her delight at him and slipped her hand through his arm. "Eric! You are coming now, aren't you?"

"Let him finish his whiskey, daughter!" Sir Thomas commanded.

"I shall do so quickly," he promised Anne Marie. He swallowed down the amber liquid, smiling as she pouted.

Suddenly his smile faded as his gaze was caught by a flash of color beyond the open door. A strange sense of the French déjà-vu seemed to seize him as he caught first an impression, nothing more. Then the dancers in the hall swept by again. As a gentleman shifted to the left, he saw the girl who had so thoroughly caught his attention. Her gown was blue, deep, striking blue, with a full sweeping skirt and a daring décolletage trimmed with red ribbons and creamy lace. Against that blue, tendrils of her hair streamed down in a rich and elegant display of sable ringlets. They curved about her naked shoulders and over the

rise of her breasts, enhancing her every breath and movement. Her hair was so very dark . . . and then, with a
shift of light, it wasn't dark at all, but red as only the deepest sunset could be red.

His gaze traveled at last from her breast to her face, and
his breath caught and held. Her eyes were the most startling, purest emerald he had ever seen, fringed by dark
lashes. Her features were stunning, perfectly molded, lean
and delicate, with a long aquiline and entirely patrician
nose, high-set cheekbones, slim, arched brows. All that
hinted of something less than absolute perfection was the
wideness of her mouth, not that her lips were not rose,
were not formed and defined beautifully, but they held
something that cold marble perfection could not, for the
lower lip was very full, the top curved, and the whole of it
so sensual that even within the innocent smile she offered
her partner, there could be found a wealth of sensuality.
She wore a tiny black velvet beauty patch at the side of her
cheek, very near her ear, and that, too, seemed to enhance
her perfection, for her ears were small and prettily
shaped.

There was something familiar about her. Had he seen
her before? He would have remembered a meeting with
her. From this moment onward he would never forget her.
He had not moved since he had seen her, had not spoken,
yet he had never felt more startlingly alive. He had lived a
reckless life, mindful of his inheritance, but fiercely aware
of his independence, and women—virtuous and not so virtuous—had always played a part within it.

He had never known anyone to affect him so. To render
him so mesmerized, and so very hot and tense and . . .
hungry, all at once.

"Eric? Are you with us?" Anne Marie said, annoyed.

Thomas Mabry laughed. "I believe he's just seen a
friend, my dear."

"A friend?" Eric managed to query Thomas politely.

"Lady Amanda Sterling. A Virginian, such as yourself,
Eric. Ah, but she has spent most of the past years at a
school for young ladies in London. And perhaps you have

been at sea on those ships of yours when the young lady has been in residence."

"Ah, yes, perhaps," Eric replied to his host. So the woman was Lady Amanda Sterling. They had met, but it had been years before. Still, it was an occasion that neither of them should have forgotten. There had been a hunt. She had been a mere child of eight upon a pony and he had been longing for the very mature and beautiful upstairs maid at their host's manor. Young Lady Amanda had jostled her pony ahead of his and the result had been disaster with both of them being thrown from their mounts. And when he had chastised her, she had bitten him. He hadn't given a fig about Lord Sterling and had paddled her there and then. She had raged like a little demon, the child had.

The child had grown.

"Eric, may we dance?" Anne Marie prodded sweetly. "I promise an introduction. Father, do remind me from now on not to have parties when Mandy is our guest, will you?"

Thomas laughed. Eric joined in, and Anne Marie grinned prettily. Eric gathered his wits about him and reached politely for her arm. "Anne Marie, I am honored."

He led her out to the floor, and they began to dance. Anne Marie gave him a lazy smile as he swept her expertly about the floor, seeking out the woman who had seized his attention. He saw her again. Saw her laugh for her partner, saw the devil's own sizzle in her eyes. He thought that he recognized something of himself within that look. She would not be governed by convention, she would demand her own way, and fight for it fiercely.

The sound of her laughter came to him again and he felt a reckless fever stir within him. Come hell itself, and time be damned, he would have to have that woman.

Who was the man who caused her laughter, he wondered.

Anne Marie, watching him indulgently, answered the question that he did not ask. "That's Damien Roswell—her cousin," she said sweetly.

"Cousin?" He smiled. His hand tightened upon hers.

Anne Marie nodded sagely. "But—and this is a grave 'but,' I must warn you!—the lady is in love."

"Oh?"

Love so often meant nothing. Girls of Amanda Sterling's tender young age were in and out of love daily. Their fathers seldom let the affairs go past fluttering hearts and dreams.

Yet her eyes were wild, deep with laughter and secrets and passion. He smiled, thinking she was one lass who should probably be wed and quickly—to an appropriate person, of course.

"And he loves her," Anne Marie warned.

"Who is 'he'?"

"Why, Lord Tarryton. Robert Tarryton. 'Tis said that he has adored her for years, as she has adored him. She will become eighteen in March, and it is believed that he will ask Lord Sterling for her hand then. It is a perfect match. They are all loyal Tories, landed and wealthy. You're frowning, Eric," Anne Marie warned him.

"Am I?" Tarryton. He knew the man, if vaguely. The old Lord Tarryton had been a good Indian fighter, but Eric didn't think that this young Tarryton could hold a candle to his lamented father. Their properties were not so far apart that they had not met upon occasion, nor did the social organization of Virginia allow for much secrecy in private life.

There were rumors in very high places that Lord Tarryton was seeking a union with the widowed Duchess of Owenfield. As the lady was young and childless, dispensations could be made to give the title to Lord Tarryton.

"Aye, you're frowning! And you're very fierce when you do so. You take my breath away, you cause me quite to shiver and make me wonder what woman would dare to wish that you might court her!"

He grinned at Anne Marie's sweet dramatics and thought that they would always be the very best of friends. He started to assure her that she would dare anything she chose when he found himself staring over her shoulder instead.

Amanda Sterling had ceased to dance. Her young escort

was whispering earnestly to her near the door. She kissed his cheek, then watched as he retrieved his cloak and hat and discreetly disappeared into the night.

She stood still a minute. Then she, too, hurried toward the door, procuring a huge black hooded cape from the halltree, and then rushed out into the night.

"What the—"

"What's the matter?"

"Why, she's just departed."

"Amanda!" Anne Marie cried in distress. "Oh, how could she! If Lord Sterling returns . . ."

Eric glanced at her sharply. She was very pale, not acting at all. "He is about on business this night. Perhaps he will not come back—he sometimes stays gone." She paused, her eyes wide. Eric realized that Anne Marie was trying to tell him that Lord Sterling frequented the area brothels and left his daughter in Sir Thomas's care.

"If he comes back?"

"It is just that he is so . . ."

"I know Sterling," Eric said, waiting for more.

"I'm just always afraid that he shall—hurt her."

"Has he ever?"

"Not that I know of. But the way he looks at her sometimes . . . his own daughter. I do not envy her, no matter what her wealth or title. I pray that Robert marries her soon!"

Eric kissed her cheek. "I'm going out. I'll find her," he assured Anne Marie. She still gazed at him anxiously. "Wait up for me," he advised her softly. "I'll come back, I promise."

He offered her an encouraging smile and swept by her. He, too, went to the door after retrieving his cloak and his hat. He turned to Anne Marie and waved, and exited the house.

As soon as he was on the streets, he could almost feel the tension on the air and beneath his feet. This night, Boston was alive. He wondered just what was going on.

He called to the Mabry groom, and his horse was quickly brought to him. "Do you know anything about what is going on?"

Dark eyes rolled his way. "They say it's a tea party. A tempest in tea, Lord Cameron. Dark days is a-comin', milord! You mark my words, dark days is a-comin'!"

"Perhaps," Eric agreed. He nudged his mount forward. It was true, something was afoot tonight. He could hear men walking, men calling out.

Damien Roswell had gone into the night. And Lady Amanda Sterling had followed. Just what route might she have taken in these dangerous times? He nudged his mount on, determined to find her.

Frederick Bartholomew shivered as he hurried along the street. The night was cold, and a mist fringed the harbor, floating about the city lanterns, making the ships that sat in the harbor and at dock look ghostly.

It had been a quiet night . . . but now it was about to explode.

Frederick could see the great masts of the proud sailing ships that ventured forth from England to her colonies rise high against the night sky, seeming to disappear into the darkness and the clouds. The cold winter's water lapped softly against the sides of the ships. A breeze stirred, lifting the mist of winter, swirling about cold and certain, and still so quiet.

Then the peace of the night was broken. A shout rang out.

"Boston Harbor's a teapot tonight!" a fellow shouted.

Then their footsteps began to thunder. Dozens of footsteps, and the night came alive.

We must be a curious sight, he thought. There were fifty or so of them, streaming out of the mist and out of the darkness and through the cold of winter, toward the harbor ships. At first glance they would appear to be Indians, for they were half naked, bronzed, darkly bewigged, and painted, as if in warpaint.

They were at war, in a way, but they were not Indians, and it was not death they sought to bring to the ships, unless it was the death of tyranny.

They rowed out to the three British ships riding in the harbor and streamed upon them.

Frederick stood in the background then.

The head "Indians" were polite as they demanded the keys to the tea chests from the captains.

"All right, men!" came the command.

Frederick still remained in the distance, watching as his friends apologized when they knocked out the guards. Then he joined in; they all set to their tasks, dumping the contents of 340 chests of tea into the sea. Fires burned high against the darkness and the mist. The men went about their task with efficiency, unmolested, for it was unexpected by the British and condoned by the multitude of the citizens of Boston.

Frederick Bartholomew, printer by trade, quietly watched the tea fall into the sea. Beside him, one of his friends, Jeremy Duggin, chortled. "A fine brew we're making, strong and potent!"

"And sure to bring about reprisals," Frederick reminded him.

Jeremy was silent for a moment. "We'd no choice, man. We'd no choice at all. Not if we intended to keep the British out of our pockets."

"Lads! Hurry now. Swab down the decks, see that all is left shipshape! We've not come to cause real injury to the captains or the men—the tea has been our business, and that is all. Now hurry!"

The older men in the crowd had planned the action. The younger ones had carried it out with glee. Many of the boys were college students from Harvard. For some it was a prank, a lark.

Others saw what the future might bring, but all carried out the work, and to a man, they cleaned the ships when they were done.

The keys were politely returned to the captains.

"Away!" someone called. "Our deed is done. Let's flee! The troops will be out soon enough."

"Come then, Jeremy!" Frederick called. They were both oiled and slick, wearing buckskin breeches and vests. Frederick was starting to shiver violently. Out on the water, it was viciously cold.

"Aye, and hurry, man!" Jeremy said.

They climbed down to the small boats that would bring them to the dock. "A teapot she is! The harbor is a teapot tonight! She steams, she brews! And what comes, soon, all men will soon see."

It was one of their leaders shouting then, passionately, heartfully.

The British fighting force was estimated to be one of the finest in the world. If it came to war . . . Frederick thought.

If they were caught . . .

There were so many of them. The entire port of Boston had been with them, except for the British troops and the minority of loyalists.

The Indians reached dry land again. They were making little secret of their actions, marching to the grand old elm, the Liberty Tree. They would not hang for their deeds this night. The governor could not see that they all hanged! If the king had thought that Boston rebelled before, let him see the people after a heinous act like that!

"Back home, me lads! And a deed well done!" one of the leaders called.

Frederick tensed, for he was not done with his night's work. As the others began to drift away, returning to their homes or heading for their chosen taverns, Frederick stood waiting by the tree.

Two men soon appeared before him, one another printer, a man named Paul Revere, and one the wealthy and admired John Hancock. Hancock was a cousin of the well-known patriot Samuel Adams, but it was the seizure of his ship *Liberty* by the British that had turned him so intensely toward the cause of the patriots. He was a handsome man, richly dressed in gold brocade and matching breeches. "Have you come by the arms, Frederick?" Hancock asked him.

Frederick nodded.

"We still hope it'll not come to conflict, but the Sons of Liberty must now begin to take precautions," Revere warned him. Frederick himself had become involved because of Paul Revere. He had begun as an apprentice in the older man's employ. Now they were both kept busy printing pamphlets and flyers for the cause of freedom.

"They come from Virginia, sir. A good friend travels to the western counties and gets French weapons from the Indians there," Frederick said nervously. This was not like their tea party—this could be construed as high treason. "The wagon is down the street, near the cemetery."

"Good work, Frederick. And your Virginian is a good friend, indeed. Go ahead now, and the West County men will follow quietly behind you. If you see a redcoat anywhere, take flight. Sam has said that we've had a leak and that the Brit captain Davis knows we're acquiring arms. Go quickly, and take care."

Frederick nodded. He was anxious to return home. He believed passionately in his cause, but he believed, too, in the love he shared with his young wife and in the future he sought for his infant son. He'd tried to explain to Elizabeth that it was for the future that he had come out this night. They were a free people. They had won the right to representation in 1215 when the barons had forced King John of England to sign the Magna Carta. They were good Englishmen, even if they were colonists. It was not the idea of taxes they minded so much—it was the idea of taxation without representation.

No one really thought that it might come to war.

And yet, already, there were whispers of bloody, horrible conflict, of American fields strewn with blood . . .

He didn't dare think of blood, not now. He still had to make it to the wagon, and then home.

He hurried along the street, turning corners, moving in silence. He knew that he was followed, and he took care to allow the West County Sons of Liberty easily keep tempo with his gait and yet keep hidden.

At last he passed the cemetery. In the cold mist of the night, the sight of the weathered tombstones made him shiver. He was almost upon the simple wagon that held the French armaments. His breath came quickly. Before him he could see the shadowed figure of his contact. The figure saluted sharply, then hurried away to disappear into the cemetery.

Frederick's feet seemed to slap against the cobblestones.

He passed the wagon by and exhaled heavily. He was almost home. Suddenly he heard a flurry of footsteps. He turned about. There was a woman running down the street in a huge sweeping cape.

"Damien?" a female voice called.

Frederick's heart began to pound. She was not following anyone named Damien, she was following him! He ducked around a corner into a lamplit street and started to run across it, then he paused. There was a sentry out. A sentry in a red coat.

"Halt!" the soldier cried.

Never—come death or all of hell's revenge, he could not halt.

He streaked across the road. Then he heard the woman calling out. "No! Oh, no!"

A Brown Bess was fired, but though he did not pause to look, Frederick was certain that the woman had caused the sentry to lose the precision of his aim. He was struck, but in the shoulder. He barely suppressed a scream as the bullet tore into him.

He clasped the injury with his good hand and sagged against a brick building. He could hear the sentry arguing with the woman, and he could hear the delicate tones of the woman's voice. Who was she, and why was she saving him?

He closed his eyes and thanked God for that small favor, but when he tried to open his eyes again, he discovered that he could barely see. He was falling, falling against the building and toward the mud beneath him.

He heard the sound of hoofbeats.

There was a horse pounding down the street. Frederick tried to push away from the wall. He had to find a place to hide, and quickly.

He staggered into the road. Looking up, he could see the spire of the Old North Church rising out of the mist. Or was the mist in his eyes? He was falling.

He would never see Elizabeth again. He would never cradle his infant son in his arms again. Was this, then, the price of liberty? Death and bloodshed? He would never see her face again. He would never see her smile, he would never feel the tender caress of her lips against the heat of his skin.

The rider was upon him. Frederick threw up his arms as a great black stallion reared before him. "Whoa, boy, whoa!" a man called out, and Frederick staggered back. The massive animal came to a rigid halt, and the rider leapt from his back.

Frederick fought to stand but slumped to the ground instead. The man coming toward him was tall and towering, and wearing a fine black greatcoat trimmed with warm fur. He wore fine boots over impeccable white breeches and a crimson frock coat. His shirt was smocked and laced. Dimly Frederick realized that he was not just a man of means, but a man with an aura of confidence and the assured and supple movement of a well-trained fencer or fighter. Dressed in his buckskin and paint, he had come across a member of the nobility.

Now he would not even die in peace. He would be dragged into prison, tried by a puppet jury, condemned by the king to be shot or hanged by the neck until dead.

"What in God's name—" the stranger began.

"Aye, in God's name, milord, for the love of God, kill me quick!" Frederick cried.

As he reached out, trying to ward off an expected blow, he saw the stranger's face. It was a striking face, composed of steel-fire eyes, a hard jaw, and strong cheekbones. He was dark-haired and wore no wig. His very presence was menacing, for he was not just tall but extremely well muscled for all that he gave the appearance of a certain leanness.

"Hold, boy, I've no mind for murder in the streets!" the stranger said, a touch of humor upon his lips. "You're no Indian, and that's a fact. I can only determine that you were in on the trouble at the harbor. Is that it?"

Frederick remained stubbornly silent. He was doomed anyway.

"Ah . . . perhaps there is even something worse," the stranger murmured.

"Search this way!" came a shout from the street. "I'm sure I've seen one of them!"

"Wait!" Frederick could hear the woman's frantic voice. The stranger stiffened, hearing it too. He seemed puzzled.

"Redcoat coming," the man murmured. "We'd best get you out of here, boy. I've business to attend to, but still . . . I'm wondering how badly you've been hurt. Now first . . ." He took off his cloak and wrapped it around Frederick.

"I'm not a boy. I'm married and I've got a child."

"Well, you're one up on me then, lad. Come on, then, take my shoulder, we'll have to move quick."

"You'll turn me in—"

"And leave your wee babe an orphan? No, man, the British will have their revenge for this night—a blind man would know that. But I can't see why your life should be forfeit."

Frederick was not a small man, but his strange deliverer swept him up into his arms and quickly slung him over saddle on the flanks of the black stallion. He mounted the horse behind Frederick and then paused briefly again. "I dare not go back by Faneuil Hall. We'll have to move westward."

Breathing desperately against the pain in his shoulder, Frederick swallowed hard. "My house, milord, is just down the street."

There. He had done it. He had told this man where he lived. He might be bringing danger down upon Elizabeth and the baby. He might have sealed their fate.

"Point me onward, and I will see you home."

But before Frederick could do so, the sentry rounded the corner with the woman in the cloak following close beside him. "Sir! A man is lost, I tell you, and you must give up this ridiculous manhunt to help me!" the feminine voice cried.

The sentry stood dead still staring down the cobbled street to where Frederick sagged atop the horse. Frederick's rescuer stepped forward. "Amanda!"

Frederick could see that she stared at him blankly, but perhaps the sentry did not fathom the look. The man stepped forward, drawing her toward him. "My betrothed, Officer. Her father would be horribly distressed if he knew that she was roaming the streets. He would charge me with negligence, and . . . well . . . My friend, have a heart. Were you to report this, my lovely prize might well be snatched from my very hands."

"What? Your betrothed—" she began in protest.

"Yes!" he snapped, narrowing his eyes. "She has lapses!" the man said quickly, and he caught hold of her with force, pulling her against him in a fine semblance of desperate affection. Frederick heard his urgent and commanding whisper. "If you wish your Damien well, you will shut your mouth now!"

She went stiff, but still. "Take the lady, milord, and save me some time and strength!" the soldier complained. "I'm looking for a dangerous, armed rebel. I followed his trail—who is that up on your horse?" he said with sudden sharp suspicion.

"My friend has partied too heartily this night. We've been at the home of Sir Thomas Mabry, and well . . . young fellows do imbibe too freely upon occasion. Isn't that right, Mandy?"

She went very stiff, but agreed. As she smiled to the sentry, Frederick saw that she was very beautiful. "It was quite a party, Officer," she murmured.

"There's parties all about tonight, so it seems!" The sentry saluted the man. "Milord, then, if you've things in hand, I'll be on my way."

"Quite right! Thank you."

The sentry moved on. His footsteps fell upon the cobblestones, then faded away.

"Who are you, sir, and what do you think you're doing?" the woman hissed. "Where's Damien? And what do you know about him?"

"I only know, mam'selle, that you were about to lead the king's men straight to him."

"And what difference would that make?" she demanded heatedly.

"I don't know, nor can I care. This man needs help."

"Help! He's been shot! Oh, my God! He's one of the rabble, one of the dissidents—"

"He's a bleeding human being, milady, and you'll help him since you're here! Then I'll see you home!"

"I don't need you to see me anywhere—"

"You do need me, milady. And I need you at the moment. Come, let me put my arm about your shoulder and sing. That should see us as far as this poor man's place. Frederick! You must lead us, for I don't know where we're going."

There was no choice. Frederick told him the number of his house, and they hurried onward. They could still hear the soldiers running blindly about the streets. The night was coming more and more alive as news of the night's deed spread quickly from house to house.

Soldiers passed them again. The man cast his head against the woman's shoulder and stumbled, singing.

"Stop it, you lout!" the woman cried.

"Ah, Mandy, love, drunken lout—it's a drunken lout I am. 'Scuse me, Officer!" He stumbled, looked about sheepishly, and pulled the woman against him again, but led the horse along with perfect direction. The soldiers snickered —and left them alone.

Frederick could almost hear the woman's teeth grate, and if he didn't hurt so badly, he'd be laughing. What were they doing with him, he wondered, for they were aristocrats, the two of them. Alive in a sea of the Sons of Liberty.

It was a patriot's city! Frederick thought proudly, and then he wondered again at the man who carried him homeward. He winced. This man was a lord.

But his accent sounded a bit . . . colonial. It was cultured, it wasn't a northern accent, it had a softer slur to it. Maybe there was hope. Why, George Washington, a growing power in Virginia, was friends with Lord Fairfax, a man of importance very loyal to the crown. The time would come when a man had to choose sides. It would come soon.

The man reined in on the horse quickly as they stopped before the house. Frederick didn't realize how weak he was until he was lifted bodily from the black stallion. "Help me!" the man demanded quickly of the girl. She complied, seething, helping as Frederick fell from the horse into the man's arms.

Quickly, competently, the man brought him to his door and knocked upon it.

Elizabeth came and opened the door. Frederick tried to rise against the stranger's shoulder. He saw her face, saw her soft gray eyes widen with alarm, but then she responded ably, drawing them into the small but comfortable home where they lived.

"Frederick!" she cried when the door was closed against the night.

"He's taken a shot in the shoulder, and he drifts in and out of consciousness," the stranger was explaining. His voice quickened. "We need to pluck the bullet out—he's probably got a broken arm and collar bone, but ma'am, first, we need to wash away the paint, in case of a visitor."

"The paint!" The girl gasped.

Elizabeth gaped at the strangers for a moment. The girl was stunning, well dressed, beautiful. There was no doubt of the man's prestige and power, for though his clothing was not overly elegant, the cut and quality were unmistakable.

"Let's lay him down, shall we?" the man said softly.

"Oh, oh! Of course!" Elizabeth agreed.

Frederick drifted in and out of reality as they laid him out and bathed him. He was offered a bottle of home-distilled whiskey, and he drank it deeply. Then the man was digging into his shoulder for the bullet and Elizabeth, with tears in her eyes, was clamping her hand over his mouth and begging him to silence.

"Let me," the girl said suddenly. Elizabeth and the man stared at her. She shrugged. "I've some skill."

"How?" the man asked her.

She shrugged dispassionately. "My father has been shot upon occasion," she said. She smiled at Frederick and brought the blade of a knife against his flesh.

Frederick passed out cold.

Eric watched with a cool assessing gaze as Lady

Amanda Sterling removed the bullet from the young man's shoulder. Her touch was both gentle and expert, and she murmured that it was best that he had lost consciousness, for he would feel no pain. "There's no break in the shoulder, I'm quite certain." She glanced at Elizabeth who stood by, wringing her hands upon her apron, tears in her eyes. "Cleanse the wound with alcohol, and I'm sure that all will be well."

Elizabeth Bartholomew fell down upon her knees, grasping Lady Sterling's hands. "Thank you! Oh, thank you—"

"Please!" Amanda Sterling's beautiful face flushed to a soft rose. "Don't thank me! God alone knows how I have come here, and I intend to leave now. This is a bed of traitors—"

"You are good, lady! So kind—"

Amanda Sterling, her hood fallen back, her hair glistening a glorious red in the firelight, pulled Elizabeth to her feet. "Please don't. I'm leaving, and I—"

"Lady Sterling would not dream of betraying you," Eric said firmly. Amanda glanced at him quickly. He saw the fury and defiance in her startling emerald eyes, but she did not deny his words.

"Warn your husband that he is a traitor against the king," she said to the woman.

"But you will not turn us in."

"No." She hesitated a moment. "No, you've my word, I shall not turn you in."

Eric stepped forward, taking her arm. "I'll be back," he told Elizabeth. "I shall return Lady Amanda—"

"I can return well enough on my own—"

"The Sons of Liberty are on the streets, milady, as well as British soldiers—as well as some common rapists and thieves ready to take advantage of the situation. I promised Anne Marie that I would find you, and for her, I shall return you."

He set his hand upon her with a force she could not deny. She seemed to sense the implacable determination in his words, so she merely stared at his hand, gritted her teeth, and agreed. "Fine."

She swept around, then paused, looking back to Elizabeth. The young wife now knelt by her husband with such a look of love and anxiety in her eyes that even Lady Sterling seemed to soften. "Keep him well," she murmured, and exited quickly to the streets.

Eric followed her, catching her arm when she would have walked ahead. She spun about, staring at him with her chin and nose regally high. He smiled. "Did you ride?"

"No, I—"

His voice deepened harshly. "You have been walking all this distance on a night like this? What an idiot! You could have been robbed of that splendor, stripped naked, raped, killed!"

"You are crude!"

"You are a fool."

She tried to wrench her hand from his hold. He had already released her to set his hands about her waist and throw her up atop his horse. Before she could protest he was mounted behind her. Her back went very stiff. "How do I know that you are not about to rob, rape, or knife me, sir?" she demanded coolly.

"Because I am worth far more than you are, I prefer my women warm, willing, and talented, and murder simply isn't among my decadent hobbies." He nudged his horse into a canter. She twisted her face against the chill of the night, shivering as she raised her voice so that he might hear her.

"You may take me back to the Sir Thomas's, milord, but it will do you no good. I must find Damien."

Eric hesitated. He had an idea where young Roswell might be, if he was in any way involved with the dissidents. He reined in so sharply that she crashed back against him. The sweet scent of her hair teased his nostrils and the shocking warmth of her body lay flush against his.

"Milord—" She gasped, but he ignored her, nudging his heels against his mount's flanks and leading the animal toward the left.

"We'll find Damien then," he said.

They rode through the streets until they came to a tavern. The street was very quiet there, the light within was dim. Eric dismounted. "Don't move!" he ordered her. Then he turned and entered the tavern.

A multitude of men were there, engaged in soft and quiet conversation. There were no drunks about, just working men in their coarse coats and capes and tricorns, huddled about the meager warmth of the fire. At his entrance, all eyes turned to him. Several faces went pale as the quality of his clothing was taken into account.

Someone rushed forward—the barkeeper, he thought. "Milord, what is it that we can do—"

"I need a word with Mr. Damien Roswell."

"Milord, he is not—"

"I am here, Camy." The handsome young man who had partnered Amanda in the dance stepped forward. He stretched out his hand. "You're Lord Cameron. I've heard much about you."

Eric arched a brow. "Have you?"

"Why were you looking for me?" Damien asked carefully.

Eric cleared his throat. "I am not. A lady is."

"Amanda!" He gasped. "Then she knows . . ."

"She knows nothing. But perhaps you should come along."

Damien nodded instantly. He and Eric exited the tavern together without a backward glance.

From atop Eric's horse, the girl cried out. "Damien! You had me so worried!" She leapt down gracefully and ran forward.

"Amanda! You shouldn't have followed me."

"You are in trouble, off on your own," she said worriedly.

Eric stepped back on the porch of the tavern, watching the two together. Damien turned to him. "Thank you, milord. Thank you most fervently. If I can ever be of assistance to your—"

"I'll let you know," Eric drawled calmly. He tipped his hat to Lady Amanda. "Good evening, milady."

"Milord," she said stiffly. Had she been a cat, he thought, her back would have been arched, her claws unsheathed. He had not made much of an impression. He smiled deeply anyway, feeling as if he burned deep inside. He did not mind her manner, and he was willing to wait. She did not know it as yet, but she would see him again. And again. And in the end, he would have his way.

He swept his hat from his head and bowed low, then mounted his horse.

"Who was that arrogant . . . bastard?" he heard her demand of her cousin.

"Mandy! I'm shocked. What language!" Damien taunted. "Who was he?"

"Lord Cameron. Lord Eric Cameron, of Cameron Hall."

"Oh!" She gasped. "Him!"

So she, too, had remembered their meeting long ago. Eric smiled and led his mount into the darkness of the streets. They would meet again.

II ❧

When Frederick came to, he was still on the sofa, he could hear the fire crackling and burning in the hearth, and he could feel its warmth.

There was a certain commotion at the door. Elizabeth and the man were both standing there, talking to the redcoat before them.

"I assure you, Sergeant," the man was saying, "that I know nothing about any tea party at the harbor, nor do I know anything about any smuggled and hidden arms. And I assure you that this young lady knows nothing of it either. Indeed, I would appreciate some discretion here. I visited here earlier with a lady friend. You know how difficult a certain privacy can be. Then I returned, for I'd hoped to convince the Bartholomews to move down to Virginia to take positions at Cameron Hall, but Frederick's printing business has been quite a success."

"He prints traitorous garbage!" the sergeant insisted, then he added quickly, "Lord Cameron, sir, that is."

"What? Is the man not still a free Englishman with rights! Come on, man, what has this to do with anything? I'm telling you, Sergeant, yes, we've been having a tea party. Elizabeth and I were sipping a warm berry brew when you so rudely interrupted us. I wish privacy now. I have been harassed quite enough for the night, as have these good people, I am quite sure. Am I understood?"

"Oh, quite, milord, yes!" The sergeant snapped to a salute. "Yes, milord. Good night, milord."

Milord. Milord Cameron. Frederick smiled. He had heard of the man. He had fought, leading a band of Virginians, in the French and Indian Wars. He sat on the Governor's Council in Virginia. He was immensely wealthy, with estates in the colonies, the islands, and in England. But he had stood in the line of battle again and again, defying bullets, so they claimed. He could do more than shoot Indians, he could speak their language. He was powerful, yes, and by God, he was a member of an elite peerage, but he was an American, too, so it was sworn. Virginia was not Massachusetts, the seeds of discontent were not so fully sown there as here, but she was a great colony, creating great statesmen.

This man sat on the Governor's Council instead of in the House of Burgesses. The Councilmen were appointed for life, a great honor. He should be loyal to the Crown. And still, Frederick realized, Lord Cameron had saved *his* life.

The door was shut and bolted. Elizabeth fell against the door, trembling. "I shall faint—"

"You mustn't madam, I beg of you!" he said, and drew her up.

"You've saved us once again. Oh, milord, our lives are yours! Whatever you wish—"

"I wish a long, potent drink!" Eric laughed. "And a word with your husband."

Elizabeth nodded and glanced worriedly toward Frederick. Then she hurried toward the kitchen, and Eric approached Frederick. He pulled up a chair and straddled it, and stared at the printer. "I want to know about it. I want to know about tonight."

"But you must know—"

"I know nothing. I'm a Virginian. I'm here on business, and I stumbled upon you."

Frederick inhaled and exhaled. The man was tough, and he wanted answers.

"We didn't want it to happen—"

"Don't tell me that. The trouble has been brewing here since the Boston 'Massacre' in 1770."

Frederick exhaled. The Boston Massacre had actually been a street fight. About fifty citizens, infuriated by the soldiers within the city, had attacked a British sentinel. Captain Preston, the British officer in charge, had brought more soldiers, and they had fired into the crowd. Three people were killed, eight were wounded, and two of the wounded later died. A town meeting had been called, and the British had agreed to let the captain stand trial for murder. John Adams and Josiah Quincy had been his defense counselors, and he had been acquitted of murder—it couldn't be proven that he had ordered his men to fire into the crowd. Two soldiers were found guilty of manslaughter, and they were branded on their hands and dismissed from the service. Speechmakers and politicians, eager to keep sentiment high against the British, had termed the event the Boston Massacre.

"We did not intend this!" Frederick insisted. "Milord," he added quietly. Then he lifted his chin. "Ask around, among your friends, and you will discover the truth. The British offered the British East India Company a rebate for tea sold in America. The tea was to be consigned to certain individuals. There would have been a monopoly on the tea, and our local merchants would have been put out of business. It was a government move to enforce the tea tax, milord, can you understand? The Committee of Correspondence refused to permit these tea-laden ships to land, and we appealed to Governor Hutchinson to let the loaded ships return to England. The governor refused. There was a meeting, a huge meeting at the Old South Meeting House. We went to the governor again, and again he refused to receive the mass of people." Frederick lowered his head. "At a signal from Sam Adams, we boarded the ships and dumped the tea."

Eric was silent for several long seconds. "There are going to be repercussions, you know."

"Of course."

"We move ever farther and farther away," Eric murmured. "God, how it hurts. But of course, they don't want to hang you for your part in this tea party. They want to hang you for smuggling arms to use against the Crown. So —tell me. What of these arms?"

Frederick started. "Arms?"

"You are guilty. Of storing arms."

Frederick wet his lips nervously with his tongue. He knew all about the arms. There was no sense denying it. "We are not planning anything. The arms are not to be kept in Boston. I should not tell you more."

"You're right—you should not. Not now."

Frederick looked at the man, and he tried to rise. But Eric wasn't looking his way, he was staring into the flames. The fire caught the curious color of his eyes. They had seemed dark, indigo. Now they looked like steel. They burned with startling, silver flames. He was lost in thought, but Frederick could not read those thoughts.

"Tell me, is a man—a Virginian—named Damien Roswell involved in any of this?"

Frederick inhaled sharply. "Milord, turn me in if you would, but I will not give you names—"

"Never mind. You have given me what I want."

Elizabeth came, and offered Lord Cameron a glass of whiskey. Lord Cameron flashed her a quick smile, and Frederick was somewhat startled by his wife's reaction. She flushed deeply, and her eyes fell over the length of him as he straddled his chair. Even at rest he was laden with energy. There was a pulse about him. In silence he spoke of tempest and passion. His eyes portrayed intelligence, fire, and wisdom; his mouth betrayed a great sensuality and an undaunted love of life.

"You'll not turn me in now, will you?" Frederick whispered. Lord Cameron looked his way, and the printer real-

ized that the man was not ten years his senior, he was
hardly thirty, if he was that.

"I'd hardly bring you here, act out such outrageous performances, and lie to a soldier to turn you in," he said.

"What of—what of the lady who saved my arm?"

He shook his head slowly, his eyes clouding over. "No.
You have nothing to fear from the lady. Not for this night's
work."

"She is so kind—"

"She is not so kind, my friend. But though she refuses to
face it, she has a stake in all that has occurred. You will be
safe from all that she knows."

Frederick nodded, then spoke to him in blunt amazement. "You're a lord, sir. You've a great deal at stake here."

"I have promised you that I will not turn you in. And my
word is seldom doubted, sir!"

"Oh, bless you, milord! Again and again!" Elizabeth
cried passionately, and she fell to her knees.

Eric smiled, touched her hair, and looked at Frederick.
"You've far more at stake than I have, lad. You have this
lovely woman, and you have her love, and you have your
son. What you possess now is precious. You must take
care with your decisions in the future."

"My son is the future, sir, and it is for him that I make
my decisions. I am not a lord, I have no memory of a
motherland, nor did my father, or his father."

Eric laughed, rising. "Dear sir! I'll have you know that
my ancestors settled the Hundred when Jamestown was
still in its infancy." He was silent for a moment. "Our
blood has been shed for this land, my father and my father's father and his before him, all lie cradled in Virginia
earth." He shrugged, and Frederick saw more than the
strength and severity of the man, he saw his humor and
his youth and all that was charismatic and powerful in his
lazy smile. "Perhaps I do have much at stake, for I do love
my land, and I would fight, and die gladly, to hold it."

"Who would you fight, milord?" Frederick asked.

"God knows, lad. God alone knows. Perhaps we should
all pray for peace. Elizabeth, may I have my greatcoat,
please?"

Elizabeth brought his coat and set it over his shoulders. He started for the doorway.

"Milord!" Frederick said, imploring him back.

Eric turned. Frederick offered him his hand. "I thank you, Lord Cameron. I am your servant, for all of my life."

Cameron shook his hand. "My name is Eric. And it is good to have friends, Frederick. I shall remember that I have friends here."

"Aye, milord—Eric. And that you do. The very best of friends."

With a smile, Eric turned and strode out of the house and into the night. Elizabeth sank down by her husband's side, and together they watched as he closed the door. She trembled slightly, but he said no word to her, and they both knew that their lives had been strangely touched. Greatness had descended upon them, and had done so with mercy.

Eric mounted Joshua, his great stallion, but pulled in on the reins.

The last of the soldiers' footsteps had gone still, and the night was coming quiet again. Cold and quiet and touched with mist. The spires of the churches rose high against mist and darkness to touch the heavens, and the city lamps were burning low. There was quiet all about.

There would never be quiet again, Eric thought. This particular tea party would be known about from the length and the breadth of the country, and its cry of rebellion would stretch across the Atlantic Ocean. In his pursuit of Lady Sterling he had seen the tea floating in the harbor, and he felt both a horrible, wrenching pain and a startling excitement. They were a new people. A new breed of men. They would be given the rights and liberties of English men by the English government, or, by God, they would forge their own liberties.

I have become a dissident this night! he thought. But maybe he had not, maybe the seeds of dissatisfaction had been sown in him long ago, perhaps during the French and Indian Wars, or the Seven Years War, as it was known on the Continent.

War. It could come to war again. . . .

No one wanted to speak of war. Even the worst of the radicals were careful not to speak of it.

Eric sighed deeply. It didn't matter. The whisper was on the wind, and it was growing louder and louder. Virginia's ties to England were firm and fast. The Virginian Patrick Henry spoke passionately about reform and against illegal representation. But not even he spoke aloud about war.

Eric glanced toward the printer's house and smiled ruefully to himself. The lad and his young bride were so in love, and so passionate, and so ready to die for a cause. He knew their feelings, though, for he would die, and gladly, for his land. Frederick's question was a good one.

Just who would he battle?

He thought of Lady Sterling, of the passion in her eyes when she warned Elizabeth that her husband was a traitor. Her mind was set! She was loyal to the Crown. Still, Eric knew instinctively that Frederick was in no danger from her. She did not know that her cousin Damien was procuring arms for the Sons of Liberty, but she suspected something. And because fear for him lurked within her breast, she would keep quiet, no matter what her loyalties. Poor lass! Her heart was due to be shattered. That fool Tarryton was destined to betray her, and her own kin was already embroiled in rebellion!

There was nothing more for him to do that night.

Eric rode back to Thomas Mabry's. The house was very quiet, but he knocked softly upon the door. Anne Marie opened it quickly, her eyes wide and brilliant. She had been awaiting him, it was obvious.

"Lady Amanda returned safely?"

Anne Marie nodded, catching his arm and pulling him inside. "She is sleeping, and thank God! Lord Sterling did return; he is anxious to get home tomorrow. And Amanda is expected by her aunt in South Carolina within the next few weeks. If she had not been here, God knows what would have happened! He wouldn't have let her go, and I fear for her when she is at home."

Eric frowned. "But why? What would he do to her? The girl is his child, his own blood."

Anne Marie poured him a whiskey. "Eric, something about it chills me! She does not see the danger. She tosses her head in the air and ignores it all." She hesitated. "Just as she ignores trouble. With—with Damien." Anne Marie cast him a quick glance. "She loves him, passionately, you see. And that is her way, her nature. When she loves like that, she is reckless and daring and so defiant! Oh! How I do go on! But I wanted to thank you, Eric, with all of my heart."

He kissed her cheek tenderly. "It is ever a pleasure to serve you, Anne Marie," he told her.

She smiled. "I just wish that you could love me!"

He started to speak, to protest. She smiled and placed a finger against his lip. "You do not, so don't deny it! And I would settle for no less than a man who did love me, milord, so there!" Her smile was only slightly saddened by the mist in her eyes.

"Anne Marie, you are a priceless treasure, and I will never allow you to settle for less than a man who adores you and will know all that he holds." He finished the drink and handed her the glass, then started for the door.

"Where are you going?" she asked him.

"Back to my lodgings. Then—home."

"Home! But it is so late. You mustn't start to Virginia now!"

"Nay, lass! 'Tis morning. A new day. A very new day," he added reflectively.

"You should stay—"

"I must go."

She walked him out. He took his reins from the post and mounted his horse and smiled down to her, saluting. "I shall see you soon. Give your father my regards!"

"Yes, Eric! And—thank you. Thank you, so much!"

He waved and started to ride. The light was coming. Boston was about to burst into activity.

It suddenly seemed urgent that he head for home as quickly as he could.

He wanted to stand upon his own acres, feel the breeze from the James River. God, how he loved that land. The land had always been his mistress, his heart's desire. He smiled ruefully, though, thinking that he envied Frederick his son. Perhaps it was time that he married, for Cameron Hall needed heirs. And he craved a son who would learn to love the land as he did.

Maybe it was not his sudden interest in an heir that led his thoughts, he warned himself ruefully. Maybe it was the memory of Lady Sterling. She, who carried within her soul the passion of this very night, all the fire and the tempest and the spark of raw excitement that seemed so very necessary to him.

Pausing beneath a streetlamp, he smiled. He remembered the girl she had been. Passionate, aristocratic, haunting even then. She had been so young, but already those emerald eyes had carried a dazzle and a fury to match. She'd had a soft, vixen's laughter, and a will of steel. It had been years since he had first seen her, but tonight he could remember the encounter vividly. He'd been so furious, and she'd been so very indignant, calling him boy, and assuring him after his first warning that she was Lady Amanda Sterling, and that no one ever spanked her.

No one had previously, he told her, but the situation was about to be rectified. She had warned him imperiously that her father would have him lashed, but he didn't care. She had so very nearly killed them both, he had still been tense and frightened because she had so nearly been crushed.

He had paddled her good and hard, but she had cried out only once, and when he had released her, she had promised him that he would die very slowly and rot, she would see to it. He had offered to tell her father about the entire event himself, and she walked off furiously, her eyes flashing, her chin in the air.

But she had never told her father about the occasion. She would have gotten into trouble as well as he, Eric was certain.

She had changed. The lady had definitely grown.

Take care, friend, he warned himself. She was becoming a fascination. And this was a dangerous time to find oneself falling beneath the spell of Lady Sterling. Very soon it could come to war.

No. It would not come to war. No one wanted war.

It did not matter. For the time he was going home. He would make inquiries about Lord Sterling's daughter—she had not seen the last of him. If Tarryton meant to marry the Duchess of Owenfield, he had best forget his interest in Amanda Sterling. And if it were all bald rumor, then Tarryton had best be prepared to fight for the lady, for Eric did indeed plan to have her.

Tension filled him as he nudged the stallion back into motion. Repercussions were sure to come, swift and serious. There had been a tea party that night, and the guests were destined to pay. Where were men of good reason? There was an answer to this new trauma, surely, there must be an answer.

And yet, as he rode toward his room by the common to gather his things for the long ride home to Virginia, Eric felt a new rustle upon the winter wind.

As he reined in on the stallion, he felt it all around him. He knew that the events of the night had forever changed him, and that there were things he could not deny.

There was that movement, a whisper on the wind. And the whisper grew louder . . . the whisper of war.

Eric rode on, unaware that his next meeting with Lord Sterling's daughter would indeed cause him as much turbulence as the dangerous deeds of the night.

III ❧

There had never been a more beautiful summer's night, Amanda was convinced of it. Oriental lanterns had been lavishly strewn about the estate in all shades of soft colors. The breeze was soft and cool for the season, the flowers were all in full bloom, and the magnolias were casting their delightful scent upon the air. Summer was hot, but not tonight. Tonight everything was peaceful and beautiful and the sea breeze whispered gently.

There was no hint of dissent or trouble to mar the night, she thought, and then she was annoyed with the very thought, just as she was nearly sick to death of the continual talk of separation from the Crown. Had the men of Virginia, of the colonies, forgotten that the dear motherland had come to their defense against the French and Indians in the horrible war? Taxes had paid for that defense. They could not expect the Englishmen at home to cover their expenses here! The people of the colonies had opposed the Stamp Act, and that had been repealed.

Now they were fighting over tea. Ever since that night when the Bostonians had decided to dump endless chests of English tea into Boston Harbor, people talked of nothing but tea. And to punish the citizens for the act, the British had closed the port of Boston. And Virginia—so far away from Boston—was becoming embroiled in the whole matter. Tension was a constant emotion among the people, something almost tangible in the air.

Amanda did not want to be interested in politics, but she had a keen, sharp mind and she knew all the basics of the current problem simply because it seemed that everyone was beginning to speak of it. And of course, she had been in Boston on the very night when the tea had been dumped, and everyone always wanted to know her opinion of what had happened. She could never say that she didn't give a damn about the tea—Damien's involvement in the matter worried her. When she thought of her cousin, it was with irritation for the trouble he seemed bent on causing her. And when she became irritated with Damien, she became further irritated because she was forced to remember Lord Cameron. The audacity of the man! He had involved her in something that smelled despicably of treason, and he had never given her a chance to protest. He had set his hands upon her and ordered her about, and despite her outrage, she'd had to go along with him because of Damien. She didn't know what he was involved in, but she was afraid.

She shivered and looked down at her hands. Cameron could have turned Damien in as well as the young printer. But he hadn't. And so they all shared a filthy little secret. The thought of it made her grow warm and tremble, but she inhaled quickly and gained control of herself. She hadn't seen the man in these many months. Pray God, she would never see him again. And when Damien came tonight, she would warn her foolish cousin to keep his nose clean—and out of politics. She would take care to keep silent on the subject tonight. Her father disapproved of her knowledge of it, and tonight she would strive to please him with her silence—except when she spoke discreetly with Damien!

Nigel Sterling had taught her often enough that a woman's place was to be beautiful and soothing, a wife of virtue would be a notable woman adept at the finer arts who was also able to manage her husband's estates.

But he was wrong, in a way. For men all about, in all phases of life, were appealing to their wives and sisters and mothers to help boycott tea. Ladies were forming societies where they worked on homespun materials and garments and where they drank home-grown herbal teas. Their opinions and assistance were proving frightfully important.

"No more tea!" she whispered aloud. On this night, this magic night, when the future might well dangle before her in glazed and golden magnificence, she would curb her thoughts. This was her night. Robert had said that he needed to talk to her, that he needed to see her alone when they had met so briefly at tea earlier in the week—with her father present.

It was her night, a beautiful night, and she didn't want to think about politics, or the frightfully willful Bostonians, or even the foolish things being done by the Virginia House of Burgesses—and she especially did not want to worry about Damien or the dark and fierce Lord Cameron who had been so terribly rude and outrageous.

From the second-floor balcony of Sterling Hall she gazed down on the drive. She felt the kiss of the soft breeze and inhaled the subtle scent of the flowers. She was delighted. It was a perfect night. The musicians would soon be warming up in the gallery above the dance hall, the guests would arrive, and men and women in the height of elegance would swirl to the dances. Beautiful women would arrive in velvets and silks and satins and brocades, their hair powdered, their faces, perhaps, adorned with tiny hearts or moons, drawn in with a kohl pencil or made of velvet or silk patches. Their hair would be high, their bodices would be daringly low, and their conversation would be light and musical. Handsome men would arrive too. And they, too, would be dressed in the height of fashion. They would wear silk or satin knee breeches, fine hose, silver-buckled shoes, and elegant shirts all cuffed and collared in lace. It was her first week home from visiting her aunt in South Carolina, her first party of the summer season, and it was going to be a magical night.

Fine carriages, all marked with prestigious family coats-of-arms, were beginning to arrive. They moved down the oak-shaded drive in the moonlight. Lord Hastings was first, she saw, her father's old friend. She knew his carriage, even in the shadows, for it was drawn by four white stallions with braided tails and manes.

Everyone would arrive soon.

Lord Robert Tarryton would arrive.

At the thought of his name, Amanda sucked in her breath and fought a wave of dizzying sensation. Yes, Lord Robert Tarryton would arrive. He would find her on the dance floor . . .

No, no, no. She would let him arrive first, and then she would go down. She would make a grand entrance on the broad curving stairway that led to the entry. She would walk slowly and innocently, but she would pause in the middle of the stairway, and she would look out across the sea of faces, and she would find that he was looking for her, only for her. Perhaps she would allow her hand to flutter to her throat, and, of course, her heart would be pounding mercilessly.

He would be the most elegant man present. Tall, and with his soft blue eyes and near-platinum hair. Lean and nonchalant, he would wear mustard brocade, she was nearly certain, for the color so enhanced his masculine beauty.

His eyes would touch hers . . .

And she would know that this night was indeed the night, the most beautiful of all summer nights—no, the most beautiful of all nights.

He would thread his way through the crowd to her, and he would capture her hand, and soon she would be on the dance floor with him. But his need to speak would be great, and he would sweep her away, out to the garden, into the maze. And she would run behind him laughing; all the way to the statue of Venus, and there he would set her upon the bench and fall down upon one knee and beg her to be his wife. She would smile, and clasp him to her to breast, and—

"Amanda! Amanda! We've guests arriving! Come down here immediately."

Her dream dissolved in a shimmer of gray ashes as her father called her harshly.

"Yes, Father!"

"I'm going down; the guests are already filing in. Amanda!"

"I'm coming, Father!" she called in return. She swallowed down a touch of pain that he should always be so brusque with her. She was his only child, and though he provided for her in all things, he never displayed the slightest affection. She wondered sometimes if he despised her for not having been born a son, or if he despised her for bringing about her mother's death with her birth. She didn't know, and she learned over the years to harden her own heart and not to care. Danielle had been with her always, and Danielle showered affection upon her. Harrington, the butler and head of the staff, was proper in public and affectionate in private. At least she knew what caring was.

And now . . .

Now there was Robert. Lord Robert Tarryton. And she believed that he intended to ask her to be his wife this very night. She was so in love with him.

There had been other men in her life. In fact, she thought with a rueful smile, there had been many. She was accomplished, she was beautifully clad, and she was her father's daughter. Dozens of the most influential young men had called themselves her suitors, and she had laughed with them and flirted with them, but she had never given her heart away and, for all of his coldness, her father had never forced her hand. Even when John Murray, Lord Dunmore, the royal governor of the colony, had teasingly suggested that she was of an age, her father had shrugged and said that she had a mind of her own, she was not quite eighteen, and there was plenty of time for marriage.

She did have a mind of her own, and she enjoyed life. Before leaving the Colonies for her schooling in London, she had ridden with Sir Henry Hershall, sipped spiked lemonade on the balcony swing with the Earl of Latimer's second son, Jon, and played golf with the Scottish commander of Lord Newberry's Highlanders. And even Robert she had teased mercilessly until she had returned home in November last year and discovered that she was in love with him, wonderfully in love, at last.

"Amanda!"

"I'm coming, Father!"

She rushed from the balcony, and through her room to the hallway, and from there, to the top landing of the winding stairway. Once there she paused, breathing deeply.

The great hallway below was already filling with guests. She hurried down a few steps and then paused again. This was her grand entrance. She was supposed to move slowly and demurely. She inhaled again, resting her fingers delicately on the bannister. She felt her heart beat. Robert should just be arriving. She should glance to the entryway and find him, and his eyes should be upon her.

Perhaps he had already arrived. She quickly gazed out over the room, smiling to friends. The dream was too real, and so she looked on to the entryway.

A man was just entering, handing his gloves and hat to Harrington, smiling and offering the man a word.

Suddenly he looked up, just as if he had sensed that she was there. She discovered his eyes upon hers.

Just as she had imagined . . .

Except that the man was not Lord Robert Tarryton.

It was her nemesis—Lord Eric Cameron.

God! What right did he have to be there? In her very house? Yet she stared at him, unable to draw her gaze from his.

His hair seemed very dark, almost black that night. He had not worn a wig and he had not bothered to powder it. He seemed exceptionally tall, towering in the doorway.

His eyes, she thought, were even darker than before, indigo blue, with just that touch of taunting silver. He was dressed fashionably enough in a frock coat of royal blue, and white laced shirt, and breeches in a light-blue silk. His hose was white, and his shoes were adorned with silver buckles. Somehow he still didn't look quite civilized. Perhaps it was the way he wore his hair, defying fashion. Perhaps it was the structure of his face. He was tanned, as if he spent much time outdoors, and his features were bold and strong, his cheekbones were high and his chin was quite firm and squared. His mouth was full and wide, and as his eyes met hers, she thought that perhaps his very smile gave him the look of something just a bit savage, for his lip curved with a slow and leisurely ease that caused little shivers to race down her spine.

She realized that her hand had fluttered to her throat, and then she decided angrily that it was his eyes that gave him such an uncivilized appearance, for they danced then with startling silver humor as if he knew that he had somehow affected her, somehow caused her breath to catch. And she couldn't even seem to look away from him.

And neither did he look away from her.

Eric Cameron stood in the entry and stared up at the girl, his hostess, and he was both amused and entranced.

He saw in her eyes the same little vixen with the dark red hair and emerald eyes who had bit him with such certainty and vengeance all those years ago.

He almost pitied Lord Tarryton, if the man hadn't made sure to tell her the truth as yet. Eric had heard word from the governor himself that if Tarryton had not jumped with joy at the prospect of the young duchess, he had been quick to covet the title and property that came with her. Yet from the look of Amanda this evening, he surmised that she did not know. She had dressed to entrance a lover, but the excitement in her eyes was a greater attraction than any lace or velvet could create. Eric thought that she might well be aware of her femininity and her assets, she had confidence, but he wondered if she knew just how beautiful she was, standing upon the landing, her fingers trailing delicately over the bannister and brought softly against her throat. She was a woman of medium height, but so slim and delicate that she appeared somewhat taller than she really was. Her neck was long and graceful, and her breasts rose provocatively high and round against the embroidered bodice of her white gown.

Her hair was truly her glory that night. It was flame and it was dark, a deep auburn that framed the ivory of her perfect complexion, in ripples and waves. It was caught high above one ear with a golden comb just to tumble and cascade over the opposite shoulder like a deep burning fire.

Everything about her that night was glorious. Her beauty was startling. Her face was such a fine oval, like something exquisitely carved. Her cheeks just now burned with a touch of pink. Her eyes were deep green, like the land at its most verdant, Eric thought. He smiled slowly. Flame hair, green eyes. And though she stood motionless, he felt her vitality. She would fight, he thought, for what she wanted.

She raised her chin slightly. She was determined to look away. Her will had not lessened a bit, nor, it seemed, had she had occasion to learn much about humility.

She had been looking for a man, Eric thought with amusement. And most obviously he was not that man. Tarryton. She did not know that she been cast aside for riches.

He bowed to her deeply. When she barely acknowledged him, he realized that she was still furious about the night in Boston. He hadn't had much choice about his actions, but it was unlikely that she would ever understand or forgive him. She arched a delicate brow, caught up her skirts, and hurried on down the stairway. The perfect hostess, she began to greet her guests. She offered her cheek for the most delicate of kisses, she regally offered her hand to those she knew less well, and men and women flocked to her, eager to greet her.

"Why, Mandy, Mandy, dearest! Don't you look just heavenly!" someone gushed to her. Eric looked through the crowd. It was Lady Geneva Norman, one of the richest heiresses in the area with countless estates in England.

She was a beauty in her own right, but Eric had never found her any more than amusing and he was careful to keep his distance from her—she was a cunning witch who delighted in trouble and in dangling her worth before her suitors. She would, Eric thought, acquire a husband, for not many a man could forget that life was a harsh game that must be played well.

He was grateful then for his own position, for he was not dependent upon making a fortunate marriage. His forefathers had acquired some of the finest land in Tidewater Virginia, and he retained estates in England he had seen but once. He could play Geneva's game. He could delight in her bald humor and her coquetry and laughter, and he did not need to feel the sting of her temper at all, for he had nothing at stake. He could enjoy her beauty and walk away.

His land in the colonies and his estates in England gave him so very much.

Of course, those estates might not remain his for long, he realized solemnly. Not if he continued with his present course of action. Ever since Boston, he had become more and more deeply involved with men whom the Crown would call questionable associates.

Some of his friends were calling it suicide, but he could not turn back. He believed in what he was doing.

"Lord Cameron!" a voice bellowed, and Eric saw that his host, Lord Nigel Sterling, had come up before him, reaching for his hand. He thought briefly of the things that Anne Marie had told him about the man. Still, Amanda did not seem to show any signs of abuse.

"Eric, my man, I've been most anxious to talk to you. I've been hearing the most fearful rumors."

Eric took Lord Sterling's proffered hand and smiled. "Rumors? How intriguing. I shall be interested in hearing them."

"Come with me, and we'll take a brandy into my office. I would have a word with you in private," Sterling said.

Eric shrugged and smiled, looking over his host. He was a squat man with heavy jowls and beady brown eyes. How he could have taken part in the creation of the thing of beauty upon the stairs, Eric did not know. Nor was he particularly fond of the man's personality. He was forceful, rude, and often abrasive, a great believer in his own nobility. Still, he was Eric's host this evening, and if they had been prone to great dissent when they had sat together in the Governor's Council, by every rule of polite behavior, Eric owed him a moment of his time.

"As you wish, Nigel. But I warn you, it will not change anything."

"Come, I'll take my chances."

They moved through the room. Eric nodded to some of his male friends and acquaintances and bowed to the ladies as he followed. He could already hear whispers as he did so. He smiled more deeply. So much for polite society. He had become a black sheep already.

"Ah, my dear! Amanda, there you are. Have you met Lord Cameron? Ah . . . yes, of course, you have, but that was years ago. Amanda was in a young ladies' school in England for several years, and since then she has been in South Carolina with relatives. Do you remember my daughter, Lord Cameron?"

"We met recently, Nigel. At Thomas Mabry's, in Boston."

"What? Oh, so you were at Mabry's fête that evening, were you?"

"Yes." Eric kept his eyes upon Amanda. She was flushed, despite her determination to ignore his knowing smile.

"Yes, Papa, Lord Cameron was there."

Eric took her hand and bowed over it deeply, just brushing the back of it with his lips. He felt the pulse race at her wrist. As he raised his head, he looked into her eyes, those passionate, telltale eyes, and he moved his thumb slowly over the delicate blue veins that he could just see beneath the surface of her porcelain skin.

"It was a night I shall not forget," he said pleasantly.

Her eyes widened slightly. She nearly snatched her hand away, but then she spoke softly and with poise. "Lord Cameron. How nice to see you again."

It was anything but nice for her to see him again, he thought, somewhat amused and somewhat sorry. She was even lovelier up close. So much of her beauty lay in her love for life, something vital and warm that seemed to sweep about her in a golden light. Well, she was passionately against him, he realized.

"Milady." He bowed to her. These were passionate times. He was determined in his own course of action, and it was natural that tempers and spirits would soar high.

"Save a dance for Lord Cameron, my dear," her father said. "Come, Eric, please, so that I may have my word with you."

Eric bowed to Amanda once again, then followed Sterling toward the doorway to his office.

Cameron! Amanda thought, watching his broad back disappear in the wake of her father. Cameron!

He had come to taunt her! On this magical night, he had come here! Well, he had nothing on her! If he ever dared to implicate Damien, she would call him a traitor in no uncertain terms! He laughed at her, she saw it in his smile, he dared her with every glance!

She tightened her jaw, thinking that the man had really changed little. He had always been less than cavalier, supremely confident and assured. So *arrogant.* She would never forget the day of the hunt. Perhaps she *had* been too eager to catch the fox, but he'd had no right to spank her. She hadn't thought that he would dare, but he would dare anything, she had learned. Perhaps it had been as much his fault. He had been about seventeen, and eager to return to one of Lord Hastings's pretty chambermaids. She'd already heard his name whispered in various households. His appeal was legendary.

Oh! Cameron was a traitor. Just two weeks ago he had stood up in the governor's chambers, a member of the prestigious council, an honor set upon one for life, and he had suggested that perhaps he should resign because he disagreed with various actions being taken. Everyone had been speaking about it. The governor had refused to accept his resignation, demanding that he think it all through. The colony had been abuzz with it! Last night Robert had talked of it, calling the man a fool and a traitor. It was amazing that he hadn't been arrested on the spot, hanged, boiled in oil, or drawn and quartered.

Well, perhaps nothing so dramatic. And perhaps it was true that the governor would be hanging men from dawn to dusk if he had to start with the men who had spoken so in the lower house, the House of Burgesses. But Cameron was not a member of that society. He was a lord. His duty was to support his king and his governor.

It was said that he had given a fine speech with a wonderful elocution—learned at Oxford, so she had heard—and agreed to wait, but suggested that time would make little difference. His heart was with the men who had gone to Bruton Parish Church for their day of prayer—just as his heart was with the men who had dumped the tea into the sea. His heart was not with many of the decisions being made, and therefore he did not think that he could serve the governor to the best of his abilities.

He was listening to radicals. Men like Patrick Henry. He was far more interested in the lower House of Burgesses than he was in the goings-on of his own council chambers. He met with radicals at the various taverns in Williamsburg. He was dangerous.

"There goes the most arresting man in the colonies," a soft voice mused behind her.

Amanda swirled around to see Lady Geneva standing behind her, batting her fan, her dark eyes following Lord Cameron.

"Cameron?" Amanda said incredulously.

Geneva nodded knowingly. "Lord Cameron," she said, as if she tasted the name as she spoke and found it very pleasing. Her gaze shot to Amanda again. "He's dashing, don't you think? Bold, a rebel. He bows down before no man. All heads turn when he enters a room. Don't you feel it? The tension . . . why, darling, the very heat! Oh, but I do just feel ignited!"

A sizzle of warm rushing liquid seemed to trail down the length of Amanda's spine with Geneva's words and she shivered, remembering how it felt to have her eyes locked with his, to feel his lips against her flesh. She shook her head, though, denying the sensation. She didn't even want to think about the man, she wanted to find Robert.

"Lord Cameron is a traitor and nothing more. And I can't even imagine why Father would want him here."

"He might prove to be an invaluable friend one day," Geneva said. "He is trusted by the radicals, and, oddly enough, he is even trusted by those very men he spurns. Your father is no fool, my pet. I'm sure he intends to stay very good friends with Lord Cameron."

"And you, Geneva, do you intend to become very good friends with Lord Cameron?"

"Ah"—Geneva laughed— "the little tigress shows her claws! Me? Ummm. I am good friends with him. I don't know about a lifetime commitment, for I like balls and pageants, I love royalty, I adore the finer things in life. Our fierce and proud Lord Cameron is casting his path in a different direction. He might well come to hang one of these days, and should he not, he might well find his bed to be one of hay. And still, I have danced with the man. I've felt his arms around me, and sometimes I do wonder if lying with him in a bed of hay might not be preferable to lying with any other man upon silk. But don't worry, pet—the competition is still wide open."

"You needn't worry, Geneva," Amanda said sweetly. "You've no competition from me. I've no interest whatsoever in a traitor to the Crown."

Geneva batted her fan prettily, smiling to someone across the room. "Because of Lord Tarryton, I believe?"

"Believe what you wish," Amanda told her, but Geneva was very smug, obviously ready to tell a secret that she was finding most amusing.

"I know things, Amanda. I'll tell them to you if you like."

"All right, Geneva. Tell me what you will."

"Lord Tarryton is engaged to marry the Duchess of Owenfield back in England. She's a widow and as her dear departed husband left no heirs, young Robert will gain the title of Duke of Owenfield."

"I don't believe you!" Amanda gasped, so stunned at the news that she could not pretend nonchalance.

"Then ask Robert," Geneva said sweetly. "Excuse me, dear, will you? Men are flocking to your father's study, and I'm quite certain they'll have Lord Cameron on the cooking spit, searing him away. I should love to see him defend himself."

Geneva hurried toward the hallway door. She bypassed it, excusing herself to various people to escape out the open doorways at the back of the hall. She would walk around the terrace to the floor-length windows and find a seat upon one of the swings, out of sight, and therefore able to listen in on the conversation.

Amanda looked around the room. She didn't see Robert anywhere. She had to find him and speak with him. Geneva was lying. Robert loved her, and though she couldn't give him a new title, she did come with a rich dowry. There was no reason they should not marry. They were Virginians, both of them. He couldn't wish to live across the sea. . . .

And yet Geneva's words had left her with a set of chills, for the woman had not teased or taunted, she had simply stated what she knew and disappeared, eager to chase Lord Cameron.

Amanda sighed, determined to follow.

It was not so easy, for she was stopped by young men and older women, and as her father's hostess, she was obliged to be polite to their guests. Finally, though, she managed to escape down the hall while the musicians played a minuet.

Outside, Amanda did not see Geneva, but as she moved near the open windows, she felt her heart suddenly pound, for Robert was inside the study with her father, Lord Cameron, and Lord Hastings.

"You turn your back on us, Cameron, when you do such things!" Lord Hastings was saying.

Seated before her father's desk, Cameron set down his brandy glass. Then he rose, setting his thumbs into the waistband of his breeches, and faced Hastings.

"Lord Hastings, I beg to differ. The House of Burgesses determined that a day of prayer for our sister city would not be out of order. Tell me, sir, who is it that we offend with prayer!"

"You were not obliged to attend!" Robert said fervently.

Cameron arched a dark brow at him, turning to face

him. "No, sir, I was not obliged to attend, I did so because I desired to do so. The British closed the port of Boston—"

"The British! *We* are the British!" her father proclaimed.

"There is no land I would claim with more ardor as my mother country than Britain, sir, but I am not, I fear, British. I am a Virginian. I am his Majesty's subject, but I cling to my rights as his subject. I attended a day of prayer—"

"Boston is not our sister city. Not when she behaves as she does!" Hastings exclaimed.

"To feel so, sir, is indisputably your prerogative," Cameron said, bowing deeply. He turned then toward his host. "Lord Sterling, I cannot apologize for what I feel to the depths of my heart. There was nothing wrong with prayer. Lord Dunmore has now dissolved the House of Burgesses, and yet I fear her members will only meet with more regularity. They have elected representatives to their Continental Congress, and I fear that the way to peace must soon be found or else—"

"Damn it, Cameron! You're a fine soldier, a wealthy man, and we all admire you. But you're talking treason again!" Sterling thundered, pounding upon his desk.

"I have spoken no treason, sir. But beyond a doubt, our difficulties with the mother country must be solved. I offered to give up my place on the council, sir, because I know how my opinions distress you all. I shall continue to offer my own absence if you feel that you cannot tolerate my opinions, although I hope that I speak with reason. And now, gentlemen . . ."

His voice suddenly trailed away. Amanda realized that he saw her staring in at him, listening to the conversation —and searching about the room. She quickly ducked behind one of the pillars but kept her eyes upon the man. He smiled, bowing his head, yet she saw the laughter in his eyes and the rueful curve of his lip and the devil's own humor at her expense. He knew that she was looking for Robert, she thought.

Damn the traitor. And then she didn't care, because Robert had seen her too. Lord Cameron quickly recovered his poise and continued speaking. Robert did not do so well. A gentle smile touched his features and he started toward the floor-length windows.

"Robert—" her father began with a frown.

"Ah, sir, I was just feeling the need for a bit of air myself," Eric Cameron said. "Shall we break, milords?"

He gave the men no opportunity to protest, but bowed sharply to them all and quickly departed the room.

"Well, I never—" her father began, but Robert interrupted him hastily.

"Sir, it is frightfully hot in this room. Excuse me, Lord Sterling, Lord Hastings."

He bowed his way out. Amanda quickly ducked back around the pillar and hurried to the doors leading out from the hallway. She could hear the musicians clearly there, playing a Virginia tune. Men and women swayed in one another's arms and parted to a far different tone and beat from the minuet. They laughed and touched and their eyes danced as they participated in the more energetic reel.

Amanda searched for Robert, and yet her eyes rested upon one couple on the floor.

Lord Cameron had found Geneva. Well and good for them both, they deserved one another! Amanda thought, and yet she paused, for they were enchanting together. He so tall and dark as he bent over her blond beauty, pulling her close. She so full of laughter, her eyes those of a cat, feline and feminine. One could almost feel the heat between them.

Hers was a finer love, she assured herself. And Geneva was a liar. Robert was not going to marry another woman.

Geneva whispered something to Lord Cameron. The two of them disappeared together.

Amanda looked again for Robert, and at last she saw him hurrying toward her down the hallway and through the doors. She was so glad to see him, and so glad to be alone, that she threw her arms around him and came upon her toes to kiss his lips. For a moment he was still, then his arms swept around her and he held her tightly. His lips eagerly sought hers, indeed, he hungered for more, smoothing back her hair, passing the barriers of her lips with his tongue.

She drew away from him, not so alarmed by his ardor as she was by their nearness to the party.

"Amanda, for the love of God, let me touch you! Last night we were not alone a second, your father was always there!" he cried, but she silenced him, pressing her fingers against his lip.

"Let's go into the maze," she urged him. Catching his hand, she hurried down the back steps, pulling him along. She knew the maze, she had played within it as a child, and now, with fingers entwined with Robert's, she scampered quickly into the very heart of the foliage. The night was warm with the softest of breezes. The high foliage rustled in the breeze and the flowers, in summer bloom, caught silver light from the moon and lay around them abundantly in a dazzling display of color.

"Amanda!" Robert called to her, but she laughed, winding around a cherry hedge and coming to the statue of Venus with its tinkling waterfall and fountain. The statue was beautiful, draped in marble as if Venus lived, an innocent virgin. Twin cupids played by her head with the long tendrils of her marble hair, and a wrought-iron loveseat awaited those who came to the Venus garden in the maze.

Breathless, Amanda fell into the seat. "Oh, Robert!" she whispered delightedly. "Now! We're alone at last!"

There was a curious rustling sound, and she frowned, then determined that it was nothing more than the wind in the bushes. She smiled up at her lover, adoring his lean and poetic features, and reached for his hand.

"Come sit by me. I have to speak with you."

"Amanda, I have to kiss you."

"Robert! Sit!"

He did so and she curled against him, resting her head upon his shoulder. He bent down slowly to her, very slowly. Then his lips found hers, and the kiss was rich and deep and sweet. She moved her hand against his cheek, and she felt his fingers against her own. Then he gripped her tightly against him. She felt the power of his heart.

And she felt his fingers, fervently wandering upon the bodice at her breast, seeking the rise of bare flesh.

Some inner warning sounded and she realized that she was not behaving like a lady. She was in love. She just wanted to touch him, and to be held in turn, and to believe in their future together.

She had to pull away. He was growing reckless with his kisses, and with his hands, and although it was private in the Venus garden in the midst of the maze, she knew that she was tempting the man too far.

"My love, please!" She gasped, capturing his straying fingers and bringing them to her lap. He still didn't quite seem to hear her. Breathing heavily, he stared at her. He tried to lift his hand to touch her, but she held tight. "Robert—"

"I have to have you!"

"I love you, and our time will come. Robert—"

"But I need you now. I need to feel your lips and I need to touch your flesh, I need to be with you. I am a man, my God, can't you understand that!"

"Oh, Robert, I long for you too, but we must wait. Surely you understand. My father . . ." No, it wasn't her father, not really. It was her upbringing. She was Lord Sterling's daughter, of Sterling Hall, and even if she was in love, and loved in turn, she had to wait. Until the words were spoken. Until they were joined before God.

"Come to me, love. Feel my lips, my kiss. . . ."

She was startled when he drew her back into his arms with an alarming force. They had teased and laughed a dozen times together, and it had never been like this. Her frown alone had stopped his ardor before, while now her harried fingers had no power at all against his touch.

"Robert!" Leaping to her feet, she escaped him. He stood quickly, coming behind her, gently holding her shoulders. His voice was harsh when he spoke to her.

"Amanda, come, we've played this game again and again. Surely you must feel it, you must ache and crave as I do, you long for consummation of this desire as deeply as I! And I would die for your touch, for your kiss, and still you play the tease, and you taunt and torture me. We are not children any longer. I cannot stand it!"

She swung around, heartfully sorry and somewhat alarmed. She didn't want what he wanted, not desperately at all. Marriage was not the same for men as it was for women. She liked to be close, and she liked to be loved. The rest, she was certain, would have to come with time.

"We cannot, Robert. Not until we are married."

"Married!"

She knew the moment he repeated the word that Geneva had not lied to her. She need not feel guilty for a single thing she might have done to Robert, Lord Tarryton. Pain spilled through her. She wanted to fall to the ground, and she wanted to scream, and she very nearly wanted to die.

"It's true!" She gasped, backing away from him. "You're to marry some duchess for her estates!"

"Amanda—" He reached for her, his misery written clearly upon his face. "Amanda, I love you. I have no choice. It doesn't have to make any difference between us."

"You have no choice!" she cried. "Oh, you dreadful, despicable, cowardly bastard! How dare you!" She slapped him as hard as she could across the face.

He gasped, staring at her, his eyes narrowing. "I have no choice!"

"Don't you ever come near me again. Ever."

"I am no coward, milady. You wait until your father has chosen for you, lady, and then tell me how to fight what we are honor-bound to do!"

"Honor bound! You say you have no choice," Amanda retorted. "You say *no*, milord, and that is that! But you don't wish to say no, do you? Ah, that's right. You'll be a duke. Well, so be it then. Marry the duchess for a title. I hope that it will be well worth the price of your soul and my heart."

"Damn you, Amanda!" Robert cried, and he reached for her, dragging her hard against him. "You've no right! And you wait! You will be promised to a man like Lord Hastings, a man with three chins and four stomachs, and then you shall be sorry that you taunted me so! I love you, and you will not forget me. You will see. And for now, my God, you've played the bitch and the tease—"

"How dare you—" she began, her voice low and husky and shaking with emotion and pain.

"You've led me on! You've taunted and teased with your eyes, you've driven me near madness with your touch, and now you tell me that I shouldn't come near you—"

"Let me go!"

"I'll not! I'll have tonight what you've offered from the start, and when you're forced into a wretched marriage, then you'll understand. It will happen. The day will come, and your father will force you into wedlock with some monster, an old goat perhaps, and then you'll come to me. You'll know the world is not perfect, no fairyland, milady."

"Let me go!"

He did not. His lips came down upon hers, hard and suffocating. She slammed against his chest, to no avail. He was making her dizzy, and she wondered how long she could fight. And she couldn't believe that she had to fight, that love had turned to nightmare, that her dreams were being shattered one by one, here in the Venus garden, beneath the summer moon.

"No!" she cried out, wrenching from his lips, horrified when his fingers latched hard upon the velvet ties to her bodice. Desperate, she twisted in his arms, certain that she had not lost as yet and determined to kick him into agony. But just as she freed herself enough to strike he leapt forward and she fell hard upon the ground, the breath knocked from her. He jumped down upon her and started to speak.

"Amanda—"

His word was cut cleanly from his lips as he was grasped from behind and lifted high and tossed into the bushes. Stunned, Amanda gazed past her fallen foe to see the tall man standing before her, watching Robert where he had fallen, with immense distaste.

Cameron. Lord Cameron!

"How dare you!" In a rage, Robert was up and on his feet. Bellowing like a wounded bull, he lunged forward.

Cameron sidestepped him neatly, then delivered a hard chop upon his nape, sending Robert down into a heap at his feet. Robert groaned, then staggered up again.

"You! What right have you here! None at all. This is a private affair!"

"Oh?" Cameron said, not even breathing hard. He crossed his arms slowly over his chest and his eyes fell upon Amanda. "I don't think that there is anything between the two of you anymore, do you?"

"It's none of your business!" Robert repeated.

"I'm afraid that it is. She asked you to let her go—I heard her."

"This is none of your affair!"

Amanda's cheeks blazed despite herself. She could not believe that she had been dragged into this horrible and humiliating position. She longed to skewer both men through.

"You . . . bastard!" she breathed.

"Amanda—" Robert began.

"Robert, you're a mewling coward, and I hate you, I swear it."

Robert glanced at Eric Cameron and took a sudden, wild swing at the man. It was almost pathetic, the ease with which Cameron caught the flailing arm and twisted it.

"Well, Milord Tarryton," Cameron said softly, "I can well believe that the lass has elicited a fire in your loins, and I do believe that she could tease and tempt a man to hell and back again. But still, she said no. And you, sir, are considered an aristocrat. Hardly the manners one should expect, eh?"

Amanda gasped enraged that he should speak of her so —and witness so much of her humiliation. She couldn't be grateful to him. She swallowed hard and took a step toward him. "Lord Cameron . . ." She kept her voice soft and quiet, demure. Ladylike. "You! You again! You are the plague of my life!" she charged him softly.

Then she slapped him.

His features went rigid but he barely blinked. "Once, milady, you may take that liberty. Don't take it again. As to you . . ." He shoved Robert forward. "The night, milord, is over."

Robert's head bowed. "I still say that it's none of your affair!"

"But that, sir, is point two. The lady's behavior is every bit my concern, as is her welfare. Tonight, Lord Tarryton, we have sparred and played. Touch her again, and I might well determine to kill you."

"What?"

"I am that horrible, wretched, monster man she will be forced to marry, Lord Tarryton. The old goat. I have asked her father for her hand, and he has most graciously agreed." He bowed to Amanda. "Truly, mam'selle, you are about to find me the plague of your life!"

IV 🍁

"**I** don't believe you!" Amanda gasped, stunned. And of course, it had to be a lie. Still reeling from the impact of Robert's words and actions, she was afraid that she was going to be sick. She hurt, as she had never hurt before. Her sense of betrayal was already complete, yet now she was discovering that not only Robert but her father had turned from her. It could not be true. Her father had not let her go her way so freely and so far to turn her over to a rebel! She backed away from him, shaking her head. "Sir, you are a liar!"

He arched a brow and though he maintained a pleasant enough countenance, his silver-blue eyes narrowed sharply. He didn't like being called a liar, no matter how nonchalantly he stood. "No, I am not, milady," he said softly, and his gaze rested upon Robert. "Lord Tarryton, my warning stands. And as you are a man affianced, perhaps you should be casting your attentions upon your future bride." He paused, pointing a finger at Robert. "Go. Now."

"Amanda," Robert said, appealing to her. "We can discuss this later—"

"Discuss this!" she cried. "No, Lord Tarryton, we will never discuss—this. Or anything else, for that matter. You fool! I loved you!" she whispered.

"Amanda, I do love you, I tried to tell you—"

"Lord Tarryton!" Eric snapped. "This is a touching scene indeed, but under the circumstances . . ."

There was a deadly note of menace in Eric's voice. Robert stiffened and walked past Amanda and Eric without another word. Amanda listened to his footsteps falling upon the earth as he disappeared, then she spun around on Cameron.

"I'm sorry that you were hurt. I'm afraid that Lord Tarryton's engagement has been common knowledge for quite some time now," he told her. "I suppose you hadn't heard the news at your aunt's."

"I am not hurt, Lord Cameron," she lied. She wanted to die on the spot from the humiliation and the pain she was experiencing. She hated him. She hated him more than she hated Robert, because he'd witnessed her humiliation.

"Lady Sterling—"

She did not want his help or his compassion. She wanted to be alone, she wanted to rage and cry in private. "Get away from me, sir, for you are far more heinous a man than he. You've no right here, you've no business here—"

"I do beg your pardon, Lady Sterling." Now he sounded cool and dangerous. "I did not intend to spy upon you, but I heard your cries of distress and assumed that you wanted assistance."

"Assumed—"

He sat down on the bench before the Venus statue, idly watching her. "Tell me, did I interrupt you rather than rescue you?"

It took several seconds for the meaning of his words to sink into her mind. And when she grasped their full meaning, she was furious. In a sudden rage, she flew at him, but

he stood immediately, catching her arms, securing them
behind her back and pulling her very close. She struggled
against him wildly, determined to free herself at any cost.
Desperate, she tried to kick him. He slipped a foot against
her ankle and she started falling. He deftly preceded her
to the ground, rolling beneath her so that when she fell,
his body took the brunt of the force. Then he rolled
swiftly, and she was caught beneath him again, staring up
at him exhausted but ever more furious, yet her breath
coming so quickly that she could not speak. She gritted
her teeth and he laughed, but there was an edge about the
sound and she wondered just how amused he was. "I
warned you," he told her quietly. "You struck me once. I
will not allow you to strike again."

"Don't you dare laugh at me."

"Why, milady, I wouldn't dream of doing so."

"Let me go!"

"Are we understood?"

"Lord Cameron, I am quite certain that I shall never
understand you!"

"Perhaps you should make an effort to do so."

"Get off me."

"Milady, your every wish is my command."

He leapt to his feet, but she found no freedom, for his
hands were upon her own, drawing her up against him.

She tossed back her head, staring up him, longing to do
serious battle again, yet painfully aware that she could not
win. Praying for composure, she held still with her chin
high, her hair tumbling and rippling down her back and
seeming to burn like a slow flame in the moonlight. Her
eyes sizzled and she spoke as softly as he, with every bit as
much of an edge.

"I'm demanding, Lord Cameron, that you let me go. Or
perhaps you imagine that I'm really dying to remain in
your arms too? Can I dare hope that some other man is
otherwise engaged elsewhere in this maze and will come
to my rescue?"

He laughed, and it was an open, honest sound. It
brought back strange feelings to her, causing a cascade of
warmth to rush through her. Geneva's words came back to

her. *The most arresting man in the colonies.* And she felt his arms acutely. They were strong arms, well muscled, like the steel of a blade. His body was hard and vital, and his thigh was pressed tightly against her own. Her breath came quickly, and she longed to escape him.

"Milady," he told her, "you have not lost one bit of your aristocratic hauteur. You had quite an abundance of it as a child, you know."

"And you were a very rude child, and now you are a very rude adult, Lord Cameron. You're not only a traitor, you're a brute."

"This is a subject, mam'selle, with which I think that you should take extreme care."

"Your activities—"

"I am no traitor but a man of convictions. And a brute, milady? For seeking to save myself from your very tender touch? Alas, I should stand still, and allow those feminine claws of yours to draw blood. That is what you seek tonight, isn't it? Blood, milady?"

"You're sadly mistaken. I seek no vengeance upon anyone."

Still, he held her close. His fingers wound tight around her wrists, and his words whispered like the breeze against her lips. She could almost feel the brush of his lips. The lace of his shirt and the satin of his surcoat lay against her bare flesh where the mounds of her breasts rose daringly above her bodice, and she was uncomfortably aware of the feel and texture of the fabric and of the warmth of the man beneath it.

"Tarryton is a fool."

"How dare you judge him!"

"Any man who would cast aside such exquisite beauty for mere wealth is a fool."

"You've no right to judge him!"

"Ah, but he didn't exactly cast you aside. He meant to have love *and* money."

She tried to kick him again. He dragged her down upon the bench, laughing again. "Careful, milady! I'm striving not to be a brute, but the role of knight is difficult to play when you are so determined to cause me pain."

"You are causing *me* great pain!" she retorted. Drawn upon his lap, she was in a very awkward position. He held her hands still, and though his touch was easy, she was still his prisoner. There was no doubting that.

"I'm so sorry. As I said, my wish is really only to fulfill your desires."

"Oh, you lie!"

"But I don't lie, milady!"

"I'll never, never marry you, so any point you wish to make between us is quite moot."

"Alas! You crush me!" he said with mock despair.

He was not in the least crushed or broken, but every bit amused. Things had not changed at all. He still viewed himself the adult, the master of the world, and her but a child playing willfully within his realm.

Except that now he touched her differently. He held her tightly. And she was all too aware of that hold. The scent of flowers was all around them and the moonlight played over his striking face, which reminded her of the fine statues in the Venus garden. His features were like those of Mars, or Apollo, hard cast and striking, as was his smile. She wanted to wrench away from him, and then again, she was struck with the startling and dizzying desire to learn more about him. She trembled already. If he touched her lips with his own the way that Robert had done, just what was it that she would feel?

"Let me go," she said swiftly. "Now."

His smile deepened. He knew, she thought with sudden panic. He knew exactly what she was thinking, and he was both amused and challenged. He was holding her ever closer, but now just one of his hands secured her wrists and the other moved upward to her cheek.

"I could scream!" she threatened in a whisper.

"Scream," he suggested.

But she did not. The softest little whimper escaped her as his lips touched hers. They brought with them an incredible heat that consumed her. There was no hesitance about him, just sweeping determination and power. He offered no subtlety, he asked nothing, but demanded, his tongue plunging against the crevice of her lips with an

intimate surge, breaking through the barrier of her teeth
and sweeping her mouth with deep and sensual effron-
tery. She felt the breath of him and the scent of him, and
she was filled with everything that was intimate about the
man. She freed her hand to fight him, and found that her
palm fell against the breast of his frock coat, and she was
achingly aware of even the feel of the material there. She
was trembling. She should be fighting now for dear life
and honor, yet she was locked in his embrace, and could
not begin to find the power to pull away. His kiss was an
invasion, a subtle rape of her mouth, and yet his touch
was so overwhelming that she could do nothing but ab-
sorb the sensations. Tears stung her eyes, for she was
somehow aware that the magic of the night was over. Innocence was gone. She had fallen in love, she had believed
in a man, and she had believed in love. And she had been
spurned. And now she was discovering that she could still
be touched, that she could feel, that she could rage and
despise a stranger and still fall prey to the demand of a
kiss, to tremble and shake in the arms of the enemy. . . .

She pulled away from him at last, gasping and horrified.
Her fingers flew to her swollen lips, her arms wrapped
protectively about her chest. "St-stop!" she charged him.
She rose and backed away, hating him and hating Robert
with all of her heart. She would never, never love anyone
again, she vowed silently. And certainly not this man who
now watched her with such striking curiosity in his silver
eyes. He did not breathe hard, he did not shake or tremble. He was, at least, no longer amused, for his gaze was
hard and grave upon her.

"Stop!" she repeated, still shaking. "You are in truth no
better than he!"

"Ah, but I am, you see," he said softly as he stood. "I can
offer you an honest proposal of marriage, and he cannot."

"Marriage!"

"Yes, marriage. The legal type of arrangement."

She ignored the taunt. "You are a rebel, a rogue, and a
backwoods adventurer, sir, and I cannot begin to take
such an idea even remotely seriously. You are the last man
that I should ever wish to marry. You thought that you

could frighten me and bully me in Boston; well, you cannot do so here! You must know what I feel for you, and I cannot begin to wonder what it is that you can possibly feel for me."

He laughed. "Your father took my offer very seriously. And as for my feelings, why, I am enchanted."

She flushed and stared up at the stars. "You are no better than Robert. You are ruled by lust."

She saw the hint of his smile. "Lust? Your word, milady, and so I will admit to a fair amount of it. But perhaps I see more. A heart that drums a different beat, eyes that dare the very devil."

"And are you the devil? So goes your reputation, Lord Cameron."

"No devil, lady. Just a man in lust."

Amanda moved back, hugging her arms more tightly about herself, wondering if his agreement with her father could possibly be true. All of Virginia's society, or their society at least, was up in arms against Lord Cameron. Although Cameron Hall was a magnificent estate, and he owned endless acres of cotton and tobacco and produce, and had a pedigree that went back to the Dark Ages, dissension was in the air, and he was turning his back on his own kind to join up with rebels.

"I don't believe you!" she whispered again, but she said it more quietly. "My father did not—agree to a marriage!"

"Milady, I do not lie," he told her. He walked toward her, and she wanted to turn and run. She hated to be a coward, but at that moment she wanted to run, and still she could not. It was not courage at all that kept her still, it was something about the way he looked at her.

He stopped several feet before her and reached out gently. She thought that he was going to sweep her into his arms again, but he did not, and for the life of her, she did not know if she was relieved or disappointed. She could not breathe properly, and it seemed that the very masculine scent of him was not just around her, but part of her, and that she would never forget it or forget his power. He touched just her cheek, his knuckles running over the softness of it, his hand then falling to his side. "But neither shall I force the issue. If you are adamantly opposed to me, milady, then the matter is solved. However, I do suggest that you think carefully before accepting Lord Tarryton's . . . proposition."

Heedlessly she tried to strike him again. He was quick, catching her hand before it could land upon him. He turned her wrist slowly, drawing a finger over the valley of her palm, then pressing his lips against it. Her breath came in a rush and her heart pounded and again. She wanted nothing more than to escape him and the sensations of his touch.

"I told you, milady, you may not strike me again."

She smiled very sweetly. "Being a loyalist's mistress might be preferable to a life as a traitor's wife."

"Really? I think that you're sadly mistaken. About yourself, Lady Sterling, if nothing else. Young Tarryton is a boy, playing at a man's games. He isn't for you. He'll never be for you. He desires you, perhaps he even loves you. But he hasn't the courage to fight for you, milady, and in the end you would be sadly disappointed."

"Oh, I see. I'd never be disappointed in you, I presume?" she challenged him sarcastically.

"No," he said. "You would not be disappointed in me. Had I set out to seduce you, milady, it would never have come to attempted rape, and in the outcome, I promise that you'd have been mine."

She opened her mouth to protest with outrage, but she never spoke. He did touch her again then, hard and sure. He drew her against him and his lips found hers. She whimpered and pounded furiously against his chest, but he paid her no heed, and he gave her no quarter. His mouth closed upon hers with swift, searing hunger and his tongue penetrated deeply against her protest, filling her with a warmth that consumed all thought and reason. She whimpered and pressed herself against him, feeling dizzy and almost falling. But it didn't matter, for as he continued to kiss her, he held her weight with ease. She thought briefly that he would never let her fall, and she realized that the overpowering heat that exploded throughout her emanated from some searing center of her being that had come alive tonight. It was unlike anything she had ever imagined before, this hot excitement that stirred her blood and swept from her lips to her breasts, and from her breasts to some secret place within her, near the juncture of her thighs, wickedly deep within her.

And then, abruptly, he released her, a negligent smile upon his lips. "You should marry me, milady, because I do believe that I could promise never to disappoint you."

"I would fight you all of my life!" she exclaimed out, and then realized that it was she who still clung to him. She needed the support.

"You would fight me, but you would not be disappointed by me. Now, milady, if you'll excuse me, I shall leave you to your own devices, since you are so capable." He let her hand fall and bowed deeply to her, turning about to leave the maze.

Shaking, Amanda determined to have the last word. "You are a traitor, Lord Cameron! A traitor to the king, a traitor to your own kind!"

He turned back around, bowing deeply. "As you would have it, milady. Far be it that I should argue with your gentle tongue."

He turned again and was gone.

Amanda sank down upon the bench, feeling the pressure of her tears come rushing to her eyes. She pressed her hands against them, determined not to cry. She was trembling still. He had awakened things inside of her, things she had never dared to dream of. . . .

And things she now despised.

She hated him. She had hated him in Boston, and she hated him now! How dare he come upon her so highhandedly again. He had known about Robert—dear God, all the world had known about Robert, all the world but she!

She touched her swollen lips, and all that she could remember was Eric Cameron's touch. Yet it was true, the magic was gone, love was gone, and her belief in things beautiful and good and right was gone. Innocence had been cruelly slain, she thought, and then, despite her best intentions, tears did start to fall down her cheeks. Robert! How could he? How could he speak of his longing and desire for her and then tell her that yes, he did intend to marry the Duchess of Owenfield?

How could he suggest that she become his mistress?

Amanda wiped the tears from her cheeks and forced herself to stand and smooth down her gown. She dusted bits of leaves from her skirt and swallowed hard and touched her fingers to her hair.

She had to go back. She had to lift her head and smile and return to the house and be her father's most gracious hostess, and she had to laugh and dance and be certain that no one ever knew what had taken place in the Venus garden.

"Amanda!"

Hearing her name called, she leapt to her feet and forced a smile to her lips.

"Damien!" she called in response to that well-loved voice. She knew her cousin would quickly be upon her, for he knew the maze as thoroughly as she did. They had often played there as children. "Damien!"

He came through the last row of hedges, bewigged and handsome, looking fabulously elegant. He knew his appearance was quite proper and perfect, and he paused by the Venus statue to pose for her quickly. "The ultimate gentleman, the lord of leisure!" he said, then he laughed and raced toward her, and she threw herself into his arms.

"Damien! You're back. I thought that you were staying in Philadelphia with your brother and that the two of you had been larking about from Boston to New York. And it frightens me when you and he are apart for I am ever afraid of what trouble you will find!"

He shook his head, and it seemed for a moment that sober thoughts clouded his dark handsome eyes. "I am ever quick to avoid trouble!" he vowed to her, then laughed. "I heard that Lord Sterling was hosting a ball, and I came quickly, thinking that my dear sweet cousin might need me."

Amanda pulled away from him, watching his eyes. Then she sighed softly. "So you knew too. All the world knew about Robert and this Duchess of Owenfield except for me, and, therefore, I made the most horrible fool of myself." If she wasn't careful, she'd start crying again.

"Amanda, he's not worthy of you," Damien told her swiftly. Setting an arm about her shoulder, he led her to sit down on the bench.

She smiled up at him lovingly. "Perhaps not, but I loved him, Damien. So what do I do now?"

"Forget him. There will be other men to offer for you, to love you—"

"Well, I've had the offer!" she said, and laughed bitterly. "But not the love. It was quite astounding. Lord Cameron appeared on the scene and offered himself."

"Cameron!" Damien repeated, startled.

"Aye, the traitor. My night is beset by betrayal, so it seems, for Father had told him yes!"

Damien stood, hooking his thumbs into his waistband as he paced before her. He swung around and looked at her. "He's been quite the bachelor, Mandy. You know that. Mamas have thrown their daughters at him for some time now, and he has never shown the least interest. You are deeply honored, you know."

"You like him!" Amanda accused. "You were good friends in Boston, or so it seemed, but, Damien, you must take the greatest care! You know that the man is a traitor."

Damien hesitated a long time, looking at her. "No, I do not know him as a traitor, cousin."

Amanda gasped, leaping up to catch hold of his shoulder. "You can't mean that! I . . . I know that he is guilty of evil deeds, I have seen him in action. And he follows the words of fanatics, of fools—"

Damien shook his head, watching her sadly. "I do not believe that these men are fanatics or fools, Mandy." She stared at him blankly, and he suddenly gripped her hands with excitement. "In Philadelphia I met with the writer and printer Benjamin Franklin. I—"

"Benjamin Franklin? The newspaper man? The fellow who puts out that *Poor Richard's Almanac?*" Franklin lived in Pennsylvania; his yearly book on weather and forecasts and sayings was like a bible to men from Georgia to Maine, and even up into the Canadian colonies.

"Yes, Franklin. Benjamin Franklin. He's considered a great man these days there, a wise man indeed."

"He prints insurrection, I take it."

"You'd love him, Mandy."

"Oh, Damien! You frighten me. I do not like the company you keep. Franklin wants war."

"No! No man wants war. But if you listen to these people, you'll come to understand."

"Understand what? We are English. We must pay taxes for English defense! Come, Damien, think on it. Without our fine English soldiers, what would we have done during the French and Indian Wars? Our militia was sad and pathetic! Scant defense!"

"Not so scant!" Damien protested. "Why, it was only what our colonials learned about Indian warfare that saved us then. George Washington was a volunteer with the British regulars when General Braddock was overtaken by the French and Indians, and it was young Washington who saw the troops back to Virginia. And Robert Rogers's rangers out of Connecticut were so adept and disciplined that they became part of the regular British army."

"British reinforcements saved us in the end, and it was a horrible and long bloody war. Without the Crown forces we would have been lost, and you know it."

He looked at her. "A Continental Congress is due to meet in Philadelphia this September to protest the closing of the port of Boston and other 'intolerable' acts."

Mandy exhaled. "I am so tired of this endless talk of war."

Damien laughed. "Cousin, you weren't even born when the French and Indian Wars broke out in 1754. And you were a babe of eight when it ended in sixty-three, so tell me, what makes you such an expert?"

She lowered her head suddenly, remembering that it had been in 1763, when the last of the campaigns had begun, that she had first seen Eric Cameron. Lord Hastings had called a hunt just before some of the Virginia relief troops were due to leave. There'd been no reason for young Cameron to go, but his father had already been killed in the fighting and his grandfather had not denied him the right to fight if he chose. He had been young, disdainful, and ardent, she remembered. Determined to fight. Assured, poised . . .

Abysmally rude to her.

She shook her head. Well, he had come back, and he had been given some officer's commission. Even though his grandfather hadn't allowed him to leave with one, he'd earned it on his own.

Mandy shivered. She couldn't understand war, and although she'd been very young during the French and Indian Wars, she could still remember the tears of the women who had lost husbands, the sons who had lost fathers, the girls who had lost their lovers. And there had been greater tragedy before her birth, when the war had just begun, for the Acadians from Nova Scotia—Frenchmen who had loved their land and stayed with it when it had gone from French rule to British in a previous treaty —were no longer trusted. They were cruelly exiled from their lands and cast upon the shores of Maine and Massachusetts and Virginia. Although some were able to make it into the French Louisiana Territory, many had been forced to seek some livelihood among the hostile English and Americans. There were still Acadians at Sterling Hall, even though her father despised them. She had heard it rumored that her father had slain an Acadian, although it had been at her birth, and she had never known whether it was true or not. She pitied the women, and the beautiful little children, and she had always done her best to be kind to the Acadians who remained with them. Indeed, Danielle was Acadian.

And still men went to war.

They had gone before, and it seemed now that they were growing eager to do battle again, that they might soon be eager to stand before flaring muskets, to allow themselves to be brutally ripped and torn and maimed.

"I'm not an expert on war, Damien, and I don't want to be," she assured him. "And I'm very worried about you."

"No! Ah, cousin, please, for the love of God, don't worry

about me. This is Damien. I land on my feet, always. Remember that."

"I'll keep it in mind when they hang you."

"They'll not hang me. And they'll not hang your new betrothed either, love."

"Betrothed!"

"You said that Lord Cameron proposed—"

"Proposed? No, I did not say that. He burst upon Robert and me with an announcement that Father had agreed to his suggestion that he and I marry. But then . . ."

"Then what?"

"He was quick to assure me that he did not want me without my consent." She paused, looking at Damien. "Why would Father do such a thing so suddenly, though? Father is an ardent loyalist. Could it be true?"

"Zounds—"

"Damien, don't swear."

"Me! Why, Mandy, when you've the mind, you swear like a seaman!"

"Don't be absurd. Ladies don't swear. But if I were to swear, I wouldn't do silly things like turn the words around. I should say, 'God's body!' and that would be that!"

"Tarnation! So you would, Mandy!"

"Damnation—and be done with it!" she said.

"If you weren't such a lady, that's exactly what you'd say!" Damien murmured with mock solemnity. But then he frowned in earnest. "Who knows anything about your father? He's never much liked me, and that's a fact."

Amanda frowned. It was true. Damien was the child of her mother's younger brother, and her father had tolerated him, keeping up the pretense of family, but had never shown him any affection. Michael, Damien's elder brother, very seldom came near Sterling Hall. He would not pretend to tolerate his uncle, and though Amanda loved Michael dearly, she seldom saw him now for he had moved to Pennsylvania.

"Surely Father does love you—" Amanda began awkwardly, but Damien interrupted her, waving a hand in the air.

"Cousin, I do not mean to be cruel, but I wonder if he even loves you. Never mind, how callous of me. What a horrible thing to say. And still, let's head into the house, shall we? He was asking about you, and I'd hate to bring his wrath down upon the two of us. And—"

"And what?" Amanda asked quickly as her cousin paused.

"And you need to dance, love. You need to dance and laugh and appear as if you're having the time of your life."

"Oh!" The blood drained from her face as she remembered that she had been rejected and humiliated. She tossed back her hair, adjusting the comb over her ear. "Am I all right, Damien?"

"All right? You are entirely beautiful. And we shall kick up our heels and make fools of the lot of them!" He caught her hand and led her quickly through the maze. "Remember when we were children? I loved this place so. You were going to marry a prince, or a duke at the very least. And I was going to kidnap the most glorious Indian maiden and strike out to conquer the world."

Gasping as she hurried to keep up with his pace, Amanda laughed. But there was pain to the laughter, just as there was pain to growing up. Dreams were like clouds, created only to be shattered by violent, unexpected storms.

She stopped short, just outside the entrance to the maze. She could see the lanterns swaying brilliantly upon the porch, and she could see the silhouettes of their guests through the windows, elegant men, beautiful women with their coiffures piled high and their skirts most fashionably wide. Growing up. It was suddenly very frightening, and she had never felt so old as she did this night. Life was still a game, but it was for higher stakes, and she suddenly shivered.

"It's all going to change again, isn't it, Damien?"

"Who knows what the future holds?" he answered her with a shrug. "Come, hold my hand, and we'll slip right onto the dance floor."

They scampered up the steps and over the broad porch together, slipping into the house at the end of the hallway.

It wasn't to be quite so easy as they had planned, for Amanda's father was there, watching them as they arrived.

"Damien!" he said sharply. "I would have a word with you now. And you, girl—" He paused, his voice low and grating as he stared at her coldly. "You I will deal with later!"

"Ah, Lady Sterling!" A voice interrupted. She spun around, recognizing the deep resonant sound. It was Eric Cameron. He bowed to her father. "Alas, your charming daughter and I shall not wed, sir, but she did promise me this dance just minutes ago."

"Minutes ago—"

"But of course, sir. May I?" He smiled at Lord Sterling and caught Amanda's hand, swirling her out to the center of the hall where couples were just forming for a reel. The musicians started up and she could not move at first. His silver gaze lit upon her and a daring smile touched his lips.

"Dance, Lady Amanda. You've got it in you, I know that you do. Toss your head back with that glorious mane of hair and cast one of your dazzling smiles upon me. Laugh, and let the whole of the world go to hell. They are whispering about you, and your scandalous behavior, rushing into the maze with an engaged man. Gossips and old hags. Let them know that you don't give a halfpenny about their opinions."

"What makes you think that I have ever cared about their opinions?" she countered. His hands touched hers, and suddenly they were swirling to the music.

"Perhaps you don't. But you do care about your pride."

"Do I?"

"Immeasurably."

"Enough so that I should not be dancing with a known rabble-rouser?"

"Rabble-rouser? Ah, milady, I've not nearly the eloquence necessary to sway the populace!"

"They talk of you from here to the nether regions, Lord Cameron. How can you say that?"

"You haven't heard the real speech masters, milady.

They rouse the heart, and that is where change lies, madame. Not in arms, and not even in bloodshed. Change lies within the very heart and soul of the people."

"So you do seek war."

"No one seeks war."

"You are infamous."

"Perhaps, but as I said, I haven't the eloquence to move worlds, milady."

She shivered suddenly, not knowing why. He was scarcely a humble man, yet his words caused her to feel chills.

Someone walking over her grave. . . .

Or perhaps a warning. As if she would live to see the day when she would depend desperately upon his eloquence and his ability to sway the masses.

Never. He was the traitor.

"You are a liar, a knave, and a scoundrel."

He laughed, lowering his head near hers, and she realized that all the room was watching them. "Am I all that, milady? Pity, for I felt that you fit so very well with me. And of course, I'm even daring to believe that you might realize it one day—once your heart recovers from its bruising."

"I shall survive, but I shall never discover that I fit well with you, milord." She smiled sweetly, and they swirled with an ever greater vigor about the floor. His eyes never left hers, and with each step she felt more fully the heat of the summer's night, the sizzle of fire, as if lightning storms raged outside. His confidence in himself was outrageous, yet even thinking of his kiss, of his touch upon her, caused her breath to catch, her heart to thunder, and she realized there was one thing about him she could not resist—he was exciting. He infuriated her, and if she cared for nothing else, she did long to show him that she would never be beaten.

"Ah . . . careful, smile sweetly! Lady Geneva has her eyes upon us."

"Perhaps she is jealous. Didn't you recently share a dance with her?"

"Recently, yes. But I've never proposed marriage to her."

"I see. But perhaps you have made other proposals to Lady Geneva?"

"The green eyes of jealousy, love?"

"I'm not your love, and my eyes are green by birth, mi-lord."

"Lady Geneva makes her own proposals," he told her softly, and she almost wrenched from his hold, for she knew then that they had been lovers, and she was furious that she should be so bothered by the thought.

"I'm quite exhausted. May we cease this mockery?"

"Alas, no! Chin up, eyes bright, 'tis be damned with the world, remember?"

" 'Tis be damned with you, sir, and if you'll excuse me—"

"Ah, but I won't."

And he did not. He held her close, and she was captured with the dance. Swirling and spinning, they passed by the other dancers, her hair and her gown flying out about her, making her a vision of beauty and fire in the night, on the arms of the tall, dark man. He twirled her from the dance floor out onto the porch, and then he had her laughing, for he did not quit then, but deftly brought her leaping down the steps and onto the lawn. Once there, he continued to swirl her beneath the moonlight. She cast back her head, smiling, for he was right about one thing. She longed to throw all caution to the wind, to show the gossips that she would do as she pleased, that she was not spurned and she knew no pain. He saw her smile, and some knowing glint came to his eyes.

"A temptress and a hell-raiser, milady? Shall we show them that life is to be lived to the fullest and that passion is its own master?"

"You are a hell-raiser. I am no temptress."

"Ah! I beg to disagree!"

"Do you, sir? Amazing, but I do not see you begging at all."

He smiled. "A matter of speech, milady."

"Humility is surely your greatest virtue."

"However you would have it, Lady Sterling, however you would have it."

And then suddenly they were dancing no more. They stood beneath the moonlight. His mouth was hard and unsmiling. His eyes were as piercing as a silver blade as they stared down into hers.

"There are whispers upon the wind, Amanda. Harsh whispers. Should you need me, know that I will be there."

"I will not need you!" she promised. But perhaps that was not so true, for even though the night was warm she was already shivering, and despite the entire debacle of the evening, she longed to cast herself into his arms and feel their warmth and security about her. And yet, she thought, for all the lightness of his words, this man would be no gentle master, but one determined upon his own cause. A woman who loved him was bound to be mastered by that iron will and determination.

No! she thought. I shall never lose my heart or my soul to one such as he! The pain that she felt this night was one thing. She realized that being entrapped by the fierce passion of this man could cause an anguish she could not begin now to fathom. The strange sensations touched her like mist, making her feel uneasy and hot. The strange tingling seized her body once again, dangerously touching places that it should not.

"You—you cannot love me, you don't even know me!" she cried.

"I know a great deal about you," he told her, and he smiled again. "And don't forget—I am in lust with you."

"You wish to best me! That is all. I have not fallen amorously into your arms, as others do too easily. You like to win, before you step upon your conquests. Well, you shall not win against me, sir."

"Perhaps not. I'll consider it a challenge well met." He was silent for a moment, then he indicated someone over his shoulder. "It's an interesting evening. Your lost love is consoling himself, I see."

"What?" Amanda swung around, stunned to see that Robert had come to the porch.

With Geneva. And they were close together in an intimate embrace. She had cast her arms about his neck. Her head was back and her laughter was throaty. And then she was kissing him.

Amanda gave not a thought to the night, the world, or propriety. Blindly she cast her arms about the man before her and came up high on her toes to press her length against him. Instinctively she arched against him, curling her fingers into his hair and then pressing her lips against his. Tentatively she pressed her tongue against his teeth.

And then the world seemed to explode. His mouth gave way, and he was not in her arms, but she was in his. She was barely upon her feet, swirling in the moonlight again, and his tongue raked her mouth as if it invaded the very soul of her and reached with his searing liquid fire to touch her heart. He laid his hand upon her breast, and something moved in her to that touch, something that pulsed with curiosity.

With desire.

"Oh . . ." She gasped against him, when his mouth lifted from hers at last.

He held her still, swept off her feet, in his arms. She stared up at him in the darkness and saw his slow rake's smile just touch the corner of his lips as he spoke seriously. "Did that suffice for what you wished, milady? I do believe you've struck fairly in return. The poor dear fellow is on the porch. I'm afraid he's just about ready to trip over his tongue. Shall I release you and ease his agony? Or do you wish to heap more torture upon him? I am ready to oblige you in any manner you choose."

"Oh! Oh, you bastard!" She gasped. "Set me down! This instant."

He started to do so. Instantly. She nearly fell flat and managed to save herself only by clinging to his neck.

"Lord Cameron—"

"Yes, love. What is it now? I never seem to be able to please you."

"That's because I absolutely despise you."

"Ah, then I shall look forward to the kisses you will give when you've discovered that you love me."

"Kisses! I shall spit upon your carcass when they've hanged you!"

"Shh! Careful, he's coming close. With Geneva upon his heels. Ah, and there is Lady Harding! Amazing how many of your father's guests have discovered that they need a bit of fresh air. Slowly now, slide down against me." He carefully set her down. She was against him still, yet it was a very proper position, with his arm just about her as he escorted her in the moonlight. She stared at him furiously, but she didn't fight him. She didn't want to face her father with any more whispers of scandal raging about her.

"You will be made to pay one day," she promised him pleasantly.

"To pay? Why, milady, I have desired to do nothing the whole night long except to ease you from any difficulty you encountered. You do have a vengeful streak within your delicate soul. Perhaps, when we are married, I shall have to beat it from you."

She started to jerk from him and she saw the laughter in his eyes. "Perhaps I shall marry you, just before they tighten your noose. I understand that your property is very fine."

"You must visit it. Come to Cameron Hall any time, milady. Or if you're in Williamsburg, you must be my guest, whether I am in attendance or not. I shall leave word with Mathilda that you are welcome any time. Ah . . . here comes your father. He is looking for us, I think."

He raised a hand. Nigel Sterling stood upon the porch, his hand stuck into his frock coat. He saw Eric Cameron's wave and started down the steps.

Amanda did not like the speculative look within her father's eyes. She did not like his glance upon her, colder than usual.

"There you are, my dear, Eric."

"The night was captivating. Not nearly so captivating as your daughter, yet the combination of loveliness was one that I could not resist. Forgive me."

"You are forgiven for being young and enamored, Lord Cameron—if not for other things," Nigel said. He smiled cordially, but when he gazed at Amanda, she still felt the coldness. "Our guests are beginning to leave, Mandy. Perhaps you will be so kind as to see them on their way?"

"Of course, Father. Excuse me, Lord Cameron."

He reached for her hand, kissed it. She waited until his eyes rose to hers and she mouthed sweetly, "Good-bye."

"I'm not leaving—yet," he returned, arching a brow rakishly.

She pursed her lips, turned about, and fled for the house. Her father remained talking a moment longer, then he followed her, standing by the door while Amanda took a position at the landing of the stairway, by the bannister.

The Hastings and the Hardings were leaving, and Amanda called Danielle to fetch their hats and accessories. She was thanked for a wonderful time, and she kept her sweet smile in place, wondering if the ladies were pitying her—or if they were eager to rush home to discuss her scandalous behavior. It didn't matter. She kept her chin up and her laughter light. No one would ever know just how devastated she had been.

Mrs. Newmeyer left next, thanking her and Lord Sterling for the sumptuous buffet. Smiling graciously, Amanda realized she hadn't even glanced at the buffet table.

Then Robert was before her, his eyes pained as they stared into hers—as if he was the one who had been betrayed. He managed to draw her aside as her father was caught in a discussion nearer the door.

"My God, how could you!" Robert whispered heatedly.

"How could I?"

"I saw you in his arms. It was indecent."

"Indecent! Robert, he asked me to marry him. You asked me—no! You sought to force me into something that was indecent!"

"He'll never marry you," Robert said harshly.

"Oh?"

"It's a lie. It's a ploy. He's disgustingly wealthy, and you are perhaps an heiress, but nowhere near as wealthy as he. He couldn't possibly be serious. You're not—"

"I'm not as disgustingly wealthy? Robert, take your

hands off me. Contrary to your belief, not every man longs to awaken with wealth alone on the pillow beside him. Now leave me be."

Robert stiffened and turned sullen. Although the pain of betrayal and shattered dreams was still with her, she was startled by the discoveries she was making. She did not like this side of him.

"You won't marry him. He's a bloody patriot."

"Patriot? I believe the word might well mean many things. And I do intend to marry him."

A slight cough interrupted them. Amanda swung around to see Lord Cameron. His eyes were alight with amusement and mockery. "Good night, my love," he said, purposely turning her away from Robert. "I shall return very soon—to discuss the wedding plans, of course."

She longed to kick him but she didn't dare. Robert was still before her. She forced herself to smile. "Good night. My love," she added.

He bowed deeply. At the door he paused, speaking with her father.

In a fury, Robert swung about and left too.

There were more guests bidding her good night. She longed to escape to her room, but she held her ground and maintained her smile.

Damien was the last to leave for his home, an hour north of his uncle's estate. She kissed him and agreed to ride to Williamsburg with him soon. Then Damien said good night to her father.

"Yes. Good night, young man."

They shook hands, and Amanda thought that Damien had been right—her father did not like him. She clenched her hands behind her back, wishing that he would not be so obvious.

The door closed. Danielle stood quietly before Lord Sterling, lowering her eyes. "Is there anything else, sir?"

Her voice still held a hint of a French accent, and Amanda thought that even that annoyed her father. He looked at Danielle distastefully, even though she was a wonderful servant. She managed the household staff and slaves, and did so very well, and still Lord Sterling never had a good word for her.

Amanda thought that Danielle stayed because of her. She wasn't sure. Danielle's husband and brother had died in the cargo hold of the ship that had brought them to Virginia from Port Royal, Nova Scotia. Her tiny daughter had died in that same hold.

"No. You are dismissed."

Danielle turned to leave. Lord Sterling quickly shifted his gaze from his servant to his daughter, and the cold distaste remained in his eyes.

"And for you, girl."

"What is it, Father?" Amanda said wearily.

"Come here."

She was somewhat surprised by his tone, but too weary to fight him. She strode across the room to stand before him.

"Yes?"

She was stunned when his hand lashed out at her, catching her across the face with such violence that she fell to her knees, her head reeling. She screamed out in her surprise and pain. Danielle, barely out of the room, heard her cry and came rushing toward her.

"Stop!" Lord Sterling commanded Danielle. "It will be a whipping for you. You are dismissed."

Danielle paused, then continued forward. Crawling to her knees, Amanda raised a hand to stop her. "I'm fine. Danielle, *tu peux t'en aller maintenant.*" she urged her in French.

Her father seemed to hate even the language. His eyes darkened further with displeasure as he stared down at her. "Don't you ever go against my word. I made arrangements. You broke them."

"What?" Amanda said, amazed.

"Lord Cameron has informed me that he is not interested in a marriage that is not desirable to you. I will make the arrangements for your life—you will not."

"No!" she cried. This night, which she had hoped would be a night of magic, had turned into a nightmare. "You cannot make me marry, Father! I do not believe this. I—"

"Don't worry. Lord Cameron no longer wants you."

"You cannot make me marry anyone!"

"When I so choose, you will marry. You will not disobey me, or else you will learn the persuasion of the lash. Now go to your room. Get out of my sight."

She stood, facing him, feeling her cheek swell while tears rushed to her eyes. "I—I hate you!" she whispered to him.

And to her amazement, he smiled. With pleasure. "Hate me to your heart's content. But you bear my name, and you will obey me. Now go to your room."

She turned and fled up the stairway. More than anything in the world, she wanted to escape the sight of him.

When she reached her room, she slammed and locked the door and leaned against it, gasping for breath.

Then she burst into tears and fell on her bed. What sin could she have committed that was so grave that she should deserve the agony of all that had happened this night?

Magic had died.

And even in her misery she was dimly aware that the nightmare was just beginning.

The world was changing, her whole world was changing. Winds of change were sweeping over the land, and no one, no one at all, would be able to stand against them.

V ❧

For several weeks Amanda managed to stay clear of her father, just as he stayed far away from her. It helped that he was gone on business for a time, but even when he returned, she had no difficulty avoiding him. He dined in his room; she dined in her own.

It was a miserable time for her as she accepted the fact that not only had she been betrayed by the man she had so foolishly loved, but her own father did not care for her at all. All of her life she had thought he was being stern for her own good, but now she realized he hated the very sight of her.

Then she was plagued by thoughts of Eric Cameron. Despite her rude refusal of his proposal, he had willingly allowed her to use him to taunt Robert when she'd had an opportunity to salvage some of her pride. She had not heard a word from him since the party, and as the days passed, she realized that she would not. His promise that he would come by to discuss the wedding had been for Robert's sake.

Yet she had expected him. He was not a man to give up what he wanted, and he had said that he wanted her. Maybe he hadn't wanted her badly enough. She told herself that it was definitely well and good, but when she lay awake at night, flushed and tossing, it was Eric Cameron she was remembering, the audacity of his touch and laughter, the bold command of his eyes. He knew too much, she thought, and she tried to tell herself that she referred to Boston—and to Damien. But it wasn't true. He knew too much about her. He knew her far too well.

Her days passed easily enough despite her expectation and dread that Eric would come—and her startling disappointment that he did not. Her pride was doubly wounded, nothing more. She just wished that she did not feel such peculiar flashes of heat and unease when she thought of his eyes upon her, when she remembered the force of his hold, the caress of his lips.

Still, her father's cruelty ravaged her soul. If home had not been such a pleasant place to be, she would have thought about running away. She did start wondering where she could go if she ever felt desperate enough to leave. She could go back to Boston and stay with Anne Marie, but if her father wished to wed her to some distasteful stranger, he would come for her, and Sir Thomas would dutifully hand her over. She had just returned from her father's sister's plantation in South Carolina. And while she loved her aunt and her cousins, she knew that if her Aunt Clarissa were pressed to side with either her or her father, she would choose her father.

Then there was Philadelphia, where Damien's brother Michael lived, but both Philadelphia and Boston seemed to be such hotbeds of rebellion right now that they did not seem to be safe places to visit. Thinking over her own position, she realized that she was very strongly a loyalist herself and that she did not want to live among rebels.

Then, too, she loved her home. She loved Virginia, she loved the soft flowing river. She loved the summer warmth and the flowers and the beauty of the land, and she loved the accents of the people. She loved Sterling Hall, the singsong of the slaves in the field, the melodic murmurs of the Acadians on the household staff and in the laundry.

Walking out beyond the oaks that lined the walkway before the house, Amanda suddenly panicked, remembering that her father had mentioned sending her to England when she had first returned from South Carolina. She hadn't protested emphatically then, for she had thought that he meant to protect her because he loved her. Now she knew that he merely wanted her out of the way, set upon a shelf until he was able to use her as pawn to his advantage. Her heart quickened. She would not go to England. She would weather the storms of discontent until reason prevailed.

She stared down the slope of ground in the back of the house, leading toward the river. Sterling Hall was self-sufficient. There was a huge smokehouse, the laundry, the stables, the barn, the carriage house, the cooper's, the blacksmith's, and the shoemaker. Beyond those buildings lay the slave quarters, and the larger houses for the free servants, and far beyond those lay the lands and the homes of the tenant farmers. Her father did very well here. The land was rich, and the fields were filled with the very best tobacco. Her father gave it no thought himself; he never dirtied his hands, nor did he keep his own books. He hunted, danced, and indulged in politics, drank hard, and played hard. Amanda knew that he had a mistress in Williamsburg, and she had also heard that he slept with one of their young mulatto slaves.

On her fifteenth birthday she had struck Damien in a fury when he had told her about it. But then, when she had asked Danielle if it was true, she had been appalled, for Danielle had not been able to deny the accusations.

She had known that her father was not a terribly nice man. She had just never realized how he really felt about her. Maybe she had always sensed it, though. And maybe that was why she had fallen so desperately in love with Robert.

Robert. At the thought of him, she felt the same gnawing

pain in her middle. She had been so desperately in love. She had imagined a life with Robert, waking beside him, laughing in his arms, taking great pride in the fact that their home was known far and wide in all the colonies for its grace and beauty. She had never dreamed of a different house—it had always been Sterling Hall. She had never imagined her father's death—he had just been gone, and Robert had been lord of Sterling. They had laughed and played by the river, and she had even indulged in fantasies about making love. The water would ripple by them and the moon would be full up above, or else the sun would beat down upon their daringly naked flesh, but it would be all right, because they would love one another so deeply. She had never really thought too terribly much about the act of making love, not until . . .

Her thought trailed away, and then she flushed furiously, grateful that she was alone with her awful realization.

She had never, never thought about the act itself until she had been with Eric Cameron in the maze. Never, never before that night had she felt anything like that physical excitement, like a hot river sweeping through her, awakening her flesh.

"Oh! Will he forever plague me?" she whispered aloud, and pressed her hands against her cheeks. They were flaming. He had sworn that he would plague her, she recalled, but she had not thought that it could be in this manner! She didn't want to think about Eric Cameron, she hated him almost as much as she hated her father this morning. She wanted to hate Robert, but love died a very hard death, and so she hated Eric all the more venomously. For all that he had witnessed, for all that he had caused—and for the horribly shameful way that he made her feel.

She wasn't going to think about him, that was all. Not now, not ever again. And as much as she loved Sterling Hall, maybe it was time to leave for an extended vacation. Then she wouldn't have to hear the rumors and whispers when Robert married his duchess.

"Amanda! Amanda!"

She swung around. Danielle was on the porch steps,

wiping her hands on her apron, waving to her. Frowning, Amanda waved in return and then hurried toward the house. Danielle's dark eyes were anxious. *"Ma petite,* your father is looking for you. He is in his study. You must go now."

Amanda stiffened. She had no desire to see her father, but such a summons would be difficult to ignore. He had total power over her; he could beat her if he chose, he could send her away. And her only recourse would be to run away.

She squared her shoulders. "Thank you, Danielle. I will see Father now."

She smoothed down her cotton skirt and composed herself as she walked down the hallway to his office. She knocked on the door, then waited for him to bid her to enter. When he did, she came in and stood before his desk in silence, waiting. An open ledger book lay before him, and he finished with a group of sums before looking up. When he did, his eyes were as cold as lead. He looked her up and down distastefully.

"Make ready for a trip."

"What?" she said. "I don't wish to leave—"

"I care nothing for your wishes. I am going to Williamsburg. The governor has asked that I come. And he has especially asked that you come too. You will do so."

Her heart took flight. He was not attempting to send her out of the country. She just wished that they would not be traveling together.

"Fine. When do we leave?"

"This afternoon. Be ready by three."

That was it. He turned his attention back to his ledger. Amanda turned around and left his office. Danielle was out in the hall, her deep, beautiful dark eyes full of anxiety again.

"It's all right," Amanda told her. "We are leaving this afternoon. For Williamsburg."

"Am I going with you?"

"I didn't think to ask. Yes, you must come. It's the only way I shall be able to—"

"To what?" Danielle prompted her.

"To bear being near him," Amanda said quietly, then she turned around and hurried for the stairs.

At three she was waiting in the hallway. Timothy and Remy, two of the house slaves, had carried down her trunks. She was dressed in white muslin with a tiny print of maroon flowers and an overcoat of the same color in velvet. The overcoat fell in fashionable loops over her wide-hipped petticoats, then fell gracefully in a short train down the back of her skirt. She wore her delicate pearled pumps and a wide-brimmed straw hat decorated with sweeping plumes. Danielle, behind her, wore a smaller hat and a soft gray cotton dress, but even she had given way to fashion in her choice of petticoat. She was still very beautiful, Amanda thought of Danielle. After all these years.

Her father appeared, looked her over curtly, gave the servants last-minute instructions, and then ordered her into the carriage. He looked at Danielle for a long moment and then shrugged. "No French," he told her as she climbed up into the carriage. "I won't hear any of that gibberish, do you hear me?"

"Yes, milord," Danielle said simply. Her eyes were lowered as they entered the carriage, and a chill shot through the Amanda as she watched the exchange. She was suddenly certain that her father had used Danielle, just as he had used his mistress in Williamsburg, and just as he used the mulatto slave girl. She felt hot and ill, and wished desperately that she would not have to face him for the next several hours as they traveled.

It was a miserable journey, the whole of it passing in near silence. Her father read his paper, scowling constantly. Danielle stared out the window. There had been rain, and the road was pockmarked and heavily grooved. Like the others, Amanda sat in silence. She stared out the window, eager to arrive, eager to be rid of her father's presence. Not until they neared Williamsburg and passed the College of William and Mary to come down Duke of Gloucester Street and turn onto Market Green did she begin to feel the least bit pleased to have come. Then she leaned back, thinking that her father would be completely occupied, she would be free to shop, to visit friends, to forget some of what happened, and to plan for her own future.

They halted before the governor's palace. Servants were quick to help them from the carriage and to attend to their luggage. Amanda and her father were ushered into the entrance hallway while Danielle was taken to the servants' quarters on the third floor. Amanda did not look at her father while they waited, but stared at the impressive weaponry displayed with artistic grandeur upon the walls.

"Ah, Lord Sterling!"

She turned around as John Murray, Earl of Dunmore and the governor of Virginia, came toward them. Lord Dunmore was a tall, striking man with red hair and amber brown eyes and a fiery temperament to match his coloring. Amanda had always liked him. He was imperious but vivid and energetic, and generally kind and most often wise in his dealings with his elected government officials. It was only recently that he seemed to have completely lost his temper with the officials.

He was impeccably dressed in yellow breeches, fawn hose, and a mustard frock coat. His hair was powdered and queued, and his hand, when he took Amanda's, was as soft as pigskin. He smiled at her as he kissed her hand. "Lady Amanda, but you have grown to be a true beauty! You grace our very presence. The countess will be so sorry that she missed you!"

"Thank you, milord," she murmured, retrieving her hand. "Is your wife not here?"

"She is not feeling well this afternoon." He smiled with pleasure. "We are expecting a child, as you might have heard."

"I had not, milord, but I am delighted, of course."

She stepped back, aware that his true interest was in her father, which was fine. She wanted to escape them both.

"Nigel, you old goat, you're looking fit."

"And so are you, John."

"Come along. I've had tea served in the garden."

John Murray took Amanda's hand, slipping it through his arm. He chatted about the summer roses and about the weather as they walked through the vast and expansive ballroom to reach the gardens out in the rear. They walked along a path of beautiful hedges, and came at last to a manicured garden. At a table places were set with huge linen napkins and silver plates. Lord Dunmore's butler waited to serve them.

Amanda sat, and thanked the man when her tea was poured. She nibbled at a meat pie and realized she could barely eat when her father was near.

"Isn't it a glorious day?" John Murray demanded, and she agreed. She listened and responded politely, and wondered when they would clear their throats and indicate that their coming conversation might be lengthy and of little interest to a young lady.

They never came to that point. She was sipping a second cup of tea and watching a bluebird, wishing that she could fly away as easily as it could, when she realized that both men were silent and staring at her. She flushed and set down her teacup. "I'm so sorry. I was wandering."

"Ah, milady, it's quite all right. It is a beautiful day. And a young woman's fancy must not be confined to a garden with two older men, eh? I've heard that Lord Cameron asked for your hand in marriage, young lady," Dunmore said.

She flushed again and lifted her chin without glancing her father's way. "I believe he asked Father permission to court me, milord."

"You turned him down."

"I—" She hesitated a minute, feeling her father's eyes boring into her. She smiled sweetly. "Milord, I hear that he is in sympathy with certain men of whom I do not approve. His politics are quite different from my own."

"His politics! Nigel, do you hear that!" Dunmore laughed. "Why, young lady, you mustn't worry yourself with politics!"

She smiled. He was still chuckling, but the men exchanged glances again and again. A prickling of unease crept along her spine. Dunmore moved toward her. "Did you know, Amanda, that he is one of the wealthiest men in Virginia? He owns endless acres. He is titled, he is deeply respected. He is young, striking, and known for his courage, honesty, and valor. Perhaps he is noted for a certain hardness, determination, and temper, but his anger is aroused, they say, only under the greatest duress. He is considered a most illustrious marriage prospect and has been approached by nobility and royalty, as well as by the most affluent of private citizens. He has politely eluded all of these offers—then shocks us all with a proposal for you. Not that you are wanting in any physical way, indeed, my dear, you are surely one of the loveliest creatures in all of his Majesty's realm. But you are not royalty. Your father's holdings in Europe are meager. Therefore one would think that Lord Cameron is quite enchanted by your beauty and your beauty alone. You should feel quite honored, milady."

Honored. She remembered the way he had taken her into his arms, the way she had felt. And she remembered the way Robert had seemed to cower before him, and she felt ill.

She remained silent, and Lord Dunmore spoke again. "His teeth are excellent, and one of my maids told me the other day that he had the most manly handsome face and fascinating eyes she had ever seen. Would you mind explaining to me, milady, your aversion to the man?"

"I—" She paused, completely unprepared for the intimate conversation. This should be between her father and her, and no one else. She couldn't have even told her father, though, that her aversion was her love for another. She could have also told them both that Lord Cameron did not want her anymore, that he manipulated her like a puppet on a string, and that she would never be able to endure his laughter or the mocking knowledge in his eyes.

"I cannot say, milord," she answered at last, smiling. "What is there in one that we do or do not love? Who can say?"

Dunmore leaned back, nodding. "Your father has the right to say, child," he reminded her. "And at the moment . . ." His voice trailed for a moment. "Eric Cameron is one of my most able commanders. I will lead men out west to fight a Shawnee uprising very soon, and Eric will be my right hand. He can summon more men for a fighting force in less time than it takes to gather the militia. He is a very important man to me."

"I imagine that he is, milord," Amanda agreed carefully. She cast her lashes down and gazed toward her father, wondering where the conversation was leading. John Murray did not play idle games. He was a powerful man who spent his time wisely and well.

Her father remained silent. He just watched her, his eyes very small and narrow and speculative.

"Do you love England, my dear? Do you honor your king?" Lord Dunmore asked suddenly, staring at her as if she were a culprit.

"Of course!" She gasped, startled by the turn of conversation.

"So I thought!" he said proudly. He leaned toward her again. "Lady Amanda, I have a task to ask of you."

Her fingers started to shake. Dread filled her.

"As I've said, Lord Cameron is to leave very soon for the west. The Indians are giving our people severe trouble, and they must be stopped. Cameron and I will be together in this venture, I know—he has given me his word."

Eric Cameron was leaving. That was wonderful. But what on earth could they want of her then?

"Until such a time, I would like you to see him."

"I beg your pardon, milord?"

"For me, for England, Lady Amanda. It is also your father's will. See him. Become his friend. Pretend that you might consider his proposal."

She didn't realize that she was standing until she heard her teacup shatter upon the ground. "Oh, no! I can't. I really can't. I'm sorry, I do love England, milord, and I will be loyal to the death if need be, but I cannot—"

"He spends his time at a tavern with a number of hotheads. Men who might be arrested soon enough for their politics. I want to know if he is still loyal to the Crown. And I want to know what plans are being made by these so-called patriots."

"But milord! Men speak openly of their opinions. I believe Lord Cameron is a traitor, but then, by the law, so are hundreds of men. Lord Dunmore—"

"Please. Other men may have opinions. Not Lord Cameron. Too many men will follow him blindly, and, my dear, if he is guilty of stockpiling arms against the king, then he is a traitor in black and white, and must be stopped."

"But . . . I—I can't stop him!"

Dunmore leaned back. It was her father's turn to speak at last. He stood up, facing her coldly. "You can, Amanda. And you will."

"Father—"

"You see, Lord Dunmore has on his person an arrest warrant for your cousin Damien."

"What?" She gasped. He stared at her, smiling. He was enjoying himself, she realized. He really enjoyed seeing her hurt and shocked, and he enjoyed using her. Her ears seemed to roar. She could smell the flowers, and she could hear the chatter of birds on the air. The day was so very beautiful.

And so awful.

She looked at the governor, and she knew that it was true. "What crime has Damien committed?" she asked hollowly. She tried very hard not to scream in panic, for they didn't need to tell her much. She had suspected him of foolish deeds for a long, long time. She had followed him in Boston because she had been so afraid of his activities. She didn't think that he had dumped tea into the harbor, but he had left the party so determinedly. . . .

"Damien Roswell is guilty of a number of crimes, dear. We know that he has smuggled arms and armaments and that he has possessed and propagated numerous pieces of seditious literature."

"Seditious literature! Why, Lord Dunmore. You would have to hang half of the colony—"

"I can prove that he has been smuggling arms, Amanda," Dunmore said softly. His tone was truly unhappy. Then he fell silent, and in those seconds Amanda felt her blood run cold. She could not bear it if harm were to come to her cousin, no matter how foolish his behavior. "His crime," Dunmore continued softly, "is treason, we have him dead to rights. But Damien is a small fish, and knowing how dear he is to you, we are loath to make him a scapegoat for the sharks."

She sank back to her seat again. They couldn't be serious, but they were. She lifted her chin, determined that she could be as cold as her father. She would never forgive him now. She hated him with all her heart.

"What do you want?"

"The truth about Cameron. What he intends to do, what he has done. I have to know if he will turn his back on me if the trouble with the radicals becomes too serious."

"If I get you the information you want—"

"Then I destroy the warrant for your cousin."

"I don't mind—I don't mind being a spy, milord. I don't mind serving England, and I am a loyal Tory. But milord, if you'll just ask something else of me—"

"I need you, Lady Amanda."

"But Lord Cameron is no fool!" she said uneasily.

"Yes, I realize that. The man is my friend, even if we are destined to be enemies. You'll have to be convincing. Tarnation, girl! I must know if he is loyal to me or not!"

"You—you are both blackmailing me!" she cried.

Lord Dunmore rose. He was not happy with the situation, she knew. He didn't like what he was asking her to do.

But her father was delighted with it. She knew then that it had all been her father's doing.

"Think about it. Your service would be greatly appreciated," Dunmore said. He rested his hand upon her shoulder. "The decision is still yours, my dear. I'll leave you to think." He walked away, and she was alone with her father. She stared at him for several long moments, listening to the chirp of the birds, feeling the sun and the breeze against her cheeks. Then she spoke with softly yet with venom.

"I hate you. I will never forgive you for this," she told him.

He rose, coming so close to her that she nearly leapt to her feet to run. He caught her chin and held it in a painful grip. "You'll do as you're told. I have waited all these years for you to be of some use, I have let you live the life of a lady, and now you will obey me. You will give me a place of prominence with the king. And if you do not, Damien will hang. Do you understand?"

She jerked free of his touch, trying to hide the tears that burned behind her eyes. "As I told Lord Dunmore, Eric Cameron is no fool! He knows that I despise him!"

"You must change his mind."

"He will not trust me."

"Convince him."

"What would you have me do, prostitute myself?"

Nigel Sterling curled his lip into a smile. "If necessary, my dear, yes."

She gasped, leaping up again, clutching her skirts. "You're a monster!" she told him. "No father would ask this of a child!"

His smile tightened. "I am a monster, but you are the spawn of a whore," he told her softly. "Use your heritage."

She gasped aloud, stunned. Then she cried, "No! How dare you! You cannot say that about my mother!" Furious, she leapt toward him.

He was no small man. He caught her in a cruel grip and held her very tight. She felt ill. His breath touched her face, his eyes raked over her, and that hateful smile remained.

"It would delight me to take a bullwhip against you. I can do that, as well as see that Damien hangs." He paused, staring into her eyes with an assurance that he did not threaten her idly. "Perhaps you should get ready for an evening out. Damien is here, in Williamsburg. I've told him that we are coming, and I've assured him he has my permission to take you for a ride this evening. You should get dressed. I expect him by seven. Such a young lad. Many will cry to see him hang, I am certain. Don't make the mistake of warning him. He is a dead man if you do."

Nigel released her and walked away, leaving her alone in the garden.

The scent of the summer flowers rose high all around her. The birds continued to chirp, the breeze to flutter the foliage. She sank down on the garden seat, her fists clenched in her lap, and feared that she would be sick.

Somewhere inside the mansion the countess was lying back on her bed with a smile upon her lips. She probably dreamed of her child, and when that child was born, both she and Lord Dunmore would cherish it, and plan a future for the babe with love and care.

What had gone so horribly awry in her life that her own father could despise her so? Label her mother a whore, and send her out to play a harlot's game?

She brought her knuckles to her mouth and bit down hard upon them, silently damning Damien for his foolish ways. But Damien loved her, honestly, with his soul and his heart. She had so little of value in life, of love sincere and untainted.

They were casting her to Lord Cameron. Casting her to the very wolf. Wolf? Aye, he was that! But if he had wanted her—even to devour her!—he would have come to her to do so. What could she do? Her father could not know how crude or harsh the words had been between them. He could not understand that it would be dangerous indeed for her to suddenly appear to have a change of heart.

She rose slowly and turned back toward the mansion. It had to be nearly seven now.

She did not mind serving England, there was so much that she would have done gladly for Lord Dunmore!

But this . . .

She started to shake, and so she walked faster. She was still shaking when she entered the mansion and hurried up the stairs to the guest room she had been given. She knew she had to wash and dress, but she threw herself on the bed, still shaking.

She remembered Eric Cameron's face, the strength of his features, the laughter in his eyes and then the hardness.

And then she knew why she shook so badly. She had said it, and it was the truth. The man was no fool. And if he suspected her of betraying him, if he caught her . . .

She swallowed hard, and she knew that she was afraid. Very, very afraid.

* * *

A hush fell over the crowd as Eric entered the public room of the Raleigh Tavern. It was known to be a place where men of different minds gathered, and Eric was looked upon with a certain distrust, for he was a lord, and it was expected that his allegiance was with the king. After all, he had great estates in England to consider.

Men, mostly planters and farmers, some merchants and shopkeepers, looked about, nodded his way respectfully, then looked nervously back to their meals or their ale. In turn he bowed, then ignored their suspicious gazes. He strode in, doffing his tricorn and cape and taking a table near the rear door.

The owner rushed forward to greet him. "Lord Cameron, come to visit with us for a spell, eh? Well, it's honored we be, and that's a fact."

"Is it? Tell me, is Colonel Washington about?"

The man went red in the face. "Well, now, I don't know—"

"It's all right" came a laughing voice. Washington himself was looking in from the hallway that led to the private rooms. He was a tall man, broad-shouldered, with dark hair—graying now—neatly queued at his nape. "He's my friend, and he's come to see me. Eric! Come along, will you? I've some people eager to meet you."

Eric rose, nodded to the innkeeper, and followed the colonel down along the hallway. Washington was a good many years his senior, a man hailing from the Fredericksburg area and now living closer to the coast at Mount Vernon, when he managed to be home these days. Mount Vernon was a beautiful plantation, and much like his own, Cameron Hall. Both homes had large main hallways and graceful porches with a multitude of windows facing the water in order to take advantage of the river breezes. Washington loved his estate, his lands, his horses, everything about home. But he had always been an ambitious man as well as a smart one. Eric shared his love of botany and respected his business sense. They were both heavily invested in the Ohio and Chesapeake Canal, and eager to see more westward expansion across the mountains.

Washington had married a very prosperous Williamsburg widow, Martha Custis, and though it had been whispered at the time that she was a somewhat dowdy little thing, she apparently offered him the warmth and domesticity that he needed. Eric knew Martha well and liked her very much. She had the touching ability to listen, to weigh a man's words carefully, and to respond with a gentle intelligence.

Following his friend down the hallway, Eric thought that George had aged rapidly in the last year. He and Martha had had no children of their own, but he had doted on his stepchildren, and last year his stepdaughter, Patsy, had died. The loss had taken its toll upon the man.

Perhaps all these whispers about war were good after all. They kept George's mind busy.

But then so did his estate. He had inherited Mount Vernon, his brother's property, after his sister-in-law and niece had both passed away. The property was his passion, as Eric could well understand. He felt that way about Cameron Hall. He never tired of studying the house, of adding on, or improving, just as he never tired of the land, moving crops, studying the growth of his vegetables, experimenting with growth cycles. The men had met in Williamsburg a few years after the French and Indian Wars. As they discussed the differences between the colonial and British soldiers, they had both reached the sad conclusion that the Crown did not treat the colonials at all well. Ever since his adventures in Boston on the eve of the tea party, Eric had joined Washington and members of the House of Burgesses more frequently in their conversations. Many men did not trust him as yet. Many others did.

In 1769 Lord Botetourt, then governor of Virginia and a popular and well-liked man, had made enemies when he dismissed the Virginia legislature because of the representatives' protest of the Stamp Act. Eric had been young then, a new member of the Upper House, and his voice had had little effect upon the decision. Eric had maintained his position—and his opinion, and eventually, the situation had evened out. The Stamp Act had been repealed.

Now the legislature had been dissolved again. During the first dissolution there had been a strained period between Eric and many of his more radical friends, but this time, he had offered to resign from the Governor's Council —an unprecedented event. Eric was walking a dangerous fence, and he was well aware of it. His ancestor Jamie Cameron had carried over a title, and because of that, Eric should be a staunch loyalist, a Tory to the core. But something about his meeting with young Frederick Bartholomew that night in Boston had changed him. There was danger in the air, but there was excitement as well. It seemed to Eric that it was becoming a time of great men and a time of change. He had heard Patrick Henry speak on several occasions, and though many people considered him a brash and foolish rabble-rouser, Eric found him to be amazingly eloquent, and more. Henry believed in his principles, and he was not afraid to risk his life or material possessions or position to speak out.

This was the New World. Cameron's own family had been living in Virginia since the early 1600s. But that was less than a score of decades. When compared with the age of the mother country, Virginia and the other colonies were young, raw, and exciting. Eric had attended Oxford; he had seen the Cameron estates in England, he had traveled to France and Italy and many of the German principalities, and he had learned that he loved no land as much as he did his own. Because of the very rawness, the newness, the excitement. Men and women traveled ever westward, seeking expansion, seeking a dream.

He didn't even like to think it, and yet Eric was convinced that the time was coming when the colonies would break away from England. And though even the supposed hotheads who met at the taverns decried the possibility of war, it was becoming increasingly evident that a split was looming before them.

"Come on in here," Washington said, opening the door to one of the smaller parlors. "It is just Thomas, Patrick, and myself tonight. I'm preparing to leave."

"Leave?"

"Our First Continental Congress meets in September."

"Oh. Of course. There are seven of us representing Virginia. Peyton Randolph, Richard Henry Lee, Patrick Henry, Richard Bland, Benjamin Harrison, Edmund Pendleton, and myself."

"A noble assembly," Eric complimented.

Washington grinned. "Thank you."

They entered the private room. Patrick Henry and Thomas Jefferson were both sitting before the fire. Henry leapt to his feet first. "Ah, Lord Cameron. Welcome!"

Eric walked across the room and shook his hand. He admired the man. His speeches were incredible, his energy was undauntable, and his passion for his cause was contagious. Henry, opposing the Stamp Act, had spoken openly about the severity of the friction between the king and the colonies a very dangerous time. "Caesar had his Brutus, Charles the First his Cromwell, and George the Third—"

He'd been forced to pause, for there had been such staunch cries of "Treason!" But then he had gone on.

"George the Third may profit by their example. If this be treason, make the most of it!"

He was from the western counties, and to many he was a crude man, rough and rugged. His clothing was not cut to eastern standards. He was intriguing, Eric thought, capable at times of a brooding temperament, but still possessed of a fascinating fire that brought men rallying to his cause.

Jefferson was a quieter man, calmer, far more elegant in his dress and manner. But as time passed, he was becoming every bit as passionate.

"Eric, sit, have a brandy," Jefferson encouraged him. There seemed to be a twinkle in his eye. He looked older too, Eric thought. As the political situation grew more and more grave, they were all aging rapidly.

"Thank you. I shall be delighted," Eric said. He drew his chair to the fire with them, accepting a glass from Washington. "How are you, gentlemen?"

"Well enough," Jefferson said. "I have heard that you are about to leave with Governor Lord Dunmore's militia for the west to suppress the Shawnee uprising."

Eric nodded. It hadn't really been decided until tonight, but it seemed like the proper move for him. "It's an easy decision, isn't it?" he inquired softly. "I was asked to lead some men against a common enemy. Here it's difficult to decide."

Washington stared at him hard. "My friend Lord Fairfax is preparing to return to England. Perhaps you should do the same."

Eric smiled slowly and shook his head. "No. I cannot 'return' to England, sir, for I did not come from England. I am a Virginian."

The three exchanged glances. Jefferson smiled again. "I've heard rumors that a certain brash lord arrived in the nick of time to save an injured, er—Indian—in Boston. Have you heard this rumor?"

"Shades of it, yes," Eric said.

"Take heed, my friend," Washington warned him.

"Tell me—was there proof of the rumor?"

"Not a whit of it!" Henry replied, pleased.

Eric leaned forward, feeling the warmth of the fire, hearing the snap and crackle of it. "I tell you, the three of you, that you must take heed. There are more rumors about. Thomas Gage has been sent as governor of Massachusetts, and the king has ordered him to arrest Sam Adams and John Hancock."

"They shall have to find them to arrest them, right?" Henry said. He rose and walked to the fire, tense with energy. He leaned against the mantel, then swung around to look at Eric. "God knows the future now, for none of us can read it, Lord Cameron. Yet if—"

"When," Jefferson said softly.

"If it comes to that point, Lord Cameron, I shall hope that a man of your wit and wisdom chooses to cast his lot with us. Yet even I would have difficulty in your position. I have watched the members of our house weigh their thoughts, and it is a difficult process indeed."

"Perhaps war will still be averted," Eric said.

Washington, who was careful with his language, swore beneath his breath. "Every man among us has hoped that a force of arms be our last resort! And so we continue to pray. But, Eric! Think back on the war. I resigned my commission because they demoted me—for being a colonial. This has long simmered and brewed."

"They repealed the Stamp Act and came back at us with the Townshend Acts, further restricting our freedoms. We thought of ourselves as Englishmen—but those thoughts faded as we were denied the rights of Englishmen," Jefferson said.

"The Townshend Acts were repealed—" Eric said.

"Except for a tea tax," Jefferson reminded him complacently.

"And they were repealed," Henry said vehemently, "merely because Lord North discovered that it cost more to collect the taxes than they were worth!"

They all laughed, and then their laughter ceased abruptly as there was a rap upon the door. Washington quickly rose to answer it. The innkeeper stood there.

"There's a woman here," he said.

"A woman?"

"Lady Sterling. She is looking for Lord Cameron."

"Cameron!" Washington swirled around, looking at Eric who was about to light his pipe. He arched his brow and shrugged. A slow, curious and rueful smile appeared on Washington's face.

"Truly one of Virginia's great treasures," Jefferson said.

"The daughter of Lord Sterling," Patrick said, his tone indicating the care one should take with such a man.

"Mmm, yes," Eric murmured. "You see, gentlemen, I did ask Lord Sterling's permission to court the young lady, but alas, her heart lay elsewhere and she rather adamantly turned me down."

"But she is here now. A young lady in a tavern—her reputation shall be forever tarnished!" Washington mused.

"Alone?" Eric asked the innkeeper. "Surely not!" He flashed Washington a wicked smile. "I rather like a slightly tarnished reputation, sir."

"She is escorted by her cousin, Mr. Damien Roswell," the innkeeper said.

The men all exchanged sharp glances. Eric shrugged and looked pleasantly at the innkeeper. "Then tell her that

I shall be with her immediately. My every wish is to serve her."

The door closed and the innkeeper left them.

"Damien Roswell is an ardent patriot," Henry said. "One who moves in ways that may well be more practical than the rest of us, at the moment."

"More treasonous ways, the king might well say. I hope the young man has the good sense to take care with his cousin," Jefferson agreed.

Watching Eric, Washington shrugged. "Perhaps she is fond of him and fond of his policies after all."

Eric remembered her expertise in removing the bullet from the young printer's shoulder in Boston. He remembered, too, her fury at her position—following his lead because she was afraid. For Damien.

She was not seeing things their way. Not at all. "Perhaps she is after something," Eric said.

"Well, you'll have to see the young lady to find out, won't you?" Henry suggested.

"Spy upon the spy?" Jefferson laughed, but his eyes were grave.

"There's nothing for her to discover," Eric said.

"Is that true?" Washington asked him. "There are some who believe, Lord Cameron, that you are more deeply involved than anyone."

"Men believe almost anything these days," Eric said evenly.

"Still, take care," Washington warned him. "I speak as your friend, Eric, and a man who would see you well."

Eric sat, drumming his fingers against the wooden arm of his chair. "Perhaps you are right. Thank you for the warning, but I always take care. Perhaps I can discover certain truths about the lady—with certain lies of my own." He stood again and bowed. "And, gentlemen, it will be fascinating, this road of discovery. I am looking forward to it immensely."

They laughed. "I bid you good luck at the Congress," he added.

"And we bid you Godspeed against the Indians," Jefferson said.

Eric grinned and left them. Outside the door, he paused for a moment before heading toward the public room and his unexpected meeting with Lady Sterling.

His smile faded, his eyes went hard. He remembered her hatred for him, and he knew that nothing had changed between them. She thought to use him.

Well, she was welcome to try.

Then he remembered the way that she had looked when he had seen her upon the stairs, and he recalled the way that she had felt in his arms. He tasted anew the nectar of her lips, saw the fire of her eyes, and felt the perfection of her body pressed to his. He had meant to have her, in his own time, in his own way. He had not forgotten for a single moment the excitement of wanting her, the ache she had created within him, nor the raw and relentless determination he would use in his careful pursuit . . .

But now she was there. And not because of any ardent desire, he was certain. She was playing with fire.

Aye, she played with fire, he thought. But it was her choice, and her game, and by God, he would play it.

And win.

Part II

✿

The Reluctant Spy

VI ❧

Amanda was very beautiful that night. Eric saw her long before she saw him, for she was seated at a table with Damien and she was speaking earnestly with her cousin. Her eyes betrayed some deep emotion that was soft and spellbinding. Watching her, Eric realized that he envied her cousin. She loved Damien. And in that moment, as she sat in the flickering firelight, he thought that he would gladly sell his soul and be damned if she would just gaze upon him once so warmly.

He knew he was being a fool and reminded himself that he barely knew the little hellion, but it didn't matter. He hadn't needed to know much once he had seen her, once he had touched her.

He was in lust, so he had said. Perhaps that, too, was true. He had been careful to wait, biding his time. He had not expected her to seek him out, and yet here she was. With Damien. He wondered what she knew of her cousin's activities. No matter how her heart bled for England, she would never endanger young Roswell.

She had turned down his proposal of marriage, but now she was back. Deviously. What a pity. Her soft smile for him would be a lie. She had come to wage battle, else she never would have stepped foot inside this tavern.

Her beauty was her weapon, and she was not averse to using it, nor did she lack the confidence, he thought, to know the very power of it.

She wore green, a fetchingly casual gown with a heavier brocade bodice that tied with delicate ribbons over her breasts. It was a color that highlighted the evocative depths of her eyes, emphasizing the emerald dazzle of them. The night was warm, but she carried a light shawl, and it draped about her elbows, exposing her upper arms. Her hair had been swept up high in ringlets, and the sleek length of her neck was bare and inviting.

Every eye in the tavern was on her, of course. She looked like a thread of gold in a coat of coarse linen. There weren't many women in the place, and not one of them could hold a candle to her striking splendor.

He felt himself grown warm, watching her, and it occurred to him that many a man was drooling in his beer. Eric quickly grew annoyed. She shouldn't be here. Even escorted by her cousin, she should not be out as she was now. She was an innocent, yet there was something about her that was more than evocative. He thought of Helen of Troy and of a face that could launch a thousand ships. Amanda Sterling had that same kind of power; she created tension and emotion. Lust, perhaps, but longing and a haunting yearning too. With a smile she could tempt a man to any act; with a promise she could be deadly trouble.

Be forewarned, my friend, he told himself. And yet still his own confidence was great. He was older. Wiser, he assured himself. He saw the danger and therefore could elude it.

"Lady Sterling, Damien," he said, moving forward. Damien rose, Amanda remained seated. She offered Eric her hand and one of those smiles for which a man could be led to kill. He kissed her gloved fingers, glanced Damien's way, and took a seat beside Amanda.

" 'Tis good to see you, lad," he told Damien.

"And you, sir."

"And your fair cousin, of course," he said, looking at Amanda. "And yet, milady, I'm very curious. What has brought you here? I had the distinct impression that you did not wish to see me again."

"Did you?" she said, her voice distant and soft. "You were mistaken." She seemed to shudder slightly, then her smile returned to her features, and she grew animated and her eyes glowed like jewels. Her cheeks were just touched with the rose of a flush, her lips seemed as red as wine, and at that moment Eric did not think that he had ever seen a woman more alluring. He did not just yearn for her with his loins—though that urge lay very strong within him—but he ached to possess her in all ways, to run his fingers through her hair, to feel those eyes upon him with trust and innocence and their touch of the siren too. He wanted to hold her against him, to watch the rise and fall of her breast, to feel the whisper of her words against his cheek.

"Was I mistaken?" he asked her.

She nodded. "I came to apologize. You caught me at a frightful disadvantage. I am grateful, of course. And I'm so very sorry that I was rude. Please, do forgive me."

"What else could I do, milady?" he replied.

"Pardon me, milady, milord," Damien complained softly. "I am here too, you know."

Eric laughed, looking at Damien. He liked the young man very much. He was bold and brash and witty, and yet, beneath it all, he was determined—and talented. Damien had already cast his glove into the fray. Roswell, he had learned, was dealing very closely with the Bostonians. Most men were still eager to negotiate. Damien ran with a crowd that seemed collectively certain that it would come down to a force of arms. Even though Washington spoke carefully, Eric was certain that he, too, thought it would come to bloodshed.

"A thousand pardons, sir. But I'm afraid my keenest in-

terest is in your cousin, Damien. Curious, isn't it, that a
lady should seek out a man in a tavern for an apology."

She still had her temper, he saw, even if she was trying
to hide it. Her lashes were lowered, but he saw the flash in
her eyes. When she lifted her head, she was smiling again.
"Is it shocking behavior that I should be here? Why, all
manner of good men and women come to this place, so I
am told. The rooms, they say, are of a far more pleasant
nature at Mrs. Campbell's Tavern, but the food here is
fine, the drink palatable, and the company . . . most re-
spectable."

"Perhaps. But for a lady of your affluence?"

"But there is a lord of your affluence here."

"And there lies the difference, Amanda," he told her
flatly.

She flushed slightly but picked up a pewter tankard of
ale, which she sipped and smiled. "Ours is a wonderful
new world, isn't that what they say? I am fascinated by it."
Her lashes rose and fell, her smile was compelling. She
was flirting with him. Her fingers fell over his like butter-
fly wings.

He caught her fingers with his own. "You are a loyalist
to the core, Amanda," he told her flatly.

She tried to maintain a smile while she struggled to free
her fingers from his grasp. "Milord! Do you mean to say
that you are not? Have you then repudiated the king? I had
not heard that the staunchest rebels had yet gone so far!"

Only in whispers. But things were moving so quickly.
Throughout the colonies, throngs of people had attacked
shopkeepers who had failed to respect the boycotts on
British goods. Few men or women had been injured, but
the goods had been destroyed. And there had been no reprisals. It was all like a gigantic wind, sweeping around
them. Rebellion was close at hand.

And he was going off to fight Indians in the west, at Lord
Dunmore's request.

He did not need to answer Amanda because Damien
was already doing so. Leaning forward, her cousin spoke
to her heatedly. "Amanda, hush! God alone knows who
may listen to our words these days! Lord Cameron said

nothing about having repudiated the king. Indeed, he is the king's good servant, leaving his own hearth and risking his own life, limb, and health and fortune to go forth and meet the Shawnee."

"You should watch for your own life and limb, cousin," Amanda warned softly.

Damien sat back, staring at her. "What are you talking about?"

She knew exactly what she was talking about, Eric thought. The night became ever more interesting.

"Nothing," she replied, and turned from her cousin, a charming smile on her lips. "It is whispered that this is where it all takes place."

"It . . . all?" Eric queried her innocently.

"The clandestine meetings. The speeches, the—"

"The rebellion, that's what she means."

She pouted sweetly. "Amusing, Damien. But so very exciting," she told Eric.

What a wonderful liar she was, he thought. But it didn't matter.

"And are you fascinated, Lady Sterling?"

"Incredibly."

"Is that a loyalist hobby?"

"No, milord, merely a growing interest in politics," she said. "Mob rule can be so very intriguing."

"Oh?"

"Yes. We hear about the glorious cause of rights for Englishmen, the demand for self-government, how very ill the poor colonist is treated. But those same brave men raided the home of Lieutenant Governor Hutchinson in Boston, and he was a man very much opposed to the Stamp Act!"

"Madness against an innocent man," Eric murmured.

"I beg pardon, sir?" Damien said.

"Oh, the lieutenant governor's words," Eric said. "Yes, it's true. Mob rule can turn very ugly. I daresay that the man did not understand just how incensed the people were about the Stamp Act."

"The 'Sons of Liberty,'" Amanda said sweetly with only a touch of mockery to her tone.

"Ah, the study of those sons fascinates you, remember!"

"Of course."

She looked around the room. Eric was aware that she was looking for the men rumored to be at the root of the Virginia dissension.

He rose, bowing to her deeply. "Lady Sterling, Damien, I was on my way out. Perhaps, if you are still interested in political discussion, you would be good enough to accompany me to my town house."

"What!" Amanda exclaimed, startled.

He suppressed a smile at her discomfiture. "I was leaving, milady. But you are most welcome to accompany me. You, milady, and Damien too, of course."

"I'd love to," Damien said quickly. "Mandy?"

"I—I—" She hesitated, staring at him. Then she found her smile again. "I'm sure you can't be so willing to forgive my bad manners that you would want me in your very home."

"My dear Lady Sterling, you would always be welcome in my home. Indeed, you—and your father, of course—are more than welcome to be my full-time guests at any time."

"That would not be necessary," she said, maintaining a sweet smile. "We are guests of Lord Dunmore."

"Ah, so you are residing at the palace, and I offer my most humble abode. I'm quite sure Lady Dunmore has you in the comfortable guest room on the second floor. It is spacious, and so beautifully appointed. I could offer nothing so grand."

"Milord, it is a charming room he has given me, yes. You know the palace well."

"I have been a guest there often myself," he said softly. "And I regret that you are not my guest for your stay in Williamsburg." He smiled charmingly himself. It was good to know exactly where the lady was staying—and might be found, if necessary. "And, milady, it is incredibly easy to forgive you. Please, my carriage is outside. Yours can follow."

Damien was enthusiastic, and Amanda seemed to realize that she had little choice. Eric retrieved his cape and hat and led the two outside. His carriage, with the Cameron coat-of-arms emblazoned on the doors, did await them. The driver started to hop down from his seat, but Eric waved a hand to him. "It's all right, Pierre. I shall get the steps. We're going home."

"*Oui*, Lord Cameron," the man replied.

Eric opened the door and dropped the steps, then ushered Amanda up and into the carriage. He breathed in the scent of her hair as she passed him. Did she always smell so sweet and so good, like tender flowers on a sunny day?

"Damien, after you," he said. He watched the young man climb into the carriage, then followed behind him.

After Eric climbed up and tapped on the carriage roof, the horses started off. His town house wasn't far from Raleigh Tavern.

"You're near to the governor's palace, aren't you?" Damien inquired.

Eric nodded. "Near enough."

"Prime, prime property!" Damien applauded.

Eric laughed. "It belonged to my paternal grandmother."

Damien leaned forward. "There's a rumor that your grandfather was a pirate," he said excitedly.

Eric arched a brow politely. "Is there?"

"Yes. I've heard tell that he was a rogue, spying on the very likes of Blackbeard for the governor. Tell me, do you know anything about the treasure?"

Eric laughed. "I'm afraid not, Damien. He did play a pirate, but he pirated only his own ships. Any gold he claimed was his own, and to the best of my knowledge, he knew nothing about any of Blackbeard's treasure."

"Blackbeard's head was severed," Damien told Amanda excitedly, "and set upon a spike as a warning to all pirates. Then the men of his crew who had been taken were tried here, and all but one was hanged."

"Perhaps you should look to your own neck, cousin!" she warned again, then paled, seeing Eric's eyes upon her. She inhaled and exhaled quickly, and Eric smiled, seeing her discomfort. He didn't know quite what was going on, but she hadn't planned on going to his town house.

Soon the carriage drew to a halt. Pierre hopped down and opened the door, and Eric quickly climbed down then reached up for Amanda. His hands slipped around her waist, and he set her down slowly, loath to let her go. Her eyes were on his, very wide, and dusky green in the moonlight. He almost felt sorry for her then. Except that he longed for her, more deeply each time he saw her, and he knew that she was using him. It was a good thing that his ego was substantial, he thought. Her disdain was sometimes so apparent in her gaze.

"Do you like the boxwoods?" he asked her, leading her along the walk as Damien followed. "My housekeeper grows them. I'm afraid that I'm not in residence often enough to do the plants here justice."

"And where are you?" she asked.

"Why, at Cameron Hall, of course," he said, opening the door. As they entered, a tall lean woman with her hair knotted beneath a mob cap came hurrying into the hallway.

"Lord Cameron, I was not expecting you so early," she said, taking his hat and cape.

"Mathilda! I promised that I should be home nice and early!" he said quickly. "This is Lady Sterling, Mathilda, and her cousin, Damien Roswell."

Mathilda bobbed quickly to them both. Amanda murmured a greeting, looking about the hall. The Cameron wealth was evident in the fine wall covering, in the display of weapons, in the polished furniture. There was a maple cabinet in the hallway that had to be worth an apprentice artisan's entire first year of pay. There were silver candlesticks set about, and, looking up the stairway, she noted that the upper hallway was lined with oil paintings.

"This way, Lady Sterling," Eric murmured.

She was led into his study, a warm room with clawfooted, brocade upholstered chairs, a massive oak desk, a standing globe of the world, endless bookshelves, and a marble mantel. She felt his hand at the small of her back, and she longed to scream out. His touch could not be forgotten. Although he was perfectly polite, the lordly gentleman to the core, she felt that he was watching her with sizzling curiosity. He knew, she thought, and the very idea made her shiver. He was leading her along, waiting to pounce upon her like a wildcat.

She had no choice. Damien was her cousin, her friend. If he had gone astray, she had to help him. There was nothing that Lord Cameron could know. She was befriending him, and that was all. There was nothing that she could learn from him. They had not joined his friends —they had left the tavern. And now she was in his home.

"Sit, milady!" he said cordially, inviting her into one of the beautifully upholstered chairs. She did so and tried to smile again. The effort was weak.

"It's a wonderful house," Damien said admiringly.

"Thank you. Damien, a brandy? Lady Sterling, I would offer you tea, except that I have chosen to boycott its usage."

"I'd love a brandy," she said sweetly.

"Would you!" Damien laughed.

"Yes," she said, maintaining her smile but warning him with her eyes. She wanted twenty brandies. She wanted to pretend that she was far, far away and that she hadn't been blackmailed into this trickery.

Lord Cameron had one dark brow arched as he looked her way. He didn't say a word though, but poured out three brandies from a snifter on his desk. He brought her a delicate glass, setting it into her fingers. His eyes touched hers, and when their fingers met, she was suddenly beset with shivers again. He was clad darkly this evening. His breeches and his frock were navy, as was his surcoat, and only the white lace of his shirt showed at his throat to lighten the effect. It was somewhat somber garb, and it became him well, with his hair so very dark and his eyes so hauntingly silver-blue. They probed the soul, she thought, and she tried to look away. He seemed to tower over her as he stood by her chair, not releasing the brandy but watching her endlessly, seeking some answer.

"Thank you," she said, taking the glass. He smiled and moved away, offering Damien his brandy. Damien thanked him quickly and studied the books that lined the cases. He strode to the globe and spun it around, fascinated.

"You are quite blessed, Lord Cameron," Damien said. This beautiful town house, and I understand that Cameron Hall is magnificent."

"Thank you, I think it is." Eric told him as he watched Amanda steadily. She wanted to look away from him, and she discovered that she could not. He was darkly satyrish this evening, and it was almost as if he had some mysterious power over her.

It was nonsense, she convinced herself.

"Do you play chess, Lady Sterling?"

"Yes."

"Play me."

Was it the game he referred to? It was difficult to tell when he stared at her with such probing eyes. She shrugged. "If you wish."

He rose and went over to a small table with the board built onto it. The fine ivory pieces were kept in little pockets at the side.

Eric set up his men and looked at Amanda. They had drawn their chairs close, and she felt his presence all the more keenly. "Your move," he told her.

She brought forth a pawn. He followed suit. She moved in silence; he moved again. Her gaze fell upon his hands. His fingers were long, his nails clipped and neat. They were intriguing hands, bronzed from the sun, large, long, and tapered. The palms were not smooth but callused, as if he often engaged in manual labor.

She looked up and found that he was watching her, that it had long been her turn. She paled and foolishly moved a second pawn. He took it with his knight, and she was helpless to fight back.

"In love and war—and chess—milady, it is dangerous to forget the object of the attack for even a moment."

"You're giving me advice?" she said. "We have hardly begun the game. Perhaps, milord, you will find yourself on the defensive much sooner than you think."

"I had not realized that I was on the offensive."

"Are you playing to win?" she murmured.

He smiled, very slowly, his gaze silver and searing while he rested back in his chair. "I always do win, Lady Sterling."

"Always?"

"Always," he assured her nonchalantly.

She tore her eyes from his and concentrated on the game. Damien watched in silence.

They moved quickly for a few minutes. They were both on the offensive, and they both played with skill. Amanda lost a knight and a rook, but in turn she took a knight and bishop and two pawns. Soon the game began to slow down as they both took greater care with each move, trying to weigh what would come after the next immediate turn.

"Long-range planning," Damien said lightly.

Eric's eyes met his over Amanda's head. "Mmm. It can take a long, long time to win a game. Hours. Days, even. Alas, I haven't many days left."

"Alas!" Damien sighed. "I was so looking forward to seeing your Cameron Hall."

"Were you? Well, sir, you've a standing invitation. I shall be gone, and I don't know when I shall return, but my home is your home."

"Milord, I thank you sincerely!" Damien said.

"My pleasure." Eric looked over the board and maneuvered his knight in a position to set Amanda into checkmate on the next turn.

She saw his move and countered it, saving her king. The rescue, however, cost her a bishop.

"Ah! Take care, milady. I am stripping away your defenses. One by one."

"I am not beaten, milord."

"I should hope not, milady. You would not be a worthy opponent if you did not fight until the very end."

She was shivering again. They weren't talking about chess, not at all. And Damien was blithely innocent to it all.

They played for an hour and had reached a stalemate when Damien drew away Eric's attention. "I am fascinated by your books, Lord Cameron!" Damien said.

"Are you? I noticed you looking at the thesis on animal husbandry. I've another matching volume on botany. Would you like to borrow them?"

"Yes, I would, very much," Damien said.

"Come then, I believe the volume is upstairs. Amanda, will you excuse us, please?"

"Of course," she murmured quickly. Her heart was beating hard and she could not wait for them to leave the room. When they were gone, she leapt to her feet. On sudden inspiration she raced around the desk and tried the top drawer, impatiently searching through the papers there. There were bills and receipts. He had written a note to buy Mathilda's daughter a toy for her birthday. He had a list of stores in his wine cellar. There was nothing, nothing, indicative of any treason.

She started to sink into his chair, then she paused and wrenched open a side drawer. There was a letter there, postmarked from Boston.

They were coming back down the stairs. Amanda inhaled and exhaled deeply, then stuffed the letter into one of the pockets in her skirt. Then she closed the door quickly and raced back to her chair.

"I'm sure you'll enjoy the volume tremendously," Cameron was saying. "If you love the land."

"Very much. Almost as much as I love horses," Damien said cheerfully.

"You sound like a friend of mine, Colonel Washington. He is enamored of horses and forever experimenting with botany."

"I am in good company!" Damien replied, and Amanda winced. Good company for a hanging! she thought, but then it didn't seem to matter too much then for her heart was hammering and she could scarcely breathe. She imagined that any minute Eric would wrench her to her feet and his hands would fall brutally upon her until he managed to find the letter. And then his long fingers would curl around her neck.

"Amanda, I should get you back. Your father will be worried." And more cruel than usual. Damien did not say it, but Amanda sensed the thought behind his words.

"To the governor's palace, then," she said as Eric gazed at her. Why did it always look as if he knew so much more behind those silver eyes?

The governor's palace—she would stay at such a place, or with friends. A lady of her standing seldom sought lodging in a public place. It was probably scandalous that she had gone as she had tonight to the tavern. She didn't care much about her reputation, though. It had mattered only when love had mattered, and now she had been betrayed. She would never love again, she still bore the bitter scars of Robert's betrayal, and so her reputation didn't mean a thing.

Eric smiled, taking her hand. She wished that she could wrench away from him. He seemed to do so much more than touch her hand. The heat from his fingers coursed through her. "It has been a pleasure, milady. I'm sorry that you are established with Lord Dunmore. As I said, I would have gladly offered you this residence. Or Cameron Hall, had you use for it."

Amanda smiled, pulling her hand back. She had to get away. She was hot and shaking, and she could feel his letter in her pocket. "Thank you," she told him.

She turned about and started for the door. Mathilda came to see them out, and Eric walked them down the road to where Damien's small carriage awaited them with his old Negro driver. Thomas was sleeping, and Amanda was pleased to see the gentle way her cousin awakened him. There was so much good in Damien. How could he be a traitor!

"Let me help you, milady." While Damien spoke to Cato, Eric Cameron lifted her up and set her into the carriage. She felt his hands upon her waist and then she felt them brush her skirt. Her eyes widened with fear. She quickly tried to hide her eyes, lowering her head and her lashes. Then she raised them again, composed, her heart beating furiously.

Damien still spoke with the driver. Eric looked in at her, a twisted smile upon his lips. "One would think, Lady Sterling, that my touch aroused you."

"What?"

"Arouse, milady. You do know the meaning of the word."

"Lord Cameron, how dare—"

"Lady, I have seldom seen such wide eyes. And there—at your throat—a pulse beats with ardent fury." He came closer to her. "One might think that you longed to be kissed again."

"You think—wrongly."

"What?" he demanded. "Your heart does not clamor for a lover's touch. Then one would think that you were hiding something from me. That you were a thief, with stolen goods within your pockets."

"Don't—be ridiculous," she managed to reply.

His smile deepened. "Then your apology tonight was sincere."

Her breath came too quickly, causing her breasts to rise in rapid succession, pressing provocatively against the ribbon-laced bodice of her gown. Soft swirls of radiant ringlets framed her face and cast shadows against the emerald of her eyes. She gripped the seat, unaware that her fear gave her added beauty, that she enticed, even as she angered the man.

"My apology was most sincere," she said, desperate to raise her chin, to defy him.

"I am glad," he told her. With that he stepped into the carriage and sank down beside her. With the length and breadth of her she felt his form beside her own, heated, tense. She opened her mouth to protest, but no sound came to her. He reached out and touched her cheek, stroking downward upon it, bringing his fingers around to the nape of her neck. She nearly closed her eyes, for the sensations were so sweet, as if she were suddenly drugged by the nearness of the man. It was the brandy. Burning, swirling throughout her body. She could not protest, she could sit and feel and nothing more.

His lips hovered just above hers. "I am very, very glad," he murmured, "for I should hate it, milady, were I to discover you false."

Amanda could not answer for several seconds. She fought for reason, for words. "I offer you friendship," she whispered. She could not pull away from him. She felt the curious combination of force and tenderness in his hold upon her. She remembered his hands. Strong hands. He could break a man's neck, if he chose. Or a woman's.

She was being foolish. He would not harm her. No matter how she betrayed him.

Or would he?

She swallowed, trying to keep her eyes innocently upon his, desperate, for his letter lay within her pocket. There was steel in his eyes. He would not forgive or forget if he was betrayed. Perhaps he would not harm her, and yet, if he discovered the truth about her, she was certain that she would regret her actions for the rest of her life.

Take your hands from me! she wanted to cry. She longed to leap from the carriage and to race all the way to the governor's palace. She could not do so. His hold remained firm, just as his eyes continued to compel her. His mouth came ever closer to her own. He brushed her cheek with his lips, touched her earlobe, and she felt unable to break away, unable to fight the raw, sensual power. His face rose over hers again, his eyes entering into her naked soul. She moved toward him then, wanting more. Wanting just to taste . . . Her lips parted as she drew breath. No breath came to her, for his kiss closed down upon her lips.

She tasted brandy and the heat of his mouth. What she had initiated, he finished. His tongue swept with sensual insinuation deeply into her mouth. His fingers stroked first her face and then her breasts.

She could not breathe. She could feel only the flow of the brandy within her, and it was like a liquid fire. It was like the man, entering into all of her, making her burn with a sweet and startling desire to feel more, to know more.

"Mandy—" Damien began, and then he halted, clearing his throat.

Eric Cameron lifted his lips from hers, smiling. He set her gently back upon the seat and leapt down from the carriage facing Damien with no apology. His dark hair was somewhat tousled, slashing over his forehead. She could well see him as the pirate his ancestor had been, she thought, and then she realized that her fingers were at her lips and that she was trembling.

And that the warmth and desire were still with her. She didn't even understand desire, she thought with pain and fury, and yet it was something there, living deep inside of her. And this dark traitor had awakened it.

A whore. Her father had called her a whore like her mother.

She didn't believe it. She would never believe it.

He watched her. Damien was still, and she was silent, and it seemed that even long moments passed before Eric spoke to her again. "I have asked for your hand, lady. The offer still stands, should you need me."

She managed to form words. "I cannot marry you."

"And still, Amanda, I tell you, if you need me, I will be there. I will suffer your disdain, I will marry you knowing that you love another. Just don't seek to betray me."

"Betray you, sir? Pray, tell me what is there that I might betray?"

"Any man can be betrayed."

"I do not betray you," she lied smoothly.

"Good," he told her. But he did not smile, and the look of steel remained about his eyes. He turned to Damien. "I will offer no excuse, Damien, for I would marry her, if she would have me."

Damien didn't jump to her defense. He looked from Amanda to Eric. "Why?" he asked politely.

Amanda and Eric both stared at him. "I'm sorry, Mandy," Damien said. "But you were so very rude to him, from what you say yourself. And you've hardly been an angel this evening. Lord Cameron, I know that the world can be yours, so I am simply curious. Why?"

"Damien!" Mandy warned.

Eric laughed. "Aye, lad, she's cruel and abrasive, but she's truly the most beautiful creature I've ever seen."

"But you cannot love me! You've admitted as much," Amanda murmured desperately. No, he did not love her, but she felt the attraction more and more herself this evening. She might despise him for what he was, for what he knew of her, for all he had witnessed of her soul, but he fascinated her! She was drawn to his touch, she wondered more and more about the way his hands might roam, the places his lips might kiss. She reddened with horror. "You can't just . . ."

He chuckled softly again, and the tone of it made her burn, as did the husky sound of his voice when he spoke. "Amanda, I can. Ah, lady, perhaps I do not love you. You most certainly do not love me. But as you boldly pointed out at our last meeting, lust can rule a man's heart and soul and mind, and lady, you have driven me to distraction. I do desire you, with a fever scarce kept under control. Watch your kiss, lady, lest it go too far."

"My kiss!" she cried.

"You do wound me to the soul. You kissed me tonight, do you recall?"

"Damien, can we please go?"

"Mm . . . surely," Damien agreed, but he was grinning.

"Damien, now!"

Damien leapt up into the carriage. Amanda stared straight ahead, determined not to so much as glance Eric Cameron's way again. She looked down to her lap, feeling a fierce burning inside her. She could not bear these feelings. She had loved Robert, she had been deeply in love. And she had never felt like this with him, so what could it be? Her father's words returned to haunt her. She was a whore's daughter. . . .

Her heart rebelled. She had seen the portraits of her beautiful mother, seen her gentle smile, the intelligence in her eyes. She couldn't have been a whore. Amanda had never known her, but she could not believe such a thing.

"I remain your faithful servant, milady!" Cameron said.

Grinning, Damien waved to him and tapped on the carriage. Thomas clipped the reins, and they started down the street. They were very close to their destination.

The carriage swayed and she felt she was going to be sick. She stared across in the shadows at Damien, aware that he was watching her.

"He is twice the man Robert Tarryton is," Damien said softly.

Longing to pull his hair out, Amanda let loose with a

startling oath. "Damien, don't you dare say such a thing to me! After all that he has said and done that you have seen or heard!"

"He has been honest," Damien said quietly. "Which you are not, cousin," he added.

She longed to rail at him and barely managed to hold back her words. "Leave me be, Damien."

"Amanda," he said softly.

"What?"

"I love you, you know," he reminded her.

She exhaled. "Oh, Damien! I love you too."

He reached across the dark carriage and squeezed her hand as Cato drove up around the driveway to the front door of the palace. "I'll deliver you to your father, and then Cato and I shall retire for the evening." He lifted her from the carriage and set her upon her feet, grinning. "I shall face my uncle the ogre with you!" he said dramatically.

"I will be all right," she assured him.

He shrugged. "Come."

The door was already being opened by a servant in handsome livery. They entered the hall and Amanda saw her father coming down the stairway, hurrying toward them.

"I've brought her home, Uncle, well and in good time, I pray," Damien said.

Nigel Sterling nodded curtly to Damien. "Fine. You may call upon her again, nephew."

Damien quirked a brow at Amanda, then wished her good night and made a hasty retreat.

When the door closed behind him, the servant discreetly disappeared and Amanda faced her father alone.

"Well?"

She shrugged. "Lord Cameron intends to leave on the governor's behalf to the west country to fight the Shawnee."

"He does intend to go?"

"Yes, definitely. Dunmore knew that already."

"Did Cameron introduce you to his acquaintances?"

"No."

"Then you failed! He did not—"

"He asked me to marry him again, Father," she said coldly, "so I did not fail."

Sterling fell silent, stroking his chins. She returned her father's stare and felt distinctly uneasy. He hated her and she was quickly learning to hate him.

She felt the letter in her pocket. She had brought it to turn over to her father.

Yet she could not do so. Not until she had read it herself.

"When he comes back, you'll see him again."

She smiled. "I understand that the Shawnee are fierce and merciless. Perhaps he will not return."

"Then there will be no worry on the matter, and we will decide a different future for you." He smiled pleasantly. "Lord Hastings has been a widower for some time now. He would be delighted to take you in marriage."

Lord Hastings was well over sixty with a girth the size of an elephant's and a penchant for whipping his slaves.

She shivered and stood staring at her father, despising him with ever greater ferocity. She had never been afraid to be near him before, and now she realized that she dreaded the days to come. He would sell her to any man, and do so with relish.

"We'll go home in the morning," Sterling said. "You may go to bed. And Damien will be safe. For the time being."

She trembled, fearing the sudden brutality of his smile. Without knowing what she was saying, she started to talk.

"Lord Cameron offered me the hospitality of his home while he is gone fighting, Father. I thought that I should go."

"You will not—" Sterling began, but then he broke off, smiling again. "Yes. Yes, you shall go. And while he is gone, you can search his belongings for his correspondence. We could capture the whole core of this rebellion and hang them all like the traitors they are if we can bring proof of high treason into court!"

"There is no high treason, Father, don't you see that! The man is Lord Dunmore's friend—"

"No. No man has friends right now, girl. Bear that in mind. Friendship will not matter—blood will not matter."

Amanda felt a chill sweep over her. Her father turned away, heading for the stairs. "Tell him that you will marry him. You won't have to do so, but the promise alone will open doors for you."

"Father—"

"And think of it, my dear," he said, holding the newel post and turning back to her. "Such a move will salvage your pride. Robert Tarryton's fiancée has arrived from England. They are to be married in the middle of October. It will look so much better to the world if you are betrothed to Lord Cameron."

He started up the stairs again, murmuring to himself. "Perhaps you should marry him. If he is innocent, he is a man of the greatest prestige. And if he is guilty they will hang him, and his property will fall to you."

The chill swept around Amanda, settling deeply into her heart. "I cannot marry him!" she cried, racing after her father.

He paused and looked down at her. "You will do as you are told," he said, and kept walking.

She gritted her teeth, longing to run away, into the night. She didn't care what happened to her, as long as she could escape him.

But then Damien would hang.

She waited until he had disappeared, then she tore up the stairs herself and slammed into her room. She fell upon the bed, breathing heavily.

Then she remembered the letter in her pocket, and she slipped her fingers into it, anxious to read the correspondence.

Her fingers faltered, and her heart began to slam. She had his life in her hands.

And before God, she didn't know if she wished the letter to prove him a traitor or no. Pulling it from her pocket at last, she began to shiver. Even as she smoothed out the envelope, she felt again the fever of his kiss, the touch of his hands. Yes! She could condemn him. She had to! She was a loyalist; he was a patriot.

And it might well be Damien's life against his.

She rolled over and looked at the envelope. There was a

name and address in the corner. Frederick something of Boston.

With shaking fingers, she reached inside.

The envelope was empty.

She lay back on the bed, and she began to laugh. She laughed until she cried.

And then she sobered with a gasp. She had spoken in haste.

And now she was condemned to play this torturous game still further. She was to go to his home; she was to make promises that she would never keep.

By God, she could not . . .

By God, she had to.

VII ❦

There was a soft tap on Amanda's door. She hastily stuffed the envelope back into her pocket and rose, hurrying to the door. "Yes?" she called softly.

"C'est moi, Danielle."

Amanda quickly opened the door and Danielle, dressed in sober blue with an immaculate white pinafore, slipped into the room. She had taken her hair down, and it streamed in dark folds down her back.

She touched Amanda's cheek. "You had a nice evening, *ma petite?*"

"It was . . . fine," Amanda lied. She forced a smile that probably did not fool the woman in the least. "You know how I love Damien."

Danielle nodded and crossed the room to a large wardrobe in the corner, opened it, and brought out one of Amanda's nightgowns. It was soft silk, trimmed with Flemish lace at the throat and bodice and sleeves. "Lord

Sterling does buy for you the best," Danielle murmured. "You have fought with him again?"

Amanda shrugged. "Not really. It is as it always is."

"No. It is worse now. He sees you growing up." She was quiet for a moment, her dark eyes luminous. "I should have killed him years ago!"

"Danielle!" Amanda gasped. "No, you cannot even think such a thing! They would hang you for it. And perhaps— perhaps not even God would forgive you."

Danielle moved the silk against her cheek. "God would forgive me," she said. She looked at Amanda, troubled. "That they should hang me, perhaps that is better than what he will do to you!"

Amanda was shaking again and she didn't like it.

"He is my father. He would not really hurt me." But she couldn't help it; the shivers remained with her. She couldn't forget the way that Nigel had called her mother a whore and suggested that she was just like her.

Danielle opened her mouth to say something, but then she closed it and helped Amanda out of her gown. Left in her stockings and corset and petticoats, Amanda hugged her arms about herself. "What was my mother like, Danielle?"

"Beautiful," Danielle said softly. "Her eyes were the color of the sea, her hair was as radiant as a sunset. Her smile made others smile, and she was both gentle and passionate. And beautiful." She hesitated, taking a petticoat as Amanda stepped from it. "You are her very image, Amanda. And that is why . . ."

"Why what?"

Danielle shook her head. "She was so very kind to me, and to Paul."

"Paul?"

"My brother. He died before you were born." Danielle untied the ribbons of Amanda's corset, then slipped the nightgown over her head. Amanda murmured her thanks, then sat on the bed to remove her shoes and stockings and garters from beneath the gown, watching Danielle as she returned her things to the wardrobe and trunks.

"I can never forget," Danielle continued. "It was so horrible. We Acadians, we were farmers in Nova Scotia. When the British took over the French rule, we vowed to serve the English king. But then war broke out again, and the French feared that we would fight with the British, while the British feared that we would take up arms with the French. And so they simply stole our land and exiled us from the place of our birth. We lived in a little town called Port Henri. It had been named for our great-grand-father. We reclaimed the marshland, we had many cattle, we fished the Bay of Fundy. Then the British gathered us at Port Royal and told us that we must leave. We were huddled into ships like slaves, and the captains made money on the misery they inflicted upon us. They made their coin, whether we lived or died. *Mon Dieu!* Day after day, the human waste and sickness gathered upon us. They would not let us out of the hold . . . except for Marie d'Estaing, for the captain raped her again and again. She began to look forward to his violence, for she told me that it was better than smothering in the hold with the smell and the worms. She died before we came to port. I was barely alive when our ship came to Williamsburg. Your mother demanded that your father take some of us in, and he was forced to oblige her. So Paul and I had a home."

Amanda rolled up one of her stockings, her fingers clenching against the pain and injustice done to Danielle's people. Many who had lived had not been accepted upon the colonial shores, and they had left again, searching for a homeland with the French, to the west.

Danielle exhaled slowly, then sucked in her breath. "I'm sorry. This is long ago. In 1754. Before you were born."

"But my mother was there. And she was kind. She was good then, Danielle. She was good and kind and beauti-ful."

Danielle nodded. "She was very good. Has someone told you otherwise?"

Amanda shook her head hastily. She knew that the pain her father caused her would hurt Danielle even worse. "I just wanted to hear about her from you, that is all."

"Then good night, *ma belle jeune fille,*" Danielle said

softly. She kissed Amanda's head and hurried to the door. Then she swung back suddenly. "How long are we staying?"

"I—I don't know," Amanda replied. "Maybe not long. We have been invited to see Lord Cameron's estate on the James. Perhaps we shall do so."

Danielle's eyes widened with pleasure. "We may go there?"

"Yes."

"Away from your father?"

"Yes."

Danielle nodded, pleased. "Lord Cameron is a far better man than the other you loved, Amanda."

Robert. His memory tugged at her heart, even if she had forced it to grow cold. She had dreamed too often of his golden head beside her own upon a pillow. She still had visions of little children, their little children, laughing and running about the house on Christmas day.

"Goodnight, Danielle," she said, more abruptly than she had intended. The woman stiffened, and Amanda immediately regretted her harsh tone. She raced over and hugged her. "I'm sorry, Dani. It's just that—I loved him, you see. And Lord Cameron—" She paused, shivering. "He might well be a traitor."

"Tell me, *petite,* what is a traitor but a man with a different cause? The British exiled me from my homeland. They took everything. The French were not there for me. I was Acadian, lost. And now I listen to the people on the streets and I know."

"You are a Virginian."

"I am an American," Danielle said with quiet dignity, and she smiled. "Who can ever say? If one wages war and is victorious, he is a hero, *c'est vrai*? If he wages war and loses, then he is a traitor, it is so simple."

Danielle pulled away from Amanda for a moment, studying her eyes. "Whatever else Lord Cameron may be, Amanda, he is a man who would be true to his own honor, and if he loved you, he would never betray you, as others have done." Danielle smiled, and then left.

Amanda watched after her, then she locked the door

with the key and went back to the bed. She stared at the candle on the bedside, then snuffed out the flame, swearing. "Damn! He is a traitor, and a rogue, and so help me, I will use him as is necessary!"

She crawled beneath the covers, still shivering. It was not so cold a night, but the fire in the hearth was very low, and there was an autumn snap in the air. It was definitely the cold, she assured herself, that brought about her shivers, and nothing else.

She closed her eyes and prayed for sleep to ease her soul. No matter how she tried, though, she could not drift into slumber. She was haunted by visions of the day, of her father in the governor's delightful rose garden, calling her mother a whore. Calling *her* a whore. Threatening her. And then her father's face faded away, and she saw Eric Cameron before her with his steely eyes, watching her, knowing . . . something. Chess pieces moved before her. Gravely he leaned toward her. "Checkmate, milady. Checkmate."

She jerked up suddenly. She must have dozed, because she had now awakened. She didn't know why; she didn't know what she had felt.

The fire had gone down to almost nothing, and the window was open—she could see the drapes flowing soft and white into the room. She could have sworn that the window had been closed when she had lain down.

She tossed her covers aside and set her bare feet upon the floor, then hurried to the window. The moon was sending down shafts of light and the breeze was picking up. The drapes swirled, and the soft silk of her gown rose against her legs, rippling around her.

She sensed a shadow in the room. She turned about, but the moonlight had blinded her, and now she could not see. But she wasn't alone; she could feel someone else there.

"Who—who is it!" She gasped. She wanted to scream, but the words came out in a whisper.

There was a sudden motion. She saw the dark silhouette as it approached her, and she inhaled to scream. A hand fell across her lips. She kicked viciously and contacted human flesh, but then she was swept up high and tossed down hard upon the bed. Dazed, she tried to roll away, and she was wrenched back as the dark shadow fell upon her. She twisted, freeing her knee and her mouth. She gasped, but again no sound managed to escape, for a hand fell back down upon her, firmly clamping down upon her jaw and mouth, and she felt forceful arms lock tight around her. Wildly she clutched at the fingers that held her, raking them with her nails. Her hands were quickly caught and she was pushed down deeply into the bed. The attacker was still behind her, a leg cast over her, his one arm beneath her as his fingers stifled her breath and words, his other arm around her like an iron band, his hand beneath her breast, holding her taut and hard against his body.

"Shush," he whispered. Warm breath, scented with a pleasant masculine combination of brandy and good pipe tobacco, swirled against her cheek. She tried to bite, but she could not, she was held too tightly. She tried to squirm away, and she realized with horror that her movement brought the hem of her gown high up, baring her legs, and tugged the bodice of her gown even lower. She could feel his fingers upon the fullness of her breasts through the flimsy lace of the gown.

"Lady, I mean it, not a whisper. And be still."

She went dead still, not to be obedient, but with shock. It was Lord Cameron!

With the realization she panicked. She tried to kick and thrash again. He swore with no heed for her fair sex, then wrested her beneath him, his thighs taut about hers, his hand now a brutal clamp upon her mouth, and the length of him leaned low and close to her. She had no breath; she feared that she would faint. She could see his eyes flashing in the curious combination of the dying fire's glow and the moonlight, and there was no love, and no humor, within them now.

"Be still," he warned her again, staring into her eyes, daring her to defy him. Slowly he moved his hand.

"Get off me! I shall scream to high heaven!" she warned him.

"Yes, that's quite what I'm afraid of," he told her. She

gasped then, for she realized that he now had a knife in his hand. He had slipped it from a sheath at his calf while he spoke. He lay the blade low between the valley of her breasts. She inhaled raggedly, fought for courage, then stared into his eyes again.

"You wouldn't do it. You wouldn't take a knife against an innocent woman."

"But you're not an innocent woman," he told her.

He knew. He had seen her take the envelope. Fear rushed through her. "You would not slay me, I know it. And I will scream. I find you despicable! How dare you come in here. I will scream, and my father will see that you hang—"

"Your father very well may wish to see me hang at some point, but I'd wager it would not be now. And what happened to the sweet apology you offered me earlier this very eve?" he demanded. "I warn you again, lady—" He paused, letting her feel the cold blade of the knife. "You shall be greatly distressed."

"You've broken into my room—into the governor's palace!" She smiled suddenly, lifting her chin. He wouldn't hurt her, and she knew it. She opened her mouth to scream, heedless of the consequences.

His fingers slapped back over her mouth. The blade of the knife moved swiftly in seconds, and she discovered that although her flesh remained unharmed, her garment was in shreds, and her breasts were spilling free from the silk and lace bodice. "Lady, I will wrest you from this place stark naked if you are not silent, and that is a promise. I will parade you down the streets of Williamsburg, and there are enough people here to enjoy it, for Tories such as yourself are not gaining much popularity these days."

"You wouldn't—"

"Don't ever tempt me too far. There are many things that I would like to do."

"You bas—" she began.

"No, no, milady. You are forewarned. Take care."

"I'll not—"

"You will!" His hand clamped hard upon her again, but

she gave it no heed. She wasn't about to take care. She surged against him with all of her strength, seeking to kick him. She thrashed violently against him, flailing and twisting in a fury.

Eric didn't fight back. He just held her, letting her arch, writhe, and twist. Her efforts were almost amusing to him, she realized. He had only to maintain his grasp upon her wrists, and the power of his body hold did the rest.

While she . . .

She had managed only to wrest herself closely against him, leaving her legs as naked as her breasts.

"Be still!" he warned again.

Amanda fell silent, a blush scorching all of her flesh, for she was already half naked and he was studying her at his leisure. She tried to twist away from him, but his hold upon her wrists was firm. She went still at last, aware that the ruffles of his shirt hung down upon the bareness of her nipples and breasts, and that her position was precarious indeed. Always with him she was wrested and beaten, so it seemed. She moistened her lips, horrified to realize their position. She thought of his hands, should they move. Should they touch her. She thought of the feel of his lips upon hers, and she wondered what the sensation would be if they moved lower against her, brushing her shoulder blades, closing upon her breasts. She felt the hardness of his thighs against her hips, the pressure of his manhood against the near-naked territory at the apex of her thighs, and suddenly she was truly silent, no longer wishing to defy him, desperate only that he should move away from her.

She shook her head. His fingers eased from her swollen lips. "I shall not scream! I shall not. I swear it."

He watched her for a long, hard moment. Then he sat back. She was still his prisoner, still captive between his muscular thighs.

"What do you want?" she whispered.

"Many things," he told her casually, "but at the moment, I want my letter returned."

Amanda stiffened, then forced herself to relax, offering him a wide-eyed smile. "Why ever would you think—"

"I don't think, I know. And by God's blood, lady, cease the dramatics with me, for though you do bat your lashes prettily, you are a liar and we both know it. I want my letter now. Or you shall forfeit something else."

She was seething with fury, hating him for his crude and quick ability to see through her. She gritted her teeth. "Truly, Lord Cameron, your behavior is not civilized!"

"If it was civilized, I would not be here. I am pretending nothing, Amanda. I am no gentleman, and no fool, so do be warned and take heed for the future. I want my letter."

"I—I don't have it anymore."

His fingers closed harshly upon her shoulders, wrenching her up against him with such violence that she cried out in pain. He thrust her back down again, heedless of the pain, his lips very near to hers as he spoke. "I may well lose my own neck over you one day, Lady Sterling, but I'll not have other men endangered because of your treachery. Where is the envelope?"

"I gave it to my father."

"You're lying!" he snapped so quickly that she gasped and trembled and bit her lip in an effort to stay still. She had forgotten his knife. It lay against her cheek now. He stroked her face with it.

"You would not use that," she challenged him.

"Perhaps not." His eyes were very dark but glittering still in the night. "Perhaps I would use other means to reach my end."

She didn't know what he meant, only that the warning was very real. She didn't want to discover what lay beneath it. "It's—it's in the pocket of my gown."

If he was dying with desire for her, he certainly betrayed no emotion then. He was off her in a second, dragging her from the bed. His hat had fallen to the floor in their scuffle and now he swept it up atop his head. Stumbling, she tried to draw her gown together. She hurried to the wardrobe with him two steps behind her. She could barely open the door, and when she found the dress, he pushed her aside, reaching into the fashionable pocket hidden within the skirt. He found the envelope and thrust the dress back inside, and closed the door.

"Why did you take it?"

"Because—because you're a traitor. And you have to get out of here. Now."

"Oh? And you intend to prove that I'm a traitor?"

"No!" she cried with horror. "I just . . . I . . ."

"Pray, do go on."

"You get out of here! Before I do choose to scream!"

But he didn't move. He was watching her very closely. She clasped the gown closely about her, backing away. Something about him was exceptionally fierce in the strange shadowland of the bedroom, and yet she no longer felt the explosion of anger about him. He stepped toward her, towering in his tricorn and cape.

"Why didn't you give this to your father?" he demanded.

"I—I never had a chance."

"You're lying."

"All right. I wanted to read it myself. But as you see, there is no letter. If fact . . . why are you here, if there is no letter?"

He turned around, striding across the room to her bed. He sat on it, watching her carefully. "There is a name upon it," he told her. She shivered, feeling the silver touch of his eyes, even in the shadows.

"Frederick's name. The printer from Boston. The Indian tea-ditcher, right?" She swallowed quickly, not liking his eyes as they fell upon her. "You've got the envelope. Now go."

He shook his head. "I haven't quite decided what to do about you."

"About me?" she exclaimed. She tilted her head back, defying him.

"You went through my personal belongings; you stole my property."

"If you're not out of here in two seconds, I promise that I will scream until the entire British army is in here."

He leaned back more comfortably. "Nice lads. Some of them are my friends." He shrugged, then rose up from the bed and approached her with slow, menacing steps. She was nearly against the door. She had nowhere else to run. And yet she had not managed to scream.

"If you do scream," he promised her softly, "I shall offer your father my gravest apologies, but I shall tell him that you seduced and coerced me to this room, and then I shall be broken-hearted, of course, wondering just how many men you have led astray." He set a hand against the wall, his teeth flashing whitely as he smiled.

Amanda stared at him, furious and appalled.

"He knows I—"

"Despise me? Ah, but Lady Sterling! You came after me this evening! With apologies sweeter than wine tripping off your fair tongue."

"Yet—" She broke off. Both were silent as they heard footsteps coming down the hallway outside.

His knife flashed suddenly before her face. "Behave!" he warned her. "A word, and someone will die!"

He turned and seemed to disappear. Amanda stared into the shadows after him, uncertain as to whether he had slipped out the window or perhaps into the dressing room beyond her own.

There was a sharp pounding on her door. She stood behind it, her mouth dry. "Who is it?"

"Your father. Open the door."

She hesitated, then threw open the door. She stayed there, blocking his entry to the room. "What is it?" she asked quietly.

He pushed past her and went on in, lighting a candle with a wick from the fire, then looking about. He went over to her, staring at her intently. "I heard voices."

"Did you?"

He cuffed her on the side of the head, a silent blow that still sent her reeling down to the bed. She jumped back to her feet, loathing him, trying to pull the torn shreds of her bodice together. He walked over to her, staring closely. He lifted a finger to talk to her as his eyes narrowed. "You'll not play the harlot, not on my time, girl. A whore breeds a whore, but you'll serve me and do my purpose before playing elsewhere."

She stood still, her teeth clenched, her shoulders squared, and she prayed that Eric Cameron was gone. She could not bear him witnessing another scandalous scene, yet if he was near, he could not miss hearing the words.

She was a fool, she thought. If she shouted out and screamed and cried, she could tell the truth! But Cameron's words were true. With her father's appraisal, it would appear that she had asked him here. She spoke softly. "There is no one here, Father. I am alone. Please leave me, so that I can sleep."

"There is no one here?"

"No."

"Don't play games with me. I have ordered you to bestow your charms on Lord Cameron, and you will obey me."

She inhaled sharply, looking into the shadows. Please God, she thought, let him be gone, let him be gone.

Her father suddenly came close to her. She felt uneasy as his eyes raked over her. They seemed to have a strange, hungry light about them. He touched her chin, lifting it up, and he stared down at her breasts, so ill concealed in the gown. His finger ran down her throat to the deep valley between the mounds. "What happened?"

"I twisted in my sleep. I have rent the seam, nothing more. I will fix it."

"It is a beautiful gown on you, daughter. I have kept you well clad."

"You have," she acknowledged bitterly.

His hand hovered closer until she thought that she was going to throw up. She cried out, backing away from the door. His eyes narrowed as if he would grab her and wrench her away, and for the first time she was physically afraid of him as a man. He made her feel unclean.

She threw open the door quickly. If he came toward her again, she would scream. The governor was a good Englishman who might stoop to a little bribery or blackmail, but if she screamed hysterically, he would at least see that she was left alone. Her father would not dare abuse her before Lord Dunmore.

"Good night, Father," she said.

Sterling stared at the door then stared at her, a pulse ticking at the base of his throat. He swallowed hard and

walked by her, but paused in the doorway, holding the
door open. "It's not over between us, my daughter. We will
return to our own home."

He closed the door sharply. Amanda fell against it, leaning her forehead upon it, ready to cry.

Then a sudden movement alerted her and she twirled
around.

Eric Cameron hadn't left at all. He had hidden, motionless and silent, beyond the dressing-room door. Now he
was standing there before her, watching her, his face
somewhat hidden by shadow, and yet she felt both the
fury and the pity within it. She didn't want his pity.

"I wanted to kill him," he said furiously.

She arched a brow, startled. Even in the darkness she
could sense the tension about him. He was more enraged
with her father than he was with her.

"He is my father," she said, shrugging. She could not
bear that he should see her pain.

"The more he should be slain for what he does to you."

As regally as she could manage, she swept her gown
about her. "My God, can't you please get out of here too?"

He strode toward her, taking her shoulders, and stared
into her eyes. Some furious war waged in the very cobalt
of his eyes. "So, you were ordered to apologize to me!"

"You've found your letter, now please go."

"I warn you now, milady," he said very softly, "I will not
be betrayed again. Why didn't you tell him that I was
here?"

"You promised to kill someone if I did."

"And you believed me?"

"What difference does it make?" she snapped scathingly.
"You would have said that I'd asked you here."

"And he would have believed me, wouldn't he?"

She didn't answer. She didn't want to see his piercing
silver-blue eyes anymore, or feel the strength of his hands
upon her. She wanted to be left alone.

"Answer me!"

He could rise so quickly from gentleness to sharp, demanding anger! "Yes! He would have believed you. He—he
despises me," she admitted softly. Then she jerked back

away from him. "For the love of God, will you leave me alone?"

"I did not start this thing, lady, but I would finish it," he said softly. She didn't understand his meaning, and it worried her. His tension seemed to have increased and he paced the floor, as if he were suddenly loath to leave her.

She trembled. "You know what I have done—"

"I know that he is willing to sell. And I am willing to buy."

"My father—"

"You must be taken from him."

Amanda felt the heat and fury of his words, though they were spoken softly. She shook her head, protesting. "You don't understand! I do find you a traitor! Whatever I did—"

"You are a fool. It is best for me, milady, to have my eyes upon you. I will speak with him, and warn him that I don't want my bride bruised, battered—or touched in any way."

"I'll never marry you."

"Little idiot. No one can make you marry. I am offering you an escape, and God alone knows why. No woman is that beautiful," he murmured. "Yet you are," he said softly. "Beautiful, and cold. And yet I have seen the passion in you. I've even felt it. Why do you pretend so fiercely that it isn't so?"

"Because I hate you, Lord Cameron!" she cried. She hated that he could make her tremble so easily, to grow hot and flushed, and breathless as if she were what her father accused her of being . . .

A whore.

"Never mind! If you would just—"

"But I will not 'just' anything," he assured her huskily. Then he came around to her again, and it did not seem that he felt her resistance when she tried to free herself from his hold.

"You will come tomorrow. You cannot wait any longer, do you understand me?"

"I don't know what you're talking about!"

"I will leave the invitation with Lord Dunmore. If they

are eager to hang me, I must give them the rope. Whatever his mind, he is a decent man. I will speak with your father. A betrothal will give you freedom. You will come out to Cameron Hall tomorrow—"

"You are mad!" she cried. "I stole your letter, and you know that I hate you, but you would have me anyway! And what makes you think that I would come?"

"The fact that I will be quickly gone and that you will have the place to yourself."

She fell silent. She knew that she would go. She longed so desperately to escape her father.

Cameron doffed his hat to her. "You should marry me, and quickly, you know. I could well be skewered through by a Shawnee arrow."

"I don't believe that I should have such wonderful good luck," she retorted.

His teeth flashed in a dangerous smile and he reached out suddenly, pulling her gown back in place. The silk had slipped from her fingers, and she had been standing before him, proud and bare. She swore softly, brushing his hand aside, but not before she felt the stroke of his fingers, warm and taunting. "You may have to marry me soon. For the sake of your good name."

"I haven't a good name left at all, Lord Cameron. And I don't give a fig," she said regally.

His laughter was soft and husky, but then it faded, and the silver-blue eyes that fell upon her held pity and tension. "You don't need to fear me."

"Don't I?" she inquired sweetly, now holding the remnants of her bodice together very firmly. She smiled, her teeth grating, as she awaited his answer.

"You should fear those around you, lady. Come on your own accord, milady, else I shall find a way to rescue you from yourself."

"I don't know what you mean."

"And I pray that you need not discover the truth of my words," he warned her. Then he bowed deeply. "Adieu, milady."

He twirled around and was gone. The breeze rustled through the open window, and she wondered briefly how he did not break his neck, or a leg at the very least. Then she wondered, too, about the British guard assigned to the governor's palace. She should hear shouts any second. Eric would be arrested, strung up.

She raced to the window, her heart hammering in her breast. She looked down into the yard below but saw nothing but the shadows of the night and, beyond, the foliage of the governor's gardens and mazes. Cameron was uncanny. For his great height and the breadth of his shoulders, he could move swiftly, and silently.

Damien once told her that many men who had fought in the French and Indian Wars had come home like that. Still soldiers.

Still savages.

He was no savage, she assured herself. But he was swift to anger, and she had already aroused him.

The letter was gone, in his hands.

Her tongue felt dry; her breath came quickly. Though she was afraid of Lord Cameron, still she knew that if the invitation was true, she would travel to Cameron Hall in the morning.

She dared not remain with her father, and Lord Cameron was right about one thing. A betrothal would buy her freedom.

The next day had turned to a beautiful sun-streaked twilight when Amanda first saw Cameron Hall. She didn't know when Eric had gone to talk to the men, but she listened in silence when her father told her that she was betrothed and when Lord Dunmore told her that Pierre, with the Cameron carriage, would be waiting for her and Danielle whenever she was ready.

Lord Cameron would be leaving any day, but he wanted her to accustom herself to his home in his absence. The wedding date, in these troubled times, must be set later.

Her father caught hold of her arm just before she entered the carriage. "You will make yourself at home. You will search his desk and his papers, and you will find the truth. Anything, anything you find—letters, names, addresses—we must have. Do you understand?"

"He'd probably kill you, Father, if he knew what you were about," she said flatly.

"You're still my daughter, mine to command," Sterling reminded her roughly. "And I can have you dragged home whenever I choose. Then there is your cousin. You think on it, girl." He released her arm. Then he smiled and stared at her, and the same unease that had touched her the night before filled her with dread. She didn't think that she could ever bear to be in a room with him alone again.

"If you touch me, he'll kill you," she said bitterly, and then she was startled by the fear she saw in her father's eyes. For a man who had been badgering his prospective son-in-law about his political views not a month previous, suddenly he seemed very wary and cautious.

Sterling stepped away from her, and she was glad. Danielle was already in the carriage.

Lord Dunmore had already turned his mind to the matters of the day, and it was her father who stood before the gates of the palace to watch the carriage turn along the green. He did not wave, and Amanda was relieved. She leaned her head back against the carriage and was glad of the respite. It would be a three-hour drive down the peninsula to Lord Cameron's home.

From the moment she first set eyes on the place, she felt a peculiar stirring in her blood. A mist was just rising as the carriage turned down the long winding drive. Great oaks sheltered the drive, and the mist caught within their branches and leaves. Then suddenly the trees parted and the house could be seen, rising high upon a hill on a waving lawn of emerald-green grasses. It was a huge place, made of brick, with a great porch surrounding the whole of it and great white Doric columns adding grace and elegance to the symmetry of the architecture.

"*Mon Dieu,*" Danielle murmured, pulling back the carriage draperies to better study the house. Her eyes were bright as she smiled at Amanda. "This is a house, *mais oui!*"

Amanda tried to smile, but she felt butterflies in her stomach. The whole of the plantation was impressive. As they rounded the drive, she could glimpse the neat rows of outbuildings all on a path and surrounded by vegetable and flower gardens. The gardens seemed to stretch out forever, just as the main house seemed almost to glitter beneath the sun and reach upward to the heavens. It was an illusion of the mist, she thought, and yet she couldn't deny that it was beautiful. To the far left she could see the fields, and already there were a multitude of men at left. From this distance, slaves and white tenant farmers all seemed to blend together as they bent at their tasks. Far beyond she could see a rise of trees as the land sloped down to the river, and she could just make out some of the dock buildings that lay directly behind the house and far down the slope. Lord Cameron was at a distinct advantage with his property sitting on the river and with his own dock and deep harbor.

Danielle's eyes were flashing happily. "It will be good here, *ma chérie*. It will be good. This lord is very wealthy, and he will marry you and keep you far from your papa."

Amanda shivered suddenly, despite the grace and beauty that surrounded her, and she didn't know if it had been Danielle's mention of her father or of Lord Cameron. She was escaping the one to come to the other. He knew that she was a fraud, yet it was his fraud that they were now perpetuating. She had never lied about her own political beliefs. He knew she considered him a traitor. He had been furious to hear that her apology the other night had been forced upon her, but he'd already known that she had been spying on him.

She could never marry him. Even if nothing had ever happened between them, if she had not fallen in love with Robert, if her heart had not been twisted by her father's dark corruption, she was still, in her heart, and always, a loyalist. They were English; they were English people, with English laws, and she was proud of that heritage. At the school for young ladies, she had learned she loved London. America was still raw and wild, but her people belonged to one of the most cultured and greatest nations on earth. To her, he was a traitor.

"There he is! Lord Cameron awaits us!" Danielle said happily.

Amanda was not so happy. She swallowed sharply as she held open the curtain. He was awaiting them on the steps to his house. He was in white breeches and stockings, boots, and a navy frock. As usual, his shirt was finely laced and impeccable, his hair was unpowdered but neatly queued. As the carriage clattered along the stone drive, Amanda admitted that he well fit the regal house, for his bearing was fine.

The carriage came to a halt. Pierre came scampering down from the driver's seat. Lord Cameron called out something to him, and Pierre laughed, then helped Danielle from the carriage.

"Welcome, Danielle," Cameron said. He took the woman's hand in both of his own. "Welcome to Cameron Hall."

Flustered, Danielle smiled and Lord Cameron kissed her hand.

"Merci, merci!" Danielle murmured, blushing and flustered. She was so happy, Amanda thought. And perhaps she had the right, for Nigel Sterling had never treated her with anything that resembled kindness.

He had always hurt her, Amanda thought, paling. Then she saw Eric's eyes on her, and she flushed. He had known that she would come. And she had.

He took her hand. "And, my love, to you my warmest welcome. I hope that you shall be very happy here. And safe."

Safe? she wondered. Could she be safe from him?

With both of her hands within his own, he pulled her close. He kissed her cheeks and then slowly released her, studying her eyes. "Pierre, find Thom if you would, and see to Lady Sterling's trunks, please."

"Mais oui," Pierre agreed, grinning and turning toward the house.

Amanda found herself looking at the carriage with its coat-of-arms and then to Eric Cameron. He was so comfortable, so affluent, and yet it seemed that he was willing to risk it all.

"Shall we go in?" he asked her.

She nodded, and then she realized that she hadn't spoken a word yet. "Yes, of course."

"Come, Danielle, I think that you'll enjoy a bit of a tour too."

"*Merci*—thank you," she said quickly. Nigel Sterling hated her to speak French. He hated the fact that Amanda had mastered the language so easily.

But Lord Cameron did not mind at all. He smiled kindly, and in those seconds Amanda felt a curious thrill sweep through her, for his smile had made him arresting indeed, charming and youthful.

It was only when he was crossed that the laughter left him and the tension settled in.

She had already crossed him.

Large double doors painted white were opened behind them and he was no longer gazing her way. "The land, my love, was originally called the Carlyle Hundred. It was granted to my many times great-grandfather by James the First. He was a Jamie himself, and he and his wife Jassy built this place. They were here when the Powhatans massacred the settlers in 1622, but they survived to lay the cornerstones and build the hall."

He had led her through the doors, and now they stood in a grand and massive hallway. Opposing double doors opened to the river behind them, and a gentle breeze blew through the hallway. A grand stairway stood at center, and a door led off in either direction to the wings of the house. The bannister was polished mahogany, the walls were covered with European silks, and the ceilings had beautifully crafted moldings. A man in crimson livery similar to Pierre's came hurrying down the stairs. "Ah, here is Richard. Richard, Lady Sterling, and her maid, Mademoiselle Danielle."

White-haired and lean, Richard bowed. "At your service, milady, mam'selle. Milord Cameron, shall you desire anything now?"

"Blackberry tea in the library in an hour, Richard, if you would be so good. I had thought that I would show milady and mam'selle their rooms, and give them time to refresh themselves from the ride."

"Very good, milord," Richard said, and bowing, he left them.

Lord Cameron led them on up the wide and graceful stairway. At the landing they came upon a portrait gallery. Amanda found herself stopping before the first portrait, startled. A dark-haired man in seventeenth-century dress stared out at her with Eric Cameron's silver-blue eyes. Beside him was the portrait of a beautiful blond woman with crystal eyes.

"Jamie and Jasmine," Lord Cameron told her. "Rumor has it that she was a tavern wench, but he was so enamored of her that he would have her no matter what her birth."

Amanda stared at him and flushed, feeling the piercing power of his eyes. "Are all Cameron men so determined?"

"Yes," he said flatly. "Ah, here, Jamie's grandson, another Jamie. And his Gwendolyn. They sheltered numerous Roundheads when Cromwell ruled and King Charles the First lay headless in his grave. Virginia has always been a loyalist colony."

"So what has happened?" Amanda asked him.

"Time changes eternally, Lady Sterling. Seeds, once sown, often flourish, and the seed of liberty has fallen here."

"So you are a traitor."

"What words, lady! I am about to travel with Lord Dunmore to face the West County savages! What traitorous work is that?"

She smiled serenely, and he laughed huskily. "Alas, I can imagine your very thoughts. You see a Shawnee hatchet riding high upon my temple. Mam'selle, that you could be so cruel!"

He mocked her, she knew, but his fingers felt like steel about her own, tense and powerful. He raised her hand to his lips and kissed it. Just the very light brush of the hot moisture of his lips made her blood seem to sizzle and flow, her knees grow weak. A flush came to her features because she knew that he evoked forbidden things within her, and it should not be. And still she stood, captured in a curious hold as he turned her hand, touching his kiss against her palm. A pulse leapt through her. His eyes rose to hers and she felt suddenly dizzy. "Please . . ." she whispered, dismayed by the note of desperation in her voice.

He let go of her hand and moved down the gallery to another portrait. He was, she thought, well versed in this game they were playing. He was making the rules. She could not allow him to do so. "Here, my lady! This is a favorite portrait of mine. Petroc Cameron, and here, his wife. Roc was rumored to be a pirate, and to have captured and seduced his own bride."

"A Cameron tradition?" Amanda inquired pleasantly.

He paused, looking into her eyes. "He pirated for the Crown."

"So 'tis *rumored.*"

"He was my grandfather, and he raised me, for my father was killed fighting the French. I know the truth about him and his beloved, for I heard it from their very lips. They aged in beauty and in love, and never seemed to change to one another. He was the pirate; I daresay that she did the taming. But they taught me much of the true values in life, and I am grateful."

He turned away from her, walking on with Danielle at his heels. Amanda paused, suddenly aching. She'd never known what it was like to watch someone age with love, to learn any of life's true values. She'd known coldness, betrayal, and brutality.

She looked again at the portraits, and wished that these people had been her own family. She wanted this background, she wanted the very beautiful people to look down upon her, with love.

Amanda trembled and feared that she would cry. It was so very senseless. She was there to escape her father. Bless the warring Shawnees, they would take Lord Cameron away, and she would have peace.

"Milady?"

He was politely waiting for her now.

She hurried along. He threw open a door on the southern side of the passage. She stepped into a huge room with a mahogany sleigh bed and Persian carpets on the polished wood floor. Huge grand windows opened to a river view, and there was a massive fireplace to warm one, a fine carved table with two elegant French brocade chairs to face the windows. It was a room fit for a princess, finer than the governor's room at the palace.

"Will this suffice?" he asked her.

She nodded, then lowered her head. He had turned to speak with Danielle. "Mam'selle, you are just down the hall, there."

The open door awaited her and Danielle smiled, thanked him, and hurried forward with delight. Amanda still had her head down but she could feel him near her, the very crisp clean fabric of his clothing, the pleasant scent of good tobacco and brandy and leather, and something subtle, something with which he apparently bathed. And there was his own scent, vibrantly masculine. She moistened her lips and turned to him. He was watching her, his hands folded behind his back, his eyes unreadable.

"Where is your room, Lord Cameron?" she asked him.

He arched a brow politely, then smiled. "Through the wardrobe, Lady Sterling." He watched with amusement as she paled, then added, "You have a key, of course."

"Of—course."

"But then, one wonders why you are so interested. Are you concerned about my whereabouts, or my belongings?"

"I'm not concerned—"

"You are, so please, spare us both, and quit lying. Search to your heart's content, but take care. If I find you too close to my bed, I might be tempted to believe that you wish to lie upon it. Pride, my love, dies hard."

"I imagine, for yours is monstrously large."

"Perhaps with just cause."

"You do flatter yourself."

"Do I? I think not. I do believe that I know you better than you know yourself, and therefore I am at an advantage."

She opened her mouth to protest, but he gave her no chance. He bowed and turned away, then paused at the door.

"Richard will come to escort you to tea. You'll need to

meet Cassidy, my valet, and let's see, Margaret will furnish you and Danielle with anything you need. From then on, milady, you shall be on your own. And, my lovely little spy, it will be quite fascinating to see where your—delicate—steps do lead you."

"Never too close!" she called after him. "Never so close as to be . . ."

"Caught?" he inquired pleasantly. His eyes leisurely drifted to her, and he smiled. "You are in check already."

"I do not concede the game!"

"Ah, trust me. You will."

He turned then and was gone.

VIII ❧

Amanda did not take long to inspect her room, though a high excitement had risen in her, just being there. She loved the gracious manor, the view of the river beyond her windows, the exquisite sense of freedom. She didn't understand it. She was there under false pretenses, playing a dangerous game with a dangerous man. But she was far away from Nigel Sterling, and at the moment that seemed enough.

A pitcher had been filled with clean fresh water and a bowl and towel and sponge had been left for her arrival. She washed quickly, smoothed her hair with the silver-handled brush upon the dressing table, and quickly turned for the door. She hesitated just a moment. There was a door at the far rear of the room. She couldn't resist it.

A key was set within the lock. She had the ability to lock him out of the room. She smiled and then twisted the key. Then she pushed open the door and entered his room.

Here, too, long windows looked out on the sloping lawn
and down to the river and the docks and warehouses. The
sun streamed in beautifully, the river breeze lifted the
light curtains under their heavier velvet backers. His bed
seemed huge; it was four-postered, and hewn of a wood as
dark as the man. But the room was not at all dark. It was
exceptionally large and, though masculine by nature, it
also had a sweeping elegance, as if it would welcome the
partnership of a woman. The mantel was large also, with
fine molded woodwork. Candles in elegant silver holders
awaited the fall of night as did beautiful glass lamps. A
small cherrywood table sat before the windows, catching
the fall of the sun. A large braided rug added warmth to
the polished wood floor, and the armoires and dressing
tables that rimmed the walls were even finer than the furnishings she had seen in his Williamsburg town house.
There also seemed to be a scent on the air. A scent of fine
Virginia tobacco, rich leather, and a touch of men's co-
logne. It was a haunting scent, arresting.

Like the man.

Amanda felt color rise to her cheeks and she quickly
exited the room, forgetting that she was supposed to be a
spy of sorts and that spies do not flush and retreat when
they fall upon the very core of their search. Still, she hurried into her own room and closed the connecting door
between the rooms, breathing deeply. Irritation rose high
within her. Her father was such a fool! Damn his fascination with Cameron. What man these days did not wonder
what the next years would bring? But, of course, it was
true, she knew. Cameron was in sympathy with the
rogues, saving the fellow in Boston, meeting with the burgesses in the Apollo Room at the Raleigh Tavern. But she
had heard that Colonel Washington himself had been dismayed at the events in Boston, saying that the destruction
of property could not be justified. But even with the House
dissolved Washington was still engaged in meetings, and
he had been elected to attend the Continental Congress.
And Lord Fairfax, loyalist to the core, called Washington a
great man, a pride of the Crown. Life was in a whirlwind.
Nothing was as simple as black and white anymore.

She pushed away from the door, wondering if she was trying to excuse Eric Cameron within her own mind. She told herself that it could not be true, yet she was suddenly running away from herself and toward her next meeting with the man.

She did literally run, past the pictures in the wide gallery and to the sweeping stairway. Once she reached the upper bannister she paused, for a man was waiting for her at the foot of the stairs. He was as tall as Cameron and so black as to be ebony. He stood as straight as an arrow, and he was dressed in a handsome uniform that enhanced his startling color. He was regal, she thought, and wondered that such a word could come to her in reference to a slave.

She struggled for breath as he bowed deeply. "Lady Sterling, I am Cassidy, Lord Cameron's valet. I shall take you to him now, and if ever I can be of assistance, you must let me know."

Amanda nodded, startled by the man's exquisite speech. She held herself with dignity as she descended the stairs. He said no more but walked along the large main hall until he came to a set of double doors. He opened them and moved discreetly to the side. "Lady Sterling, Lord Cameron."

Amanda entered the handsome parlor. Eric was waiting for her by the mantel, this one made of fine smoke-gray marble. Persian rugs lay scattered over the floorboards, the walls were covered in a fine silk cloth, and there were deep window seats toward the rear of the room. A tea cart with a silver server and delicate porcelain cups was parked before a richly upholstered French sofa.

"Do sit down, Amanda," he welcomed her, nodding to the black man. "I see you've met Cassidy."

"Yes," Amanda said, nervously taking a seat near the edge of the sofa. She smiled at Cassidy. He reminded her of his master. He appeared to be exceptionally strong, a man who could be of great value in the fields. Her father would never have had him as a house servant.

Cassidy bowed deeply and left them.

Amanda turned back to Eric to find that he was studying her intently, his silver-blue eyes brooding. She wondered if she hadn't been a fool to come. She loved the house, she loved the excitement, she loved the freedom. But she didn't know at all what she felt for the man anymore. He tempted her like the original sin of Eden, and that temptation burned into her, for her father's words were never far away. She could not believe that her beautiful mother had been a whore, but when Eric Cameron came near her, she was forced to wonder at the blood that simmered within her.

"So that is Cassidy," she murmured. "He looks more like a prince than a house slave."

"I believe he would have stood in line to be a Nubian prince. And he is not a slave. He earned his freedom. He remains with me by choice, and earns wages."

"How . . . interesting," she murmured. She had difficulty meeting his gaze so she lowered her eyes quickly, wondering what he read within them. "So this is berry tea, milord? How intriguing."

"No. It is horrible. But one gets used to it."

"Shall I pour?"

"Please do."

Her hands were shaking. She gritted her teeth and willed her fingers to cease their trembling. She lowered her head to her task, but when the curious berry tea was within a cup, she almost cried out, for when she raised her lashes he was before her, hunched down upon the balls of his feet and looking at her. He wasn't a foot away. She hadn't heard him move, hadn't realized he was so near.

His teacup clattered within its saucer. She swallowed, noting his remarkable eyes and the pulse that beat a wicked rhythm against his throat.

"You startled me." She gasped.

He rescued his cup, setting it down, his eyes never leaving hers.

"Marry me," he told her.

"I cannot!" she whispered desperately.

He caught her hands and came up beside her on the sofa. A rueful smile curled his lip even as the tension remained in his eyes. "There is no reason that you cannot. There is every reason that you should."

"I do not love you!"

"Ah, so you are still in love with that fop."

"Fop! Robert Tarryton—"

"Is a fop, by God's body, I swear it. Still, no man but Robert Tarryton will ever convince you of that. He is due to wed within the week. And your father is a dangerous man."

"My father!" She flushed, fully aware that he was telling the truth and fully aware of him as he sat beside her. She had never felt more alive, she thought, more attuned to every fiber of feeling within herself. Her flesh burned with greater sensitivity, her heart beat as if it were touched. She was drawn . . . she frightened. His very passion on her behalf could well stand against her. He excited her beyond reason, he scared her to the depths of her soul. A pact with him would be like a pact with the very devil.

She shook her head, losing both breath and reason. She didn't want tea or sustenance of any kind. She discovered that she was fascinated only with the long dark fingers that curled over hers. His thumb brushed again and again over her flesh, stirring strange fires and causing truth and wisdom to sweep away.

"Your father will not let you play this game long, though I am not certain of what game he plays himself. If you do not set a date to wed me, he will seek another for you. There was talk, you are aware, of betrothing you to Lord Hastings, a man almost thrice your age and—I've got it from very reputable sources—a man who snores with the vehemence of the west wind."

She couldn't help but laugh at Eric's bold description of the man. He moved closer to her, drawing a finger provocatively over her cheek, then defining the breadth of her lower lip with the same sensual touch, his eyes following his movement. "I am not as young as Tarryton, and I admit to a scar or two upon my back and at my side, but I swear that my teeth are all mine and quite good, I've kept to one chin, and I do bathe with frequency. I am wealthy, landed, and I come with this house, a stable full of horses, and fields full of tobacco and grain. Marry me. And—I have it from very reputable sources—I do not snore." She laughed again, but his eyes grew darker as they seemed to possess her own. "I promise to be an excellent lover."

"Oh!" She gasped, but laughter still mingled with her indignity. He had broken into her very bedroom and forced her down upon her bed. What brazen words he offered now could not cause her more outrage. "You, sir, are the most egotistical man I have ever met! Tell me, sir, does that piece of information come from reputable sources too?"

"I'm sure I can arrange for references, milady, should you require them."

"Lady Geneva?" she inquired sharply.

"I do believe you're jealous. Marry me," he insisted. "And do so quickly. Before I leave. Then, if the Shawnee split my head, you shall have safety and peace."

"I cannot marry you so fast—"

"Ah! You will consider it then."

She couldn't help smiling again. The world faded away when he was before her so vehemently, so adamantly. And she did feel safe. As if no man—not even her father—would dare to come against her. "You're forgetting something."

"What?"

"I am a loyalist. That is not my father's voice, nor Lord Dunmore's, but my own. I fear the radicals and what is to come. And you, sir, are a patriot."

"You are welcome to be a loyalist."

"And your wife?"

"Yes. You may follow your convictions, just so long as you take no steps to betray me."

Amanda inhaled sharply. How could she make such a promise when she had been cast into his arms for that very purpose? She looked down to where his hands lay over hers. His palms were rough from work he must have chosen to take on himself. Perhaps they were a soldier's hands, roughened by his hold upon his horse's reins. She didn't know. She only knew that the roughness against the soft flesh of her hand was somehow good. She drew her eyes back to his, and she was suddenly very frightened, and not so much of the man as by the depths of the feel-

ings that stirred within her. If he kissed her now, s
would want to explore that touch.

Like a whore . . . like the whore her father claimed
her to be. Her mother's daughter.

Some darkness must have fallen over her eyes for Eric
frowned, watching her. "What is the matter?"

"Nothing. Nothing!" she cried. She leapt to her feet,
shaking her head. "I can't marry you. I can't. We—we're
on different sides. It's impossible. If you want me to
leave—"

"Leave!" He stood, watching the sudden torment that
constricted her features. "Leave?" He smiled slowly.
"Why, of course not. I should not want to cast you to Lord
Hastings with his four-score chins. My God, what a travesty that would be!"

Amanda almost smiled; she could not. She turned
around and fled the room, to race up the stairs. She entered her room. Her trunks had arrived, and a servant
would come to hang her clothing on the hooks in the armoire and to set her hose and undergarments into the
drawers of the dresser. But no one was there now. Night
had come. A fire had been lit in the hearth to burn away
the dampness. The windows were open to the river. She
walked toward them and looked out on the night. Slowly
her heart ceased to beat its rampant rhythm. As she stared
at the James, a sense of peace settled over her. She was
safe here. Eric Cameron might taunt and tease her and
discard propriety, break into the governor's palace and
perhaps even manhandle her. But he would never force
her to do anything against her own will. He would not
strike her in anger, and he would not use her for his own
cause. It was almost like being loved. She smiled to the
night, then changed into a cool cotton nightgown. So mel-
low had she become that she dropped her stockings,
garters, shoes, corset, shift, and gown upon the floor with
no thought and curled into the comfortable bed to sleep.
She did not dream, and she did not hear the knocking
upon her door later when Danielle came to see if she
would have supper.

ᵥₒr did she hear the connecting door open when the
ₒcks about the house were striking midnight.

Eric stood and looked down on her as she slept. The
dying firelight lay gently upon her face, and she looked
very young. Fragile and vulnerable. Anger rose within him
as he thought of Nigel Sterling, and he wondered how any
man could so mistreat a daughter, especially one so beautiful and proud as this. He wanted to touch her, but he did
not allow himself to do so. He did not want to wake her,
and so he just watched her, the ache to possess her tem-
pered by the very innocence of her appearance. She
evoked so many things within him. From the moment he
had seen her dancing at Thomas Mabry's in Boston, he
had wanted her with an urgent fever. From the night
he had touched her in the garden, he had wanted her forever with something that burned and sizzled inside of
him. But from the time he had seen her with her father, he
had wanted to protect her with all of his heart. Her loyalty
to the Crown was so very fierce! If she could but love a
man so fiercely, then he would gladly lay down his life for
her and smile in the dying.

He reached out but did not allow his hand to fall. He
smiled and felt the cool breeze ripple over him, and then
he turned to go back to his own room. The game had
changed, if subtly so.

In the morning when Amanda walked into the dining
room, Eric was nowhere about. The girl he had mentioned, Margaret, a fresh-faced farm lass with bright dark
eyes and bouncing black curls, came to inform her that
his lordship was about seeing to the mustering of his Tidewater troops. Margaret left then, and Thom served her—
coffee that morning, rather than the berry tea—delicately
seasoned fish and fresh-baked bread. When she was finished with the meal she decided to explore beyond the
house. After exiting by the rear, she started down a path
that led by the outbuildings, the smokehouse, laundry,
bakehouse, kitchen, the cooper's and the blacksmith's, and
the barns and stables. Men and women stopped in their
work to look her way curiously, then quickly bowed or

curtsied to her. She smiled to all she met in turn, wondering how many of the blacks were slaves and how many were freemen. Nor were the servants all black, and not just within the house. A white woman who spoke with a soft French accent was directing the smoking of a butchered hog. There were numerous Acadians here, she thought, and she was happy, for Danielle would be pleased to meet so many of her own people.

Just as she thought of Danielle she came upon the stables. To her surprise she saw Danielle there, deeply engrossed in conversation with a tall white man. Amanda hurried forward, then paused. The two were speaking French very quickly. And furtively. They whispered, they gesticulated.

Amanda instinctively slipped behind the wall of the barn and looked at the man. He was very handsome, perhaps forty years old, with dark hair and sensitive light eyes, eyes that haunted his face and gave it much of its appeal. His features were fine. He almost had the look of a scholar about him, except that he was tall and well muscled, and wore the plain breeches and hardy hose and shoes of an outdoors worker. He did not seem to be the blacksmith, which made Amanda wonder at his work.

"Lady Sterling."

Startled—and caught in the act of spying upon the servants—Amanda swung around. Cassidy was there, towering over her. He seemed to glisten beneath the sun.

"Aye, Cassidy!" she said, annoyed and embarrassed.

He betrayed no emotion at all. "Lord Dunmore has come to look over Lord Cameron's troops. Your father has accompanied him, along with Lord Hastings."

"I shall come right away, Cassidy." She fell into step beside him but he quickly let her precede him. She fell back, determined to be on her guard. "Then Lord Cameron has returned?"

"He has. They await you in the parlor."

"Thank you."

She walked ahead again. When she came around the trail, she could see that the rear yard was filling with canvas tents. Men were arriving, camping out on the open lawn. A captain drilled a company of foot soldiers near the river while others sat about on crates or on the ground, cleaning their rifles, drinking from tins, laughing with one another. She could not make out faces or men, but she estimated that at least fifty men had come, and they seemed to be dressed in the buckskin clothing that was associated with the West County men. She paused again and waited pointedly for Cassidy.

"Who are all these men? They are not regular militia."

"No, Lady Sterling. They are troops raised by Lord Cameron—tenants, farmers, a few artisans. And many cousins."

"Cousins?"

"Distant, perhaps. Half of the men out there are Camerons. They own property, some estates, near here, all on the old Carlyle Hundred grounds. The first lord and lady had several children, and since that was well over a hundred years ago, you can imagine that their descendants are many."

"Of course," Amanda murmured.

"Milady, they're waiting."

She had hardly fled her father and he was upon her again like a vulture. She did not answer Cassidy but hurried up the back steps to the hall and went from there straight to the parlor. The men were all there, her father and Lord Hastings with his "four-score chins," Lord Dunmore and Eric himself. Lord Dunmore was striking as usual with his flashing brown eyes and elegant apparel. Eric wore navy breeches and a white cotton shirt. Her eyes were drawn to his, a habit that seemed more and more customary as time wore on.

"Ah, Amanda, my dear!" Her father drew her close and kissed her cheek. She wanted to scream and refuse his touch. However, she managed to hold her ground and escape him, allowing the governor to take her hand and bow low over it.

"I've come to see how Eric is managing to gather men. I did not believe he could summon so many," Lord Dunmore said.

"Only half have arrived as yet, John. The others will

come by the end of the week, I believe. We shall be ready to travel very soon."

"Good. Lewis has his West County men out on the frontier; we'll come at the Shawnee in a pincer movement and settle this once and for all," the governor stated.

Glancing at Eric, Amanda didn't think he believed that things would be settled once and for all, but he didn't say so. Instead he announced, "I believe that our meal is ready to be served. Gentlemen, Lady Amanda, shall we?"

Eric would have taken her arm, she thought, except that she stood before Lord Hastings, and the old man hooked his arm into her own, smiling down at her with his little beady dark eyes. "May I, milady?"

"Ah . . . of course," she murmured, and so she was escorted into the dining room on his arm. She was very grateful when he released her and they all took their seats about the table.

The dining room took up almost the entire left side of the house. The table was long, able to seat at least twenty, but this afternoon the five of them were gathered at the far end. Upon the walls were several displays of arms, and a large family crest sat high above the fireplace. There were sideboards on all four sides of the rooms, and deep window seats where Amanda imagined guests could relax and socialize before and after the meal. Perhaps the ladies gathered by the fire in the plush seats when the men exited the room for their brandy and pipes.

She drew her eyes from the room to realize that Lord Dunmore was watching her. She flushed and asked after his countess's health.

"She is quite well, thank you."

"I had not heard that she was ill," Eric commented, frowning.

"Not ill, soon to create a new Virginian," the governor said.

"Ah, then to your fair lady's health!" Eric murmured, lifting his glass of Madeira. About the table the toast was repeated and they all sipped wine. Thom and Cassidy served the meal of delicious wild fowl and summer squash and pole beans. Amanda was somewhat forgotten as Dunmore heatedly discussed tactics with Eric.

Eric calmly disagreed on many points. "I have fought the Indians before, Governor. They are not cowards, and their practices are not so different from our own at times. The white men on the frontier take scalps as often as the Indians. The Indians themselves are fierce fighters who were never taught to stand in neat lines. They attack from the brush, they attack in darkness, and they must never, never be taken lightly as simple savages. Especially not the Shawnee."

Amanda shivered, suddenly aware that she did not want Eric Cameron falling beneath a Shawnee's scalping knife. He was leaning back quite calmly and comfortably in his chair, dauntless, she thought, yet aware. She set down her fork, paling.

"Gentlemen! Our conversation is distressing the lady!" Lord Hastings protested.

"Is it?" Eric, amused, was looking her way. "I do apologize most deeply, Amanda."

She smiled, standing quickly. "I do believe I could benefit from some fresh air. If you gentlemen will just excuse me. . . ."

They all stood, but she gave none the chance to protest, sweeping quickly from the dining room and out into the hall. She raced out to the front porch and stared down the endless drive before the house.

"Lady Amanda!"

She turned, truly distressed to discover that Lord Hastings had followed her. She tried to smile as he waddled to her, panting. She backed away from him, but he reached for her hands. "Are you unwell?" he asked.

"No, no, I'm so sorry that you left the meal—"

"I'm so sorry that you were distressed. Yet perhaps, my dear, it is best that you realize that young Cameron may not return." He clicked his tongue unhappily against his cheeks.

"Oh, I . . . I'm sure that Eric will return. He's fought the Indians before. He will take care."

"Still . . . my dear, I hope that you do not think of me unkindly."

"No . . . of course not, Lord Hastings. I shall never forget all the wonderful hunts at your estate when I was a child."

"You are a child no more, Amanda. And you must not be worried for the future. I would have you know now that if Eric does not return from the front, I will be there for you. I know that I am an old man, but I am one who is humbly and deeply in love with you. I have spoken with your father and if anything does not go as planned, well, then he has agreed that I should be your husband." She tried not to gaze at him in horror, but a light in his beady dark eyes made her feel as if she would spew her meal all over his fine silk shirt. She swallowed hard, gaping at him. Then she realized that the other men were coming out on the porch, Eric between her father and the governor.

"How . . . kind," she told Lord Hastings. She felt cold, sick, imagining his fleshy hands upon her. She would die first, she thought.

"How very, very kind, but . . . you see, we, er, we cannot wait. We cannot wait—"

"Cannot wait for what?" her father boomed out.

She moistened her lips. Eric was watching her, amused once again. She ignored his look, smiled regretfully at Hastings, then hurried past him and slipped her arm through Eric's. "We—we have agreed that we cannot wait for Eric to return. We're going to be married right away."

"What? But there are just days before we are due to leave for the frontier—" the governor protested.

"Yes, yes, of course," Eric murmured, his cobalt eyes falling upon her with a sizzle. "And we should have spoken earlier, Amanda, we should have told them right away." His eyes remained upon hers, daring her. "Alas, it is the very thought that I could die that has prompted us to this measure. I would leave an heir behind if I could."

"But you cannot marry so quickly—" Sterling began.

"Your pardon, sir! Lord Dunmore can give us a special license, and the service can be quiet and performed at Bruton Parish within the week."

"It's quite inappropriate—" Nigel began.

"I like it," the governor said. His Scots burr sounded for just a moment and his brown eyes sparkled. "I like it very well. We shall marry our little loyalist to this doubtful fellow and keep him in line, what do you say?"

They all laughed. The tension lay far beneath the comment, and at the moment, it was ignored by them all.

"Perhaps, under these circumstances, Amanda should return with me to Williamsburg," Sterling said.

"No!" Eric retorted. So quickly that it was almost rude. He softened his speech, smiling. "Gentlemen, we should all spend the night here and go into town tomorrow."

"Splendid!" the governor agreed.

He clamped his hand on Sterling's shoulder. "A good match, Nigel. Come, let's imbibe upon your son-in-law's spirits and toast to your future grandchildren!"

Lord Dunmore led Sterling back toward the house. Lord Hastings looked from the older men to the young people, then sighed and headed toward the house. When they were alone at last, Amanda struggled to free herself from Eric's hold. He did not release her. She tossed back her head to stare into his eyes.

"I'm delighted," he murmured. "What brought on this sudden ardor upon your part? Have you discovered if not love, then lust for me at last?"

"Don't be absurd. I've discovered . . . I've discovered Lord Hastings's four-score chins," she retorted.

His smile deepened. A dimple showed against his cheek and his eyes were touched by a silver glitter born of the very devil. "You have cast yourself into this. You will not renege?"

She swallowed, shaking her head. She could not breathe. "No. No, I will not renege."

"You needn't say that as if you were going to your execution."

"That is how I feel."

He threw back his head and laughed, then he lifted her chin with his finger, searching out her eyes. "You are mistaken. I will prove to you that it will be fun."

"Fun!" She shivered. "It cannot be fun. Not for a wife."

"But it will be," he promised her. His eyes seemed to pour down upon her with fierce and unyielding promise. His fingers stroked over her throat and then his lips touched down on hers. Her eyes closed and she felt as if demons set fire throughout her, causing a cascade of searing liquid to dance against her limbs. Then his lips left hers and touched down upon the arch of her throat, and the sensations increased. She swallowed suddenly, tearing away. Puzzled, he caught her hand and pulled her back. Color blazed in her cheeks.

"What in God's name is wrong with you?" he demanded.

"It isn't—right!" She gasped.

Angrily he held her against him, lifting her chin once more to meet the tumult in her eyes. "Not right? Lady, you are not a harlot I have chosen for the night. We are to marry."

She lowered her lashes. "Let me go, please! We are not married as yet."

He did not let her go. "Tomorrow we will be. And when the words are said and you are my wife, don't think that you can turn to me and trust in my honor to leave you be. I am taking a wife because I desire one. You do understand that."

"Yes!" She wrenched free from him and turned and ran down the steps. He started to follow her and then paused, then turned to reenter the house.

That night Amanda was too nervous to remember the dark-haired man with whom Danielle had been having her curious animated conversation. She paced the room endlessly, having preferred supper on a tray to the gentlemen's company that evening. She walked back and forth telling Danielle that she was insane, but that she did not know what else to do. Danielle was quiet, but Amanda did not even notice.

She ceased her pacing when a knock came on the door at about eight o'clock. She did not answer it—her father opened the door and stepped into the room. He took one look at Danielle and said curtly, "Go." The woman glanced toward Amanda but obeyed him quickly enough.

He closed the door behind Danielle. "So you are going to marry him tomorrow."

"Yes, Father. It's what you want, isn't it?"

"Yes. But I want you to remember that even if you are his wife, you remain my daughter."

"Meaning?"

"You will do as I say."

She smiled, glad of her coming marriage for one reason. Eric Cameron could protect her from anything. "He is a forceful man. He might disagree."

"He cannot save Damien Roswell's neck from the hangman."

She paled, her pleasure cleanly erased. Sterling kept talking, ignoring her. "Damien is accompanying Lord Cameron to the front, did you know that? No, I did not suppose so. Perhaps one of them will die. It will be interesting to see."

He turned to leave her. "Don't forget how very much of your future I still hold, my dear, dear child."

The door closed. Amanda sank down on the bed, shaking.

Eric Cameron could not protect her from everything.

In the morning Danielle came to her very early. Amanda dressed numbly. Danielle had chosen a soft blue-gray gown for her with pearls stitched into the lacing. She did not bind or cover Amanda's hair, but let it stream down upon the gown like a ripple of dark fire. When Amanda was ready, she walked down the stairs. The servants were lined up on the stairs. A glass was raised to her, and she was welcomed among them as Lady Cameron. She thanked them but had gone so pale that she could not manage a smile.

She remained numb for the long drive back to Williamsburg. She and Danielle rode alone, for Eric had gone in with the others even earlier to make the arrangements.

Danielle was pleased about the marriage, if distressed about the rush. "There should have been time for a wedding gown, for the church to properly announce the ceremony. But it is good, *mais oui,* it is good. You will be out of that monster's clutches forever!"

"That monster," Amanda knew, was her father. But Danielle was wrong. She was not out of his clutches.

In Williamsburg she was taken to the governor's palace. His countess very kindly and enthusiastically helped her freshen up from the journey. She chatted very happily about her wedding day, and apologized for the indisposition that had kept her from entertaining Amanda on her last visit. "I do hope that John was gracious."

"Very gracious," Amanda agreed. He had threatened her cousin's life—graciously.

But then the countess offered her a stiff brandy. "A gentleman's drink perhaps, but for the prewedding tremors, a lady's drink as well!"

Amanda drank a lot of it. It seemed to be one way to endure the ceremony.

Despite the haste of the wedding, the Bruton Parish Church was quickly filled. Many of the men who had been in town for the dissolved House—who would soon be attending the Continental Congress—came to see Lord Cameron take his bride. As she walked down the aisle on her father's arm, Amanda noted that it was a curious assembly indeed. The governor laughed and joked with the very men whose meeting he had so recently dissolved. Lady Geneva had come, and squeezed her hand as she passed by. Colonel Washington was there, she saw, nodding to Eric with a pleased grin on his sober countenance. She did not see Damien, and that worried her, as he had been invited. Actually, everything worried her.

She was going to pass out, she thought. But she could not. Nigel Sterling passed her hand over to Eric, and the reverend stepped forward to tie their wrists together with white ribbon.

And then he began to speak.

Amanda did not hear his words. She felt the heat of the small church, and she heard the muffled whisperings of the people in the pews. She felt Eric standing beside her, and she heard the clear, well-modulated tones of his vows. Then she heard a pause, and she forced herself to speak even as she wondered at the words she said. She swore to love, honor, and obey.

Suddenly the reverend was smiling and suggesting that Eric might kiss his bride. Then his lips were upon hers, and fierce as she had never felt them before. The breath was robbed from her body and very nearly her life. It was not so different from any other of his demanding kisses except that it seemed ever more so. It was not a taunt . . . it was a possession, she thought.

There was a cry, and Lady Geneva surged forward, laughing, kissing her, then kissing her groom with something a little less than propriety. But that didn't seem to matter, for the peculiar assemblage was in a joyous mood. Dunmore kissed her deeply, then others in the council, and then members of the House of Burgesses.

There were so many people around her. Unable to breathe and feeling terribly trapped, she finally managed to escape through the crowd and exit the church into the cemetery. There she leaned against the cold wall, closing her eyes and breathing deeply. She opened her eyes to discover that Washington had followed her. Tall, with soft blue-gray eyes, he smiled her way ruefully. "Are you all right, Lady Cameron?"

Cameron. It was her name now, she thought. She opened her mouth to answer the man, but no words would come, and she knew that her eyes were wary. She nodded.

Washington smiled at her. "If I can ever help you, please do not hesitate to come to me. I see your husband coming. I wish you long life and happiness, milady, and I hope that you will visit us at Mount Vernon. We shall all pray for peace."

"Yes, we will pray for peace!" she agreed. The trees rustled over their heads, and for a moment they smiled at one another and shared something. Then the moment was broken, for Damien had discovered her.

He flashed Washington his rogue's smile, then kissed his cousin warmly. "Felicitations, Lady Cameron!"

"Damien! I did not see you!"

"I was in the church. I would not have missed it!" He

swept her off her feet and swirled her around, then he suddenly paused, laughing. "Uh-oh. Lord Cameron! Well, er, here she is! Your bride!"

He thrust Amanda into Eric's arms. So she wouldn't be dropped between the two men, she curled her arms around her husband's neck and met his gaze. He smiled down at her, and the tenderness in his smile warmed her. She offered a tentative smile in turn, and then he was laughing at something someone was saying, and then agreeing that the wine and ale were flowing freely at his town house.

It wasn't much of a walk to the town house. Eric carried her all the way there with a score of wellwishers behind them. She remembered little more of the afternoon, for despite his smile she was very, very nervous and so she kept her glass of Madeira filled and refilled, perhaps far too often. She thought that they would party into the night, but the wellwishers were still in abundance when Eric came to her, sweeping her into his arms again. Panic seized her as she felt his arms close around her.

"What—"

"We're going home."

"Home?"

"Cameron Hall."

"But—" she said, then fell silent, for she was glad of it. The long drive would delay their time alone together, the time that she was dreading, that now held her in pure terror. She had sold herself today, to a devil or a traitor, she knew not which. She had done so with open eyes, yet now she was afraid.

"Speech!" someone shouted out, and Eric gave one, waxing on eloquently about love—and then Shawnees, ending with an apology that all must be so quick since the darned Shawnees didn't care a whit about his love. Laughter followed them out to his carriage. He deposited her inside first, then climbed in beside her. Danielle would follow in her own coach.

Amanda closed her eyes as the horses clattered down the street, afraid to acknowledge the man beside her. He shifted suddenly, and her eyes flew open, for she was afraid that he meant to take her into his arms. He did not. He watched her from the shadows of the carriage. "It will be a long drive. You've been, er, imbibing quite freely. Perhaps you should try to sleep."

"Ladies do not imbibe," she told him.

"Nor do they swear, and Damien tells me that you could put a cattle drover to shame."

Lowering her lashes, she flushed and informed him that it was very rude of him to say so. He laughed and slipped an arm about her, drawing her upon his lap. She looked up at him in the shadows, ready to protest, then felt his fingers smoothing back her hair. "Rest, Amanda."

She did so. She fell asleep and did not waken until he had lifted her from the carriage and carried her up the stairs. Then her eyes widened with renewed panic, for this was it, she was home. She wondered where he would carry her. He took her past the portraits and into his room, and lay her down upon the huge bed there. He straightened then. "I will send Danielle to you, her coach has arrived behind us, I am sure."

He left her and she sprang up. A steaming hip bath awaited her by the fire. She began to pace, ruing the fact that she had slept away many of the effects of the wine.

The door opened. Danielle came in and hugged her quickly. Amanda stepped back, wringing her hands. "I can't do this!"

"There, there, love, you can!" Danielle protested. She turned her about and unhooked Amanda's gown, sliding it down from her shoulders. Amanda stepped from it.

"I can't breathe."

"It's your corset." Danielle pulled away her shift, then untied her corset. It didn't help. She still couldn't breathe. Danielle had to lead her to the bed to sit down so that she could remove her shoes and hose and garters. Then she shivered desperately as the breeze hit her naked flesh.

"Come, into the hip tub before you catch your death!" Danielle chided.

Amanda found herself in the bath smelling the sweet scent of rosewater. She sank back as Danielle lifted her hair carefully away from the water. The woman dropped her a round ball of French soap and a cloth, and Amanda automatically picked them up and sudsed the cloth, then her body. Then she started to shiver. Danielle handed her a little glass.

"Brandy."

"Oh, thank God!"

She nearly inhaled the liquid. "Again!" she begged Danielle, gasping. Danielle refilled her glass, and she swallowed it down quickly again. Then she was furious with herself. She was behaving like such a coward. Just who did he think that he was, terrifying her so? He had wanted the marriage. She just wasn't ready for this side of it. He would understand. She would make him.

She scrubbed herself to a glow then stood and grabbed for the towel Danielle offered her. Then she stood shivering as Danielle dropped a shear silk and lace gown over her head. The night was cool, despite the fire. She did not shake with fear, she absolutely assured herself.

"*Bonsoir, ma petite!*" Danielle told her, kissing her cheek tenderly.

"You're leaving!" Amanda gasped.

"But of course," Danielle said, shaking her head. But she had not left when the door suddenly opened, and Eric appeared.

His dark hair was damp, as if he had bathed elsewhere. He was clad in a long velvet robe that tied at his waist and fell nearly to his ankles. A smattering of dark hair showed at the neck of the robe where it lay open against his chest. Amanda discovered herself staring at his chest and losing the strength to stand.

"*Pardonnez-moi!*" Danielle said quickly.

"*Bonsoir,* Danielle," he said, his eyes locked on Amanda.

Danielle left them and the door closed behind her. Amanda moistened her lips and cleared her throat. She discovered herself backing toward the windows. "Eric . . ."

"Yes?" He was walking toward her. He had the grace of a wildcat and the same sure stride of determination.

"I . . . uh . . . I can't."

"Can't?"

"I can't go through with this."

"Oh?" He paused, his smile polite. "What do you mean, can't?"

"I . . ." She looked down at her gown. Horror filled her as she realized that the gossamer gown delineated the rouge crests of her nipples and the red-gold triangle at the juncture of her thighs. She drew her eyes quickly back to his, wishing that she could snatch the curtains from the walls to cover herself. He was coming toward her again. She shook her head.

"Eric, I beg of you, be a gentleman and understand . . ."

He paused again, as if carefully weighing his decision. "No."

"No!"

He shook his head and kept coming for her. "I told you yesterday what I would expect. You gave me your word that you would not renege."

"I didn't intend to renege. I swear it. Eric, please try to understand. I don't know you—"

"By the end of the night, my love, you will know me very well."

"Eric, honest to God, I would like to! I can't—"

He caught her arm and pulled her hard against him. Beneath the robe she felt the pulse and vitality of his body, for her gown lay as nothing but mist between them. She felt his male shaft, rising. She looked into his eyes and saw the darkness within them and the silver glitter of his laughter as he lowered his head to whisper against her lips.

"But you can, my love. Honest to God, you can." He lifted her into his arms. "Now, if you don't mind, Amanda, I'd just as soon have no more of the deity on my wedding night." He tossed her down into the softness of the bed. Even as she struggled to rise she heard his laughter, then his weight was upon her, bearing her ever farther downward into the depths of the bed.

IX ❧

She felt as if she were immersed within lightness and magic and clouds, and yet at the same time Amanda keenly felt everything about her. She felt the rush of the river wind and the warmth and flicker of the candles and the fire. And she felt the hard-muscled body and heat of the man on top of her, barely clad in the robe, and nearly naked against her. But even as she brought her arms against his chest, she felt the simple fascination of touching him there, of feeling the dark, crisp hair with her fingertips, of knowing the ripple of sinew and muscle beneath it. When she looked up she saw that he was smiling, no, laughing.

"Don't you dare gloat and laugh at me!" she cried, but his smile deepened and his laughter was haunting, as was the silver-blue decadence in his eyes. He planted a kiss upon her forehead, for she was powerless to move, and then his lips brushed her cheeks and her mouth, causing her to ache for more. His words fell softly against her flesh, and they, too, were a curious caress. "I'm not laughing at you, my love, and if I gloat, well, then you will have to forgive me."

"I forgive you nothing!" she retorted, meeting his eyes in the candlelight that made a devil's flame of them. It was best to meet his eyes. She did not dare look upon him. It was enough that she felt him.

"No, you would not!" he whispered. "Nor would you give up any fight, and yet you are, my little hawk, suddenly a sparrow in this bed."

"Sparrow!" She surged hard against his chest. A gasp escaped her as she saw that he had purposely goaded her to action, that pressing against him only served to accent all that was male and relentless, all that was hard and unyielding about him. Her fingers closed over his arms. As she felt the tension and size of the muscle there, she knew that she would never dislodge him. Despite herself she began to tremble. She moistened her lips to speak, but that was when he chose to kiss her at last. His tongue penetrated into the far recesses of her mouth, touching her as if he entered into her soul. Each movement was so slow, and so filling, and each robbed her of more breath, each made her tremble with a greater fever. His face rose above hers in the darkness, and he smiled, tracing his finger over the wetness of her lips. "So the hawk returns. You are never afraid, Amanda. Why fear me now?"

"I do not fear you," she whispered.

"And you must not," he told her. "I have not lied to you. Life is meant to be lived, to be enjoyed, my love, aye, even here! And I promise you, I will teach you that it is so."

"If you would do this tonight, it will be rape, and I swear that I will never forgive you."

"It will not be rape."

"It will!" she cried in sudden panic, slamming a fist between them, seeking any way to fight his weight and strength. In a burst of desperate new energy she thrust against him with all her strength, her knee connecting with his masculine anatomy.

At first she didn't comprehend what she had done.

He was suddenly still and taut, his features harsh, pained. At first all she realized was that he had eased his hold upon her. She slammed hard against him again, managing to escape his hold.

Before she could roll off the bed, she felt a hard tug upon her gown. The material ripped down her side as she cried out and tried to rise. She rolled and fell to the floor.

His foot landed hard upon her gown and she looked up into his face. He was furious. And he was reaching down for her. "Amanda, my love, you are a true bitch."

"No," she whispered. She didn't know if she denied his words, or the things yet to come between them that night. "No!" she breathed again, frantically trying to tug her gown free. She could not endure him towering over her so, and she couldn't cease her trembling. She realized then that she had really hurt him and she was suddenly afraid. She had been a fool. She should have continued to try to reason with him.

"I did not mean to hurt you!" she cried.

"Oh? Was that your idea of a gentle, wifely caress? Then, my dear, you are sorely in need of instruction."

She did not like the look upon his face at all, he had not forgiven her. "Eric—"

"Get up, Amanda!" He reached down a hand to her.

She stared at it, and knew that she could never take it.

She ripped free from the patch of gown beneath his foot, rose, and tore across the room. She spun around to face him again with her back to the wall. With almost casual strides he pursued her, pausing there, not touching her, but imprisoning her by placing his hands upon the wall on either side of her head. He smiled. "We spoke of this. Nothing, nothing, my love, will change the course of this night. Be it whatever it shall be."

She gasped, startled, and tried to strike out as he swiftly pulled her into his arms. She kicked and writhed, but he carried her back to the bed and cast her down upon it. She tried to rise, but he was on top of her, catching her wrists and holding them high above her head with one hand.

"We will be man and wife this night," he promised her savagely.

Then he captured her cheek with his free hand, and he kissed her. Kissed her thoroughly, passionately, open-mouthed, stealing her breath and strength and reason, and shattering her will with the reckless plunder of his tongue. She did not know how long the kiss went on between them. When he took his lips from hers, his eyes were passionate, his words were harsh. "You're my wife, Amanda. Your commitment to lie with me in this bed was made when you spoke your vows to me, and, lady, you may not now change your mind!"

She stared at him, knowing that she would fight him no matter what his words, yet wondering at the fierce new pounding in her heart. She hated him.

Yet . . . she might even want him.

He released her wrists, placed his palms over hers, and threaded her fingers with his own, holding them steady by the sides of her head. Her hair flamed out over their entwined fingers, radiantly red in the firelight. He smiled again as she stared at him, her eyes wide and emerald in that same haunting light.

He had never wanted her more, never needed her with such a frightening urgency. He had sworn to himself that he would go gently; he had not expected her to fight so viciously, nor had he expected the anger that would cause him to treat her so. Nor had he expected to feel a surge so strong within himself that it could not be denied. She had said that it would be rape.

Grimly he determined that it would not be so, and yet he knew that one way or another, he would have her. There was no way that he would let her go this night. No way that she would not sleep beside him, his wife in fact, his marriage consummated.

He spoke to her on a tense breath of air. "I will not take you, madame, until you give me leave. But you will not stop me from seeking that permission."

Her fingers curled tightly against his. "I will never give my leave to you."

"Be still, you are not to deny my kiss, my touch . . ."

A denial did form on her lips, but it never found voice. His mouth touched down upon hers, then wandered with abandon, effortlessly, slowly. His lips teased her flesh and her earlobes. She stared at the ceiling as his kisses covered her throat, hovering ever closer to the lace and gossamer of her gown where it fell low against her breasts. She felt his sex, engorged and hot against her thighs, and she ignored the heat and trembling within her own body and hoped that, pray God, it would be over swiftly.

But it was not. His own desires did not seem to affect his easy leisure, and as his hot breath swirled against the lobe of her ear, some sweet stirring took root and found life within her. She closed her eyes and gasped, for his hands were moving with the same lazy purpose as his lips. He lay his palm against her breast and his fingers closed over the mound, his thumb playing against the nipple. She twisted with the startling sensation, burying her face against his throat, a choking sound escaping her as his lips followed the movement of his hand upon her right breast, closing hotly about her nipple, teasing the swollen bud mercilessly. He repeated the evocative act upon her left breast, as if he would not leave that mound cold and forsaken. When he was done with the taunting play she was nearly limp against him, determined never to see his face again, for she was aware of the surge of her body against his. She felt his fingers upon her naked thigh, drawing her gown high above her hip. She twisted against him, trying to capture his hand, to prevent its wandering over her. The tear in the gown gave him such easy access to her flesh, and she felt the rough stroke of his palm so acutely upon her naked hip and belly. She writhed to free herself from him, but he did not seem to notice.

Impatience seized him when the gown caught beneath his own weight and he swore, destroying the rest of the garment as he rended the delicate fabric to pieces in a single movement. "Damn you!" Amanda swore, her eyes upon his, wide with anger and alarm, her protest frantic. "You've ruined the gown—"

"My love, God rot the gown!" he said flatly, pulling the remnants of silk from her body and the bed. Amanda grasped for the disappearing fabric, then found herself entirely naked and captured by his arm and his thigh. She was amazed at the emotion that welled within her, the fury, the fear . . . and the tense excitement. "You'd said you'd not take me until I gave you leave!"

"You, love, have not held to your part of the bargain."

"My part! I want no part of this!"

"You do, Amanda. You are flesh and blood, lady. You are ripe and I shall prove to you that married life is no hardship. Lie still, lady, and let me touch you. Better yet, do not lie still, but twist and writhe beneath me, press yourself against me," he ordered her, his eyes hard and demanding upon hers.

She felt what his words implied. Felt his body with the length of her own. Completely naked beneath him, she tried to whisper words to disavow him. She wanted to fight him so badly, and yet she was so suddenly still. His leg was cast upon hers, powerful, muscular, she could not escape him if she chose. She did not know if she chose. There was a rushing all about her, a startling fire within her. She felt it as she saw his naked thigh draped upon her own beneath the rising hem of his robe. She felt it deep within her stomach, and deeper still, at the juncture of her thighs. Hot and frantic, it coiled tighter and tighter and she both dreaded and eagerly anticipated his touch.

She swallowed sharply and he watched the length of her throat, watched where her heart showed its frantic beat against the swan's column.

"Eric—"

"Be still!" he commanded her. He pressed his lips against the pulse at her throat, moving his hands upon her, his fingers stroking the length of her with a hunger he could not deny. He touched her thighs and allowing his touch to brush the striking red triangle at the apex of her thighs, and he went onward to explore her belly and waist, the deep valley between her breasts. Her fingers curled over his shoulders, her nails digging heedlessly into his flesh.

Suddenly he drew up, casting his robe aside.

When he stared down upon his wife, her eyes were closed, her lush lashes dark above her cheeks, her lips parted, her breath rushing from them. Her breasts rose in swift and beautiful agitation. He found himself pausing for the simple pleasure of seeing her body before he lowered himself to touch it again. The tendrils of her hair lay like laps of flame upon the pillow, like liquid fire, spilling into him, haunting him. The fever that had seized him the first time he had seen her in Damien's arms came home to him then, causing him to tremble with the prospect of his longing. He hurriedly sank back down, afraid of breaking the spell that lay upon her, so fragile was her consent to his will. She was his wife; he could have her as he pleased, and no man could gainsay him. He wanted more.

He caught her shapely limbs, parting them and lying between them so that her eyes opened with alarm. A gasp escaped her and her eyes closed as a word of protest tore from her. With a wicked smile he cast his hands beneath her buttocks, lifting her hips. He buried his face within the fascinating texture of the tempting sable-red triangle, his tongue ravaging her with a shocking, seductive invasion. Her fingers tore into his hair, she writhed, she cried out.

"Nay . . . !"

"Aye, my love," he murmured, his breath hot against her delicate flesh. She could not fight the weight of his shoulders, nor would he show mercy now.

"My God, 'tis wicked—"

"God, madame, has blessed our union. And love, lady, is wicked and beautiful, as it will be between us."

She gasped again, but the sound of it was lost in a cry, for he curled his fingers within those that tugged upon his hair, and he had his way with leisure and purpose, finding the sweet bud wherein her own desire lay, touching upon her very innocence. She thrashed upon the bed, seeking to escape him, seeking then to know more of him. He felt the change within her as he ruthlessly captured her sensuality, felt the surge of her body, tasted the nectar of her warmth as she writhed against him, seeking release from all that he had nurtured within her. Frantic whimpers fell from her lips, and her hips undulated in an ever-growing rhythm. Then she stiffened, straining, crying out, and the sweetness of climax exploded from within her. He lost no time but rose above her, the full weight of his body wedged between lovely length of her thighs. "Madame, would you stop me?" he demanded.

She lay silent, her eyes closed. He leaned low against her, demanding more emphatically, "Amanda! Shall I have my wife this night?"

Her lips parted just slightly. He lay his palm against her breast, bringing his words to the hollow of her throat. "Amanda—"

"Yes!" It was a pained whisper that tore from her throat. Then she cried out, her eyes opening for a moment of emerald anguish, then closing again as her arms wound around him. She could not meet his gaze, he knew, and he did not care, not at that moment. He gritted his teeth, his muscles clenching, demanding that despite his state of desperation, he take his wife with care. He moved against her, the tip of his shaft coming into the contact with the barrier of innocence. A cry of pain and protest rose to her lips no matter how he had prepared her; he closed over that cry with his kiss and entered into her like silk and steel. Her nails dug into his flesh again, her head fell back. He moved slowly, so slowly, until she had taken all of him into her, whispering assurances all the while. Her eyes remained closed, her face pale, but once she had accepted him, he began to move. He fought the wave of stark dark desire that seized him and brought his rhythm to her slowly. He had proven that passion dwelled within her, he need only ignite it again.

He touched her as he moved, stroking her breasts, her cheeks, her breasts again. He touched her lips with his own and seared her with his kiss. Her lips parted, a soft moan escaped her, and then triumph seized him, for she was moving again. Moving with his thrust and surge, undulating, like a wave of fire, beneath him.

Somewhere in the tempest that followed he allowed himself the sheer pleasure of having her at last, of burying himself within the beauty of her molten sheath. All the reckless abandon that he had denied himself burst forth, and he took her in raw, blinding desire, his tension and energy relentless, then finding fruition in a volatile combustion that cast him shuddering deep, deep within her time and time again. The pleasure was so great that he saw blackness as the veil of release first lifted from him, then, in alarm, he stiffened against her. He exhaled, feeling the trickle of sweat seep down his chest, and then he exhaled again, feeling that she still lay, wracked with tremors, beneath him. He held her tight, kissing her forehead, then pulling back to see how the moon and the firelight fell over her sleek body.

Her hair was entwined about them both. She did not open her eyes until he touched her cheek, then they came wide upon him, and she groaned, trying to twist away in some new horror. Alarmed and impatient, he dragged her back. "Madame, what—"

She bent her head against him, whispering fervently, "It is not right! Oh, God, what you have done to me—"

"I am baffled, love. What have I done that no other husband, young Tarryton or multichinned Hastings, would not?"

"It isn't that!" she whispered.

"Is it me? Forgive me, milady, but I thought that I caused you as little pain as possible. Nay, call me an egotist as you are so wont to do, and yet still, I would swear I caused pleasure."

"Oh!"

She almost turned from him. He caught her shoulders and lay her back, crawling above her and demanding now that she meet his eyes. "What is it?"

She moistened her lips. "It is not you. It is me!"

He sank back, careful to keep his weight upon his haunches. "You . . ."

She closed her eyes. He had never imagined such a look of bleak misery. "Milord," she said hollowly, "only a woman of a different variety should . . . feel so."

The last he did not even hear, for the whisper had grown so soft upon her lips. "Who told you that?" he demanded so harshly that her eyes flew open again.

"It's the way—you must be horrified."

"No, milady, it is not the way of anything, and I am not horrified but delighted. You are my wife. Warm and fascinating in my bed, and I confess, I am evermore enchanted. If I am horrified, it is because I must leave you so soon."

Her eyes were so wide, so very vulnerable then. What was it that she had feared so greatly? He wanted then to protect her so fiercely from all the hurts of the world. He swept her into his arms, whispering to her fervently, "Tell me! What has done this to you!"

"I cannot tell you!" she whispered, but she did not press away from him. Rather she curled close, her small hands knotted but against his chest, her head bowed beneath his chin. He inhaled the fragrance of her hair, and he swore then, to himself alone, that he would love her until the day that he died, defend her against all odds.

He stroked back her hair. "Shh . . . I will not ask you again. When you can trust me, tell me. Until then, believe me when I say that you are more exquisite than I dared dream, that I am well pleased." He hesitated a moment. "I did promise that it would be enjoyable."

She shuddered suddenly and he laughed, running his finger around her ear. "Well, madame, is it not enjoyable?"

"That's a terrible thing to ask me, sir!"

"Then I will show you again!" he swore, and swept her beneath him. Her eyes went very wide, but then a smile curved her lips. He kissed her.

And he loved her again, bringing her once more to an exquisite peak of pleasure and finding that agony and ecstasy again himself. Exhausted and spent, she lay against him, and he held her tight, his hand below the sweet curve of her breast. He thought that she slept when she whispered to him.

"Milord?" Her voice was soft and pale and lazy.

"Aye, love?"

"Indeed . . . I do suppose that one might call this . . . enjoyable."

He smiled, and he allowed his eyes to close. He did not think that he had ever slept so deeply, or so well.

In the days that followed Amanda came to wonder that she had ever thought to refuse Eric. He was demanding, voracious, unexpected, and always exciting, and most of all, he lived up to his promise that life should be lived and that it could be enjoyable. There was an exceptional energy about him in those days when he knew he would leave so soon. Awaking to discover that he was down with the troops, she would take great care with her dress, and start down the stairs only to discover that he had finished with drilling for the day and was running up the stairs even as she began to descend them. No protest stilled him then, and she would be swept into his arms, laughing, and all her careful detail to her appearance would be for naught since it seemed to take him less than seconds to disrobe her.

They rode over his acreage and the land of the original Hundred and she met many of the landowners and planters, artisans and merchants who made their homes near Eric's. They were always welcomed warmly and, though tea was no longer served and more and more women were dressing in homespun, there seemed to be little talk of politics then, and much more discussion of homes and estates and repair and planting. Many men were eagerly working their prize horses, for racing was a prime diversion of the Tidewater aristocrats, and nothing ceased their talk of good horseflesh.

Despite the seemingly endless troops camped out on the lawns of Cameron Hall, Eric saw to it that he showed Amanda their immediate realm. As they walked down to the cemetery one afternoon, he told her tales of a great-great-aunt who had married a Pamunkee Indian and whose several times great-grandchildren were the half-dozen blue-eyed, blond Clark children they had met on a nearby estate the day before. They left the cemetery and he walked her on toward the river until she found herself in a pine-arbored copse. She could feel the river's breeze there, and distantly she could hear the fife and bugle of the men who marched and drilled upon the hill. Eric drew her into his arms, and before she could protest the wicked determination in his arms, she found herself lain upon the soft pine-strewn earth, looking up into a dazzle of sunlight that wavered with the motion of the tree branches. He laid his hands upon the laces of her gown and she gasped, protesting with outrage that they could not. She continued to protest, but his arguments were fast, his hands faster still, and before she knew it she was naked upon the raw, sweet-smelling earth, laughing and arguing in one, and then unable to laugh or argue for the passion that blazed there between them was shocking and intense, bursting upon them like the radiance of the dappled sun rays. And when they lay still the river breeze swept sensually over their dampened bodies, adding something of the feel of an intimate Eden to the place. She shivered, and he warmed her with his body. She stroked his cheek and he caught her hand, bringing it down against him, teaching her to hold and stroke the bold arousal the breeze and her nearness had wrought. She did not think to argue then, for his kisses filled her as deeply as the shaft of his body, and the warmth and liquid fire that burned into her mingled from the force of his mouth and that of his loins. Twilight came, and with it the cool of the night, before they roused themselves at last, dressed, and returned to the house.

That night they had their first argument as man and wife, yet there was nothing new in the gist of it.

Damien arrived to serve with Eric, commissioned a captain to command one of the companies he himself had raised. Amanda, delighted to see him, greeted him in the parlor. He was all enthusiasm for the cause, but he was even more enthusiastic about the events taking place in Williamsburg and beyond. Washington had returned to Mount Vernon, so Damien said, and Patrick Henry and Edmund Pendleton had stopped there before all three men headed for the Philadelphia Continental Congress. Rumors were running rampant that no gentle words for the Crown would be spoken.

Eric stood by the mantel as Damien spoke, lighting his pipe from the fire with a wick. He was silent as Damien went on. "Things are about to change. Mark my words, milord, I daresay that the very men who govern our colonies will all be looking over their shoulders to see to the sheriffs with arrest warrants!"

"I daresay that it would be quite difficult for a handful of soldiers to arrest the whole congress," Eric told him.

"It will depend on which way many hearts lie, sir? It will depend on where the power lies. If the leaders side with the Crown—or the patriots."

"Stop it, Damien!" Amanda commanded him. "You a talking about treason."

"Mandy, Mandy, do stop with this treason nonsense! The will of the people must prevail." Damien leaned forward on his seat. "Lord Cameron, it will be interesting indeed to travel west once again. When the Shawnee are subdued, treaties might be made that could be of grave importance later. And the French arms to be purchased on the coast are often in abundance—"

"Damien!" she snapped, rising from her chair and staring at Eric. "Make him stop this, Eric."

Eric's dark brows shot up. "Amanda, I cannot make him stop his mind from working—"

"You are his commander, Eric! I demand that you stop this talk of arms and war this very second."

"Amanda, this is my home," Eric reminded her, "and though I would do my utmost to give you any request, milady, I will not accept a demand."

She twirled about in a fury and exited the room, slamming the door with a vehemence that the servants could not miss. When Danielle came to her, saying that dinner was being served, she refused to dine and asked for a tray. She ordered a bath be brought up but not to the master bedchamber, rather to the one that adjoined it, the one with the locking door. Fuming and incensed, she locked herself in with a cup of warmed Madeira and the steaming water. She settled back, swearing that her husband would find himself duly chastised when he thought to be so crude to her.

Yet that was not to be the case. She had barely adjusted her long hair and lain back, the steam delightfully easing the pain from her, when the locked connecting door shattered and banged open upon its sagging hinges. His eyes dark and furious, his features those of a stranger's, Eric stood there. She gaped, then hastily closed her mouth in a fury of her own. "The lock meant that I did not wish you to enter!" she warned him heatedly.

 married me, milady. I will enter where I wish."
strides brought him quickly to her. In panic she
wet and streaming, ready to fight him with all of the
of the worry and fear within her. "Stop it, Eric, don't
ou dare come near me, I am telling you—"

Her breath was swept from her as his arms came about
her. He lifted her from the water, giving no thought to his
fine brocade waistcoat and silk shirt. She struggled against
him, wanting to hurt him, then suddenly wanting to escape him as she saw the light that her fight had brought to
his eyes. "No!" she breathed, slamming hard upon his
chest, yet he bore her down anyway, lying over her as he
brought her atop the bed where she had thought to find
her privacy. "I shall claw you to ribbons!" she warned him
desperately.

"If you do so, Amanda, make sure it is with wifely passion, with cries of ecstasy upon your lips."

"Oh!" she cried, and tried to slam her knee against him,
but he shifted his weight, and the gaze he gave her then
shot daggers into her heart. "You fool, you will get Damien
hanged and yourself hanged and I will not let you do this
to me!"

He held her head between his hands and looked angrily
into her eyes. "Politics will not enter into the bedroom,"
he told her firmly.

"I am a loyalist and you knew it when you married me,
and you said that you'd not deny me my beliefs!"

"I do not deny you your beliefs, but I swear, lady, by all
that is holy, you will not bring them to bed, and you will
not slam doors or think to make a stricken, gelded fool of
me because of them. Do you understand me?"

She thought for a moment, straining against him, her
teeth gritted. Then she shouted out a vehement "No!"

His eyes darkened. She thought that he meant to strike
her, his teeth were so tightly clenched. "Let me up!" she
demanded in fear and fury.

"Madame, I will not!"

He dragged her hands up high over her head and held
them easily despite her struggles and curses. His lips covered hers, trailed the valley between her breasts, then fon-

dled the rouge crests, watching her eyes as he did so. She found that gaze upon her and knew that he read more within their depths than she wanted him to know. Suddenly, savagely, she twisted free from his hold, slamming her fists against his chest. She sought to roll free from him, but he threaded his fingers through her hair, dragging her back beneath him. His eyes sought hers again with war within them. He held her still, and his mouth captured hers. She thumped her fists against his shoulders, but he ignored the pain, demanding more and more with his lips and tongue. His hands stroked her sides and buttocks, and thighs, and his knee wedged them apart. He kissed her, and touched her, his kiss consuming, his touch ever more evocative. His lips parted from hers and she spoke his name, desperately trying to remember her argument. His kiss moved over her throat, to her collarbone, to her breast, and the passion of her fight became a flame of desire deep within her. Perhaps the need was even heightened by the torment of emotion. He did not disrobe, but adjusted his breeches and had her there with a startling fever and vengeance, and as he spent himself within her, she thought that she had passed over some strange line between what she had been before . . . and what she would be as his wife. Something indelible poured into her along with his seed that evening. She did not understand it. She whispered that she hated him even as her arms wound around him, she cried against him even as her body was wracked with the sweet shudders of ecstasy. The battle had receded between them, she thought. But it was far from over.

She felt his fingers upon her cheeks and only then did she realize that tears had escaped her. He was quickly up, guarded and hard, but anxious too. "Did I hurt you?"

She shook her head, trying not to meet his eyes.

"Amanda!"

"No! No, you did not hurt me."

He rolled from her, his back to her, then stood, adjusting his clothing. "Come down to the meal. There will be no talk of arms, and I swear that I will keep my eye upon your cousin."

"And smuggle arms yourself!" she whispered.

"What?"

"Nothing! Please, leave it be, nothing!"

"Come down then, and we shall close the subject."

"I—I cannot!" she whispered. "My God, all of the house will have heard that door shatter."

He reached for her hands, pulling her tight against him. His smile was suddenly wicked and taunting and challenging. "I did not suggest that you should slink down in shame, milady. Rather, my love, you should do so with laughter on your lips, your chin as high as ever, your glance one of the greatest disdain."

She pulled away from him. "The meal will be quite cold, I am certain."

"Dress, or I shall dress you myself."

She swore, she called him every name that would come to her tongue, but when he moved toward her, she determined that she would choose her gown, and do as he suggested. He helped her with corset and with her hooks despite the stiffness of her back, and when she was duly clad, he insisted that she sit so that he could comb out her hair. His fingers lingered on her shoulders as her hair fell down upon them. In the mirror she saw his hands upon her flesh, bare for the gown lay low upon her bosom, and she saw how very dark and masculine and large they were, and yet felt how very tender their brush upon her could be. She shivered, meeting his eyes in the mirror, and he smiled, with what emotion she did not know. "Lady, none could deny your beauty, nor the boldness of your spirit. Come, take my hand. You do grace this ancient hall and will, I expect, continue to do so. Even if they do decide to hang me."

She stood, shivers upon her heart, for even in the very depth of this battle, she knew then that she could not bear to see him hanged.

They started down the stairway together. Thom and Cassidy met them at the doors of the dining room. As they neared the pair, Eric suddenly laughed, as if he and Amanda shared some great joke, and he whispered against her ear. She turned to him, and a smile formed upon her lips, and she knew that the act had been very well executed. No one would wonder at the goings-on of the master and mistress, they were newlyweds, and prone to take their time.

She did not forgive Damien though. Not until the hour grew late, and she rose, begging that they continue to talk, but forgive her, for she was exhausted. Then she hugged her cousin fiercely, because she was afraid for him.

"Forgive me!" he whispered to her sorrowfully. "We have chosen different paths." He had never seemed older to her, or more serious or grave.

She said nothing, but turned away, not offering her cheek to her husband. There were no servants about to witness the act.

But when she went upstairs, she did not seek out a separate bed. She lay within the one they shared, and for a long while she remained awake, tormented by all that lay between them. Her eyes closed, and the hour grew very late. The fire dimmed, and she slept.

She awoke slowly, with the feel of his lips against her spine. She did not think at first but rather felt the delicious slow motion of his hands over her hip, stroking down upon her buttocks. His lips and tongue moved with rich and languorous ease over the silky flesh of her shoulders and back. Then she felt his body, bare and heated and rigid, thrust against her own. She started to twist, but he whispered against her ear, "Amanda. I leave with the morning light."

He drew her against him, kissing her nape, her throat, her shoulders. His hands fondled her breasts while he thrust into her from behind. The urgency touched her. Love was bittersweet, but something she would not deny. She did not want to think of the nights ahead.

"I do not retreat—"

"Nor surrender!" he agreed, but the words were meaningless, for she had given in to him that night, though his fervent words and his fierce cries of pleasure gave her some sense that perhaps she had not lost at all, that indeed perhaps he held the strength, but she held her own curious power.

* * *

The next morning when Amanda awoke she saw Eric standing before the window while the draperies rustled in the wind. Her muscles constricted tightly for she saw that he was dressed in a buckskin jacket with fringe and rugged leather leggings and high boots. She looked at him with confusion. It was so very early. But then she remembered that it had to be early, he was riding out this morning. He knew that she had awakened; he turned to her and walked back to the bed where she lay, sitting beside her. His gaze fell over her where she lay, and he reached out to touch her cheek. Cascades of her hair fell wildly over his fingers, and he smiled with a touch of bitter irony. "How very hard it is to leave you so. I sit here about to cast all honor and right to the wind and tell Dunmore that I cannot risk my neck for my soul is in chains."

She flushed, listening to his words. His thumb moved over her cheek and she was tempted to grab hold of his hand and beg him not to leave her, not when he had just taught her so very much about life and . . . was it love? she wondered. She had hated him so fiercely, feared him, needed him, and now she did not dare judge the seed of emotion that stirred so desperately in her heart. They had lived the days since their marriage in a fantasy, and now the world was intruding upon them. But in those days she had come to find an ever greater fascination in the strong planes and angles of his face, in the curve of his lip, in the light of his eyes. She had lain upon the bed with her lashes low, her eyes half closed, and she had watched the effortless grace of his body as he had dressed or undressed. She had touched the scars upon his shoulders and she had learned which he had sustained in the closing days of the French and Indian Wars, and which he had obtained as a child playing recklessly upon the docks. He did not love her, he had told her once, and she had labeled the emotion as lust. Were that what it was, then the same spellbound fever held her. She wanted to touch him, and so she reached out and laid her palm against his freshly shaven cheek. Then she dropped her covers, rising to kiss him, to breathe into that kiss the truth that she would miss him with all of her heart, that she would pray until the day that he returned that God keep him safe.

His lips parted from hers and he caught her palm, kissing it softly. His brow arched with humor but with tenderness too. "Dare I take this to mean that you will not be too disappointed if the Shawnee leave my scalp intact, despite all that occurred last night?"

She nodded, suddenly afraid to speak. She had loved once and had discovered then that love brought betrayal. Her own father had turned from her.

"Take care, my love. Take the greatest care," he told her.

"God watch you, Eric," she whispered.

"Tell me, what are your feelings of this marriage into which you so desperately plunged? Is it better to endure my temper than Lord Hastings's chins?" he asked, his lips still moving just above her own, the warmth of his words entering into her.

"I am not . . . displeased," she said, unable to meet his eyes. "Except upon occasion. What of you?" she demanded, looking at him at last.

"I knew what I wanted, madame, from the very moment that I saw your face," he told her.

His lips brushed hers. "Betray not my heart, Amanda, that is all that I ask." He rose and then was gone.

For long moments she lay in the bed, feeling the tingle of his kiss upon her lips. Then she cried out and leapt to her feet, throwing open her armoire to find a heavy white velvet dressing gown. She quickly hooked the garment about her and tore down the stairs. Thom stood in the hallway with a silver tray and a very traditional stirrup cup upon it. "May I?" she begged him, awaiting no answer but running out to the porch steps in her bare feet.

Eric was mounted upon his huge black stallion at the front of a disciplined line of troops. Amanda, her hair like a stream of wildfire against the white velvet, ran down the steps to her husband's side. The officers who had been shouting out orders fell silent, and Eric turned from his study of the men behind him to see her before him.

That was how he would remember her in the long nights to come. Proud and wild with tousled flaming hair, a soaring spirit with her emerald eyes, pagan with her bare toes showing upon the earth, exquisite as the white velvet outlined her body. She handed him the cup, and a cheer went up that warmed his soul and tore upon his heart.

He drank the whiskey and set the cup upon the tray. "Godspeed to all of you!" she cried, and again a chant rose, a cheer for the lady of Cameron Hall.

And he thought that he just possibly detected tears within the emerald beauty of her eyes.

Eric leaned down and kissed his wife's lips. Then he rode forward, toward the west.

X ❦

Two divisions came against the Shawnee that fall, marching toward the Ohio River. Lord Dunmore led his men from the northern part of the valley. Eric was not with him. It had been decided that he would take a number of his old Indian fighters and accompany General Andrew Lewis, a man Eric highly respected, one of Washington's stalwart colleagues from the campaign against the Frenchman Duquesne. Lewis led his men by way of Fort Pitt while the governor's men came through the Great Kanawha Valley.

The western militia were an interesting breed of men. The majority of the men were clad in doeskin, and many of them had taken or displayed an Indian scalp upon occasion. In the Virginia Valley, life was still raw, and men eked out their livings. The Indians had a name for Lewis's men; they called them the Long Knives, an acknowledgment of their prowess with the weapons.

But they weren't after just any Indians. As Eric rode with Lewis, the general explained much of a situation that had not changed. "We encroach upon the land. Hostiles kill white settlers, then the settlers turn around and they don't seem to know if they're after a Delaware, or Cherokee, a Shawnee, or another. Inevitably they kill an Indian from a friendly tribe and then that tribe isn't so friendly anymore. A lot of trouble started with the establishment of trading posts out here—greedy men selling so much liquor that they create a savage out of any man. But now we're going after Cornstalk, and there ain't any man alive could call that man anything but a savage when he fights. You mark my words. The Delaware and Cherokees themselves, they tremble at the name Cornstalk."

"So I have heard," Eric agreed. Cornstalk was a powerful voice among the Indians. He was trying to form a confederacy of all the Ohio tribes.

Lewis looked up at the sky. "Dunmore could be in some difficulty for this one," he advised Eric. "The territory might well be Canada—according to the Quebec Act. If not, it's still disputed between Virginia and Pennsylvania."

"He is determined to fight the Shawnee, and that is that."

"Didn't you get enough of Indian fighting back when the wars were going on?"

"I was asked to raise men."

"There ain't been a war whoop heard in the Tidewater region, not in a long, long time. Well, if we meet up with Cornstalk, we'll hear plenty."

Eric learned the truth of that statement at Point Pleasant where they found the Shawnee under Cornstalk. Tension raced high throughout the forces as the commanders conferred, but the Shawnee were the first to attack.

And Eric heard the war whoops, blood-curdling, savage, just as Lewis had said. The Indians appeared like painted devils, glistening in the sunlight, attacking with their cries. Yet above the roar of those cries and above the roar of his own orders, Eric heard Cornstalk. The Shawnee warrior, painted generously himself, cast his voice out over his people like that of God—or Satan. His men spurred forward, unafraid of steel or bullets, unafraid of death itself.

The militia fought well. Men stood their ground, and did not falter or fall back against the onslaught of the savage fighters. War whoops rose from the white men, and hand-to-hand combat came quickly. Eric was unhorsed when a Shawnee warrior fell atop him from a tree. As he rolled in the mud, he saw the brave raise his knife against him. Eric latched his wrist about the warrior's, aware that his life lay at stake. He strained against the Indian's slick muscles, and just as the blade neared his throat, Eric found the burst of energy to send the Indian flying. He did not waste time, but leapt upon the Indian, bringing his own blade swiftly home within his enemy's chest. A gurgle of blood rose on the brave's mouth, then his dark eyes glazed over and Eric was quickly up on his feet again, wary for his next opponent. One of his men, a distant Cameron cousin, hurried his horse to him. "Down the lines, sir, we have to hold here!"

They did hold, but Eric fought even as he shouted new orders, and the hours passed by slowly and painfully. Still he heard the haunting shouts of Cornstalk, and he realized that the Shawnee were still coming.

Then darkness came at last, and the Shawnee slipped away across the Ohio, shadowy silhouettes in the night. The militia had taken the day. But even as he realized that there were no more opponents to fight, Eric looked about the darkened field before him. Men lay everywhere.

"All right! We've got to tend to our wounded," he called sharply. Then it all came home to him, the horrible cries of the dying, the screams of pain that had not ceased. He began to hurry, hearing from one sergeant that two hundred of their own number lay dead, entwined with the glistening bodies of their enemies.

It took well into the night to sort the living from the dead, to bring what aid they could to the wounded and the dying. He was anxious to find Damien, whom he hadn't seen since very early in the day. He did not want to return home without his wife's cousin. Amanda had, he thought, very specifically entrusted his life to Eric, and she would expect the young man to survive.

Dismay and despair claimed him as he searched the men. At last he found Damien on a stretcher with a surgeon examining a bloody head wound. He grinned at Eric. "Knocked me for a loop, it did! I thought I was dead. But it's hard to keep a good man down, eh, sir?"

"Aye, Damien, it's hard to keep a good man down," he agreed.

He went past the tents of the men, conferred with Lewis who wanted to start building a fort the next morning, then hurried onward to his own canvas shelter. He had a bottle of good Caribbean rum with him and as he cast himself down upon his pallet, he was glad of the liquor. Home seemed a distant place now. All that danced before his eyes were the bodies of the Shawnee. He saw red, the color of blood, and it colored everything.

A chill shook him. He had come very close to death himself. Once he had fought so haphazardly and with undauntable courage. He had been a lad then. He had not seen himself as being mortal. Age had taught him that all men die, and age had even allowed him to accept the prospect of his own death. Now he was fiercely determined not to die.

He smiled, because even here, even in this wilderness with the stench of oil and blood so strongly with him, he could close his eyes and see her face. "I will not die, madame, to thwart you, love, if for no other reason!" His hands shook, and so he drank more deeply from the rum bottle. His marriage had brought more to him than he had dared hope, but the idyll of their days had been rudely marred by the quarrel before he left. There was more going on than he could see, though he could not pinpoint what. She despised him for being a "traitor," yet she laughed in his arms and she came alive when he reached for her. The line between love and hate was thin indeed. He wondered on what side of the line her true emotions lay. He had taken her from her father—and from Lord Hastings—and for that she seemed pleased enough. But still there was something there, something that he did not trust. He almost imagined that Sterling held something over his daughter, but he did not know what it could be.

He shrugged, tossing over, praying that he could sleep. He did not. He tossed again and wondered what went on back in the Tidewater. He did not want to stay in the west any longer. Men were meeting in Philadelphia, things were happening, his wife was home—alone—and he was caught up in this wretched battle against the redskins. Robert Tarryton would have married his duchess by now. He wondered if Amanda had attended the wedding, and he wondered how she fared at Cameron Hall.

His heart quickened suddenly. Maybe she had conceived an heir for him. A son . . . a daughter. A child to teach to love the land, to ride, to plant, to stand by the river and learn to read the wind.

She did not love him, he thought, and he wondered if she still carried any feelings for Robert Tarryton. The thought angered him, and he breathed deeply, tossing again. She did not need to love him to conceive an heir. And if she ever went near Tarryton . . .

She would not. She had a fierce pride and would surely keep her distance—if only to make Tarryton pay.

Then he wondered if Tarryton was haunted at night like this, lying awake, wondering about Amanda. No, he could not wonder so fiercely, for he had never known the explosion of heaven that it was to possess her. To touch her and fall . . . in love.

He smiled bitterly in the darkness. Love would be a very dangerous weapon in her hands. He had to take care that he not give her the chance to use it.

He tossed again, and remembered her eyes, then the rise of her breasts, the rose color of her nipples, the fragile ivory beauty of her skin. He wanted to go home.

It simply wasn't to be. In the morning they started a crude fort. When the fort was done they rode north again against the Shawnee across the Ohio. They met with Dunmore's forces.

There, finally, the governor announced that they should disperse and return to their homes.

The militia were angry, for they were so close to ending

more of the fray. General Lewis was in sympathy with his men, Eric thought, but he was a commander, and a Virginian, and his opinions were certainly not clear to those around him.

He asked Eric to accompany him as they backtracked home. Eric bit down hard upon his desire to return as rapidly as possible to Cameron Hall and agreed that he would do so.

She should have been delirious with joy, Amanda chastised herself as she sat in the arbor by the river, her shoes and stockings cast aside, her bare toes wiggling in the cool grass. Above her the trees danced and swayed and the sun fell down upon her with the same curious dappled light that had touched them both when she had come here with Eric. It seemed so long ago. The weeks had become months, and summer had given way to fall, and now it was November.

She had everything that she had wanted. She had her freedom, she had the run of this magnificent estate, and in Eric's absence, her every wish was considered to be law. It had not been difficult to slip into the role of mistress here for there was not much that differed from Sterling Hall. Though the estate would have run quite competently in Eric's absence with or without her, she loved involving herself and she had tried to enter into the management of the hall unobtrusively. She had earned Thom's mistrust when he had discovered her assiduously going over the books, but then she had been careful to praise him lavishly with her very best smile, and then point out where they could perhaps reduce an expenditure here or there and use the savings to improve upon the house.

She had been shocked to learn from Danielle that she had an enemy within the house. Young Margaret whispered in the servants' quarters that the lady of Cameron Hall was looking to its future because she was looking forward to its master's demise. Amanda was horrified and longed to either slap Margaret's round little cheeks or send her packing. She did neither, determined that she would not betray her fury. A servant's sly whisperings

should not distress her, and she determined th.
would ever see her upset.

When one of the mares went into labor for a lat.
she heard the news and instantly headed down to the
bles. The dark-haired Frenchman who had whispered wi.
Danielle was there. His name was Jacques Bisset. An Acadian, he was the estate manager, responsible for the running of the acreage and the groves and the stables just as
Thom was responsible for the running of the house and
Cassidy was responsible for everything regarding Eric's
personal needs.

She did not have much occasion to come across him,
and at the stables he did not seem pleased to see her,
though he treated her with courtesy. She ignored his manner and spoke to him in French, asking after the mare,
demanding to know if he thought that they would lose the
horse or not.

He informed her curtly that the birth was breech, and
that so far he had not managed to turn the foal.

"Well, sir, my hands are much smaller than yours. Perhaps I shall have better luck," she informed him.

Aghast, he stood blocking her way to the stall. *"Mais,
non,* Lady Cameron, you must not come in here at this
time—"

"I must do as I choose, Monsieur Bisset," she told him,
but at his look she could not resist a wicked smile, then
she laughed and tried to ease his tormented soul. "Really.
We had fine Arabs and bred many racehorses at Sterling
Hall. And my father was never about and seldom cared
about what I did—" She paused, dismayed at her own
words. She ignored him and moved past him, heedless of
her gown, of her safety, of anything. She spoke softly to
the troubled mare, then plunged in. To her delight she was
able to shift the foal about, and though the birth still took
several long hours and she was exhausted and a mess
when it was over, Amanda was delighted. The beautiful
little filly with a blaze upon her forehead had a fine broad
chest and stupendous long legs. She and Jacques laughed
with delight as the filly tried to stand, then managed to
teeter up. When she smiled at Jacques she saw that the

...ed from his eyes and that he gazed at her with ...nd remorse. Her own laughter faded, and a ripple ...ase washed over her. She was not afraid of him, ...r he fascinated her. And she was determined to dis- ...ver why he had argued with Danielle. Perhaps the two were falling in love, she thought. The idea dazzled her. She would be delighted if this curious marriage of hers brought happiness to Danielle.

She teased Danielle about it from her bath, but to her surprise, the woman quickly lost her temper, emphatically denying a love interest.

"Come now! He has the most gorgeous eyes, Danielle," Amanda said. "Huge and green and rimmed by those dark, dark lashes. And his features are so fine and fair. It looks as if he were sculpted by a master artist, planes and coloring all put together so beautifully. You should marry, Dani! You should."

"Cease to taunt me, *ma petite*! There can be no marriage, ever!"

"But, Danielle—"

"He is my brother!"

"Brother!" Amanda gasped, astounded. "But—but you told me that your brother was dead!"

"I thought that he was dead," Danielle said, folding and refolding Amanda's towel in her agitation. "I did not know that he lived until I came here."

"Then we must—"

"We must do nothing! Amanda, I beg of you, never mention it. Never, never mention that my brother lives."

Startled, Amanda stared at her maid. Danielle dropped the towel and came to kneel by the tub. "Please—"

"Danielle, calm down. I would never do anything to hurt you, you know that. I don't understand your distress, but—oh, no, Danielle, he wasn't a criminal, was he?"

"I swear, no. Yet you must keep the secret. He did not know these many years himself who he was—"

"What?"

"He nearly died. He very nearly died. But Lord Cameron's father found him and kept him alive, and he never did know from whence he came, nor could he remember his circumstances."

"Until—he saw you?" Amanda said.

"*Oui, oui.* You must keep his secret safe. He has been Jacques Bisset these many years, and he must stay so, please!"

"Tell me—"

"I can tell you no more! If you bear me any love at all—"

"You know that I love you dearly and that if you wish it, your secret is safe."

Danielle hugged her, soaking herself. Amanda fell silent but her curiosity was definitely piqued. She was determined to discover the truth.

Lying in the grass and feeling the breeze upon her, she reflected that she should be very happy. She had never, never been so free. She had done very well for the estate; her time and her life were her own. She had come to Cameron Hall just for this freedom, then she had married Eric to achieve it. But curiously, it did not taste so sweet as she had imagined. She could not believe that there had ever been a time when she had hoped that Eric Cameron might fall before the Shawnee. She did not want to miss him, but she did. She remembered all that he had done to her there in the grass, and she colored feverishly with the explicit memories. She was anxious about his return and prayed each night that God would keep him safe.

She was falling in love with him, she realized, and then she rose, fiercely annoyed with herself. Last month she had dressed in her finest to attend Robert Tarryton's wedding to his duchess, and she had smiled and offered him best wishes without a flutter of emotion. It helped that the Duchess of Owenfield was lank and skinny with horrible jutting teeth and limp brown hair. Amanda had felt fiercely sorry for the young woman, but she was still not certain that she could befriend her. She was just glad to realize that her heart had grown cold, that watching Robert marry meant nothing, and that feeling him kiss her cheek meant even less. And still, she did not want to love again. Love was a wretched emotion that left one vulnerable and weak and entirely miserable. She wanted no part of it. But there was more to love. It came whether asked or nay, and she had fallen beneath her husband's spell.

Sudden agitation came to her as she watched the river. She reached for her hose, pulling them on too quickly, snagging one. News had reached her that the parties had split, that Eric was traveling with General Lewis. She had even received a letter after they had fought a battle on the Ohio. Pierre, who had ridden into Williamsburg for a copy of the *Virginia Gazette*, had told her that the governor was back. That had quickened her heart, but then her hopes sank for she learned that Eric was not with the governor.

She turned and raced back to the house, suddenly hungry for more information. Running inside, she shouted for Thom. When the butler came to her, she smiled winningly. "Thom, please call Pierre and tell him that I'll have the carriage and that we'll go to Williamsburg tonight. I'll have my trunks ready within the hour. Have you seen Danielle?"

"Aye, she's gone to the laundry. I'll send her to you immediately, Lady Cameron."

He didn't seem to approve of her trip, she knew from his deep frown, but he had no power to stop her. She smiled radiantly. "I won't be gone long. I—I'd like to know more about my husband's whereabouts, if I can discover some news."

He nodded, but she still didn't think that he was pleased. She tossed her hair back. She had married for this freedom, and it was hers and not to be denied her. "Thank you, Thom," she told him brightly, and turned to hurry upstairs to pack.

Danielle did not seem any happier about her proposed trip, but Amanda ignored her as well. It would be fun to stay at the town house, to walk the streets, to visit the shops.

"And see your father!" Danielle warned her.

Folding a shift, Amanda paused, her heart fluttering. No. She had still not obtained freedom. She was still afraid of the power he held over Damien's life, and therefore over her.

"I hate him!" she whispered.

Danielle did not chastise her. She merely closed a tr\
opened the door, and called down to Thom, asking .\
help.

By nightfall Amanda had reached the town house. Though she was certainly surprised, Mathilda quickly made her welcome, asking her into the parlor while a room was freshened for her.

"The city is wild these days, milady! Every corner has an orator, every coffeehouse is full of conversation."

"What has happened?" Amanda asked.

"Why, 'tis the men back from the Continental Congress. Now they have formed an association. Measures are not so voluntary now. We are to strictly boycott British goods, to band together to do so. And there will be committees to see that the rules of the association are carried out. We are even to call off the Dumfries races, if you can imagine the good men of Virginia doing so!"

Amanda could not, but she was careful of what she said before her husband's housekeeper. "Whatever shall come of it?"

"Well, 'tis rumored that the governor is quite irate, and that he is. Him with his grand Scots temper! He's holding quiet, but you know that the assembly is prorogued until spring, I think that he is quite distressed that the burgesses would come in spouting all this rebellion and that there could be war on the very streets!"

A small black woman came to the doorway, bobbing toward Amanda and informing her that her room was ready. Exhausted, Amanda rose, determined to get a good night's sleep, then explore the mood of the city herself in the morning. "Have you heard anything of Lord Cameron?" she asked his housekeeper.

"Why, yes, I have. You needn't fret any longer, child, for they say that the fighting is all over. And he handled himself splendidly, riding at the front of his troops and meeting those red devils without so much as a blink. He's heading back, taking a route through Richmond. He'll be here soon enough, even if he is waylaid. By Christmas."

Christmas still seemed a long, long way off. Amanda

...ked the woman, then hurried upstairs. She realized ...t it was Eric's room that had been prepared for her. ...he ran her fingers over his desk, tempted to delve within the drawers. That's what she was supposed to be doing, searching his belongings. But she had no heart for it. She was haunted by the presence of him that seemed to live in the room. When she disrobed and stretched out on the bed, she moved her hands over the coolness of the sheets, and her body burned and she tossed about with a certain shame. She wanted him there. She even knew exactly what she wanted him to be doing.

She lay awake at least an hour before she sat up suddenly, furious. He hadn't written to tell her that he was well; his one missive had been while he was traveling. The servants knew more than she did.

Fuming, she tossed and turned, the slow burn of anger simmering within her. But it wasn't the anger that kept her awake, she realized. It was the longing.

She had barely come downstairs in the morning when she heard the cheerful tones of Lady Geneva Norman's voice. She stiffened, remembering that she was certain that Geneva and Eric had been lovers at some time, then she gave the matter no more thought. When she reached the landing, Geneva, splendid in silk and brocade, hugged her tightly. "Marriage does become you, Mandy, darling, even if you stole away the inestimable Lord Cameron!" She lowered her voice. "Father told me that you had come in last night. Do let's get out on the streets and see what is happening today!"

Intrigued to see what was happening, Amanda hugged Geneva in return, wondering if she wasn't a terrible hypocrite. "Fine, let's head out."

"There's a wonderful new little coffee house off of Duke of Gloucester Street. Come, we'll see the rabble!"

"I'd love to see the . . . rabble," Amanda agreed, and so they were off.

It was fun just to be back in Williamsburg, to feel as light and free as she did, to look in the shop windows and study the fashions and hats and jewelry.

"Homespun is the rage," Geneva said, wrinkling her nose.

And it was.

They stopped to buy a copy of the *Virginia Gazette*. As they did so, there was a sudden commotion ahead of them. Amanda rushed forward as she heard a woman scream, then she saw that a crowd had formed around the steps to a shop door. A man had apparently walked into the store, removed bolt after bolt of fabric, and tossed them into the center of the road. He stamped on them and the material sank into the road, soaked by mud and excrement.

"Stop him!" Amanda cried, rushing forward. She was accustomed to people giving way for her; but now no one moved. The restless mob of people ringing the shop held tight.

"Ye'll find no peace in this town, Mrs. Barclay, you'll not, not with English goods in your store!" someone called out.

The shopkeeper backed away. Pushing against the crowd, Amanda shouted in fury. "That is destruction of private property! Would you be a people ruled by the force of a mob!"

A few people turned to her, shamefaced. More and more of them looked at her defiantly.

"Dear girl, committees keep an eye upon the articles of the association, but then this type of thing will happen. I find it entirely exciting myself!"

Amanda, hearing the voice, swung around with pleasure despite the words. "Damien!" she cried. She almost hugged him, then backed away laughing as she looked him up and down. He was clad in the buckskins of the West County men, and he looked very provincial and entirely fierce. She had never imagined it of her cousin who did so love his finery. "Damien! You are home, alive and well!"

"I am. A slight gash to the temple, but I'm quite fine now."

"Oh, Damien! Poor dear! Is—is Eric with you?"

"Oh. No, I'm sorry. I, er, traveled ahead of him. He has been held up on General Lewis's request. He will come soon enough, though." Smiling, Damien bowed to his cousin's companion. "Lady Geneva. This is indeed a pleasure."

Amanda expected Geneva to lift her delicate chin with scorn at Damien's appearance, but the woman did just the opposite. She came up on her toes, caught his hands, and kissed his cheek. "Damien. You're with us again. Thank God. We were on our way to the coffeehouse. Will you join us?"

"I wouldn't dream of leaving a Tory like Amanda on her own, Lady Geneva. I fear that trouble might find her."

"Trouble! These people are acting like rabble! And they pride themselves so fiercely on being Virginians, the descendants of free enterprise rather than the cast-off dregs of society or poor religious dissenters!" Amanda cried.

Damien laughed. "That's true, love, we Virginians do keep our noses in the air. But we're sniffing rebellion these days, and that's the way that it is. Come, let's have that coffee, shall we?"

He slipped an arm within each of theirs and they hurried on down to the side street and then to the coffeehouse. The place was filled, but the harried owner still came forward quickly and politely, eager to serve. Even as he brought them steaming cups of coffee and morning pastries, conversation rose around them. Then one young man was up—a student at William and Mary, Amanda was certain—and began to weave an eloquent tale of the trouble in the colonies. "We are, by the grace of God, free Englishmen! And we shall have the rights of free Englishmen, we will not grant Parliament the right to take men from our colony to England to stand trial for the crime of treason, or for any crime!"

"Here, here!" Boisterous shouts rang out. Amanda felt a chill settle upon her.

"You would think that we were at war!" she whispered.

She did not like the look that Damien gave her. Then he excused himself to speak with some men behind them. A tall, bulky fellow from the cabinet maker's shop approached Amanda, rubbing the rim of his hat nervously.

"You're Lady Cameron, eh, mum?"

"I am, yes."

"I just wanted to tell you that I served under your husband at Point Pleasant. I never served beneath a finer commander nor a braver man. I'm pleased to be his servant, should he ever require."

"Thank you," Amanda murmured, moving forward anxiously. "Can you tell me more?"

The room had fallen strangely silent, and it seemed that the men and the women in the coffeehouse had all turned to look at her. A cup was raised and the young man who had spoken insurrection shouted out. " 'Tis Lady Cameron! A toast to our hero's wife. Madame, you should have been there, and yet you should not, for the blood did run deep."

Suddenly everyone wanted to talk to her. Many of the men there had served in Dunmore's Indian campaign. One young fellow came before her to give a description of her husband in battle. "Why, one of those Shawnees a-come straight at him, leaping down from his horse. I was certain that our Lord Cameron had seen his last blessed light of day, but suddenly he throws off the savage, and God bless me, but if he didn't slice the fellow faster than a cow could sneeze!

"And he was upon his feet again in an instant, never used a musket at all, did he, but fought hand to hand with savages, and shouting orders all the time, even when we came up knee deep in our own dead. He wouldn't allow no scalpin' though, and when we moved north, he wouldn't allow no killing of squaws or chillun, even if we did try to tell him that little savages grew up to big 'uns."

Amanda smiled. "My husband has many relatives with Pamunkee blood. Maybe that ruled his thinking."

"Maybe it did! How is his lordship?"

She tightened her smile but managed to maintain it. "I believe him well."

"Ah, well, no message, but I expect as you'll hear from him any day now."

Another toast was raised to her. Geneva seemed to love all of it. Her eyes sparkled and she clapped with delight. Amanda had been so eager for news, but knowing that despite the bloody battles he had fought, Eric was alive, and heedless of her feelings, a simmering fury brewed within her. She ceased to listen to the men as Geneva flirted and laughed and chatted. Then she realized that she could hear the muted voices of the men behind her—and Damien.

"I have managed . . . a cache of a hundred . . . fine French rifles, I managed to trade soon after Point Pleasant with some Delaware."

Someone said something and Damien's voice lowered. There was an argument over price. Amanda felt her face burn as she listened. "Fine. We shall secrete them in the Johnsboro warehouse after dark. The place is abandoned. If there is trouble, no man shall have property confiscated or face the threat of removal to England."

Damien! she wanted to shout. She had to tell him that Dunmore knew him to be an arms smuggler. Perhaps then he would cease his foolish and dangerous activities.

She rose suddenly, startling Geneva. "I wish to leave. Excuse me."

She brushed past the men who had surrounded her and hurried out to the street, trying to breathe deeply. Damien came upon her quickly. "Amanda—"

"Damien! You are an idiot!"

He twisted his jaw. "Amanda, *you* are the fool," he said irritably. "All of America is up at arms—"

"But they do not practice treason!"

"What is treasonous here? To want to protect oneself?"

"They are on to you, Damien!"

He backed away from her. "Who?"

She did not answer for Geneva appeared suddenly before them, laughing indignantly. "Fine friends! Leave me to the rabble."

"Geneva, never." Damien bowed deeply over her hand. "I shall consider it my first duty and greatest pleasure to see you both home."

They walked back to the Cameron town house first. Amanda kissed Damien and gave him a fierce glance, and she thought that he would come back.

But as night fell he did not return. Anxious, she paced

the downstairs. Then she tried to read, and when she did she found the book on botany that Eric had lent to Damien that summer. A gasp escaped her when a small map fell from the book. She stared at it for a long while, thinking it was merely a pattern for planting boxwoods. Yet there were curious symbols on it. Then her blood ran very cold, for she realized that some of the curious markings referred to money and some of them referred to powder and arms.

She sat back, shaking. Eric was a traitor beyond a shadow of doubt. He was involved more deeply than she had ever imagined.

The map was exactly the proof that her father had demanded she find.

She held the map, then thoughtfully went upstairs and slipped it down into the bottom of one of her jewel cases. Then she went downstairs, put the book back into the shelf, and returned to her room, to curl up beneath the covers of her bed.

Two days later her father appeared at the town house. She was in the parlor, poring over the *Virginia Gazette* and trying to assimilate everything that had occurred since the Continental Congress. Reading between the lines, she was certain that Governor Dunmore had to be grateful that he had disbanded the Virginia Assembly, for it seemed that the members of the convention had come back breathing the fire of insurrection. Thankfully they would have to let some of the fires die down before they came together to meet again. It was frightening.

And, she thought, every man who had attended the convention and set his signature to many of the agreements had to be aware that he courted the charge of treason. But still, she had seen what had happened in the streets of Williamsburg. It might very well be the loyalists who were in danger if all of the colony began to rise in this rebellion. That is . . . until English troops arrived. British troops were admired the world over for their discipline and ability. Once troops descended down upon the colony . . .

She shivered, sipped some of the berry tea, winced, then realized that the taste of it was actually growing palatable to her.

Then Lord Sterling arrived.

It was Danielle who opened the door. From the parlor, Amanda heard her father enter, and she rose, planning to go to the entry to meet him. But he did not give her the chance. He stormed into the parlor. Danielle followed him, announcing him softly.

"Go. I'll speak with my daughter alone!" Nigel snapped.

She hadn't seen him in quite some time, yet even as the door closed quietly behind Danielle, they made no pretense of greeting one another with warmth. Amanda watched him with open hostility.

"Good morning, Father. If you've come for my husband —the suspected traitor—he has not yet returned from the western front where he fought for the governor." She smiled sweetly. "Would you have some tea, father? Something stronger? Tell me, to just what do I owe this . . . pleasure?"

"Damien Roswell," Sterling answered flatly, tossing his tricorn down upon the sofa. He walked over to the fire to warm his hands, smiling as he watched her face. "Ah, you're not so cocky now, girl."

She knew that she had paled. She raised her head, eyeing him coldly. "You wouldn't dare see that an arrest warrant was served upon him now. The colony would be up in arms. If he was transported to England for some trial—"

"If he disappeared in the night none would be the wiser, eh?"

"Dunmore would never condone this."

"You're mistaken. Dunmore is a nervous man, with Peyton Randolph spouting off about natural law and seeking elections for the Virginia Conclave. Aye, who would notice the disappearance of one eager young lad?" Her father lost his pretense of a smile. He stared at her hard. "I'd do him in myself easily enough. I've killed before, girl, don't you doubt it. I'll kill again if need be. This is my path to royal favor, and I will have it!"

Chills riddled Amanda and she longed to go to the fire,

just to feel some warmth. But Nigel Sterling was by the fire, and she would not take a step near him.

"My husband would kill you."

"So—you've turned on England, joined the rabble."

"I am loyal to the Crown."

"Then give me something—or else I swear that Damien Roswell will not live to see the morning sun. One way or other, lady, I will see that he dies. And don't deceive yourself about the state of this colony. Prompt and forceful action from London will quell this rebellion before it begins."

She paused, staring at him. She believed him. He would kill Damien, or seize him and see him transported to Newgate. It might not be legal, but her father still had the power to see it done.

He started moving toward her. "Don't come near me!" she warned, and he stood still, smiling again.

"Give me something! If you love the Crown, serve it!"

She thought quickly, her heart seeming to fall. She remembered the conversation in the coffeehouse, and it occurred to her that she could save Damien, serve the Crown indeed, and be sure, too, that no foolish young swain died in the serving. "There is a cache of arms," she blurted out.

Sterling's eyes glistened with pleasure. "Where?"

"On—on the river. At the Johnsboro warehouse."

Sterling smiled, collecting his hat. "If you've told me the truth, girl, you've bought yourself Christmas. Good day, daughter."

He left. For an endless moment Amanda could not move. She was so cold that she didn't think that even the warmth of the fire could help her now. She didn't feel that she had helped the cause of England. She felt as if she had betrayed not just the patriots . . .

But Eric.

She moved across the room to the brandy decanter, poured herself a liberal portion, and swallowed it down quickly. Then she repeated the action, and at long last some semblance of warmth, of life, poured back into her.

But that night when she slept she was haunted by the faces of the young men in the coffeehouse. They marched on her with fixed bayonets upon their muskets, with eyes of condemning fire, with features frozen into cold masks. They marched upon her and she backed away with a silent scream. And then they stopped, breaking apart, for a new man to make his way among them. She heard the sure purpose of his boots ringing as they fell against the ground, and then she saw his face, and it was Eric's, and it was as cold as a winter's wind, as devoid of love or passion. Like shimmering steel his eyes gazed upon her, and then he reached out to touch her, his fingers winding tightly about her. . . .

She screamed, thrashing about, for the dream was so real. Then she realized that it was no dream, she fought a real man, and that Eric was above her, truly with her, his eyes a curious glistening silver but his lip curled into a smile.

"Shush! My God, lady, what is this greeting? I reach to touch you, ready to die for the time and distance between us, and you treat me like a monster!"

She went still, the fear subsiding, yet remaining to haunt her, as it would forever. "Eric!" She gasped. And she reached up to touch his face. His hair was damp, he was naked as he sprawled atop her, and she realized that he must have come home, found her there, bathed elsewhere, and come to her. He was no dream, nor did he look upon her coldly or with disdain. His eyes were alight with fire, his body was hotter than flame, the length of him seemed to tremble against her with startling fervor. She moistened her lips, gazing at him, and she cried out, forgetting anger, forgetting everything. "Eric!" she cried his name again. She placed her hands on the clean-shaven sides of his face and pulled him to her, almost swooning as she tasted the warmth and hunger of his kiss. She drew away from him then, trying to speak, trying to recall her anger and not her fear.

"You did not write!"

"I had little time."

"I worried—"

"Did you?" He paused, staring down at her, his eyes alight against the dim glow of the fire, a dark brow arched in a satyr's mask against rugged angles of his face. Then he lay low against her and whispered with searing desire against her lips. "Forgive me this night, for I can bear the distance no more!"

His hands closed upon her gown, material ripped, and she felt the startling deliciousness of his body against hers. His hands, his teeth, his lips were everywhere. They moved upon her with wanton abandon, with wild demand. Soft moans escaped her as she discovered her body caught by his heat, alive in every way, her flesh begging to be touched, and the spiral of desire within her soaring. She arched her breasts to his lips, dug her fingers into his hair, and gasped and writhed as his fingers delved within the woman's core of her, teasing the sable-red triangle at the juncture of her thighs, mercilessly finding the tiny bud of deepest sensation. Where he stroked and teased with his touch he followed with his tongue's bold caress, sweeping the nectar from her until she surged against him, begging senselessly for she knew not what. He towered above her full of laughter, but she pushed him from her, crawling atop him, lashing him with the soft stroke of her hair as she rubbed the length of her body low over his. She kissed his chest and stroked his buttocks and thighs, nipping his flesh, lapping it with tiny kisses, and moving upward again. Gently, tenderly, wickedly, she stroked and teased him, then went on with her hair a shower about them both to lap and stroke and lick and tease the very shaft of him, so softly that it was torment, then with a sizzling force that brought forth a torrent of shudders and groans from his lips. Then the very force of his hands was upon her as he lifted her, catching her eyes, meeting them, then thrusting into her with deep, shocking passion that still seemed to burn her from the inside out, impale her until she was fused with him. His eyes held hers as he thrust, and thrust again, and sobs of sweet hunger and desperation fell from her lips. He held her steady and they rode the night and the stars and the painful distance between them and the shimmering passion that was explosive and primitive and so very undeniable.

She thought that she had died when she fell against him

at last. Though she gasped for breath and lay slick and spent and awed and exhausted, his touch was upon her again, his fingers idly upon her breasts, her buttocks; his lips seared her shoulders, his hands stroked the slope of her buttocks.

"Eric . . ." she whispered his name, and she twisted, thinking that there were things to say. But even as she gazed at him the heat went cool within her. Even now her father was seeing that the rebels' arms were seized. And that the man who touched her so fervently now might well wind his fingers about her throat if he only knew. She reached out to touch his damp, dark-haired chest, and she felt the shudder and violent ripple of muscle there and her throat constricted. "Eric—"

He rolled over, sweeping her beneath him with a sudden savage movement. His eyes touched deep into hers, dark and tempestuous, relentless. A hoarse cry escaped him and he buried his face against the fiery cascade of her hair and her throat. "Love me tonight!" he demanded of her raggedly. "Do nothing but love me this night!" he repeated, and his lips found hers, moving against them voraciously, then finding the sensitive spots at her ear, coming to the pulse as her throat, sweeping to secure the hardened bud of her breast with hunger and magic. She exhaled on a gasp, feeling the excitement rise in her again, the promise of the exquisite peaks of ecstasy.

There was nothing that she could say to him, and in moments she did not remember that there were things that she wanted to say to him.

He demanded that she love him; that night, she did.

XI ❦

That Christmas season was one of the happiest times of Amanda's life, or would have been, had the threat of what was to come not hung over them so surely. For the first few days of her husband's return, Amanda waited anxiously for what would happen. But Virginia itself seemed quiet then.

They stayed in Williamsburg long enough for a round of parties, many in celebration of Lord Dunmore's newborn baby daughter. The *Virginia Gazette* wrote of the blessed event. Throughout the coffeehouses where the students were still preaching sedition, cups were still raised to the countess and her baby.

Snow began to fall toward the end of the month, and that was when Eric determined that it was time to return home. Amanda was glad to go; she missed Cameron Hall.

Their homecoming was wonderful. Amanda and Eric sat together in the coach, bundled beneath a blanket,

while Pierre drove. Eric taught her a few of the bawdier
tunes he had learned traveling with the western militia,
and she blushed and laughed, accused him of making up
things as he went along, and he assured her that he did
not, and held her closer in the warmth of the blanket. All
along the road the snow fell in soft, delicate flakes. The
forests were frosted with it, the trees glistened, and when
the snow had stopped falling, the sky was not wintry gray
but crystal blue, and the sun melted the very top layer of
snow to ice, and the world about them seemed to be a
dazzling, crystal palace.

At Cameron Hall they were greeted warmly by the servants. Danielle, who had gone ahead, stood beside Jacques
Bisset on the steps as they arrived. Thom had come down
with a silver welcoming tray full of wassail drinks, and
Cassidy stood beside him, ready to serve. Margaret and
the cook and several grooms stood by, and when Pierre
opened the carriage door there was a cheer to greet them.
Amanda drank deeply of the warm, sweet wine, and when
it came time to face her husband at the table for their
evening meal, her eyes were softly glazed, her lips curved,
her manner most gentle and bemused.

Watching his wife, Eric became sorely frightened, for it
shook him to the bone to realize how much he loved her.
So much about her had changed since they'd met. She
laughed so easily, her emerald eyes bore for him the spar-
kle that he had once so envied when she cast it upon another man. This night she wore velvet, deep forest-green
velvet, the fur-trimmed bodice falling very low off her
shoulders and molding handsomely over her breasts. Delicate flame-deep curls curved in fascinating tendrils over
the alabaster crescents of her breasts as they rose almost
indecently high against the gown. She barely touched her
food, but smiled throughout the evening. They ate by candlelight, and he noted things he might not notice otherwise. The crystal of the candle holders seemed to shimmer
with greater colors, the silver of their goblets was dazzling, the white linen laid out upon the table was impeccable, soft as the snowdrifts that had followed them home.
But nothing was more outstanding than the color of her

eyes, nor the sweep of her lashes, nor the curve of
smile, the sound of her laughter. When they had finish
with the meal he swept her from her chair, mindless of th
green velvet dress, mindless of the servants who discreetly
disappeared, and with drama and finesse he walked her
up the stairs. And all the while her arms curled around his
neck, her eyes met his with a fascinating radiance. When
he came to their room he sat her down upon the fine bed
they shared, and he knelt down before her, slipping off her
black satin pumps. He looked up and saw something in
her eyes that he had not caught before, as if the moon had
cast strange shadows upon them, and in that moment he
shuddered suddenly. She had married him under duress;
they had never once exchanged words of love, though they
whispered often and fervently enough of passion.

She reached out, touching his face, a cry upon her lips.
"What is it?" she whispered.

He shook his head, searching out her eyes still, then
setting his fingers upon the laces to her bodice. The sweet,
fascinating scent of her rose to sweep around him like a
haunting caress. Her breasts spilled forward and he rested
his cheek against them, then found her eyes again. "I just
wonder, lady, will you always be so gentle, so tender, with
your love?"

"Always!" she whispered, stroking his dark hair and
holding him close to her.

He rose with her, bearing her downward, velvet, fur,
and all. The dress fell away from the perfection of her
upper body and her hair streamed free and wild upon her
nakedness. He pressed his lips to hers and wondered at
the curious fever and fear that gripped him that night.
"You have spun magic webs upon me, Amanda. Webs of
silk and steel, so soft and yet so strong. With a word from
your lips, I would long for death; for the brush of your
fingers upon me, love, I would move mountains. Forever,
lady, I am yours."

She returned his stare, curious at his whimsy, of which
he was capable, but not so often given. He was custom-
arily a man who took what he wanted, even when what he
wanted was his wife. But this night the words played eas-

.pon his lips, just as his fingers stroked her slowly, .hout the demand, without the solicitation. It was her yes he delved now, raking and searching, and still the easy mist and magic of his words lay with them, and the soft mood that had come from the wassail drinks wrapped sweetly about her. She touched him and vowed to him, "I will love you sweet and tender always, my lord."

He stroked her cheek with his forefinger, tracing the pattern of her lips. "Betray not the heart, Amanda. Of all in life, that is the greatest sin."

She parted her lips to protest, but that was when she lost her easy lover, when he seized her with passion and demand. The words were lost to her as the mist swirled away and the startling reality of sensation touched and ravaged her. Through it all he was ruthless in what he would take from her, and yet he was also a tender lover. No hands more gentle could ever touch a woman, no fingers could stroke upon her or touch her most intimate secrets with greater sensitivity. No whispers more driving could caress her ears; no lips could touch the whole of her with greater thoroughness or greater determination to elicit and evoke sensation. They rode the wind, and the wind danced within them, bringing them to erotic peak upon peak, and in the end she was sated, sleeping upon crystal snowdrifts of the mind, cocooned in both beauty and warmth.

In the morning Amanda discovered him at the small table within their room, sipping coffee as he read the latest issue of the *Virginia Gazette*. He was fully attired in plain clothing, navy breeches, a white cotton shirt with no lace or frills, a wool surcoat, and his high boots. His greatcoat lay over a chair by the door, and she knew that he meant to travel over his land. He would spend time with Jacques, and he would see each and every one of his tenants, and she knew that if any one of them was in need, he would see to it that they ate well for Christmas. The holiday was upon them; there would be a great party here for landowners and tenants and servants alike. It was tradition. He had told her about it earlier.

He sensed that she was awake and he looked at her, smiling though his eyes were grave. Amanda smiled in

return, rising, sweeping the sheet about her as she ca̶
stand behind him. He swallowed more coffee, indica̶
an article. "Some of Dunmore's navy men raided a wa̶
house on the coast. The Johnsboro warehouse. There we̶
all manner of French weapons being stored there."

She was glad that she stood behind him. Her fingers
clenched and she shivered painfully. Her eyes would have
given her away, for they widened in fear and dismay. She
could not speak.

But her husband did not suspect her. He shook his head.
"At least no one was killed or injured. No one knows
where the guns came from—'tis an abandoned place.
Thank God. I am sick to death of seeing men die."

He set his cup down and rose and kissed her absently. "I
am off. Perhaps you would like to ride with us tomorrow."

She nodded, unable to find her voice. He was watching
her again. "There is no reason that you should not, is
there?" he asked her.

"I—I don't know what you mean," she managed to gasp.

He looked her carefully up and down. "I mean," he said
softly, "there is no sign of a child for us as yet, is there?"

"Oh!" Relief flooded through her. She shook her head,
blushing. "No . . . no."

He kissed her again and turned away, picking up his
civilian tricorn. Then he turned back with a wicked smile
and he drew her into his arms, and kissed her with the
fever and shockingly intimate surge and sizzle that had
first taught her the stirrings of desire. Her knees went
weak and her heart came to thunder against her ears, and
fear and unease were gone. She fell against him, and when
he raised his lips, she met his eyes with an emerald smile
that was secure and dazzling . . . and ever tender.

He smiled. "I am about to forget the day."

"There is always the night."

"There is nothing like the moment."

"My lord, how could I dare to argue with you?"

He started to laugh, and she did not know where the
breathlessness would lead, but there was a discreet tap on
the door and Eric broke from her regretfully.

The next day she did ride with him, plowing through the

when they were inland, shivering against the breeze they came upon the river. Winter was coming upon in full force, but despite the cold and the harshness, she enjoyed herself tremendously. She loved the tenant farms with their thatched roofs and wattle-and-daub walls, their central rooms with spinning wheels and hearths and kitchens all in one. They were, above all, homes of warmth and laughter, filled with the melody of the voices of children. Jacques accompanied them wherever they visited. Amanda found him more curious each time she saw him. He was so strikingly good-looking with his dark-fringed light eyes and fine features. Every bit the Frenchman in dress and manner, but an Acadian still, and wary of both the peoples who turned from him. He watched her too, she thought. But it did not distress her. It warmed her.

Christmas came. Religious services were humbly observed, then it was time for the people to celebrate, and they all drew to Cameron Hall. There was mistletoe to dangle from the doorways, and the house was decorated with holly and wreaths and ribbons. Fires crackled brilliantly, musicians played the old European tunes and the livelier colonial music too. The lord and lady of the house took part in all the festivities. Amanda danced with the very proper Thom, with the round little cook, with a very shy and blushing groom. She was laughing, delighted to catch her husband's approving eye across the room, when suddenly there was a pounding on the door. Eric, leaning against the bannister in the hallway, waved away Thom and Cassidy and started for the door himself. He opened it and stepped back, welcoming their new guests.

"Well, well!" boomed her father's voice. "Daughter!"

Nigel Sterling walked into the room, Lord Hastings and Lord Tarryton, the Duke of Owenfield, with his new lady duchess following behind him.

The music died, the servants ceased to shriek with laughter, and a curious quiet fell upon the room.

"Hello, Father," Amanda greeted him coolly. Her fingers were trembling. She could not forget that the weapons had been seized, that she was lying to the man with whom she had fallen in love. Dear God, why on this day! she prayed in silence, but he was already upon her, taking her hands, brushing her cheek with his cold kiss. Thom was quickly there to take coats and hats; she greeted Lord Hastings and Robert and his duchess, and quickly suggested that they retire to the dining room where there was still warm food and a blazing fire. She saw that Eric watched her, carefully, and she wondered at his thoughts.

There was a scuffle as she led their new guests toward the dining room. Startled, Amanda twirled around. She was shocked to see Eric standing there with his arm locked about Jacques Bisset's throat, holding him despite the fact that the muscled Frenchman was straining to break free. Eric smiled despite his determined fight. "Do go on, my love. I'll be right with you."

"But, Eric—"

"Our guests, Amanda."

Confused, she nevertheless hurried forward to escort their new guests to the dining room. As she closed the doors, she could see that Danielle had come over to talk swiftly to the man she had claimed as her brother. Amanda could not catch the words. With a sigh, she gave up. She turned about, facing those who had come. Her father watched her with his ever-calculating eyes; Lord Hastings with his ever-lecherous eyes; Robert with a startling lust; and Anne, the Duchess of Owenfield, with her soft brown doe's eyes, ever frightened and timid.

"Anne, you must have some of our Christmas grog!" Amanda said cheerfully. "And the rest of you must try this too. Father, I know you prefer your whiskey, but this is a wonderful concoction with a trace of whiskey in it." She didn't wait for a reply, but played the grand hostess, pouring from a silver decanter that sat atop a small pot of burning oil to keep the contents warm. She placed a stick of cinnamon in each drink. By then Eric had come into the room, looking only slightly worse for the curious tussle.

"Welcome," he said to the group, taking Anne's hand in the best manner of the Virginia aristocrat. He kissed her fingers and smiled at the young woman—a trifle more gently than he smiled at her, Amanda thought, but then she realized that he was very sorry for the timid woman married to Robert. "Duchess, it is indeed a pleasure to have you here. I'm so sorry I missed your wedding. I understand it was quite the occasion of the decade." His eyes sparkled. "Tell me, do I detect something special here already?"

"Quite." Robert had the grace to hold his wife's shoulders and pull her against him. "We are expecting our first child."

"Oh! How wonderful!" Amanda said, raising her glass to the pair. "A toast to the two of you, and to a healthy, happy babe."

"Here, here!" Eric agreed, and he lifted his glass to the pair. "To a healthy, happy babe! Come, lady, be warmed by the fire."

Eric was wonderful with Anne, light and warm, making her feel very much at home. But the conversation did not stay light long; Nigel Sterling brought up the fact that Williamsburg was alive with gossip about the conclave that was already being planned. "The time is coming, and coming fast, when a man will have to make up his mind! He will either be the king's servant or his enemy."

Eric waved a hand in the air, but Amanda noted that her husband's eyes were glittering with tension. She knew to beware of him in such moods; she doubted if her father would see the danger or heed it. "Nigel, I have just recently returned from service at Dunmore's request," Eric stated. "I met the Indians upon our borders while politicians argued. Why do you tell me this?"

"Because, sir, you should abhor these proceedings! You, with your strength and power and your influence, you should be out there fighting the hotheads, not joining them!"

"Or leading them!" Robert suggested sharply.

It was out—it was almost an accusation of treason.

Amanda stood, bursting in between them. "I'll not have it!" she announced, lifting her chin imperiously. "This is my house, and it is Christmas, and every man here shall behave with propriety for the occasion, or leave. This is not a tavern, and you'll not act like it! Are we all understood? Nigel, you are my father, and as such you are welcome here, but not to reap discord!"

There was silence for several long seconds. Amanda realized that Eric was looking at her and that his temper had faded. His eyes were glistening with laughter.

"Amanda—" Sterling began.

Eric rose. "You heard my wife. We've quite a traditional Christmas here and we are delighted to have you, but only in the Christmas spirit. Come along. We've excellent musicians, quite in the spirit of the holiday. Come, Lady Anne, 'tis a slow tune. If your husband will allow, I will gladly lead you gently to it." The group returned to the party.

Robert nodded distractedly. As soon as Eric had taken Anne to the dance floor, he swept his arms about Amanda. He held her too close. Trying to ignore him and the pressure of his arms, she danced focusing her attention on the music and the movement of her feet. The fiddler was wonderful and the plaintive tunes of the instrument, joined by the soft strains of flute and harp, were haunting. Or they could be . . . if she did not feel Robert's arms about her.

"Marriage becomes you, Amanda. You are more beautiful than ever."

"Thank you. And congratulations. You are to be a father."

"No child yet, eh? Tell me, do you sleep with the bastard?"

"With the greatest pleasure," she replied sweetly. She felt his hands quicken upon her so that she was in pain; he nearly snapped her fingers.

"You're lying," he told her.

"No woman could find a more exciting lover."

"You have not forgiven me yet. But you love me still, and I can warn you now, the time is coming when you will run to me."

"Oh? Is it?"

"The British soldiers will descend upon this town very soon, and men the likes of your husband will be burned in the wake."

She wanted to retort something horrible to him, but she did not have the chance. Her father touched his shoulder, and despite Robert's irritated expression, he was forced to relinquish his hold upon her. She was no more pleased to be held by her father, but she had little choice.

"You did good work, daughter," he told her softly. Her heart leapt uneasily. "The arms were stashed where you said."

"Then we are even."

"There is no such thing as even. You will serve me when I demand that you do."

"You're a fool, Father. It will not be so easy! Haven't you begun to understand anything yet? There are arrest warrants abounding in Boston—and no one to see them carried out. The people are turning away from this mess that men like you are causing!"

He smiled. "Don't forget, daughter, that I do not make idle threats. When I need you again, you will obey me."

He halted, turning her over to Lord Hastings. Amanda, wretchedly miserable from her father's words, tried to smile and bear the man. She was certain that he drooled upon her breast, and by the time the music came to a halt at last she was ready to scream and go racing out into the snow. She excused herself and raced outside to the back porch, desperate for fresh air, be it frigidly cold.

The river breeze rushed in upon her. She touched the snow on the railing and rubbed it against her cheeks and the rise of her breasts, and then she shivered, staring out at the day. It was gray now, and bleak. And it had been such a beautiful, shimmering Christmas.

"Amanda."

She turned around, startled. Eric had come outside. His arms were covered in naught but the silk of his shirt, but he didn't seem to notice the cold. The wind lifted a dark lock of his hair and sent it lashing back against his forehead. He walked toward her, pulling her into his arms. "What is going on here?"

"What?" she cried.

"Why has he come?"

"Father? Because it is Christmas."

He kept staring into her eyes, and as he did so, the biting cold seemed to seep into her, wrapping around her very heart. Now was the time. She should throw her arms around him; she should admit to everything.

She could not. For one, there was England. Above everything, she could not turn upon her own beliefs.

And there was Damien. She could not risk his life.

She moistened her lips and wondered desperately what would happen if it did come to war. She was Eric Cameron's wife; and she knew beyond the shadow of a doubt that he would cast aside everything for his own beliefs. Would he so easily cast her aside? And what of her? Perhaps she dared not utter the words, for they were painful ones, but she did love him. Deeply. More desperately than she had ever imagined.

It was terrifying.

"He has come," she whispered, "to make me wretched."

Eric's arms tightened upon her. "And Tarryton?"

"Robert?" she said, startled.

"I saw the heat and the passion in your eyes when you spoke with him. Tell me, was it anger, or something else?"

"Anger only. I swear it."

"Would God that I could believe you."

She pulled away from him, hating him at that moment.

"You never pretended to love me," he reminded her. He kept walking toward her, and he was a stranger to her then. He caught her arm and pulled her back to him.

"He is a married man expecting a child!" Amanda lashed out.

"And you are a married woman."

"That you could think—" she began, then she exploded with a violent oath and escaped him, running past him and back into the house. The party was dying down. The servants were no longer guests, but they hurried about to pick up glasses and platters and silver mugs that had been filled with Christmas cheer. Amanda had assumed that her father and the others were staying; they were not. They took their leave soon after, telling her they meant to make Williamsburg before nightfall. Eric had come in quietly behind Amanda. He bid them all farewell cordially, ever the lord of his castle.

Amanda escaped him, rushing up to bed. She dressed in

a warm flannel gown and sat angrily before her dressing table, brushing her hair.

A few minutes later the door burst open. Eric, who obviously had imbibed more than was customary, stood there for a moment, then came in and dropped down upon their bed. He tore off his boots, his surcoat, and his shirt, letting them fall where they would. Amanda felt his eyes upon her. He watched her every movement even as she tried to ignore him.

"Why is it, Amanda, that we are not expecting a child?" he asked at last.

Her brush went still as the tense and brooding question startled her motionless. Then she began to sweep the brush through the dark red tresses again. "God must know, for I do not."

He leapt up, coming behind her. He took the brush from her fingers and began to work it through her hair. The tendrils waved softly against his naked chest as he worked. She sat very still, waiting.

"You do not do anything to keep us from having a child, do you?" he asked.

"Of course not!" She gasped, trembling. Then she rose and spun around on him. "How can you suggest such a thing! 'Tis you—you marry me, and then leave me!"

His eyes softened instantly and he drew her against him. "Then you do not covet him, do not lie awake dreaming that the duchess should die, that perhaps . . ."

"My God! How could you think such a heinous thing of me!" she cried, outraged. She tried to jump to her feet and leap by him. He caught her and shoved her back to the chair, and suddenly she discovered that she was not just furious, but hungry for the man. She teased her hair against his bare midriff, soft sounds forming in her throat. She touched him with just the tip of her tongue, lathing his hard-muscled flesh until she felt the muscles ripple and tremble. She loosened his breeches and made love to him there until he shouted out hoarsely, wrenching her up and into his arms. He entered into her like fire, and the passion blazed steep and heady and wild. Crying, throbbing, sobbing, she reached a shattering climax. She felt

the volatile shuddering of his body atop her own, and ╮
shoved him from her, curling away, ashamed. He tried ╮
draw her back. She stared into the night, amazed that she
could be so angry, hate him so fiercely, and be so desperate for his touch.

"Amanda—"

"No!"

"Yes," he said simply. He drew her back and kissed her
forehead. His soft husky laughter touched her cheek. "Perhaps you will better understand me after this night," he
murmured. "Anger, passion, love, and pain. Sometimes
they are so very close that it is torment. I have wanted you
in fury, in deepest despair, when wondering if I am a fool,
when despising myself for the very weakness of it. That is
the nature of man."

She curled against him, glad that he did not laugh at
her. He sighed softly, his breath rustling her hair. "If the
world could just stay as it is. . . ."

His words faded away. For the first time since he had
come home she guiltily remembered the map she held in
the bottom of one of her jewelry cases. A shudder ripped
through her. His arms tightened about her. "Are you
cold?" he asked.

"No," she lied. She was suddenly colder than she had
ever been, even with his arms about her.

She determined to change the subject of their changing
world. "What was that with Jacques today? You never told
me; what a very curious incident."

"Oh. Well, he wanted to kill your father. I stopped her."

Amanda wrenched around, certain that he was fooling
her. She glanced at his handsome features in the darkness,
and she saw that though he smiled, he was very serious.
The firelight played upon his bronze and muscled chest as
he lay with his fingers laced behind his head. "Why does
he want to kill my father?"

"Heaven knows. Or, perhaps, everyone knows," he said
quietly. He reached out and touched her chin very gently.
"I have wanted to kill him upon occasion. He is not a very
nice man."

Amanda flushed and her lashes fluttered above her

...eks. Eric reached out for her, pulling her back into the ...ug warmth of his arms. "You are not responsible for ...our father," he said briefly, dismissing the entire situation.

"You did not punish Jacques?"

"Punish Jacques? Of course not. He is a very proud man. He is not a slave or an indentured servant of any type—he could up and leave at a second's notice. And I need him."

She smiled in the darkness, thinking that he did tease her then. "How did you calm Jacques, then?"

He was quiet for a long time. "I told him that I wanted to kill Nigel myself," he said at last. His arm held heavily around her when she tried to rise. "Go to sleep, Amanda. It has been a long day."

She lay still beside him, but she did not sleep.

They traveled into Williamsburg to welcome in the New Year of 1775. The governor hosted a party, and despite the political climate, it was attended by all important men, be they leaning toward the loyalist side or the patriot. Watching the illustrious crowd that had come for the festivities, Amanda felt a tightening in her breast. It was, she thought, the last time that she should see all these people so, Damien laughing and sweeping Geneva about the floor, then bowing very low to the governor and his lady. The music was good, the company was sweet, but the mood was such that she clung to her husband's arm and remained exceptionally silent. Damien brought her to the floor and she chastised him for not appearing for Christmas. But the young man was very grave, almost cold. She wanted to box his ears, for she wouldn't be in her present predicament at all if it weren't for him. I should have let them hang you! she nearly shouted, but then her father appeared, asking for the dance, and Damien demurely handed her over to her father.

"I need something more," Sterling told her.

"What?"

"British troops are moving with greater frequency into Boston, and I suspect help here. There isn't going to be any help for Virginia if I can't get more information."

"I haven't any more! Eric has just come home; it been winter."

"Find something."

"I won't do it."

"We shall see," he told her softly, and left her standing alone on the dance floor. She quickly fled over to the punch bowl, but the sweet-flavored drink was not spiked. Robert Tarryton found her there.

"Looking for something stronger, love?"

"I'm not your love."

He sipped the punch himself, assessing her over the rim of his glass. Her hair was piled into curls on top of her head, her shoulders were just barely covered with the fringe of the mink that trimmed her gown. "The time is coming. There's to be a Virginia Convention in March. In Richmond. The delegates are hiding from the governor."

"They can hardly be hiding when Mr. Randolph approached the governor himself about the elections."

He smiled. "Your husband has been asked to be there."

"What? But it will be closed sessions, surely—"

"Nevertheless, madame, I have it from the most reputable sources that he has agreed to be there." He bowed, smiling deeply. "The time is coming, Amanda . . ." he whispered. Then he, too, slipped away into the crowd.

Glancing across the room, Amanda saw that Eric was heavily involved in conversation with a man she knew to be a member of the House of Burgesses. Feeling doubly betrayed, Amanda retrieved her coat and headed for the gardens. A tall handsome black man in impeccable livery opened the door for her, and she fled out into the night. She wandered aimlessly, for the flowers were dead, and the garden was barren and as wintry as her heart. She had never deceived herself, she tried to reason. Eric was a traitor, she had known it. She had despised him for it. She had never thought that she could learn to love a traitor so dearly.

But what would she do while the world crumbled?

As she came around to the stables, she suddenly heard a strange commotion among the horses and grooms. For a moment she was still, and then she hurried over to see

was happening. An older man with naturally whit-
ed hair was instructing a few boys on how to make a
allen, saddled mount stand. The horse was down,
sprawled upon the ground in a grotesque parody of sleep.

"What has happened?" Amanda cried.

The older man, wiping a sheen of sweat from his face
despite the winter's cold, looked her way quickly, offering
her a courteous bow. "Milady, we're losing the bay, I'm
afraid. And I canna tell ye why! 'Tis a fine young gelding
belonging to Mr. Damien Roswell, and of a sudden, the
horse is taken sick as death!"

The boys had just about gotten the mount to its feet.
Beautiful dark brown eyes rolled suddenly. They seemed
to stare right at Amanda with agony and reproach. Then
the horse's legs started to give again. The eyes glazed over,
and despite the best efforts of the grooms, the beautiful
animal crashed down dead upon the hard, cold ground.

Amanda started to back away. A scream rose in her
throat. It was Damien's horse. Dead upon the ground. It
was a warning of what might soon befall Damien if she
did not obey her father.

"Milady—" someone called.

She heard no more. Just as the horse had done, she
crashed to the ground, oblivious to the world around her.

When she came to, she was being lifted in her husband's
arms. His silver blue eyes were dark as cobalt then, upon
her hard with suspicious anxiety. She closed her eyes
against him, but held tight to him. "I'll take you inside—"

"No, please, take me home."

There was a crowd around them, Damien among them.
She did not want to see her cousin's concerned face, and
so she kept her eyes closed. Eric announced that she just
wanted to go home, and then he was carrying her to their
carriage. Inside he was quiet, and he did not whisper a
word. When they reached the town house he carried her
upstairs, asking that his housekeeper make tea, the real
tea that had come from China aboard his own ship. Danielle came to help Amanda from her gown and into a
warm nightdress, clucking with concern over her.

Amanda kept saying dully that she was all right. But w̶ she was dressed and in bed Eric himself came with t̶ tea. She did not like the very suspicious and brooding cast to his eyes, so she kept her own closed. But he made her sit up, made her sip the tea, and then demanded to know what had happened.

"The horse. It—it died."

"There's more to it than that."

Amanda flashed him an angry glare. "If Geneva or Anne or the governor's lady had passed out so, you and every man there would have assumed it was no sight for a lady to see!"

"But you are a lady created of stronger stuff. You are not so sweet—or so insipid—a woman, and hardly such a delicate . . . lady."

She lunged at him in a flash of temper, very nearly upsetting the whole tea tray. He rescued it just in time, his eyes narrowing upon her dangerously.

After setting the tray upon the dresser, he turned to her. "Amanda—"

She came up upon her knees, challenging him. "What of you, milord?" she demanded heatedly. "I was fascinated to hear that you were traveling to Richmond!"

She had taken him by surprise; he seemed very displeased by it, and wary. "I see. You managed to slip away with your old lover long enough to discern that information. You are a wonderful spy."

"I am not a spy at all!" she insisted, beating upon his chest. "While you, milord, are a—"

He caught her wrists and his eyes sizzled as he stared down at her. "Yes, yes, I know. I am a traitor. What happened with Damien's horse, Amanda?"

She lowered her eyes quickly, tugging to free her wrists. She did not want to tell him that Damien, and he himself, stood in line to die in the same agonizing manner as the horse.

"I'm tired, Eric."

"Amanda—"

A lie came to her lips, one she would live to regret, one

abhorred even as she whispered it. "I'm not feeling ell. I think that I might—that I might be with child."

His fingers instantly eased their hold upon her. He lay her back upon the bed, his eyes glowing, his features suddenly young and more striking than ever. His whispers were tender, his touch so gentle she could barely stand it.

"You think—"

"I don't know as yet. Just please . . . please, I am so very tired tonight!"

"I shall sleep across the hall," he said instantly. He touched her forehead with his kiss, then her lips, and the touch was barely a breath of the sweetest tenderness. He rose, and her heart suddenly ached with a greater potency than it thundered as she watched him walk across the hall.

She lay there for long hours in wretched misery, then she rose, and quickly dressed. With trembling fingers she reached for her jewelry case and found the map that had been in the botany book. She needn't tell anyone where she had found it. On the floor of some tavern, perhaps.

Silently she crept from the room and down the stairs, and then out into the night.

She brought her hand to her lips, nearly screaming aloud, when a shadow stepped from behind a tree, not a half block from the house. Nigel Sterling his arms crossed over his chest, blocked her way.

"You have something for me, daughter? I was quite sure that you would."

She thrust the map toward him. "There will be no more, do you hear me? No more!"

"What is it?"

"I believe that it points out stashes of weapons about the Tidewater area. Did you hear me? I have done this. I will do no more."

"What if it comes to war?"

"Leave me alone!"

She turned to flee.

Sterling started to laugh. Even as she ran back toward the town house, she heard him wheezing with the force of his laughter.

She didn't care right then. She had appeased him for the

next few months at least. And God alone knew what would happen then.

She hurried back up the steps of the town house, opened the door, and closed it behind her. Her lashes fell wearily over her eyes with relief, then she pushed away from the door, ready to start up the stairs.

She paused, her throat closing, her limbs freezing, the very night seeming to spin before her. But blackness did not descend upon her now. She could see too clearly, she was too acutely aware of the man who stood on the stairs, awaiting her. He wore a robe that hung loosely open to his waist, his sleekly muscled chest with its flurry of dark hair naked to her view and strikingly virile. His fingers curled about the bannister as if they would like to wind so about her throat. His eyes were like the night, black with fury, and his words, when he spoke, were furiously clipped.

"Where were you?"

"I—I needed air."

"You needed rest before."

"I needed air now."

"Where were you?"

"A gentleman, even a husband, has no right to question his lady that way!"

"It has been established that I am no gentleman, you are no lady. Where were you?"

"Out!"

His steps were menacing as he came toward hers. She backed into the hallway, trying to escape his wrath. "You can't force me to tell you!" she cried out. "You cannot force me . . ." Her words trailed away as he neared her. Blindly she struck out, afraid to trust his rage. He ignored her flailing hands and ducked low, sweeping her over his shoulder.

"No! You cannot make me—stop this instantly! One of the servants will hear us . . . will come . . . stop!"

His hand landed forcefully upon her derrière. "I don't give a pig's arse if the servants do come, and perhaps I cannot force you to tell me why you prowl the streets. But while you do so, madame, I shall be doubly damned if I shall be cast from my own bedroom!"

She pounded against his shoulder to no avail. A quick and vicious fight followed when they reached their chamber, but then his lips touched hers, and she remembered his words. Anger . . . it was so close to passion, so close to need. She wanted to keep fighting. She could not. The fire was lit, in moments it blazed. She never did betray her mission, nor did it matter. Despite all that soared between them, she lost something that night.

By morning Eric was gone. He left a letter telling her that he was headed for the convention and that she was to go home. She would do so with little fuss, he suggested, because certain of the servants would see that she did so by her own power or theirs.

The note was not signed "Your loving husband," "Love, Eric," or even "Eric." Warning words were all that were given to her. "Behave, Madame, or else!"

With a wretched cry she threw her pillow across the room and then she lay back, sobbing. All that she had discovered, she realized, was lost. Love had been born, it had flourished . . . and then it had foundered upon the rocky shores of revolution.

Part III

✤

Liberty or Death

XII ❧

St. John's Episcopal Church
Across Shockoe Creek
Outside Richmond, Virginia
March 1775

The debate had been endless, hot and heavy and passionate, and then, curiously, the delegates fell silent again. There was resistance, Eric thought, quietly watching the men around him, but something was taking form here today that was destined to cast the course of a nation.

Richmond, the little town founded by Colonel William Byrd II in 1733, did not boast the fine accommodations of Williamsburg. There were not so many taverns, and certainly the inns were far less numerous, and far less elegant. Yet it seemed much better to be here, at the falls of the James River, than in Williamsburg, beneath the governor's nose.

The town itself hadn't had a place large enough for the conclave to convene, so the delegates were meeting in the church. To the loyalists among the populace—who sensed the depth of the rebellion going on within hallowed halls

—the fact that they met in the church made the assembly an obscene one.

And despite the warnings of caution, Patrick Henry had the floor again, the West County giant, the rough but eloquent speaker who seemed to possess the ability to move mountains with the power of his words.

"It is in vain, sir, to extenuate the matter. Gentlemen may cry Peace! Peace! But there is no peace. The war is actually begun. The next gale that sweeps from the north will bring to our ears the clash of resounding arms! Is life so dear, or peace so sweet, as to be purchased at the price of chains and slavery? Forbid it, Almighty God! I know not what course others may take, but as for me, give me liberty, or give me death!"

The tenor of his voice, the sound, the substance of words, rang and rang against the day, with startling, dizzying, almost blinding passion. Eric thought that men would leap to their feet, that they would scream and cry from the force of the emotion.

But there was silence. Men appeared stunned by the boldness and the honesty of the words.

Henry looked around the assembly, then sat.

And still his words were met by silence as they seemed to echo and echo through the church. Then slowly a few delegates rose to oppose him, but then Richard Henry Lee was on his feet, speaking up for Henry's resolution, and then Thomas Jefferson asked for recognition. Jefferson was a damned good writer but not much of an orator. Still, when he rose, and spoke for Patrick Henry's resolves, a peculiar eloquence touched him. Tall, with his flaming red hair neatly queued, he gestured awkwardly, but still, his words, his manner, touched many men. Eric could feel it in his own heart; he could see it in other men's eyes.

When the gentlemen at last broke for the day, it was resolved that they would form committees.

It was resolved that troops would be raised for Virginia's defense.

And it was known that within the next few days, the

vote would be cast for the delegates to travel to Philadelphia a second time.

Eric, leaving the church at Washington's side, was quiet as he heard the words spoken by Patrick Henry repeated again and again. They were whispered at first, but then the whispers rose.

Two years ago they would have all claimed his words treason. But now only the staunch loyalists thought so.

"He shall go down in history," Washington commented.

Eric grinned as they carefully moved through the early-spring muck, heading for one of the local taverns.

"I imagine he shall," Eric agreed.

Washington stopped suddenly, leaning against a tree that had just sprouted soft green leaves. He turned and looked at Eric intently. "It will be war, you know."

"Yes, I think it shall."

"What will you do?"

Eric twisted his jaw, watching his own friend levelly. "I think, George, that over the years I have more than proven my loyalty to Virginia."

"Your loyalty is not in question. But you have grave interests. I've spoken with many dear friends who are planning to return to England. Fairfax and Sally . . . they are going soon. Many friends."

Eric nodded grimly. "I've spoken with a few cousins who are leaving. I've an appointment tonight with a distant Cameron relation. I'm selling him property I have in England and I'm buying up the land that he has bordering my own."

"You are lucky to be able to make such arrangements." Washington watched him intently. "What of your wife?"

Eric did not mean to stiffen so abruptly and so completely, and give away so much of himself. "I don't know what you mean," he said too quickly. Life had moved fast and furiously in the last few months. Momentous things were happening. He was caught in the wild winds of change, and he was eager to ride them. He had steered his mind from thoughts of Amanda by day, but she had haunted him every night, and along with the pain and the longing had come bitterness. He would never be able to trust her. What in God's name had she been doing, running into the night? Meeting with an influential Tory—or with a lover? Or perhaps the lover and the Tory were one and the same. His anger at her had been so great he hadn't dared to stay with her.

She had lied about the child. She had known something about the death of Damien's horse. She was betraying him with every breath she took.

"What do you mean, 'What of my wife'?" he queried coldly.

"Eric, I'm your friend. It's just that it is well known that Lady Cameron's sympathies have not changed—"

"She is suspected of something?" Eric asked flatly.

"Eric, I do not try to offend you—"

"George, you do not offend me. But Amanda is my wife. She will support me."

"But—"

"Or else," Eric said, squaring his jaw stubbornly. "I will take care of her."

"What if—"

"I will take care of her, George. You've my solemn vow on that. If it becomes necessary, I will see that she is removed."

Washington looked at him,. then sighed softly. "I pray, my friend, that you can. I for one could not. But come, let's have a drink together, while we still can. I've a feeling that things that have so far crawled will take off with a mad gallop soon."

Twenty minutes later they were all within the tavern at a table, he and George, Richard Henry Lee, Patrick Henry, and a few others. An elderly gentleman, Pierre Dupree, from north of the Richmond area, had joined them. And yet, as the men drank and laughed and teased and tried to take harbor from the growing sense of tension they themselves were creating, Eric noted that Dupree was watching him and paying little attention to the true firebrands who were the root of revolution.

Dupree, white-haired, impeccably dressed in mustard breeches and crimson coat, could down his fair share of whiskey. As the others flagged and begged leave to retire for the night, Dupree remained. Finally Washington rose, and all that remained in the dimly lit place at the table were Eric—and Dupree.

"Well, my young *ami*," Dupree murmured, "perhaps another drink?"

The candle burned low upon their table. Slumped back in his chair, Eric grinned, feeling lighter than he had for some time. "Monsieur Dupree, you have studied me so seriously. You have waited for so long. Why?"

The old man offered him a Gaelic shrug. "Curious, monsieur. And with no right to be so."

"Curious?" Surprised, Eric raised his pewter tankard and downed a long swallow of whiskey. "I admit to being baffled, monsieur. Tell me, what is it you wish to know?"

"I don't wish to offend you."

Eric smiled. "Don't offend me, sir, merely speak."

Dupree inhaled deeply. "Perhaps I can be of service to you, and that is what really draws me."

"Then I am grateful. Please, tell me what this is all about."

Dupree plunged in then, quickly and somberly, his words so soft that they did not carry in the empty room. "I understand that Amanda Sterling is now Lady Cameron."

Eric's reaction was instantaneous. Again he felt the stiffening of his muscles, the razor pain that touched him. The loneliness, the bitterness. He wanted his wife. He wanted her with him, beneath him, crying out softly in hunger and need. He wanted to strike her and walk away from her.

"She is my wife." He did not realize that his eyes had narrowed darkly, that any semblance of a smile had fled his features, that his words came out in a growl. "If you've something to say, then do so, for I tire and I lose my patience quickly!"

"It is a delicate matter—"

"Delicate be damned. If you would speak, do so. If not, leave me in peace!"

"There is a story—"

"Then tell it!"

Dupree had hesitated, but the man was no coward. He

did not balk at Eric's anger, but plunged in quickly. "Years and years ago I knew her mother."

"My wife's mother?"

"Yes. She was beautiful. So beautiful. Light and elegant, with the sun in her eyes, in her words, in her every movement. She was passion, she was energy, she was vitality! Remembering her gives me back my youth. She was so alive."

Like Amanda, Eric thought. Always the flames in her eyes, the heat in her soul, the passion for life itself.

"Go on." Again, the short words came as a growl.

Pierre Dupree moved closer. "I came to Williamsburg often in those days. I was a Frenchman born on Virginia soil, loyal to the King of England. But when I knew that Acadians were arriving in Williamsburg, desperate for homes, I had to come. I had to help those men who spoke my language. You understand?"

Eric merely nodded. Dupree went on. "I was Lenore's friend. She trusted me. She—she came to me for advice."

"About what?" Eric demanded.

"Well, she was kindness itself, you must remember. She saw the suffering; she saw the loss and confusion of the people. When the ships came laden with the exiled Acadians, Lenore demanded that her husband take some of them on. Perhaps it was not so great a kindness. I'm assuming you know Nigel Sterling."

Again Eric nodded gravely, saying nothing, giving nothing. Dupree did not need his approval. He continued. "She never should have married him. Never. Sterling was always everything pompous and cruel in a man, despite his property, despite his title, despite his claim to wealth. He coveted glory, and greater titles, at the expense of all else. He did not deserve a woman like Lenore."

"Pray, sir! The good woman is long dead and buried. And freed from Nigel Sterling. So of what do you prattle?"

"She came to me, sir, because she was going to bear a child. A child who did not belong to Nigel Sterling, but to a handsome young Frenchman. To an Acadian, that is, sir. To the man Sterling had taken on as hired help."

Eric inhaled sharply, watching the man ever more intently.

Dupree saw that his words had sunk home. "She was in love. Deeply in love. Oh, it is easy to imagine. There was Sterling, hard, unbending—cruel. And there was the handsome Frenchman with light eyes and ebony hair and the kindest touch upon her! He loved her, I am certain. Who could not love Lenore? And yet when she came to me, I saw nothing of love and everything of scandal. I told her that she must not sin again, that she must give Sterling the child as his very own son or daughter, that for her sake—and for the very life of her lover!—she must never let Sterling know." He sighed, shaking his head. "I was so very wrong! She should have fled with the Frenchman, she should have run to New Orleans with him. She might have found happiness. Instead . . ."

"Instead! What the hell happened, Dupree? Damn you, man, finish this thing now that you have started!"

"I know nothing for fact," Dupree said regretfully, looking into his whiskey. "All I know is what was whispered of the Acadians. Sterling discovered her. He damned her, he fought with her. She tumbled down the stairway and was delivered too soon of her daughter. And as she lay abed, dying, bleeding to death, he swore to her that he would kill her lover. And he promised her that he would use her daughter and see that she paid for every sin her mother had ever committed. And when Lenore lay dead at last, he found the young Frenchman and beat him to death and buried him in some unmarked grave."

"My God," Eric breathed at last. He didn't want to believe the man's words. The accusations were too horrid.

But he could not disbelieve him. He had seen Nigel Sterling with his daughter. He had seen how he had treated her.

Did that mean that he had committed murder, though? Would he sink so very low?

His heart lurched suddenly, seeming to tear, to split asunder. God! He wanted to believe in her. He wanted to love her, to give her everything. What hold did Sterling have upon her?

He wanted her. He wanted her then to hold and cradle and keep and assure. He wanted to make certain that no one could hurt her again. That Nigel Sterling could never again reach her.

He jolted up suddenly, thinking of his own man, Jacques Bisset.

Jacques—who had seen Nigel and who had flown into a raving fury, determined to kill the man. . . .

Jacques, who had been found when Eric had been just a boy. Found on the roadside, barely alive, unconscious, barely breathing. Jacques, who had never known who he was, or from where he had come. All that he had known was that he was a Frenchman. Striking, with laughing dark eyes, fine features, full, sensual lips . . .

"Her father."

"Your pardon, my lord?"

Eric shook his head vehemently. "Nothing—"

Suddenly Dupree's light eyes clouded over and he looked very grave. "Lord Cameron! You must not believe that you have been tricked or defrauded! No one knows of this . . . oh, I am so distressed now. I had not realized that you might now despise your wife for being the love child of her mother and not the legitimate issue of Lord Sterling. Oh, please, you mustn't despise her for this—"

"I assure you, sir, that I will never despise her for this." He might be furious with her for any number of other reasons, but for being Jacques's daughter rather than Sterling's, he could only applaud her.

"Sir! I brought you this secret because I owed the girl's mother. I have been plagued with guilt for years; I have worried about *la belle jeune fille,* and I beseech you—"

"And I assure you, Monsieur Dupree, that your secret about my wife's birth shall remain my secret now. I do ask your permission, though, to tell the truth to Amanda, if I ever feel that it will be to her benefit to know."

"Tell a lady that she is a love child? I cannot see where this would please one raised as she!"

"Bastard, actually," Eric suggested with a trace of humor. "Still, Monsieur Dupree, the news might please her. At some later date. If that time comes . . . ?"

Dupree lifted his hands in a typical French gesture. "S.
is your wife, Lord Cameron. You must know her very
well."

Not half as well as I would like, Eric thought. "Thank
you, *merci*," he said aloud. Dupree rose then and left him
at the round oak table. Eric downed the rest of his whiskey and sat there as the candle died, pensively watching
the dying flicker of the flame.

Then he rose quickly, called for writing materials, and
set about carefully to write to his wife.

He had not forgiven her; he did not know if he could.
But he loved her, and he wanted her. Jacques and the servants had been keeping a steady eye upon her, but she was
his responsibility. His temper had somewhat cooled. It
was time to see her again.

He never knew quite what she would do.

The convention ended on March 27; Eric had returned
to Williamsburg, where he had bade Amanda to meet him.

He did not go immediately to his town house, but
stopped by the Raleigh for ale to cool his parched throat—
and for a hot bath out in the privacy of one of the store-
rooms with only a lad who couldn't begin to comprehend
Eric's determination to totally immerse himself more than
necessary. He could have gone home and enjoyed bathing
in far more luxury, but didn't want to greet Amanda with
the dust and mud of travel upon him. There was too much
between them now, far too great a gulf. And he was far too
eager to see her.

"Damn her!" he muttered aloud, through the steaming
bath cloth that lay over his face.

"Your pardon, my lord?" the serving boy said with confusion.

He laughed softly, a dry sound, and removed the cloth.
He grinned to the boy. "Nothing, lad. Just take your time
before you marry, son, and even then, take more time!"

The boy grinned. Eric popped the cloth back upon his
face, and she was there again before him. Amanda.

Many times he lay awake at night and cursed himself.
The world was exploding, he was living in a time of dras-

revolution and change. He was central to many of the things happening, and despite that, he spent his nights and often his days in anguished thought and dream and nightmare regarding his wife. He did love her so much. And that was the rub. It was bitter, bitter gall to wonder at the emotion she bore him, to never know for certain what was hidden beneath the sweep of her lashes, within the beautiful color of her eyes. There was always that which she held away from him, always that which she seemed to deny him with thought and stoic determination. He had walked away from her in anger, but he had been the one to pay the price. Now, knowing more about her, he wanted to try to find the truth within her heart and mind once more.

And still, he reflected, there was the matter of a man's pride. He had, upon occasion, betrayed himself for her. He swore silently that he would never betray Virginia, or the colonies, or his men for her.

The steam had grown cold. He called for a towel and his clothes, dressed quickly, tipped the serving lad, and headed for the street and his horse. He was but minutes from the town house.

And when he arrived, he sat on his horse for several long moments. He wondered if she had even obeyed his summons to come here. His words had been curt, demanding her appearance. His pride had forged his words.

The moon, soft and glowing, rose high over him. The first of the spring roses were just beginning to blossom in the garden, and vines were curling around the latticed trellises upon the porch. The light of a gas lamp glowed softly from within the parlor, and suddenly, even as he watched, even as his heart and body quickened, he saw her silhouette. Slim, graceful, she moved across the room, leaving it. And then, seconds later, she was at the front door, opening it.

"Eric?"

He dismounted from his horse, patted its rump, and let the animal amble forward to graze on the small stretch of lawn before the house. The horse would make it to the stables by itself. He watched her where she stood upon the porch, awaiting him. It was spring, and a soft breeze rose, and her gown looked like spring, soft white and lace with delicate blue flowers upon it. Her hair was swept up demurely, but strands escaped it, like drifting curls of flame, touching her cheek, dusting across her shoulders. He could not see her eyes for the shadow, but he prayed that there had been a welcome in her voice.

He did not respond to her; he did not need to. The streets were lit with gas lamps and the moon itself was giving off a majestic glow. He started slowly along the path, seeking her eyes. She did not move. He came to the steps, and still she did not move, and then he stood before her, and he smelled the lush sweet scent of her hair and of her flesh. And he felt the racing tenor of her heart, saw the pulse thump erratically against her throat, and he wanted to sweep her into his arms and up the stairway right then. But then he forced himself to wonder if she trembled with pleasure at his return, or if she trembled with some secret fear or excitement due to some new espionage. Her beautiful eyes were so very wide, so anxious, almost as if she loved him, welcomed him. . . .

He allowed his eyes to travel over her and touch her, though he forced his itching fingers to remain still. "You are here," he said simply.

She stepped back, her shoulders squared, her eyes suddenly as hard as diamonds. "You commanded that I come, my lord. You commanded that I retire to Cameron Hall, and so I did. Then you commanded that I come back here, and so I have."

He caught her chin, lifting it, and his lip curled into a slow, cynical smile. "I commanded you to tell me what you did running about in the middle of the night too, and you defied me in every way imaginable."

She snatched her chin from his grip, attempting to turn about. "If you have ordered me here simply to argue—"

"I have not, madame," he said sharply, catching her arm, spinning her back about so that she faced him again. Her breasts rose provocatively with her agitation. A silken skein of hair fell like a burning cascade over her shoulder, loosened by the force of his touch. He clamped down hard upon his teeth, grateful that his breeches were tight, hating the fever that rushed through him, the desire that seemed to override both common sense and pride every time he touched her.

"Listen to me, my love!" he commanded her heatedly, coming closer against her, feeling the startling warmth of her body touch and inflame his. "There will be no argument. You're my wife. You will not disappear by night again, or by day, for that matter. There are men out there who might gladly hang you—"

"And there are men out there who might gladly hang you!" she retorted, her eyes flashing. She tugged her arm away from him. "Must we squabble in the very street?" she demanded in a tense whisper.

He laughed, startled by her hauteur. "No! By all means, let's do go in. I'd much rather squabble in our own bedchamber!"

A bright flush covered her cheeks but she did not reply to that, and he wondered if she hadn't missed him in some small way. She opened the door, entering before him. She headed for the parlor, but he caught hold of her hand, pulling her back. Her eyes came wide upon his as he indicated the stairway. "I said that I'd rather squabble within my own bedchamber. That way, madame."

She clenched her teeth. Her eyes snapped beautifully and he did not think that he could stand much more. She was going to defy him and deny him, he thought, but then she spun about in a regal fury and began to take the stairs swiftly. She burst into the bedroom. The door started to slam on him as he arrived behind her, but he caught it with his hand before it could do so and followed her in, then closing the door tightly behind him, and leaning against it. She stared at him for a moment, then spun around again to sit at her dressing table, removing the pins from her disheveled hair, brushing it with a high level of energy.

There was a sudden rapping upon the door. Eric turned impatiently and opened it. Mathilda stood there anxiously. "Oh! Lord Cameron! I hadn't realized that you had

come home. I heard the commotion and I w.
about my lady—"

"Ah, Mathilda! Thank you for your concern, but
see, it is unnecessary. I am home and all is well."

"And glad to see you, I am, my lord—"

"Thank you, Mathilda." He quickly steered her around,
away from the door. "Perhaps we'll dine later."

"Oh!" Mathilda flushed crimson, realizing that her master wanted to be alone with his wife. "Oh, of course!"

Eric closed the door once again to discover Amanda
staring at him with a flush nearly as bright as Mathilda's
and the fire of battle naked in her eyes. "How could you be
so crude!" she accused him.

"Crude? Lover, I have not yet begun."

She spun back to her mirror, and her brush tore
through her hair. "Spoken like a true patriot!" she hissed.

Swift steps brought him behind her. She leapt to her
feet, spinning about to face him. "Don't you dare come
home like a strutting cock!" she warned him, her eyes
ablaze with fury and passion. "I am tired of being ordered
about and dragged here and there at your whim. Don't
you dare touch me!"

"Dare touch you!" he exclaimed, his fingers gripping
tightly into the back of the chair she had so recently va-
cated. "Madame, I shall do far more than dare to touch
you. And if you keep up with your present attitude toward
my return, I shall be sorely tempted to deal with you as I
did when you were a child."

Her eyes widened and he could almost see her temper
soar as she remembered that time when they had first met,
when Eric had dragged her over his knee in the midst of
the fox hunt. He took a step toward her and she seized her
brush from her dressing table, hurtling it toward him.
Eric ducked just in time.

Amanda knew she had gone too far when she saw the
dark cast to his expression as his eyes met hers again. She
hadn't meant this, this awful fight, it was just that she was
always afraid, it seemed. And he goaded her so.

What she had wanted was him, but she had gone too far
now to admit that. She straightened her shoulders. She

. "Eric, let's leave this be. I've things to do, we
~own, we can talk later—"

~t want to talk, Amanda," he snapped.

~'re being crude again!" she charged him.

~nd I don't want to cool down."

"Don't you take another step toward me."

He did, and she looked quickly for a second object to
throw. She found a book set upon the chair by the fire and
hurled it so quickly that she found her mark, catching him
right in the temple.

He swore furiously. Even as she cried out, he had
grasped her wrist. "No, Eric, no!" she gasped, but he was
not to be waylaid. Within seconds he was in the chair, and
she was strung over his lap, and his palm was descending
deftly upon her posterior. Outraged, she cried out. Desperately she freed herself from his hold, falling to the floor at
his feet and staring at him with wrath nearly choking
away her words.

"Now, madame—" he began.

"You must be insane. After what you've done! This is
neither the time nor the place—"

"It is precisely the place, and the time," he stated flatly.

It was not. She was quickly on her feet. Her eyes met his
and she realized that he was still every bit as furious as she
was. She decided on a hasty retreat, streaking toward the
bedroom door. He was there beside her, slamming it
closed. She stepped quickly away as he remained there,
his back to the door. "The time, and the place, love. You'll
note, our bed lies there, my love, awaiting us."

"I've no intention of joining you in bed. No intention, do
you understand me?"

"Then the floor shall be just fine."

He was already in motion. Even as she turned to flee a
second time, his hands were upon her arm, jerking her
around and into his arms. Gasping, she tried to kick him.
She was off balance so, and he quickly swept her up, bearing her down to the floor. She found herself staring into
his eyes, startled by the depth of the passion within them.
"I have missed you deeply," he breathed to her.

"Bastard!" she snapped back with soft venom. "I will

not—" she paused, moistening her lips. "I will not love with you here on the floor." His lips were above . He smiled slowly. Her heart was thundering. He wo. surely strike her, or kiss her. He did not. Instead, he strac dled her, and began to untie the ribbons to her bodice. She lay still, feeling his fingers move upon her, knowing how deeply she had missed him.

"I think that you'll make love anywhere I demand," he said.

"Oh!" Furious, she slapped his hands away. He laughed dangerously and warned her, "Make love, my lady, or take the risk of further interrogations!"

"Eric Cameron—" she began.

But then he did kiss her, and in moments she didn't feel the floor, she felt the warmth and heat of the man and fire escalating between them. His hands were upon her, beneath her shirt and petticoats, finding naked flesh. She did not know what seized her there, she knew only that the flames of anger and passion were combining with her and that she could no longer fight him. He was quickly wedged between her thighs. His hand cupped her mound, his fingers stroked into the moist heat of her body even as his lips caught hers, searing her with another kiss. She felt him wrestle with his breeches, and then it was the steel shaft of his masculinity within her, and fevered winds quickly rose to rock the world between them. Desperately she rocked with him and clung to him, felt the pounding, pulsing rhythm, the need rising so high and sweet that it was nearly anguish. And then it burst upon her, so shattering, so strong, and filled with honeyed sweetness, that the world itself swung to darkness for long, long moments.

Then she kept her eyes closed as she tried to breathe slowly once again. She felt Eric shift from her, and she felt his eyes upon her. Then she felt his lips touching hers. Softly. So softly. She opened her eyes and met his. There was a certain sorrow within them.

He rose, lifting her up into his arms, and setting her down at the dressing table. She met his eyes in the mirror. He found her brush on the floor and stroked it through the sable strands of her hair.

y do we fight so?" he asked her.

shook her head, unable to answer.

et me be tender," he whispered softly.

He was going to make love to her again, she realized.

And she wanted him to do so. She still hungered for him. Hungered for him greatly.

He stroked his knuckles over her cheeks, then over her shoulders where they were bared. So gently now. His fingers stroked softly lower to the ribbons of her bodice, and those he finished untying. He slipped the straps of her shift from her shoulders, and pressed down upon the mounds of cotton and muslin until the gown and garment fell to her waist, baring her breasts to him in the mirror. She did not move, but continued to meet his gaze. His fingers closed over her breasts, molding them, cupping them. Then he flicked his thumbs upon her nipples, stroked around the aureoles, and delicately, softly, caressed the pebbled crests again. She moaned low and softly and with just a touch of desperation. Her eyes closed at last and her head fell back against his torso. And still, he saw, in the shimmering image of the mirror, the beauty of her. The fullness, the lushness of her breasts beneath his hands, the ivory gleam and perfection of her flesh, the startling fall of her hair against the slender column of her throat. He bent down, finding her lips, and kissed her. She tasted of everything sweet and intoxicating in life. Her lips trembled beneath his and parted.

He straightened and came around before her upon one knee. Her eyes wide and dilated, she looked down upon him.

"I'll never ask you again where you went from the town house, Amanda," he told her. "But I'll never let you leave again. Do you understand me?" She nodded very slowly. Something about the way she looked at him swept the last of the anger from his being. He cried out in sudden frustration, rose, and pulled her to her feet against him. "You needn't fear him, Amanda, do you understand me? You needn't fear Nigel Sterling!"

Dismay filled her eyes. Her head fell back. Eric rushed on. "Dammit, don't you understand me? You can never go to him again, never go near Tarryton again, or I shall ▪ forced to kill one of them, can't you understand that. Amanda! I am your husband, I will protect you. You needn't fear Sterling or Tarryton!"

A soft sob escaped her and she tried to bury her face against him, but he could not allow her to do so. He caught her shoulders and shook her slightly. "Do you understand me, Amanda?"

"Yes! Yes!" she cried out, and tried to jerk free. He held her tight and his lips descended upon hers. They were bruising and forceful and even cruel to hold on to hers . . . but then she went still in his arms, soft and warm and giving, and his tongue bathed her mouth where he had offered force, and his lips became gentle and coercive, and then so soft that she was hungrily pressing against him for more.

And her fingers were upon his frock coat, shoving it from his shoulders. And soft and subtle, they were upon the buttons of his shirt, and then the stroke of her nails was delicate and exquisite upon his naked flesh.

He brought his hands against her flesh, shoving her gown and garments to the floor. He plucked her up and lay her upon the bed in her stockings and garters. She watched him in the soft candle glow as he divested himself of his clothing. When he came down beside her, she wrapped him in her arms.

They made love slowly that second time. So slowly. Exchanging sultry kisses and soft caresses, and then urgent whispers. She made love to him sweetly, and more savagely, and Eric reveled in her every touch. Desire, volatile and explosive, rose high within him. He thrust into her with his very being, so it seemed.

It was exquisite, it was a tempest. It drew everything from him and returned everything to him. But when it was over and he held her naked form close to him while the candle upon the dressing table faded out, he again decried himself for loving her so deeply. No matter how sweetly, how wantonly she made love to him, she held something back. He had yet to touch her soul.

Yet to touch the truth.

he moved slightly against him. He held her closer. "Are
ou cold?"

"No."

"Hungry?"

"No," she replied again.

He rose slightly upon an elbow, enjoying the beautiful
slope and angle and shadow of her back and derriere in
the near-total darkness.

He watched her in the darkness, then came back beside
her. Her eyes were more than half closed as exhaustion
claimed her. He softly stroked the flesh of her arm, then
lay down beside her again and very gently took her into
his arms. He wanted to apologize again; he could not. He
held her for a long while, then whispered to her softly,
"Amanda, trust in me. Dear God, trust in me, please."

She did not reply. He didn't know if she truly slept, or if
she simply didn't have an answer for him.

In the days that followed Eric gave Amanda news about
the convention, warning her that the time was coming
close when they might be facing armed conflict. A summons came from the governor, which Eric quickly answered. Lord Dunmore was fuming. He had been furious
that he had been ignored when he had issued a proclama-
tion that all magistrates—and others—should use their utmost endeavors to prevent the election of delegates to the
Second Continental Congress.

Amanda was sure that Dunmore would be furious with
Eric, but he did not balk from the summons. What went
on in the interview, she did not know, but she was certain
that the total rift between them was begun that day.

When he returned to the town house, she ran down the
stairs to the parlor to meet him. "What happened?" she
asked anxiously.

He set his gloves and plumed tricorn upon the table, and
looked her way. "It will come to war, Amanda. I wonder,
will you be with me, or against me?"

"I—I can't deny my loyalties!" she told him, begging him
with her eyes to understand. She was grasping at straws,
she thought. He had caught her slipping from the house.

He knew that she had lied about thinking she might be with child.

She had betrayed him, and he knew it, and he would not trust her, or love her, again.

He nodded, looking at her, looking past her. "Let your heart lie where it will. But follow my commands, my love!" he warned softly.

She did not answer, but fled up the stairs.

Several nights later, just as dawn came on April 20, Amanda lay beside him, naked, content, secure within his arms. She had not known until he had returned just how bitterly she had missed him. She loved just being held, just sleeping with the fall of his bronze arm upon her. She liked to awaken and see the angle of his jaw; she thrilled to the striking planes of his face, to the crisp mat of dark hair upon his chest, to the rugged texture of his hard-muscled and masculine thighs entangled with her own.

Shouts in the street suddenly startled her. She started to rise, half asleep, confused. Beside her, Eric bolted up and strode quickly to the window.

"What is it?" she asked.

"I don't know. A crowd. A huge crowd." He found his breeches and stumbled into them. He threw open the window and shouted down to the street. "My good man! What goes on down there."

"The powder! The arms. The bloody redcoats marines came in off the *Fowey* in the James and stole our supplies from the magazine! We're not a-goin' to take it, Lord Cameron! We can't!"

"Son of a bitch!" Eric muttered. He grabbed his shirt and boots. Clutching the sheet, Amanda stared at him.

"They'll march on the palace!" she said.

He cast her a quick glance. "Bloodshed here and now must be avoided!" he said, but she didn't think that he was really talking to her, but rather thinking aloud. He reached for his frock coat and she leapt from the bed at last.

"Eric—"

"Amanda, go back to sleep."

"Go back to sleep!" she wailed, but he was already leaving her, closing the door behind him.

She watched him go, then quickly dressed and followed him out.

When she left the house, she knew that she was followed. Jacques Bisset had followed her every move since Eric had left her in January. She didn't mind. She was fascinated by the man, and she always felt safe with him behind her.

And she'd had no more demands from her father since she had given him the map.

It was not difficult to follow Eric. The roar and pulse of the crowd could be heard and felt from afar. Amanda hurried toward the Capitol. It seemed that the whole population of Williamsburg had turned out in a fury.

Someone shouted, "To the palace!"

Stepping back against a building, Amanda inhaled sharply. The cry was going up on the air. The mob seemed to seethe, the people within it angry, impassioned, ugly in their reckless force.

"Stop, stop!" a voice called out.

Amanda climbed upon shop steps to see. It was Peyton Randolph. Carter Nicholas was at his side, Eric was behind him.

The noise from the crowd dimmed. Randolph began to speak, advising the people that they might defeat their own purpose. They needed to issue a protest drafted in the Common Hall.

Carter Nicholas echoed the warnings, and then Eric spoke, urging everyone to caution.

Slowly the crowd dispersed.

Jostled in the sudden stream of humanity, Amanda was startled when she was suddenly clutched from behind and turned around to meet her husband's angry eyes. "I told you to go back to sleep!"

"But, Eric—"

"Damn you, Amanda, I am trying to avoid the shedding of your dear Tory Dunmore's blood. Jacques is taking you back to Cameron Hall. Today. I want you out of this!"

She tried to protest, he wasn't about to allow it.
And by noon she was on her way home.

News trickled to her slowly at Cameron Hall. She listened avidly to the servants, and she eagerly awaited the news in the *Virginia Gazette*.

The people drafted a demand to know why the governor had taken their weapons. Dunmore replied that he had been concerned about a slave insurrection and had removed the powder for safety's sake.

Eric arrived exhausted one evening to tell her that meetings had been taking place elsewhere. Randolph and Nicholas had managed to keep the people of Williamsburg under control, but the people of Caroline County had authorized the release of gunpowder to the volunteers gathered at Bowling Green. Edmund Pendleton, however, chairman of that committee, would not allow action until he heard from Peyton Randolph.

Fourteen companies of light horse had gathered in Fredericksburg, and they were ready to ride on the capital. On April 28 the reply from Randolph reached those ready to fight—he requested caution. While there was any hope of reconciliation, it was necessary to avoid violence.

The people had ridden home. The message had been tactfully written, and men such as the Long Knives were quieted.

"Thank God!" Sitting in the elegant parlor at Cameron Hall, Amanda turned anguished eyes on her husband and fervently whispered the sentiment.

Eric, worn and dusty from riding, stared at her with a curious look in his eyes.

"There is more," he told her.

She rose, her hands clenched in her lap. "What? You—you've been in Fredericksburg. You would have ridden on the capital!"

He did not answer the question. "Amanda, shots were fired in Massachusetts. At Lexington and at Concord. The British went after the arms stored there, and the colonists—the 'minutemen'—fought them every step of the way back to Boston."

"Oh, no!" So blood had been shed after all, not in Virginia, but in Massachusetts.

"Patrick Henry marched with forces toward Williamsburg, but Dunmore added sailors and marines to the palace, and dragged cannon out upon the lawn. An emissary came out on May second to pay for the powder that had been taken."

"You were with Patrick Henry!" she gasped.

"I was a messenger, Amanda—"

"How could you—"

"I can caution reason on both sides, my lady!" he snapped, and she fell silent.

"That is not all."

She stared at him, extremely worried by his tone of voice.

"Amanda, Patrick Henry has been branded a rebel." He hesitated briefly. "And so have I," he continued very quietly. "I suspect that within a number of days there might well be an arrest warrant out for me."

"Oh, no!" Amanda gasped. She stared at him, her husband, tall, dark, striking and ever commanding, and in that moment she didn't care about the world. England could rot, and Virginia could melt into the sea, she did not care. "Oh, Eric!" she cried his name, and flew across the room, hurtling herself against him. He caught her in his arms and held her tight.

There were no more words between them. He carried her upstairs, and he made love to her gently and with tenderness. With that same tenderness he held her against the night, brushing a kiss against her forehead as the dawn broke.

His eyes were dark and serious as they searched hers. He lay half atop her, smoothing her hair from her forehead.

"Men are already beginning to return to England. Loyalists who believe that this breech cannot possibly be closed again. I ask you, Amanda, do you stay with me of your own accord?"

"Yes! Yes!" she told him, burying her face against his throat. "Yes, I will stay with you."

He held her in silence. "Do you stay for me, or for England?"

"What?"

He shook his head. "Never mind. I am a man labeled rebel for a moment, not that I think that Dunmore has the power to do anything about it. There are very long days ahead of us." He was silent again. "Long years," he whispered. "Come, love. A rebel dare not lie about too long. I've much I would get done about here in case—"

"In case?" she demanded anxiously.

His eyes found hers again. "In case I should have to leave quickly."

XIII ❧

By the end of the week, Eric and Amanda stood on the dock and waved good-bye as some of their friends and neighbors—some of them bearing the Cameron name—set sail for England. Amanda cried softly, but though Eric said nothing, he felt the sense of loss keenly himself.

He did not have to worry about Governor Dunmore's branding of him as a rebel. Dunmore had fled the governor's palace and was trying to administer the government of Virginia from the decks of the naval ship *Fowey*, out in the James River.

Lord Tarryton, Anne, and their newborn daughter went with him. Amanda heard nothing from her father, and so she assumed that he, too, had fled.

Amanda worried endlessly, because Eric discovered that Damien was in Massachusetts, and he had been there at Concord and at Lexington. The Massachusetts men had played a cunning game with the British. In Boston, they had arranged a signal to warn the people when the British tried to come inland to seize their arms. Lanterns were hung in the Old North Church:— "one if by land, two if by sea." The printer Paul Revere had ridden hard into the night to give the warning. Midway through the journey, he had been stopped by soldiers, but the cry was taken up by a friend and the men were forewarned. Shots were fired on April 19, 1775, and many felt the revolution was thus engaged.

In the days that followed, Eric was seldom with Amanda. He had been asked to raise militia troops, and he was doing so. News trickled back to the colonials from Philadelphia where the Continental Congress sat. George Washington had been appointed general of the Continental forces, and he had been sent to Massachusetts to take charge of the American troops surrounding the city of Boston. It was rumored that British troops were about to march on New York City. Most members of Congress had been escorted by large parties of armed men—to protect them from the possibility of arrest. Ethan Allen, commissioned by Connecticut, and Benedict Arnold, authorized by Massachusetts, had marched on Fort Ticonderoga. The British garrison, caught by surprise, had capitulated immediately. Congress had been elated to hear tales that the Brits had been so surprised that they had not had time to don their breeches.

The fort was very important, Eric explained to Amanda, because it commanded the gateway from Canada. It was vital to the control of Lake Champlain and Lake George, principal routes to the thirteen colonies.

In June a battle was fought at Bunker Hill. The people were vastly cheered, it was rumored, because the colonial forces had met the British—and they had held their own. Defeated only because they had run out of ammunition, they had fought bravely and gallantly, even if they were rough and ragtag.

On July 3, on Cambridge Common, George Washington took command of the forces, and the Continental Army was born.

By the end of August Virginia's leaders had returned

from Philadelphia. Patrick Henry appeared at Cameron Hall, and when Amanda saw him, she knew that things had really come to a head. Henry had been commissioned the colonel of the of the first Virginia regiment, and as such, he was commander-in-chief of the colony's forces.

He met with Eric alone in the parlor. When Amanda saw him leave the house, she tore down the stairs. She found Eric standing before the fire, his hands folded behind his back, his expression grave as he watched the flames.

He did not turn around, but he knew that she was there. "George has asked that I come to Boston. Congress has offered me a commission, and I am afraid that I must go."

No . . .

The word formed in her heart but did not come to Amanda's lips. He was going to accept the commission and go, and she knew it.

She turned around and fled up the stairway, then threw herself on the bed. She didn't want him to go. She was afraid as she had never been afraid before.

She had not realized that he had followed her until she felt his hands upon her shoulders, turning her to him. He touched the dampness that lay upon her cheek, and he rubbed his finger and thumb together, as if awed by the feel of her tears.

"Can this be for me?" he asked her.

"Oh, stop it, Eric! Please, for the love of God!" she begged him.

He smiled, handsomely, ruefully, and he lay beside her, wrapping her within his arms.

"Perhaps I shall not be gone so very long," he told her.

She inhaled and exhaled in a shudder against his chest, breathing in his scent, feeling the rough texture of his shirt against her cheeks. She hated it when he was gone. She had yet to learn to tell him of her feelings, she could only show them, letting the fires rise and the passion ignite between them. But not even the intensity of that heat had dissolved the barriers that had lain between them since he had caught her returning to the town house that night in Williamsburg. She did not have his trust. She felt him watch her often, and she knew that he wondered just how seriously she had betrayed him in the past and just how far she might go in the future. She could not let down the wall of her pride and beg him to forgive—it would do no good, she knew. He would still look at her the same way. And yet, when they were together at Cameron Hall, life was good, despite the tempest of the world. There was planting to be done, meat to be smoked, a household and estate to run. There were intimate dinners together, evenings when she sat quietly with a book or embroidery while he pored over maps and his correspondence. There were times when he talked to her, when his eyes glowed so fiercely and his words came so eloquently that she was nearly swept into the storm of revolution herself.

And yet she had not lied to him, ever. Her loyalty had always lain with the Crown. She had never wanted to betray him, and she did not want to turn from him now. She was afraid for him. Dunmore might be attempting to rule from a ship now, but the British fighting force was considered the finest in the world. More troops would arrive. They would cut down the men outside Boston, they would take New York.

"They will hang you if they get their hands upon you!" she told him, swallowing back a sob.

He shrugged. "They must get their hands upon me first, you know." He stroked her cheek and her throat. "There are some, you know, my love, who think that—were you a man—you might be a prime prospect for a hanging yourself."

She said nothing, aware that she was safe among any of the rebels because of their respect for Eric. Suddenly she felt a rise of chills, wondering what might become of her if he ever withdrew his protection.

"Aren't you ever afraid?" she whispered.

"I am more afraid of leaving you than I am of arriving at a battlefront," he told her. But he was smiling, and his smile seemed tender. She thought that in that moment, he believed in her. Perhaps he even loved her.

She searched out his eyes anxiously. "You mustn't worry

about me at all. You must give all of your attention to staying alive!"

He laughed softly, ruffling her hair, catching a long strand between his fingers. "One might almost think that you care," he said.

She could not answer him. She wrapped her arms around him, and kissed him, teasing his lips with her tongue, taking his into her mouth, touching him again provocatively with her own. A soft low groan escaped him, and he rose, meeting her eyes, his own afire. "This is what it should be, always then. There's so little time. So let's be decadent with it, my love. Let's stay here, locked within our tower, and die *la petite mort* again and again in one another's arms."

She smiled, arrested and aroused by his charm. Then they both started at some sound by the door. Eric frowned and rose, and strode quickly to the door, throwing it open.

There was no one there. He closed the door and slid the bolt. Then he turned to her. He pulled his shirt from his breeches, slowly unbuttoned the buttons, and cast the white-laced garment to the floor. Propped on an elbow, Amanda watched him. Eric pulled off a boot, then another, then faced her, his hands on his hips. "Well, wife, you could be accommodating me, you know."

She laughed, so pained that he was leaving, so determined to hold tight to the moments they had left. Her lashes fell in a sultry crescent over her cheeks and she stared at him with lazy sensuality. "My dear lord Cameron, but I am too thoroughly enjoying this curious show! Why, 'tis scarce midday, and you seem to think—" She broke off, gasping, for he had taken a smooth running leap onto the bed, pinning her down with a mock growl.

"Conniving wench!" he accused her. His fingers curled into hers, his lips locked upon them. When the kiss was ended she no longer felt like laughing, but met his eyes with the hunger and the wonder fierce within her own. He rolled to shed his breeches, her gown was quickly cast aside, and they were then upon their knees together, eyes still meeting, a leisure seizing them again. They stroked one another softly, their knuckles upon naked flesh, running the gamut from shoulders to thighs. It was she who cried out first, and he who swept her down. But the day was long, and there was not to be a minute of it in which they were not touching in some manner. Hunger seized them, slow, sweet need. They each teased and taunted with lazy abandon, and each was caught in the tempest when the taunt and fever swept from one form to the other.

Morning did come. Amanda awoke to find her husband's eyes upon her. For a moment she thought that she saw an anguish in their depths, but then the look was gone, and he was nothing but very grave as he stared at her. He touched her cheek and warned her, "Amanda, take care in my absence. Do not betray me again. Betray not the heart, my love. For I could not forgive you again."

She pulled the covers closely about her. "How would I betray you!" she cried. "Patriots hold Virginia now!"

"But Governor Dunmore is in a ship out upon the James, not so very far at all, my love. Not so very far." He sighed, curling a lock of her hair with his finger. "Amanda, I have claimed that I am your husband, that you will go where I beckon. But I am telling you now, if you would leave me, do so. Do so now with my blessing. I can set you on a ship out to meet the governor today, before I ride myself."

"No!" she cried quickly.

"Can this mean that you have taken on the patriots' cause?" he asked her.

She colored and shook her head. "No, Eric. I cannot lie to you. But . . . neither would I leave you."

"Then dare I take this to mean that you offer me some small affection at last?"

She cast him a quick glance and she thought that he teased her, his eyes seemed so aflame with mischief. She flushed furiously. "You know that I . . ."

"Mmm," he murmured, and it sounded hard. "I know that you are probably glad to be with me—the rebel— rather than within your father's care. I can hardly take that as a compliment, madame."

"Eric, my God, don't be so cruel at a time such as this—"

"I am sorry, love. Truly, I am sorry," he muttered. She seemed so earnest. Her hair spilled in a rich river of dark flame all about her. The white sheet was pulled high upon her breast and the eyes that beheld his were dazzling with emotion, perhaps even the promise of tears.

He pulled the sheet from her and crawled over her. "One more time, my love. Pour yourself upon me, let your sweetness seep into me, one more time. For the cold northern nights ahead, breathe fire into my soul. Wife, give yourself to me."

Her arms wrapped around him. She gave herself to him as she never had before, and indeed, he felt as if he left something of himself within her, and took from her a flame, a light, that might rise in memory to still the tremors of many a night ahead.

And yet that, too, came to an end, and he was forced to realize that he must rise.

She remained abed, cocooned within the covers, as he called for a bath. When he was done, she bathed herself, and then she helped him to dress. She helped to buckle his scabbard, and when that was done she closed his heavy cloak warmly about him. He caught her to him, and as the seconds ticked by he pressed his lips to her forehead.

Then he broke away and left the room. She followed him slowly down the stairs and out to the porch where he was mounting his horse, a party of five of his volunteers ready to accompany him. She offered him the stirrup cup.

"Will you pray for me?" he asked her curiously.

"Yes, with every fiber of my being!" she whispered.

He smiled. "I will find Damien for you. And I will correspond as regularly as I can. Take care, my love," he told her. He bent and kissed her. She closed her eyes and felt his lips upon her own, and then she felt the coldness when his touch was gone.

At last he rode away, and she stood on the porch and waved until she could see him no more. Then she turned and fled up the stairs and back to her room.

But the room, too, had grown cold. She started to cry, and then she found that she was besieged by sobs. They seemed to go on and on forever. But then her tears dried, and she told herself with annoyance that she must pull herself together. Her fears were irrational. Eric would come home, and nothing would go wrong. They would ride out the storm; they would survive.

He would come home . . .

And when he did, she would find a way to earn his trust again. She would find a way to tell him that she loved him.

Eric had been gone two weeks when Cassidy came to her in the parlor to tell her that she had a visitor. Cassidy's manner made her frown and demand, "Who is it?"

He bowed to her deeply. "Your father, my lady."

"My father!" Stunned, she stood, knocking over the inkwell she had been using as she worked on household accounts. Neither she nor Cassidy really noted the spill of ink.

"Has he come—alone?" she asked. The coast was dangerous for Nigel Sterling now. He had been out on the river, the last she heard, with Lord Dunmore—and Robert Tarryton.

"His ship rests at the Cameron docks. A warship."

She understood why Sterling hadn't been molested upon his arrival. Biting nervously into her lower lip, she shrugged and sank slowly back to her chair. She had no choice but to see her father. She wondered if Cassidy realized it.

"Show him in," she told Cassidy.

He cast her a quick, condemning glance. He didn't understand.

Anger rose quickly within her. Couldn't Cassidy, and the others, understand that she simply wanted to save the house?

They hadn't managed to fight Sterling and his warship!

She wasn't going to beg Cassidy to believe in her or understand her. She stared at him and waited. He turned sharply on his heel and left the room. A few moments later her father entered. He came into the room alone, but even as he stepped in, she heard a commotion beyond the windows. Amanda hurried to one of the windows and

looked out. A troop of royal navy men were assen.
the yard.

She turned around to stare at her father.

"What are you doing here?"

"Ever the princess, eh, daughter? The supreme lady. Nc
'Welcome, Father,' or 'How are you, Father?' but 'What are
you doing here!' Well, your highness, first I shall have
some of your husband's fine brandy." He walked to a cherrywood table to help himself from the decanter. Then he
sat comfortably across the desk from her. "I want more
information."

"You must be mad—"

"I could burn this place to the ground."

"Burn it!"

"Your husband's precious Cameron Hall?" Sterling
taunted.

"He'd rather that it burned than that I give anything to
you."

"Why, daughter! You've fallen in love with the rogue."
Sterling set his glass sharply upon the desk, eyeing her
more closely. "Then let's up the stakes here, Highness. I
have Damien. I'll torture him slowly before I slit his throat
if you don't cooperate."

She felt the blood rush from her face. The pounding of
her heart became so loud that it seemed to engulf her.
"You're lying," she accused him. But it had to be true. It
had been so long since she had heard from her cousin.

Sterling sat back confidently. "The fool boy was in Massachusetts, harrying the soldiers straight back into the city
of Boston. He was captured—he was recognized as kin of
mine. Out of consideration for my service to the Crown,
the officer in charge thought that the dear boy—my kin,
you realize—should be given over to me. I greeted him
like a long-lost brother—before tossing him into the brig."
Sterling stared at her, smiling, for a long while.

"How—how do I know that you really have him?"
Amanda managed to ask at last.

Sterling tossed her a small signet ring across the desk.
She picked it up and pretended to study it, but she knew
the ring. And she knew her father.

do you want out of me?" she demanded harshly.
rmation. About troop movements. About arms."
at I don't know—"

You could find out. Go into Williamsburg. Sit about the
averns. Listen. Write to your dear husband, and bring me
his letters."

"You're a fool, Father. Even if I wanted to spy for you, I
could not. The servants suspect me to begin with. They
follow me everywhere."

"Then you had best become very clever. And you
needn't worry. I will find you. Or Robert will find you."

"Robert!"

"Yes, he's with me, of course. He's very anxious to see
you. The duchess has returned to England with her child,
and he is a lonely man. Anxious for a tender mistress."

"You are disgusting. You thrust me to my husband
against my will, and now you would cast me—despising
him!—back to Robert. What manner of monster are you,
Father?"

He rose, his smile never faltering. "Highness, I would
hand you over to all the troops from England and beyond,
and gladly."

She stood, wishing she dared to spit in his face. "When
do I get Damien?"

"You don't get him! You merely keep him alive."

"No! That is no bargain. I will not be blackmailed forever."

"Why, daughter! I thought that you were loyal to the
Crown!"

"I am! I was! I can no longer betray my husband—"

"Your husband!" Sterling laughed, then shook his head.
"Why, daughter, you are a whore. Just like your dear
mother. Lord Cameron keeps you pleased 'twixt the
thighs, and so you would suddenly be loyal to a new
cause!"

She slapped him as hard as she could. He sobered
quickly, catching her wrist, squeezing it hard. "Pray that if
your fine, rebel-stud Cameron catches you at this, daughter, I will take you away. Despise Tarryton if you would

now, Amanda, but you'd be better off in his hands than in Cameron's once he discovers you!"

She jerked her hand free. "If I ever leave Virginia, I will go to Dunmore—"

He knew that she would do anything to save Damien. "Daughter—Highness!—I shall see you again soon. Very soon."

He smiled, and turned around and left her. She heard new orders shouted outside, and the sounds of the men and their armament as they marched back down to the docks. Amanda sank back into her chair and she closed her eyes. She didn't hear the door open, but she sensed that she wasn't alone. She opened her eyes and discovered that Cassidy was standing before her. Pierre, Richard, Margaret, and Remy all stood silently behind him.

"What?" Amanda cried, startled and alarmed. They stared at her so accusingly!

"They left," Cassidy said. "They didn't burn us or threaten us."

"Of—of course," Amanda said. She let her face fall into her hands. "It was my father. He—he just wanted to see if I wanted to leave with him, that is all."

Five pairs of eyes stared at her. She didn't like the defiance in young Margaret's. Or was she imagining the look? The blue-eyed, dark-haired Irish maid looked as if she were about to pick up a musket and go to war herself. And Remy, older, dark as the satin night, with Cameron Hall as long as anyone could remember, staring at her with such naked suspicion!

She wanted to scream at them all. She was mistress here in Eric's absence. They were the servants!

But they were right. She was about to betray them all.

"Have you all nothing to do!" she charged them wearily. "If you are at leisure, I am not. I have accounts!"

Slowly their lashes flickered downward. One by one they turned to leave her. When the door closed, she rested her face on her arms and damned her cousin Damien a thousand times over. She damned him for being a patriot, then she damned him for being brave, for being a fool— and then she damned him for being the one person who had always loved her unquestioningly and who had made her love him so fiercely in return.

Then her heart began to thunder anew, and she wondered what she could discover that she could give to her father that would cause the least peril among all men, the patriots and the redcoats.

And to her husband.

Perched atop Joshua on the heights overlooking the city of Boston, Eric was cold, bitterly cold. It was winter, and there was a very sharp bite to the wind, a dampness that seemed to sink into the bones and settle there.

Sieges were long and tedious, but Eric had come to admire the men of New England who ringed the city. They had already met the gunfire and the bloodshed of the war, but they held strong, despite the hardships, the cold, the monotony. It had been feared by some that the northern men might not take to the idea of their commander being a Virginian, a southerner, but not many people had questioned his military experience, and it seemed now that the colonies had really banded together at last to stand against a common tyranny.

"Major Lord Cameron!"

Eric turned, lifting a hand in a salute and smiling as he saw Frederick Bartholomew hurrying toward him. The young printer had come a long way since the day he had run through the streets, wounded and desperate. He had been commissioned a lieutenant. Just as Washington had found certain men indispensable to him, Eric had discovered quickly that Frederick was a man he could not do without. Though the siege itself was tedious, military life was often hectic for him. There were the endless meetings with Washington and Hamilton and the others, the continuous necessity of communications, the need to gather information about his ships, and his desperate need to know at all times what was happening in his native Virginia.

Frederick waved an envelope in his hand. "A letter from your wife, my lord!"

Eric leapt off Joshua's back, grinning good-naturedly as a chant went up from the men ringed about him. "Thank you, Frederick," he told the young printer, taking the letter. He didn't mind the camaraderie of the men, but he did want to be alone with the correspondence.

His nights were miserable. He lay awake and worried, and he slept and dreamed. He dreamed of Amanda with her fiery hair wrapped about his flesh, her eyes liquid as they met his, her kiss a fountain of warmth that aroused and enwrapped him. But then his dreams would fade and he would hold her no more, she would be dancing away in the arms of another man, and her eyes would catch his again, and the laughter within them would tell him clearly that she had played him for a fool all along.

Eric led Joshua away from the siege line, back to an empty supply tent. He sat at the planked table there with his back against the canvas and ripped open the letter. His heart quickened as she wrote that her father had come to Cameron Hall with a warship, but that he had simply left and gone back to join Dunmore when she had told him that she was going to stay.

Her letter went on, but she wrote no more of her father. Instead she wrote about the military state of Virginia, the fish being brought in and the smoking going on, about the repairs done to the mansion, about the cold. It could have been a warm letter. Yet it was stilted somehow, as if there were something she wasn't saying.

As if she were lying to him . . .

Eric cursed softly. If only he could trust her!

"Trouble, my friend?"

He started, looking to the entrance to the tent. George Washington had come upon him. As he entered the tent, he swept off his plumed and cockaded hat and dusted the snow from his cloak. Then he sat across from Eric. Alone together, neither man bothered with military protocol.

"You've a letter, I understand."

"A personal letter."

George hesitated. "There's a rumor, Eric, that someone in Virginia is supplying the British with helpful information. Areas to raid for salt and produce. Information that has helped Dunmore create such fear all along the coast."

Eric shrugged. "We all know of his burning Norfolk. That could not possibly have been caused by a spy!"

Washington was quiet for a long time. Then he leaned across the desk. "I trust your judgment, my friend. I trust your judgment."

He left without saying any more. Eric sat back, then rose and called for Frederick. He asked for writing supplies to form his reply to his wife. When the printer returned, Eric sat to his task.

He closed his eyes for a moment, shivering. He had wanted her to come to Boston for Christmas. Washington, however, had specifically requested that he not do so, promising that he could return home in the spring.

Eric exhaled, then he began to write. Very carefully. False information that might look like it could be invaluable to the British.

He finished the letter and sealed it with his signet. Then he called to Frederick again to see that his correspondence moved south as quickly as possible.

When the letter was gone he stared out at the snows of winter, feeling as if they swirled about his heart and soul. "Damn you, Amanda!" he said softly.

As soon as winter turned to spring, Amanda decided on another trip into Williamsburg. She announced her intentions to travel with just Pierre and Danielle, but when she came downstairs on the morning when she was to leave, she wasn't surprised to discover that Jacques Bisset was dressed and mounted and ready to ride behind her coach.

"Jacques! I did not ask you to accompany me," she told him.

He looked at her strangely, and replied as he had every time Amanda had left Cameron Hall after Eric had departed in the fall. "*Pardonnez-moi,* but Lord Cameron has charged me to guard you, and that I will."

To guard her. It was a lie. He was to watch her and discover if she betrayed her husband or his cause, Amanda knew. It didn't matter. There was really no way for him to discover anything of what she was doing, and she liked Jacques, liked him very much. She nodded slowly. "Fine," she said softly. "I will feel ever so much safer if you are along."

Danielle stepped into the coach and sat across from her. Amanda smiled wearily. The coach jolted, and they were on their way. The road was slushy with spring rains, and the day was still chill. Amanda shivered again as she looked out the window, back to the house.

She loved Cameron Hall even more fiercely than Eric, she thought, for she spent so much time there. Her portrait and his had now joined the others in the gallery. It was her home.

"You're thinking that you should take care, eh?" Danielle questioned her.

Amanda cast her a quick glance. "Danielle, I do not know what you're talking about."

Danielle exhaled impatiently. Amanda ignored her. She swallowed tightly, closing her eyes. It seemed that so very much distance lay between her and Eric now. Miles . . . and time. She had missed him so much when he had first gone. In the days that followed, she had tossed and turned through the cold lonely nights. But then her father had come, over six months ago now, it was then that the distance had settled in, then that she had grown cold, then that she had begun to feel that things were so very horrible they might never be righted.

Amanda opened her eyes and saw that Danielle was still staring at her reproachfully. The Acadian woman started to speak.

"I'm very tired," Amanda said quietly, and the other woman remained silent. Leaning back against the coach, Amanda realized that she was very afraid of Eric now. She would never be able to make him understand. She wasn't always sure she understood herself. In her desire to give information that would keep Damien alive and avoid bloodshed at the same time, she had resorted to using information from Eric's letters to her. Small things. Casual paragraphs on supplies of salt, herbs, fruits that the navy needed to avoid the plaguing diseases on the ships. She had only discovered major troop movements once, and then, it seemed, her information coincided with something the governor had learned himself. She tried not to think about battles, but she knew that it was war. Men were going to die.

Eric would never forgive her.

Somewhere during the journey she must have slept. She awoke to discover that they had come to the town house, that it was night. The door to the coach opened, starting her awake.

"We're here, Amanda," Danielle said to her.

Amanda hurried toward the house. She walked up the steps, pulling off her gloves, calling to the housekeeper at the same time. "Mathilda, I've come!" She twisted the knob, found that the door was open, and walked on into the house. "Mathilda!" she called again, walking on through to the parlor. She tossed her gloves absently upon the desk, thinking idly of that first night here when she had begun her game of chess with Eric. He had been right. She had been in check all the time.

A sound suddenly startled her and she looked across the room. Her heart leapt to her throat and caught there, and she had to clutch the desk to steady herself.

Eric was there, an elbow leaned upon the mantel, a snifter of brandy in his hand. He looked wonderful in his tight white breeches, deep-blue frock coat, white laced shirt, and high boots, his lips curved in a slowly lazy smile as she realized his presence at last.

"Eric!" Her hand fluttered to her throat.

"Amanda!" He tossed his snifter into the fire, heedless of the cracking of the glass, of the hiss and steam and ripple as the alcohol sent the flames rising high. In seconds he was across the room, and she was in his arms. In seconds she was achingly aware of him, of the scent of him, of the texture of his face, the ripple of his muscles, the rough feel of his fabric, the intoxicating feel of his lips. She felt as if she were sinking into clouds, rising into acres of heaven. It had been so long since he had touched her. . . .

She was going to fall. It didn't matter. Not at that moment. He was kissing too hungrily. When her trembling caused her to slip, he lifted her into his arms. Then she forgot her fears again as his fingers moved through her

hair, and she found a simple fascination in the way
sprang beneath her fingers. She was barely aware
they moved upstairs, she was desperate to touch more
him, to feel more of his kiss. And then, in the darkness
there was nothing but the feel and the warmth and the sex
of the man, and the throbbing pulse of an ancient music,
wrapping them in a world where words meant nothing.
She tried to speak, whispering his name with wonder. She
didn't know how he was there, but he was, glistening muscle rippling beneath her fingers, his lips feverishly upon
her, upon her body, upon her breasts. The night seemed to
come alive with the ragged harmony of their heartbeats,
with the pulse that pounded between them, with the fever
and flames that leapt and crackled and caused beautiful
colors to explode even within the darkness. . . .

The night . . .

It remained alive with the beauty, and the hunger, and
when passion was sated, it was still not time for words, for
they needed just to touch, to hold one another, to relish
something that had become exceedingly precious just to
be wrenched away.

It was morning before they talked. Before Amanda worried again. Before Eric was able to explain his presence.
He was still in bed, leaning against the frame, his fingers
laced behind his head. Amanda had risen at last and sat
before the dressing table, trying to detangle the wild mass
of her hair.

"It ended. The siege ended. St. Patrick's Day brought an
Irish surprise. The Brits had evacuated Boston."

Amanda met his eyes in the mirror. "I'm glad for you,
Eric."

"But not for the Brits, eh?"

She shrugged.

"Well, Amanda?"

"Eric, I am trying very hard to be a neutral."

He leapt up from the bed. She felt as if she were being
stalked by a tiger as he walked up behind her. "Are you,
Amanda? Are you really?"

His hands were upon her shoulders. She prayed that he
would not feel the way that she shook, and yet she was not

...en she spoke. "Yes! I swear that I would be neu-
...ow, if I could."

...me passion must have touched her voice, for though
... still seemed frustrated, he seemed to believe her too.
...He stalked back to the bed, then stretched out upon its
length, casual, bold, and brazen, and catching her heart all
over again. "I have heard that some of the things I told you
in my letters came to be discovered."

Fear clutched her heart like an icy hand. "Much of what
you have told me has been common knowledge!"

"Aye, that it has. But since I have come home, I have
realized that many a good Virginian politician and military man is alarmed by the rumor that a spy rests closely
among us. A woman spy, my love. They are calling her
'Highness.' Actually, her fame had even reached Boston.
Washington thinks that it might be you."

His voice was cool, ironic. Her heart thundered drasti-
cally and she could scarcely breathe. She shook her head.
"Eric—"

"You have never denied being a Tory, my love."

He sprang to his feet and moved up behind her. He set
his hands on either side of her head and stroked her
cheeks and her throat. How easily his fingers could wind
about her throat!

"I am your wife," she reminded him, her eyes falling.

"But are you innocent?"

She met his eyes again in the mirror. "Eric!" she told
him passionately and sincerely, "By God, I swear that in
any matter of choice, I would never seek to hurt you!"

"Or my cause?"

"Or—or your cause!" she swore softly.

"Am I a fool to believe in you, Amanda?"

She shook her head, unable to speak. Her hair moved
against his naked belly and he bent over her, finding her
lips. He spoke just above them in a whisper. "Don't ever let
me catch you, lady!" he warned huskily, then kissed her.
He pulled away.

"Oh! God!" he said suddenly. "How could I have forgotten, when it is so very important! I have seen Damien!"

"What?"

She nearly screamed the word, spinning aroun. grinned, pleased. "Yes, well the Brits had him, but he . aged to escape. He had some friendly guards and tr. shared some ale. He managed to swim his way to som. flotsam, and then he was picked up by a colonial ship. He was delivered to Baltimore and hurried back to Boston. I was able to see him just before I left."

"He's—free?" Amanda asked.

"Yes—free as a bird."

She screamed out something incomprehensible, then jumped to her feet and hurtled herself upon his naked form, bearing them both back down to the bed. He grunted and groaned, and then laughed. She showered him with kisses that caused his groaning to take on a different timbre. Laughter faded and they made love again, desperately again, until they were exhausted and glistening and unable to find words for they could not find breath. And yet finally Amanda managed to speak again. "Eric, how long do you have?"

He exhaled unhappily. "Less than a week. And so much is happening here! I've already heard that when the Virginians meet again, they plan to declare the land a commonwealth—to vote for independence! Before it is even done in the Continental Congress! History, my love, in the making, and I shall be back in New York, for that is where Washington believes they will attack next. We must plan a defense for the city."

Less than a week. So little time between them. So much that might be discovered. . . .

But Damien was free.

She twisted in his arms suddenly, smiling. "I shall never betray you, Eric!" she promised him. She almost continued. She almost told him that she loved him, but some dark shadow in his eyes held her back. He did not really believe her. He did not trust her. He was not saying as much, but it was true. He was watching her, and now she was going to have to prove that she was loyal to him, if a Tory still at heart.

"See that you don't," he warned her. She lay still against him. In a while, she realized that he slept. There were new

ɔout his eyes, about his mouth. Battle was taking its
ɔpon him.

ɔhe rose, needing to leave him to sleep, and reflect upon
ɹer new good fortune.

She dressed quickly and hurried out of the room. A pair
of boots rested before one of the bedroom doors. Someone had traveled with Eric, she realized. One of his men.
More danger, she thought, her heart beating fiercely.

She hurried on down the stairs and slipped into the parlor. There she knelt down before the desk and drew open
the door.

And then she felt the knife against her throat, brought
around her from behind. She froze.

"Good day, Lady Cameron" came a husky voice. It was
the tall black man. Her father's emissary.

She forced herself to speak. "You're a fool. My husband
is home. Williamsburg is run by colonials. All I need do is
scream, and they will hang you—"

"Ah, but your blood will rise in a pool long before that
moment, and as I'm quite sure Lord Cameron might be
surprised, there is a chance that his blood might also stain
the floor. Think carefully, Lady Cameron . . ." The knife
came so tightly against her throat she could barely speak.

And still, she was determined on her own freedom.
"Damien is free, and I am done, 'Highness' no more! Kill
me if you will, but tell my father he will get nothing more
from me!"

"We were afraid that you had heard of your cousin's
escape, my lady. Your father sends this message—if he
comes to Cameron Hall again, it will be to burn the
wretched mansion to the ground. And Lord Tarryton
wants you to know that if he comes, you will be his prisoner, his mistress. He is most anxious."

"If they come anywhere near Cameron Hall," she said,
"they will die!"

He did not reply. A second later she no longer felt the
knife against her throat. With a soft rasping cry she leapt
to her feet, spinning around.

He was gone. The man was gone. The window was

open, the spring breeze was rushing in. She ran
could see nothing.

She sank into a chair and sat there, motionless, fe
the breeze. She should tell Eric. She should admit eve
thing that had happened, she should explain that it was a.
because of Damien.

She should, if she could just find the courage!

But it was over now. All over. She never had to play the
spy again. Never. Eric need never know. And if she told
him, he might despise her, he might never forgive
her. . . .

Later Mathilda came and served her breakfast. She discovered that the boots belonged to Frederick, who had accompanied Eric, and she sat and drank coffee with him.

Eric slept most of the day. And when he came down,
and his eyes fell dark and brooding, upon her, she knew
that she could say nothing. It was finished. It had to be.
She prayed with all her heart that it should be so.

Unless . . . unless the British did come to Cameron
Hall.

They did not stay in Williamsburg long. General Charles
Lee, a highly respected military man and an Englishman
who had cast his lot with the colonies, was in Virginia to
oversee militia troops. He was learning that the Virginia
political machine was very competent and that he would
do best to work with the local leaders. Eric was interested
in seeing Lee and other of his friends and acquaintances,
but he was most interested in returning home to Cameron
Hall.

They rode the estate there, and Amanda was delighted
when he applauded her various efforts to keep things moving smoothly. It was still spring, and cool, but they came
to the little cover by the river, and they laid their cloaks
there and made love beneath the rippling branches of the
trees overhead.

Amanda still agonized over telling him the truth of what
she had done, yet she was not sure that she could make
him understand, and since Damien was free, no one could
coerce her again.

ic watched her. When she would move about the she would catch his eyes upon her. When they when they lay down to sleep together, and some-es even when he held her. If she awakened with her ack to him, she would sense that he leaned upon an elbow, watching the length of her, and she would turn and would discover it to be true, and the shadows would fall over his eyes again.

On his fifth day home the *Lady Jane* sailed brilliantly past Dunmore's ships and came in to her home berth. She had just returned from Italy, so Eric told Amanda. But when she awoke that night, Eric was not beside her. She caught a sheet about her and hurried to the window to see the activity down by the docks.

"Spying, my love?"

The question startled her. She spun around to find Eric in a simple white shirt, tight breeches and boots, his hands on his hips, framed in the doorway of her room. He strode over to stand beside her. She tried not to allow her pulse to leap. "I was looking for you. I awoke, and you were gone."

He nodded, his eyes heavy-lidded and half shielded beneath his lashes. His hands rested on her shoulders and he pulled her against him.

"The real cargo was arms, wasn't it?" she whispered.

"And powder," he agreed.

She spun around to face him, her head tilted back. "If you so mistrust me, why on earth tell me the truth?"

"You are hardly a fool. I could not convince you that I unloaded leather goods and wine by night, could I?"

He turned away, sitting at the foot of the bed, stripping off his boots, shirt, and breeches. He glanced around to see her still standing by the window, hurt by his tone of voice.

Even if she was still a spy, she would never betray Cameron Hall. He had to know that.

"Come to bed, Amanda. There is something left of the night," he told her.

She walked slowly back to the bed. She sat upon her own side, still swathed in sheets, and she watched how the moonlight played upon his shoulders and chest. more bronzed than ever, more tightly muscle stretched out beside her, and despite her anger with she wanted to touch him. But she didn't want to make first move.

She didn't have to.

He emitted some impatient sound and reached for her. She cried out softly, allowing the sunset and fire of her hair to sweep over the naked length of him, and then she nipped delicately upon the flesh of his chest, at his nipples, his throat. He caught her tightly to him, sweeping her beneath him, and they made love as if in a tempest, as if a storm guided them, and perhaps it was true. Time was their enemy; they had so little of it. They were strangers in the long months between his visits, and in this maelstrom they thought, perhaps, to find one another again.

And still, when they lay spent and quiet, she knew that he watched her. His fingers moved slowly off the slope of her shoulder to her hip, and he watched her, pensive, distant.

"Lord Dunmore is dangerous," he said at last. "Some men are afraid that he intends to sail to Mount Vernon and kidnap Martha Washington."

"Surely he wouldn't dare!" she murmured.

She felt him shrug. "I am afraid, too, that he might come here."

"Because of the arms?"

Eric was silent for just the beat of a second. "But the governor knows of no arms, my love."

She swung around, facing him. "I would never betray this hall, Eric, never!"

"But who, then, is 'Highness'?" he asked her.

She shook her head, lowering it against his chest. "I would never betray my very home!" she promised him.

"Pray, lady, that you do not," he whispered, and he held her close. She said nothing, and she luxuriated in his warmth. But it wasn't enough. She was shivering, and she was afraid.

When he left, he was gone so very long. Days passed and the weeks passed and then months.

˪remble," he told her.

˪h the cold."

˻ut I am holding you."

`But you will leave," she told him desolately.

She couldn't see his eyes in the darkness. He stared down at her, and the depths of his feelings for her were on the tip of his tongue. He loved her so deeply. Her beauty, her fire. He loved the way that she came to him now, so naturally, so givingly. She made love with passion and with laughter, and in the midst of it, her eyes were ever more beautiful. And yet . . .

They could be ever treacherous.

She held so much in her hands now. She knew about the arms and weaponry stored at the docks. If she betrayed them now . . .

She would not! he thought with anguish. She would not!

XIV

New York
May 1776

She would not betray him! Bah!

That was his thought two months later when he sat in Washington's large white canvas tent in New York and stared at his old friend. The general had just written him orders, commanding him to take a ship south. His old friend and partner, Sir Thomas—now Colonel Sir Thomas —had managed to have their ship, the *Good Earth*, brought down from Boston.

"For one," Washington told him, "Congress has now sanctioned privateering. Whatever damage you may do upon the sea will be appreciated."

It was late May, and they had spent the last weeks preparing earthworks and trenches for the attack they knew was to come upon New York. Brooklyn Heights and Manhattan had been fortified and manned, and Congress had ordered Washington to hold New York. The colonials were aware that the British general Howe was due to sail south

...ork from Halifax, Nova Scotia. His brother, Ad-
...chard Howe, was to sail from England with rein-
...ments. The ragtag colonial army—in trouble now as
...y enlistments came to an end and the men yearned to
...urn home—would be hard put to meet the British men-
...ce. They all knew it. Despite the victories in Virginia and
the Carolinas, they desperately needed to hold the north.
Benedict Arnold was losing his tenacious hold of the area
outside of Quebec, and General Burgoyne had arrived
with reinforcements. It was a tense time for the colonials.

And in the midst of this, Eric was sitting before Washington, hearing a confiscated message that warned Lord
Dunmore of the arms and powder stored in the warehouses at Cameron Hall. There was also an urgent appeal
from General Lewis of the Virginia militia that Eric come
with all haste to seek to oppose an expected attack from
the sea.

His hands felt cold. In the heat of coming summer, he
felt as if icy fingers stroked him up and down the back in
cruel mockery. He had given Amanda the benefit of every
doubt. He had known that she had once practiced treachery, but he had believed her when she had sworn herself
to him. He was ever the fool. The greater her passion, it
seemed, the greater the betrayal. While he dreamed of the
nights they had lain together, tortured himself with im-
ages of her hair curled about his naked flesh, her eyes as
bright as emerald seas, her breasts full and rich within his
hands and the scent of her so sweetly intoxicating it invaded even a dream . . .

He was alone with Washington. The general watched
him sadly, reaching into his private stock of whiskey to
offer Eric a drink.

"You were last home at the end of March?"

Eric nodded. He pulled the confiscated correspondence
—signed "Highness"—toward him, then he swore violently.

"Perhaps you judge too quickly," Washington warned
him.

Eric shook his head. His next words were harsh, and as
cold and ruthless as he felt. "On the contrary, General, I

have dragged my feet, and I may cost us much because of it!"

He stood, swallowing down the last of his whiskey, then saluted sharply. "With your leave, then, I will sail south."

"What will you do?"

"Thrash Dunmore, Sterling, and Tarryton!"

Washington stood, offering his outstretched hand. "Take care, Eric. I'm afraid that you must look for the worst. The attack isn't expected for a few days, but Dunmore is in Virginia waters. Eric, I'm trying to tell you that you may reach your home to find it burned to the ground."

"I may."

"And your wife—"

"I swear, I shall see to her."

"Eric—"

"I know that she is dangerous. I will see to her. I intend to send her to France under heavy guard."

Washington shook his head. "Perhaps she is not guilty."

"You are the one always warning me about her! The evidence points cleanly to her!"

"Perhaps, perhaps not. Perhaps she deserves a fair trial."

Eric stood, ready to exit, ready to sail. "Sir, she has already received her fair trial!" he said angrily.

He took his orders and left Washington, promising to return at the earliest possible moment. After returning to the headquarters house he had chosen in lower Manhattan, he summoned Frederick and asked for a sound crew for the ship. "Virginians, West County men, if you can. I don't care if they've ever sailed before. No one on earth is more accurate with a long rifle than a West County Virginian."

"You'll need swordsmen for hand-to-hand combat," Frederick warned him.

"Give me some men from the Carolina regiment. They're seamen, and they've all learned their swordplay well."

When Frederick left him Eric nearly bent over double, ready to scream. With all his will he tried to cast a dark shield of control over his temper, and yet he could not get her out of his mind for a moment. "I would never betray

this hall, Eric. Never!" The passion of her words returned
to haunt him again and again. Sweet, sweet mockery that
he could not bear. How had he believed her? He knew her!

He wanted to curl his fingers around her throat and
throttle her. He wanted to tear her limb from limb. He
wanted to rip that glorious hair from her head. . . .

And he wanted to take her into his arms, brutally, perhaps, but he wanted her, beneath him, to shake her, to
have her, until she realized at long last that her battle was
over, that she could never defy him again.

As he gathered the last of his personal belongings for
the trip, there was a soft rapping upon his door. He strode
across the room with its rough wood table and simple cot
and threw open the door, his features surely displaying
the tension of his mood. To his surprise it was Anne Marie
Mabry, Sir Thomas's daughter, who stood there.

Anne Marie had come a long way from that night in
Boston. She had organized many of the women's protests,
the boycotting of British goods, and she had been engaged
to marry a young man who had lost his life in Boston. She
was no longer the coquette but a beautiful, mature young
woman with a soft smile and a winning way. She had followed her father to war and was considered quite an angel
by the men.

And I could not have chosen her for a wife! Eric charged
himself bitterly. A woman sworn to the same cause as I,
and one who is gentle, with guileless blue eyes and a
tender smile.

Yet even with the thought, he knew that he could not
have turned back and he knew, too, in that moment, that
whatever came, he loved Amanda still. If he caught her, he
would deal with her as was necessary, but he would not
cease to love her. He had been ignited by the magic in
emerald eyes and flame-dark hair, and no one else could
ever touch him so deeply again.

"Anne Marie, come in," he said stiffly. "There's little here
to offer you, though there is coffee in the pot. A fire can
heat it quick enough. Or there is brandy—"

"Eric, please, I haven't come for coffee or brandy." She

hesitated. "I've come to ask you to think slowly and carefully before you do irreparable harm!"

He paused, staring at her with surprise and a certain amount of amusement. "Anne Marie, they are planning on burning down my home, a house with a cornerstone set in the late 1620s! They will seize weapons and arms meant for the use of the Virginia militia and this very army. And, Anne Marie, they know that the weapons are there because my wife—the very mistress of that hall!—has told them!" His temper rose as he spoke. Too late he realized that his long strides were bearing him harshly down upon her and that he nearly had her cornered.

"By God!" he roared, casting his hands into the air. "I'm sorry, Anne Marie. But leave this be."

He walked to the side table and poured himself a brandy. Undaunted, Anne Marie hurried to his side. "Eric, I have heard rumors about all this too! Servants' gossip, but often the truest source. Amanda has not been away from Cameron Hall since you left her."

"Then someone else there is her accomplice."

"Eric, she is my friend. I know her well—"

"Anne Marie, I caught her red-handed one night. And I let it go. That was my mistake. I should have beaten her with a horse crop that night and sent her to France!"

"Eric!" Anne Marie cried. "I know you too. You could have done no such thing—"

"It might have been the right thing," he said coolly. "Anne Marie, I have to leave. I want to catch the tide."

"Oh, Eric," she said miserably, "I've done nothing useful here at all. Listen to me, please. Perhaps she was a spy. But she wouldn't have turned against her own home! Someone else is using her past against her, can't you see that?"

"I can see, Anne Marie, that Amanda has always had every opportunity to talk to me. If she was threatened, I would have defended her. I would have protected her and fought for her against any man, or any menace. She chose another course. Now, if you'll be so good as to excuse me—"

She blocked his path. Her eyes were liquid with appeal

and misery. "Oh, Eric!" she murmured again, and she came up on tiptoe to kiss him.

He didn't know what overcame him. Maybe it was just the bitter pain of betrayal, but when her lips touched his, he seized upon her. He did not give her the sisterly kiss she had offered but parted her lips and delved deep within her mouth, as a lover might. And she responded. Just as a lover might. Her lips parted sweetly, she welcomed him, her arms wrapped around him. Moments passed in blindness, and then he realized that he could not take from Anne Marie what he was seeking in another. He could not use Anne Marie, because she was too good a woman. And she had always cared for him; he had known that. She was his friend, and the daughter of one his best friends. Shamed, he drew his lips from hers and slowly released her from the band of his arms. He wanted to apologize. Her eyes were upon his, and they both knew his mistake.

Before he could utter a word, a furious sound at the door interrupted them. Startled, Eric looked to the door to see that Damien Roswell was there, tall, straight, outraged.

"My lord Cameron, I came to see if you needed any assistance, but I see that you are well tended."

He didn't owe Damien any explanations. His young friend was rash and hot blooded, and he'd nearly spent years as a British prisoner because of it.

"I am on my way now," Eric said curtly.

"Damien, you must understand—" Anne Marie began.

"Oh, I understand!" Damien said with a dry laugh. "He's still a Brit in his own way, still 'Lord' Cameron. Just like Henry the Eighth! Down with the one, up with the next! Were you planning on killing Amanda, or just divorcing her, Lord Cameron?"

"Whatever I did, Damien, she would deserve," Eric said smoothly.

"I'm going to sail with you."

"No, you are not."

"You might—"

"Damien, for the love of God! Washington will not let

you go! Can't you understand how serious a situation has become?"

"If you hurt her, Cameron," Damien swore, raising tightly clenched fist, "revolution be damned! I will kill you, I swear it!" It looked as if there were tears in his eyes. Eric's heart seemed to tighten with agony. He did not want to do battle with Damien. Again he damned Amanda with all of his heart.

"Damien—" he began.

But Damien was gone. Eric stood alone in the rough little room with Anne Marie.

"It's all right. I'll explain to him," Anne Marie promised.

"It isn't all right, and it never shall be," Eric muttered. He swept up his hat, and bowed low to Anne Marie. "Take care."

"Eric, go gently!" she cried.

But he did not reply. He felt as if he were a tempest of seething emotions, and he did not trust himself to speak.

On the morning of the twenty-fifth, Eric and his crew met one of Dunmore's fleet, a small warship called the *Cynthia*. Because the Continental forces were desperate for ships, they took care not to sink her. They suffered damage to the *Good Earth*'s mainmast, but nothing major, and they managed to take the *Cynthia* with little effort. Her crew were sent to the brig, and a skeletal crew of colonials was left to sail her into a patriot port where she could be reoutfitted and sent into colonial service.

On the morning of the twenty-eighth they sailed the James. Through the glass Eric could see that fires burned at Cameron Hall. The *Lady Jane* was just leaving her berth.

Was his wife aboard her? Eric wondered.

He shouted orders to the gunners. The cannons were aimed and loaded by their gun crews, and he held his hand high. "Fire!" he commanded, bringing his hand down. It was his own damn ship he was bombarding!

And it might be his own wife he was about to kill! Would she be aboard? Aye, he thought bitterly, she would! The house was still standing, he could see it upon the far dis-

dawn. The warehouses were ablaze. Nothing could be salvaged from them.

And the ship, his ship, the *Lady Jane*. She was coming about, ready to fire in turn.

"Gunners, we'll take it again. They weren't prepared for us—they were barely into the river. One more strike and we come along broadside. We'll grapple her and board!"

Powder filled the air, and already visibility grew bad. He shouted his order to fire once again. The *Good Earth* vibrated and trembled, and the balls shuddered into the water, and into the wood and canvas and decking of the *Lady Jane*.

The water between them seemed to froth in shades of gray. They came closer and closer, the wheel ably handled by a West County captain. There was a massive shuddering as the ships came together.

Eric raised his sword, let out a battle cry, and leapt from the one deck to the other. Swinging from the rigging, leaping from the railing, his men followed suit.

They met the British at close combat, hand-to-hand fighting, swords and dirks drawn, their long rifles used perhaps once or twice. Fury guided Eric. It was his ship. By God, he would reclaim her!

He had just dispatched a young, talented Highlander when he saw Robert Tarryton across the ship, by the bow. Dodging and avoiding the others, he grinned with reckless abandon at this new opponent, his mortal enemy.

"Cameron, you bastard!" Tarryton charged him, parrying his first thrusts easily enough.

Their swords met high and clashed, and came low and clashed, and they were cast tightly together.

"She's with me, you bastard!" Tarryton whispered heatedly. "You thought to make a fool of me and take her from me time and again, but she's with me. I've got your ship, and I've got your wife, and I intend to make good use of both!"

Anger caused a shudder to wrack the whole of his body. Robert Tarryton made a lunge that nearly skewered him. Fool! Eric charged himself in silence, aware that the man meant to unnerve him in any way that he could. With cunning, sweeping strokes of his sword, he began to move forward, quickly. Tarryton parried his thrusts, but Eric saw the fear that slipped into his features. He was the better swordsman, and he knew it.

And he was going to kill Tarryton.

"You've nothing, Tarryton, nothing at all," he replied, and proved it with a quick slash that caught the man in the chin, humiliating, damning.

Tarryton backed quickly away and Eric discovered that he could follow at his leisure. Tarryton was now the one unnerved. He touched his chin and felt the blood.

Eric grabbed hold of the rigging and leapt upon the foreward rail for a new assault. And it was then that he saw Amanda.

She had come from the captain's cabin, and she stood among a sea of men, exquisite in green, her hair caught by the sun, a burning cascade that rippled and fell down the length of her back. She seemed both alien and natural to the deck and the turmoil that abounded upon it, tall, proud, and beautiful, her head lifted to the wind, her eyes seeking those around her. His wife. The traitor.

She was there, undeniably, she was there. She has cast her fate with Tarryton at long last. He was probably taking her on to London, now that her usefulness at Cameron Hall had come to an end.

Never, my love, he vowed silently. Unless I am dead and buried in this sea, you will never be with Tarryton, I will see to that!

But just at that moment, Tarryton made another lunge toward him. Eric parried the blow swiftly and retaliated with fury and vengeance. His temper was under control now, cold and lethal. Tarryton seemed to realize that.

"Lay down your sword, Tarryton!" he demanded.

"God's blood! Someone take this man!" Tarryton cried.

It was more than he should have expected, Eric thought dryly, for Lord Robert Tarryton, His Grace the Duke of Owenfield, to fight his own battle. At his call, five navy men sprang forward, their rapiers raised.

"I will kill you one day, Tarryton," Eric vowed pleasantly.

But Tarryton had already turned away, and Eric couldn't give him much attention, for his opponents were able. Frederick sprang forward, taking on one of the men. Eric dispatched one eager lad with a lightning thrust to the abdomen. The next he caught in the chest, and the last two disappeared into the fray.

He heard a loud splash, and he realized that Tarryton was lost to him now. The *Lady Jane* was coming under the control of the patriots, and Tarryton was not going to stay to assist his failing men.

"Highness!"

The cry was going up, Eric realized. The ship was being won, and the men were becoming aware of Amanda—and that she must be the notorious "Highness" who had betrayed Virginia again and again.

He had to reach her himself first. Frederick knew her identity, as did other friends. But not the others. And he meant for no other man to take her or touch her. She was his.

There was a sword in her hand! he realized with both fear and fury. Damned fool, would she fight them even unto death? Was she so reckless and so determined that she would kill men that she would risk her own life?

"By God, love, I will throttle you!" he vowed to himself.

She thrust her sword forward in warning, and turned to run. Eric gave chase, shouting to his men to secure the deck.

Would she throw herself into the sea? No, in panic she was running back to the captain's cabin, so it seemed. Some engagement was taking place there, a Highlander gave battle to his one of his men, and was duly silenced, falling back into the cabin. "I shall take this!" Eric called to his men.

She was within that cabin.

He reached the cabin door and burst it open with a powerful slam of his boot.

And he saw her there, cradling the fallen Highlander in her arms. Her eyes rose to his, ever emerald. Defiant . . . maybe just a little fearful. His name left her lips on a

whisper, and then she staggered to her feet, drag
Highlander's heavy Brown Bess along with her.

"Highness," he muttered in return, cleaning his sᵥ
to keep his hands steady, fitting it back into his scabbaᵣ
He didn't know what he said to her then, something thaᵗ
meant nothing, something about the state of the war. And
something about his fury to be here now, because his wife
was a traitor.

She tried to interrupt him—he would not allow her to
do so. He tried so desperately to keep control of his temper. He didn't want to touch her. He would kill her . . .
or he would rape her, there aboard the ship with all his
men about.

"I am innocent of this!" she cried at last. The denial tore
into his heart. By God, she had been there—with Tarryton.

Control, he thought! And he arched a brow politely.
"You are innocent—Highness?"

"I tell you—"

"And I tell you, milady, that I know full well you are a
British spy and the notorious 'Highness,' for I oft fed you
misinformation that found its way to Dunmore's hands.
You betrayed me—again and again!"

She was holding the Brown Bess on him. Her eyes were
in tempest, her hair was a beautiful fall about her. She
was his wife, and he had lain with her night upon night,
and she was holding the lethal weapon on him. "Give it to
me, Amanda!" he demanded furiously. "Amanda!"

"Get away from me, Eric!"

Fury filled him and threatened to burst. "Now, Amanda!
I warn you that my temper is brittle indeed. I almost fear
to touch you, lest I strangle the light from those glorious
eyes. I'll take the gun!"

"No! Let me by you. Let me go. I swear that I am innocent—"

"Let 'Highness' go? Why, milady! They would hang me
for the very act." Now! He had to take the weapon from
her now! Fiercely he strode to her. She moved away as he
lunged.

"No! I'll shoot you, Eric, I swear it—"

⎽o believe you, milady!" he retorted bitterly. Aye,
⎽ld shoot him! And be free . . .

⎽oot me, then, if you dare, milady!" he challenged
⎽. "But take heed, madame, that your weapon be
⎽aded."

"Aye, 'tis loaded, Eric!" Was she trying to warn him?
God! He wanted to believe in the tears that stung her eyes,
in the warnings she tried to issue. He could not!

He caught the gun by the barrel and sent it flying across
the room. The damned thing exploded. He spun around,
staring at her coldly. "It *was* loaded, milady. And aimed
upon *my heart*!" She would have killed him. His own wife,
she would have killed him. "And now, Highness . . ."

"Wait!"

"Wait for what, milady? Salvation? You shall not find
any."

She stared at him a long moment, her green eyes still
liquid, as if she would shed tears. Lying tears. And still,
she was so beautiful, her breasts heaving, the pulse ticking
at her throat. Her face so very fine that he longed to feel
the lines beneath the stroke of his fingers. . . .

Suddenly, like a doe, she leapt into action, trying to
sweep past him. He took a step and seized her, catching
her hair. She screamed out in pain and he swirled her
back into his arms. She pummeled, kicked and fought
wildly, and he felt the warmth of her against him, felt the
rise of her breasts, the span of her hips, and so help him,
all that he could remember for a fleeting moment was the
laughter they had shared. Laughter, and sweet tender moments by the slow-moving river.

She nearly caught his chin with her flailing fists. He
caught her wrists savagely and wound them back together
at the small of her back. She tossed back her head to meet
his eyes. "So beautiful," he told her. "So treacherous. But
it is over now. Surrender, milady."

She smiled suddenly, and it was a smile that caught his
heart, slow and nearly tender, and oh so wistful. She
brought back all the years that gone between them, all the
tempest, and all the precious moments of peace. "No sur-

render, my lord," she said softly. "No retreat, and ̶ ̶ ̶ render."

It was then that they were interrupted by one of ̶ young Carolina lieutenants. The man came to a halt b̶ hind Eric and excitedly spouted, "We've found her! Highness! She gave the ship and the intelligence to the British."

His eyes remained locked with hers. "Aye, we've found her." Fury gripped him. He no longer dared touch her. With an oath he cast her from him. She nearly fell against the back paneling and steadied herself there, ever tall and ever proud, and so damned dignified and beautiful despite it all!

The lieutenant whistled softly. "No wonder she played our men so false so easily!"

How bitter those words!

"Aye," he said quietly. "It was easy for her to play men falsely."

"I wonder if they will hang her," the soldier said. He seemed very perplexed, anxious. "Would we hang a woman, General?" He hesitated a moment. Eric barely noticed, for still his gaze was caught by his wife's brilliant green eyes, ever wider now. Was she afraid at last? Did she feel the itch of hemp about her throat?

"Milord, surely you *cannot* have her hanged!"

He smiled ironically, feeling her warmth, even now remembering that the very sun itself seemed to live in her kiss, in the glory of her hair, in the splendor of her arms.

"Nay, I cannot," he agreed, adding quietly, "for she is, you see, my wife."

The young man gasped. Eric knew that he dared not stay there, his temper fraying so quickly and so visibly. He would deal with Amanda later, on his own territory.

On territory familiar to them both.

"Tell Daniel to set a course for Cameron Hall," he ordered. "Have someone come for this lieutenant," he said, referring to the Highlander. Apparently this man had fought and died—to protect Amanda from him! "The Brits must be buried at sea; our own will find rest at home."

He turned back to Amanda. "My love, I shall see you

...he bowed deeply to her and then strode from the
...as quickly as he could. He did not stop by the wheel,
...valked straight to the tip of the bow and stood against
...e wind, feeling the wash and spray of the surf as it
...looded over him.

The deed, at least, was done. The arms and munitions
were probably all lost, but the *Lady Jane* was his again.

And Amanda was his again.

His fingers itched. He remembered Tarryton, and his
words, and a staggering pain gripped his gut as he wondered what was true and what was not.

They had been married more than two years. She was
his wife! His, and no part of that bastard Tarryton. He
should cast her from him, he should demand a divorce. . . .

He could no more divorce her than he could cut away
his own right hand. He shouldn't touch her.

He couldn't wait to get his hands upon her. He needed
time. Time to steady himself, time to prove the victor indeed. And there were things to be done. He had to find
General Lewis, and join with him to make the final plans
for hunting down Lord Dunmore.

He closed his eyes and leaned back against the rigging.
In time, Daniel came to him to tell him that they were
nearly docked.

"See that Frederick takes my wife home and that the
servants are made aware that she is not to leave. I will ride
immediately to find the troops. Our own men may stay
aboard, or set tents upon the lawn, as is their choice."

"Aye, sir!"

Eric stayed where he was when Frederick went for
Amanda. He watched from his vantage point as the man
led her across the deck, and to the gangplank. And he
watched, his heart pierced as if by fire, as she was saluted
as a worthy foe.

Damn her. Damn her a thousand times over.

When the carriage disappeared with her within it, he
strode off the ship himself. A horse was quickly supplied
to him, and Daniel was ready to ride beside him.

They didn't have far to hunt for General Lewis, his old

friend from the Indian days. Lewis had bee~
along the peninsula, and now he was eager to p~
Dunmore's position.

"We'll chase him to his anchor off of Gwynn's Isl~
We'll see that he and his pirating fleet are sent far away f~
good!" Lewis swore vehemently.

"We'll join my men with the militia in the morning then,
General," Eric agreed. "I'll ride back now to my men."

"Lord Cameron!" Lewis stopped him.

Eric, halfway out of the brigadier general's tent, paused
beneath the flap. "Aye?"

"I would have you know that there is no proof as to the
identity of the spy," the general said quietly.

"No proof?"

Lewis cleared his throat unhappily. "Well, news of your
victory aboard the *Lady Jane* traveled even more swiftly
than you did, my lord. The battle was witnessed from the
shore, and the rumor is, of course, that your wife was
aboard and that the men seemed to recognize her as 'Highness.' Bear in mind, sir, that some thought as how Dunmore would have liked to have kidnapped Mrs. Washington. Perhaps your lady was taken quite the same."

Eric nodded, not believing a word of it. His "lady" had
already lifted a Brown Bess against him. God knew what
surprises she might have waiting for him within their
room.

"I thank you for your concern, General Lewis. My wife
will soon be leaving for France, where she will be safe
from either side."

He saluted and left then, nodding to Daniel. He
mounted his horse, with Daniel behind him, and he
started off for home. Seconds later he was galloping
across Virginia fields, more than anxious to reach his
home.

At the steps he dismounted. Pierre was there to take his
mount, to greet him enthusiastically. "What happened
here?" he demanded of his good servant. "The truth,
Pierre. The truth of it."

Pierre shrugged unhappily. "I don't know the whole
truth of it, my lord. Danielle was struck and has just

...onsciousness, and she swears your lady inno-

...nielle would swear her innocent were she caught in ...king's own arms!" Eric exclaimed.

Pierre shrugged unhappily. "She meant no harm to any of us. That monster Tarryton would have struck young Margaret, but Lady Cameron would not allow it."

"But she went with Tarryton easily enough herself."

Pierre lowered his head. "So it seemed," he admitted softly.

"That is all I need for now, Pierre," he said. "I want her taken to France tomorrow, as soon as I have left. I shall leave the *Good Earth* here for that purpose. You will go with her, and Cassidy—"

"Cassidy thinks that he should be serving you, milord."

"If he can keep my wife from mischief and harm, he will be serving me."

"And Danielle?"

"Aye," Eric said after a moment. "Danielle may accompany her."

"How long shall we stay?"

"Till hell freezes over, so it seems!" Eric muttered. Then he sighed. "I don't know as yet. You will go to the Comte de la Rochelle, who is with the court at Versailles. When this thing is solved, I will come for my lady and the rest of you."

"Aye, my lord. And Cameron Hall?"

"Richard will remain here. He knows the place even better than I. He has kept things running so well."

"If I may, milord, Lady Cameron has kept things running so well."

"Then, Pierre, it shall not run so well, but there is nothing else that I can do. Is everything clear?"

"Aye, milord."

"Good night then, Pierre."

"Good night, milord."

Eric started up the stairs to the house. Upon entering his home he saw the scorched walls and places where the fires had been beaten out. The faint smell of smoke still lay about the place, but very little had been harmed.

He looked up the stairs and hesitated, his fingers winding into fists by his side.

Then he started up the steps, and when he reached his own door he paused again.

Control . . . he warned himself.

He silently opened the door and stepped within the room.

Instantly his eyes fell upon her. Passion and desire combined with raw fury to sweep all his thoughts of a cold and distant reunion aside.

Steam still rose softly from a bath, but she was no longer within it. She stood by the window, her form draped in a towel, her features grave as she gazed upon the lawn, her hair high and sable and fire and gloss in a cascade of curls. She turned to him, her eyes wide and emerald and startled. There was an innocence, a vulnerability, to the way she clutched her towel to her breast. As if she held her innocence against him, as if they were strangers, never man and wife.

You are my wife! he vowed in silence.

Her eyes met his, clouded and wary. He turned and closed and locked the door, then leaned against it. His anger and desire joined to make his voice tremble with menace as he spoke to her.

"Well, Highness, it has come. Our time of reckoning at last."

He waited for her reply, for her denial, for her cry of innocence.

A smile curled his lip. He could no longer remain still; he could not bear the distance. A searing tempest all took root within his soul, and he took his first, ruthless step toward her.

"Aye, milady, our time of reckoning at last."

Part IV

*

But One Life

XV ❧

Amanda stared at Eric wordlessly, unable to believe that he could have become the stranger standing there with the brutal lock to his jaw and the icy expression in his eyes.

She wanted to cry out so badly that she had betrayed no one. As Eric strode on into the room, she thought that he meant to come straight to her, to wind his fingers around her throat, and she tried not to flinch. His eyes were dark now. They had that ability to go from silver gray to deepest cobalt, and now, by candlelight, they were dark indeed and fathomless.

He did not come to her. Perhaps he was afraid to do so. Afraid of what he might do to her if he touched her.

He pulled out a chair at the table and sat, wincing slightly as he lifted his foot to set it upon the opposite chair. She could scarcely breathe as he stared at her relentlessly, and neither could she move. Her fingers clenched about the snowy towel that enwrapped her, and other than that, she could do nothing but return his stare. He poured himself some wine, using her glass, and cast his gaze upon the tray of barely touched food. He sipped the wine, staring her way once again. "Is there a knife you harbor at your breast, my love?" he asked softly.

She shook her head. "I have never desired your death."

"No? That's not what you've said at times."

"I've spoken in anger."

"And you leveled a musket upon my heart this very day."

"I never wanted to kill you! And I do not carry a knife. Were I to desire your death, I would not be fool enough to carry a knife. You could too easily use it against me."

"Ah." She didn't like the way that he softly whispered the sound, nor did she like his manner as he continued. "Because you are weak, and I am stronger. Amanda, you do have the most exceptional talent for crying out about femininity the moment that you are cornered."

"I am not cornered. I am innocent."

"Innocent?"

Her fingers clutched convulsively about the towel before she realized that it did seem she hid some weapon at her breast. She did not reply quickly enough and he suddenly and violently stood. This time there was no hesitation as he strode across the room toward her. His walk was so filled with menace that she gasped, seeking to elude him, but he was upon her too quickly, wrenching her arms from their taut wrap. The linen towel fell to her feet, her hair streamed damp red streamers down her back and over her shoulders, and but for that she was left naked before his gaze.

And his eyes went darker still.

She longed to reach for the towel quickly, to retreat, but they had now taken their battle farther than they had ever gone, and she could not play the coward. She lifted her chin and spoke mockingly instead. "No blade, milord, as you can see." She waited, condemning him with her eyes. Then she did begin to slowly bend to retrieve her towel. "If you'll excuse me—"

"If I'll excuse you? Madame, do you think that I intend

to engage in some drawing-room conversation. No, my love, that is the point here. I am done with excusing you!" he thundered out vengefully. His hands were upon her shoulders, wrenching her up to face him. His fingers lay upon her naked flesh, biting and cruel, and he drew her hard against him. Fire burned brightly within his eyes as they tore into hers. "I knew from the beginning that you followed the Crown, and I even knew that you were Dunmore's spy, and that didn't matter to me, lady. When we married I had you watched and followed, not so that you could not give away the information you had been given, but because I feared for your safety."

Her face went pale. He nearly ceased in his tirade. He could not. He had missed her too long. And she had played him false when he had believed that if not her love, her loyalty to the very house she called home would have kept her true. He was too shaken to cease. Too shaken to take his hands from her. He clenched her shoulders even more tightly. "My God, lady, if there is an excuse, tell it to me now!"

"I didn't do it!"

"You lie!"

"I do not!"

She brought her fists up between them to beat against him, but he swung her around and she stumbled, falling to her knees before him. She cast her hair back again, fighting tears. There had been so many times when she had deserved his wrath! She had fought him and hated him at every turn, but not now. Now she was in love with him, and, innocent, she had no defense.

"There is nothing that I can say!" she cried out to him. "Cast me before your courts, hang me for a traitor if you will, but by God, leave me be—"

"Leave you be!" He hunched down before her. His ruffled shirt was torn and powder smudged, his waistcoat and frock coat both showed signs of the day's wear. "I am called back from service in New York because my wife is planning my very doom! Handing my very property to the enemy! My God, you might very well have set fire to the house with your very own hand!"

"No!"

"You might have sailed the ship!"

She couldn't believe that there seemed to be no mercy, no reason in him at all. And still, she was desperate to make him understand. "I did not fire the house! Eric, I pleaded that they not burn the manor. I said that I would go if only—"

"Stop it!" he hissed, and his hand lashed out in a fury, stopping just short of her cheek. "You did what?"

"I said that I would go along willingly if they did not burn the house! And it didn't burn, Eric! It—"

"Bitch!" He swore to her, low and trembling. "You went with him willingly! Into Tarryton's arms! You forget how we met, my lady wife!" he charged her scathingly. "That you would need bargain with Robert Tarryton! The army lies languishing and I need run to capture my own wife, the Brit's courtesan!"

"How dare you!" she cried, near tears of anguish and fury. She could not fight. Not even the truth stood in her defense. Rising, she lashed out at him. The fight had been simmering and brewing between the two of them, and he was glad of it. He seized her arm and dragged her up to him. In panic she struggled against him. She had never seen this dark rage take hold of him, and it terrified her. "Let me go! Eric, you're hurting me, let go of me, Eric!"

He flung her hard on the elegant bed and fell atop of her, his thumbs and forefingers caressing her temples as he stared down at her.

"I've wondered. I've lain awake nights, and I've wondered if you were here, alone, in this bed. I agonized over leaving you so, yet I believed that you had vowed yourself into this marriage and that you would honor the promise sworn between us. I've faced bullets and steel time and again, and never have I sweat as I did nights, lady, torturing myself with visions of you as I have found you this night, sweet and fragrant from the bath, your flesh like alabaster, your heart beating that pulse to your veins. I've tried not to think that Tarryton might find his way to you, that his hands might close over your breasts, as mine do now."

"I never betrayed you with any man!" she cried out, and she felt as if her teeth chattered harshly within her mouth. "I cannot bear Robert now! You know that—"

"I do not know that. I know that you walked out of this house with him this morning—willingly."

"The servants—"

"The servants would not lie."

"But I . . ."

"You what, milady?" he asked scornfully.

The words fled from her; she could not whisper them. I love you. They echoed within her skull, but she could not say them. They came too late, and they would not be believed.

"I did not do this!" she cried, and his lip curled in disbelief.

"I wanted to kill Tarryton—and you," he told her. "From the time that I was summoned here, I felt an almost primal desire to draw torment and blood."

"Eric—"

"Fear not, milady. I do not intend to go so far."

"Eric, please—"

"Please what?"

"Let me up!"

He hated her at that moment, she was certain. Almost as much as she hated him for the disbelief and mockery in his eyes. And still he lay against her bare flesh, pinning her against the bed that they shared as man and wife. Love and hate . . . the emotions were close indeed. Though she thought she despised him desperately and burned to be free of him, she was filled by a greater need, to feel him close again, his hands and lips upon her, caressing, demanding.

"You're forgetting that you're my wife," he reminded her. "And that I am a soldier, returned from the front."

"I am forgetting nothing! We are bitter enemies, milord, and no matter how I try, you refuse to believe me."

"You speak of war again. You chose to fight this particular battle. Well, I won, madame. You lost. And you are my wife."

"Your despised wife! Eric, for the love of God—"

"For the love of God, lady, no. I will not free you this night. If it is war, madame, then know the truth of it. If we shall win this fight, then I am a hero. If the king is victorious, then I am a traitor indeed. But this night, lady, I am the conqueror, and the rewards of conquest are as old as time."

Anguish and tempest struck her anew. She could not surrender, not to his touch, not even to the ardent fever that swept about them both like a relentless tide. She had not seen him in so long. It had been more than two months. Two months in which she had done her best to be a Cameron wife, to cherish and nurture the land and the hall, to stand fast against any enemy. And then . . .

After everything, the British ships had appeared that morning and Robert had come to her bedchamber. And now everything that she had ever feared in Eric had been unleashed. He hated her with a passion, she could feel it in his touch each time his fingers brushed her or curled around her. His temper was on a taut string, barely held from total explosion.

But not even the bitter fire of his anger nor his absolute mockery could still the things he evoked in her when he came too close. Dear God! That she could go back to a time when she had despised him! But that time was gone. And now she longed to forget this day, this horrid, horrid day. She longed to embrace him. She hadn't tasted in so long the sweetness and decadence of once-forbidden pleasures, felt his lips, his hands upon her. But she could not give to him now. Not when she knew so little of his mind, when his fury was so sharp, so blinding.

She parted her lips to speak, but she did not. She saw the wrath of his gaze and fell silent, unable to read his thoughts.

They were easy to fathom, he could have told her. But he hadn't told her what others dreams had kept him awake at night. Dreams of her, as he saw her now. Her eyes so green, shadowed and shaded by the rich sweep of her lashes as they fell over the emerald orbs, fluttering open again. Even now her hair dried in tendrils both deep, dark sable and flaming red, depending how the locks curled or waved or lay upon her flesh.

He moved his hand to her cheeks, tracing the excellence of her features, the high set of her bones, the slight heart shape of the face, accented by the widow's peak at her temple and the sweeping richness of her hair. Her lips were beautifully shaped, naturally rose, the lower lip full and the curve of the whole evocatively sensual. At rest she was exquisite, as a statue was exquisite. Her flesh was like marble in its perfection, from the slope of her shoulders and rise of her breasts to the shapely curves of her hips and calves. In motion she was more than beautiful, for she was energy and tension and passion, and her eyes were haunted with what emotion ruled her thoughts, always exciting, always eliciting his own passion, be it yearning need or a cyclone of fury.

And now . . . now her lips lay parted beneath his. Her breasts rose and fell with each whisper of her breath, and the length of her perfection lay beneath him. Theirs had never been a soft or quiet relationship, yet he had never thought it would come to this. He knew he would take her that night by any force, rather than see tomorrow come without the memory of the night.

His mouth came closer. Their eyes met at just a breath of space.

"No! We will not—do this!" Amanda managed to protest. "Not like this! Not when you do not love me!"

"Love, madame? When did that enter into your priorities? Certainly not when you married me. Not when you discovered maps within my library to give your father. Not when you betrayed this very house."

"But I did not! Oh, Eric, you fool! Listen to me! Perhaps I am guilty of giving away past . . . secrets. You don't understand! They held Damien—"

"What?" he demanded sharply.

She swallowed. "My father had Damien. He always threatened me with Damien. First he swore that he would have him arrested and hanged. And then he did have him, Eric. The horse! Remember at the governor's palace on New Year's? Damien's horse died, and I knew that Father wouldn't hesitate to do the same to a man. And then they actually held Damien! They were threatening me—"

"I see. But Damien has been freed for some time now, milady."

"And that is what I am telling you! There is another spy out there, and it isn't me!"

He smiled. "A pretty tale," he told her.

"Eric, please—"

"Amanda, I do not please, milady! But before God, I swear it! I have missed you."

"Oh!" she cried, then gasped and swore in fury, surging against him to escape him, feeling him ever more pressed against her body. Little was hid by the tightness of his breeches. Her eyes widened as she felt the strength of him. She shuddered violently, hating him and hating herself all the more because she did not care about pride or reason, only that he held her, even if it was all a lie.

"We cannot!"

"But you are my wife."

"Who betrayed you, so you say."

"It does not matter. Not now. Not tonight."

"No! Eric!" She was very close to tears. "Not after today. My God, let me up!" She surged against him anew, trying to dislodge him, to free herself by any means. Darkness seemed to surround her in a rise of mist like the steam of a summer's sun. She felt his hardness against her again, pulsing, vivid, and it seemed as if a thousand pagan drums began to beat within her heart and core and blood. She fought him, and she fought herself, but he held her firm, his eyes ever upon her until she blushed radiantly even as she choked and swore and struggled. "Eric! No!"

He smiled, and his gaze was taunting, provocative. "Ah . . . Mandy! Don't you seek forgiveness?"

She went very still and moistened her lips.

"What?" She gasped.

"Perhaps I will."

She watched him for a moment, but she didn't trust him. He leaned against her, imprisoning her hands. "You cast yourself upon Tarryton, why not me? We even have the sanctity of marriage upon us, my love."

"I never cast myself upon Tarryton!" she swore. She tried to kick him. He laughed, for his weight was well upon her, and he was in no danger. Fury filled her. "You want me to beg your forgiveness in this manner!"

"It is a way to start," he commented dryly. But his eyes were silver and blue flame and a vein ticked rampantly against his throat. She caught her breath, but then her heart fell again and she defied.

"Then you would call me a whore!" she retorted. "Giving in for—for what I might get in turn."

"The words are yours," he said.

"Oh! Never! Eric—"

"Shh! The words do not matter, truth does not matter, nay, not even love! You are my wife, and I have been away too long, and, lady, this thing between us is ever fierce, and I will not be denied."

His lips pressed against hers with searing hunger, stealing away her words. She tried to twist her head, but his hands were powerful upon her head, holding her still to his leisure. She felt the heady fullness of his tongue as he played against the barriers of her lips and teeth and filled her mouth, seeking and giving, bringing a rush of heat to rise within her. She tried to push against him, but he caught her hands, and laced his fingers with hers, pinning them to her sides. She tossed and turned and writhed, and felt the fires burning ever more brightly, more fervently about her. She sank into the heat, into the desperate rise of passion, where thought knew no place and the heart and hunger ruled all.

She loved him. Pride be damned, for it was lost, cast along with dignity upon the shores of emotion, for come what may, in truth she could not deny him, nor herself.

Her hand was free. He stroked her open palm with his fingers, and then his hands moved over her, trembling, and yet with sureness and relentless hunger. He cupped her breast, and explored her hip, and his lips left her mouth to trail against her throat and breasts. She gasped with the startling pleasure as he took the rosebud of one crest within his mouth, teasing with his teeth and bathing it again and again with the lavish sweep of his tongue. Her

hands were upon him, she realized. Her fingers fell upon
his shoulders, and she felt the ripple of his muscle beneath
the fabric of his uniform. She threaded her fingers into his
dark hair and marveled at the texture of it. And still he
moved against her.

"Give to me, my wife, my love!" His whispers coursed
her ears and the heat of them filled her with heightened
excitement. "Fill me with your beauty, with the magic of
the night. . . ."

The threat of war receded, and battle was forgotten. The
night breeze rushed in with its scent of river salt, caressing her flesh where he did not, but nothing else of the
world could touch her. It had been too long since they had
lain like this, lovers entwined. She closed her eyes, and he
moved against her. He shifted his weight and stroked her
abdomen and her hip and the flame trail of his kiss followed along. The stroke of his lips and teeth and tongue
fell again and again upon her. She tried to thread her fingers into his hair, to somehow capture the heat and flow
of passion, but it was far beyond her. She trembled at his
touch, she moved as he manipulated her, feathering his
fingers down the length of her spine, gently nipping
against the rise of her buttocks, lying her back down again
to bathe her breasts anew with the hot liquid tempest of
his mouth. He rose then, and she watched him with half-
slit eyes, certain that he would cast aside his uniform and
come to her. And she would watch him as he shed his
clothing, and came back to her, walking with his particular grace and determination, almost like a wildcat assured
of his every movement.

He did not cast aside his clothing then, but caught her
foot and delicately teased the arch and heel and toes. Then
his tongue ran a straight trail down her calf and along her
inner thigh, and even as she gasped he wedged the hardness of his shoulders there and delved his kiss into the
very center and secret place of her most haunting desire.
She bit her lip, longing to cry out. She tugged upon his
hair and her head began to thrash. Sweet waves of ecstasy
wracked her, sweeping through her body like waves upon
the shore. She fought him, yet her head tossed upon the

pillow and wild cries escaped her as her body surged of its own accord against her. He led her on and on, and when she thought that she could stand no more, he was gone again.

And this time it was to shed his clothing.

Naked, he came back to her. His shaft as hard as steel, he thrust within her, and was welcomed by the warm encompassing sheath of her body. The waves began again, they came to crest and build and crest again with each stroke of his body. He rose high above her and his eyes met hers, dark with passion, or with anger, she knew not which. Did he make love . . . or hate? She did not know. But the passion could not be denied. It stormed upon them, and music of their every breath and whisper and cry. It made the air a silken cloud, it made the night a bit of magic in a world gone destitute of fantasy. Still his eyes held her, and still he stroked within her, urgency filling him. The waves coming upon her seemed to rise and shatter and sprinkle down again in tiny flakes of silver rapture. Again and again climax seized her, and she shuddered and trembled and shook in his arms. He thrust again with vehemence, and she felt the startling heat and liquid as his seed rushed into her, filling her.

He touched her cheek and tenderly kissed her lips, then he fell from her, coming to her side.

Moments of silence passed. Then she started to speak, and he touched his finger to her lips. "No. Not now. Not tonight."

"Eric!" she cried. "Please listen. I—I love you!"

Tension filled him, the muscles of his arms tightened and bulged and his features constricted until they were taut and anguished. She thought that he would strike her then, or that his fingers would wind around her throat and crush away her air.

"By all the saints, madame, play your games no more this night!" he swore violently.

"But it is no game, no ploy, no taunt!" she insisted, challenging his anger. "Eric!" She choked upon his name, tears rising to her eyes.

He exhaled, forcing his body to ease, and he shook with

a sudden venom. "Would God that I could believe you!" he said, his voice low, harsh.

"Please . . ."

"No! No more tonight! If you would give love, lady, then prove love."

And so she fell silent, and in seconds he let out a hoarse cry, pulling her close once again. And after the breeze had come in to gently cool the heat that had remained so slick and damp upon their flesh, he kissed her upper arm and then began to make love to her again. This time she touched him in turn. Freely. Allowed herself to stroke the hard muscles of his arms and chest, the lean sinew of his hips, the tightness of his buttocks. She teased and seduced, taking him into her hands, sweeping her hair over his naked flesh and touching him with the tip of her tongue, with her kiss, the lash and lave of her tongue. . . .

When the tremors of ecstasy faded next, he held her. And in the darkness and quiet of the night, sleep, deep and dreamless, came to them both.

When she awoke, he was dressed again. A new white shirt, clean white breeches, his doublet and his frock coat in blue and red, his cockaded military hat upon his head. He stood by the window, as if he waited for her to awake.

She knew instantly that things had changed, that the night was over. She drew the covers against her breasts, and she stared at him. He turned slowly toward her. The eyes that fell upon her were the eyes of a stranger, deep, dark, and distant.

"You're leaving," she said.

"We're going after Lord Dunmore. You knew that."

"Yes," she whispered. "Am I—am I to be a prisoner here?"

He shook his head. For a moment the beginnings of elation filled her. If they had time . . . if they just had time, perhaps there could be a separate peace between them. Perhaps she could explain that her heart had not changed, but that she was no longer fighting. She was his wife and would take his side. She could even learn to be a patriot.

"Then I am free," she said.

"No."

"What?"

He moved across the room, picking up his saber, his musket and dirk. "You are going to France."

"France! No, Eric, I will not—"

"You will."

Stunned, she swept the covers around her and tried to leap from the bed. She stumbled within her swath of sheets. He caught her, and her eyes, in tempest, met his. "Eric, I beg of you, leave me here. I did not betray you and I'll not—"

"Alas, I cannot believe you," he told her softly.

"But you said that I—" She broke off, and his brows raised expectantly. His lip curled as he awaited her words. She flushed furiously. "You said—"

"You have my forgiveness. Just not my trust."

"I will not go to France, I'll escape to England!" she threatened, afraid of the tears that burned behind her lids. He was casting her away, she realized.

"No, you will not. You will not be alone," he promised her.

"Eric—"

"No! Don't beg, plead, or threaten! This once, my love, you will obey me." He hesitated, and his words were bitter when he spoke again. "In France, my love, you can cause us no more harm. I suggest that you dress. Your escort will be here any minute."

"My escort?"

"Cassidy, Pierre—Jacques Bisset."

Bisset. She would never escape him to run to England. She knew that. Jacques had never forgotten what the English had done to the Acadians. Nor did he forgive. He was a better guardian than a father might be.

"You cannot do this!" she charged him. Her fingers curled about his arms and she shouted with fear and fury. "Eric, please! Listen to me. I did not do this! You are a fool if you will not believe me. You will be hurt, because the person who did give out this information will betray you again." He ignored her, moving about. Fear rose, and desperation, and before she knew it, she was shouting in fury, severing anything that remained between them. "Oh, you bastard! I will hate you, I will never forgive you!"

"Cheer up. Dunmore may reach me yet."

"You should die by the hangman's rope!"

"Should I? Will you cry—since you do love me so much?"

"Oh, Eric! Please! Don't send me away!"

He swept her up into his arms and redeposited her upon the bed. He looked into the tearful liquid emerald of her eyes, and for the life of him, he wanted to recant.

His heart hardened. Cameron Hall could have burned to the ground. She had gone with Tarryton. By her own admission, she had gone with the man. More than anything in the world, he wanted to believe that she loved him. He wanted to believe her innocent.

But he could not trust her. He had done so before, and he had been betrayed. Time and time again she had betrayed him. Other lives were at stake.

He smiled, then bent down and kissed her lips. He had to leave, but he could not resist. He cupped her breast with his fingers and felt the anguish of longing burst upon him. He kissed her long and slowly, and stroked her flesh as if he could memorize with his hands as well as his mind.

Then he rose and gazed down upon her ruefully. *"Au revoir,* my love."

He turned and walked to the door. She was on her feet again, flying after him. "Eric!"

He closed the door. He heard the thud of her hands against it and then he heard her curses. He stiffened as he listened to the words upon her lips. Then he heard her fall against the door. And he heard the anguish of her tears.

He squared his shoulders and wondered how he would bear it, knowing that she was in France. At least she would be far away from Tarryton. And she would be safe. Bisset would see to that. He leaned against the wall in anguish.

He straightened at last, breathing deeply. Then he walked down the hallway, down the long portrait gallery. He paused, looking up at his ancestors, at the men and women who had carved out this Eden from the raw wilderness.

The fires of war were burning brightly in his Eden.

He turned and walked again. Lewis would be awaiting him and his men. They had to break the British menace, and he had to return to Washington soon. The Congress was meeting; any day the colonies would declare for freedom.

And he would risk all in that struggle.

But he would not lose! he swore, and he paused, looking back to the bedroom. Poignant, wistful pain swept into his heart. If only she were with them!

If only she did love him.

In the gallery he stared at the portraits. Theirs were the last ones. Her hair was swept up in ringlets and fashionable curls, her beautiful eyes had been caught in all the majesty of their color. Her smile was one that could make a man willing to die in any manner for a mere whisper from her lips.

He was beside her, in the very uniform he wore now.

Lord and Lady Cameron of Cameron Hall, one of the finest properties in Tidewater Virginia! he thought with some bitter irony. They graced the gallery as finely as any of his illustrious ancestors, when they might well be the very fall of the house. Was he the first Cameron to sell his soul for love, his birthright for some vague dream of new country?

Amanda . . .

He had not left the house, and already his blood warmed and his muscles tensed and tightened when he thought her name and conjured before his eyes a vision of the woman he had left behind. He was tempted to turn back, but he could not. There were battles to be waged. In Philadelphia men were busy writing the words for the Declaration of Independence. Thomas Jefferson was drafting the document, he had heard. The Virginians were very proud of that fact, just as they were proud that many of the ideas were coming from words penned for Virginia by George Mason.

The British would hang him, he thought, if they ever got their hands upon him. Dunmore, his old friend, would hang him higher than any other.

He looked up at the portraits again and smiled wryly. "What do you say, monsieurs? Am I a fool? Casting this heritage to the winds of war?" Perhaps not, he thought, his smile deepening. His forebears had left behind a safe and guarded world to strike out into a wilderness. They would understand that he gambled all in a dream of liberty and honor. Even if his wife did not.

He turned, fighting the urge to go back to touch her just once again. He left the portraits behind and hurried down the stairs. Cassidy waited for him at the front door, holding his mount.

"There's a flagon of whiskey in your saddlebag," Cassidy told him.

"For breakfast, eh, Cassidy?"

Cassidy grinned. "Thought you might be needing it."

Eric agreed. "Aye, that I might. But I'll have to get the troops moving first. Wouldn't do to show them a drunken example, eh, Cassidy?"

"No, sir, it wouldn't do at all."

Eric mounted upon his horse and looked down to Cassidy. "You'll go with her to France?"

"Wherever you send me, milord, I will go."

Eric stretched out his hand and took Cassidy's dark one. "Thank you. And Pierre. And see that Jacques sails with her too; that is very important. He will let no harm come to her."

Cassidy nodded. "Jacques will guard her with his life. His loyalty to her is deep seated."

"It should be," Eric murmured.

"Milord?"

He hesitated, looking down at Cassidy. "I believe that she is his daughter," he said quietly, then grinned at Cassidy's dumbfounded expression. "Say nothing."

"No!" Cassidy agreed. "You mean Lord Sterling—"

"Is a monster," Eric agreed, but said nothing more on the subject. If there was a God, and if there were a multitude of battles, surely Sterling would be taken home to his eternal rest before it was all over. "I will come as soon as I can. God alone knows when that will be. If I am killed—"

"Lord Cameron, please!"

He waved a hand impatiently in the air. "It is only a matter of time before independence and war are proclaimed. Virginia will set herself free before the others, I believe. Death is a fact of life, and very much one of war. If I am killed, care for my lady still, Cassidy, for I love her."

"Always, milord," Cassidy assured him, his dark eyes grave and misted.

Eric saluted quickly and rode away toward the fields where the troops were encamped.

He did not turn to look back at the house.

He did not dare. If he saw her face in the window, he would not be able to ride away.

XVI ❧

During the first few days of July, Andrew Lewis took command of the troops gathered on the mainland elevation that fronted Gwynn's Island, where Dunmore had brought his fleet. Charles Lee had reported him as living caterpillarlike off of the land, stripping it bare, taking everything.

Lewis fired the first shot himself.

It was later reported that the first cannon shot ripped into the governor's cabin, the second killed three of his crew, and the third wounded Dunmore in the leg and brought his china crashing down upon him.

It was a complete rout. Those who could do so fled. Eric wondered briefly if either Nigel Sterling or Robert Tarryton had been killed or wounded in the fray, but there was no way of knowing. Nor did it matter, he tried to tell himself. The threat was gone.

Or was it?

By night he often lay awake, and when he slept, he kept remembering Amanda's face and her eyes, and her whispered, desperate words of innocence. She entered into his dreams, and she tortured him. His anger had kept him from listening to her, but now, with Dunmore far from Virginia shores, he wondered if he shouldn't have listened.

News arrived from South Carolina that was exciting and uplifting to the colonial soldiers—Admiral Sir Peter Parker's squadron had attacked the palmetto-log fortification on Sullivan's Island, the key to the harbor defenses at Charleston. Under Colonel William Moultrie, amazing damage was done to the British fleet. The ships limped away, with British general Sir Henry Clinton determined to rejoin Howe at New York.

With Dunmore bested, Eric was due to return to Washington's side, but he decided to return home instead. There was a slight possibility that Amanda had not sailed as yet. And he was suddenly eager to listen to her again. Desperate. He had said horrible things to her, made horrible accusations, and many had been driven by simple fear and fury.

He rode hard, leaving Frederick in the dust. But when he reached the long drive to the house, his heart sank. Beyond the rise he could see that the *Good Earth* was no longer at her berth; Amanda had indeed sailed.

He reached the house and threw open the door anyway, but only Richard and the maids were there to greet him. The house seemed cold and empty in the dead heat of July. He slowly climbed the steps to the gallery, and he felt the emptiness close around him. She had come to be so much a part of the house. The scent of her perfume remained to haunt him, almost like an echo of her voice, a sweet and feminine whisper that taunted and teased. It was best! In France she would be safe—and the colonies would be safe from her!

No words, no logic, mattered. His world was cold, his house was nothing but masonry and brick and wood without her.

"Lord Cameron!"

He swung around and looked down the stairs. Frederick

had come bursting into the room. "Lord Cameron! Independence! The Congress has called for independence! A declaration was read in Philadelphia on the sixth day of July, and it's beginning to appear in the newspapers all over the country! Lord Cameron, we've done it! We've all done it! We're free and independent men!"

Aye, they had done it. Eric's fingers wound around the railing of the gallery balcony as he stared down at the printer. They'd already been fighting over a year, but now it was official. They could never go back now. Never.

They were free.

A fierce trembling shook through him. He was suddenly glad that he had heard it here, in Cameron Hall. Despite the emptiness. He knew again what was so worth fighting for, worth dying for.

He hurried down the stairs. "Richard! Brandy, man, the best in the house! The Congress has acted at last! My God, get the servants, get everyone. A toast! To . . . freedom!"

Worth fighting for . . .

By the time Eric returned to New York and Washington's side, he had come to realize just what the words meant. The British commander Howe had already landed 32,000 troops on Staten Island. Half of the Continental Army of 13,000, under General Putnam, was sent across Long Island. The remaining half remained on Manhattan.

The Battle of Long Island took place on August 27. Howe landed 20,000 of his troops on Long Island between the twenty-second and twenty-fifth of the month, then turned Putnam's left flank.

Eric rode back and forth between the divisions with intelligence and information. He had never so admired Washington as he did when the general determined to evacuate Long Island. The brilliant operation took place between the twenty-ninth and thirtieth.

It was a bitter fall. In early September, Sergeant Ezra Lee attacked the British fleet in the *American Turtle*—a one-man submarine created by David Bushnell. The operation was mainly unsuccessful, but the *Turtle* created tremendous alarm and gave a burst of amusement and renewed vigor to the American forces.

But from there, things became ever more grim. On September 12 the Americans decided to abandon New York. On the fifteenth, American troops fled as the British assaulted them across the East River from Brooklyn. On the sixteenth, at the Battle of Harlem Heights, although Washington managed to slow Howe, Washington's communications were threatened, and he was forced to pull back.

Eric was in George's tent at the end of the month poring over maps of New York and New Jersey when a message arrived. He watched the general's face, then he saw the shoulders of his giant friend slump and his face turn ashen. "They have caught my young spy," he said.

Eric thought back quickly. Washington had asked a highly respected group from Connecticut, the Rangers, to supply a man to stay in New York to obtain information on the Brits' position. A young man named Nathan Hale had volunteered on the second call, and he had gone in pretending to be a Dutch schoolmaster.

Washington rubbed his temple fiercely. "He couldn't have been more than twenty-one. He was betrayed. Howe condemned him to hang." He exhaled on a long note, looking at his sheet of correspondence again. "He gave a speech that impressed them all, ending it like this—listen, Eric, it's amazing—'I only regret that I have but one life to give for my country.' One life. My God."

"It is war," Eric said quietly after a moment.

"It is war. We will lose many more," Washington admitted. "But this young Hale . . . that such courage should be cruelly snuffed from life!"

Cruel, yes, Eric thought, riding with his troops the next day. Cruel, but something more. Nathan Hale's words were being whispered and shouted by all men. In death Nathan Hale had given an army an inspiration. He had gained immortality.

By night the smell of powder seemed to penetrate Eric's dreams. With his eyes opened or closed, he saw lines and lines of men, heard the screams of men and horses alike, saw the burst of cannon and heard its terrible roar. But sometimes, when the black powder faded, he would see Amanda. And she would be walking toward him through the mist and death and carnage, and her eyes would be liquid with recrimination.

They had hanged Hale, the British. Traitors are usually hanged, and that is the way that war goes.

But what if she hadn't lied? What if her days as spy had ended? What if someone else played them all false?

Groaning, he would awaken. And with his eyes open to the dawn, he knew that he would ride and fight again— and lead men unto death.

On October 28 they fought the Battle of White Plains. The Americans fought bravely and valiantly, and with a startling skill and determination. Eventually the British regulars drove them off the field. Waving his blood-soaked sword in the air, Eric shouted the order to retreat to the men under his command.

Anne Marie and Sir Thomas were often his consolation then. Anne Marie continued to follow her father to war. On the field she loaded weapons, supplied water, and tended to the wounded. When conditions permitted, Eric ate with the two, and when the meal was over, he would often sit with Anne Marie. One night, as they walked beneath the trees, she turned into his arms. She rose up on her toes and kissed him. He responded, as he had before, his heart hammering, his body quickening. She drew his hand to her breast, and he touched her softness, but then he folded her hands together, drew away from her her, and gently touched her cheek. "I'm a married man, Anne Marie. And you are too fine a woman to be any man's mistress."

"What if I do not care?" she whispered.

He exhaled slowly and felt her eyes upon him in the darkness.

She smiled. "I am too late, Lord Cameron, so it seems." She teased him, her smile gentle. "When you were wild and reckless and seemed to collect women, I was seeking a ring about my finger. And now I would have nothing more but a few nights with a hero in my bed, and it really wouldn't matter if I were the most practiced whore on the continent. Eric, go after your wife. Bring her home. I do not believe that she would have betrayed you so completely."

He folded her hands together. "Anne Marie, I cannot. Perhaps I should not come anymore—"

She pressed her finger to his lips. "No. Don't take away your friendship. I need you and Damien."

"Ah! My bloodthirsty young cousin-in-law. He is still scarcely speaking to me; he does so under orders only. But he is a fine young man—"

"And in love, didn't you know?"

"No, I did not," Eric told her.

Anne Marie dimpled prettily. "With Lady Geneva. I suppose it began long ago in Williamsburg. Now he pines for her when he cannot travel south. I believe she will come north to be with him."

"Really? Geneva does love her comforts."

"You know her so well?"

"I did," he murmured. "Well, perhaps she has caught patriot's fever herself. Only time will tell."

"Only time." Anne Marie kissed him chastely upon the cheek. "Go for your wife, Eric."

"I cannot," he said, and in such a manner that she knew their talk had come to the end. She saw the twist of his jaw and the ice in his eyes, and she fell silent.

In November Fort Washington, on northern Manhattan overlooking the Hudson, fell. Twenty-eight hundred Americans were captured. And the Americans were forced to evacuate Fort Lee, in New Jersey, with the loss of much badly needed material.

The Americans began their retreat into New Jersey, southward. Charles Lee was left behind to cover the retreat. He and four thousand men were captured near Morristown.

Washington paled at the news. Furious, he refrained from swearing. He led the remaining three thousand men of the Continental Army southward and crossed the Delaware into Pennsylvania. Congress fled from Philadelphia to Baltimore, and Washington was given dictatorial powers.

Eric changed into buckskins and slipped behind the lines to discover the British position. He kept remembering Nathan Hale, and he prayed that he could be as heroic as the younger man should he be captured. The British would dance at his hanging, he was certain.

But he was able to gain information easily enough. Howe, confident of a quick final victory in the spring, had gone into winter quarters, the bulk of his men in New York and southern New Jersey.

As Christmas neared, Eric sat with other commanders and watched as Washington paced the ground and pointed at the maps. "We are desperate, gentlemen. Desperate. Our army has been sheared to threads, those men who remain with me talk constantly of the fact that their enlistment periods are up. Now, I have a plan . . ."

His plan was risky, desperate, dangerous—and brilliant, Eric thought. On Christmas night they recrossed the Delaware, nine miles north of Trenton, with 2,400 men, during a snowstorm. The cold was bitter, the wind was horrid, the water was ice. Eric felt his face chafed, he felt the numbing sting as the water rose from the tempest-tossed river in a spray to strike him. But in the pale light ahead he saw Washington standing at the bow of his boat. All of the men saw him. They crossed in safely.

At dawn they fell on the Hessian garrison at Trenton.

Victory was complete. Drunk, stunned, and hungover, the mercenaries fighting for the British tried to rise from their beds, but the colonials were all over them. Eric had little need to shout orders, for his troops moved with swift efficiency, and the attack was a complete surprise. When it was all over, of fourteen hundred Hessians, a thousand had been captured, thirty had been killed, and the Americans had lost only two men frozen to death and five wounded. Most important, perhaps, was the booty they captured, a good supply of small arms, cannon, and other munitions.

That night the small band celebrated. Within twenty-four hours, however, danger threatened again. The British general, Lord Cornwallis, was moving quickly. By January 2, he faced the American position with 5,000 men while another 2,500 awaited an order join him from Princeton.

"There is no way to fight this battle," Washington said. "Campfires . . ." he muttered.

"We leave them burning?"

"We leave them burning."

They slipped away by night. On January 3, battle cries went up as they came upon the British regulars who were marching to join Cornwallis. The battle was fierce, and furious, and when it was over, the Americans were victorious. They hurried on to Princeton and captured vast supplies of military equipment, then hastened away to Morristown.

That night they again celebrated.

"They will tout you as one of the most brilliant commanders ever," Eric told Washington.

"Unless I lose a few battles. Then I shall be crucified."

"My God, no man can do more than you have done!"

The general smiled, stretching out his feet. "Then until the spring, I shall be a hero. Cornwallis is abandoning his positions in western New Jersey because we have cut his communications. It is time we dig in for winter ourselves." He hesitated. "I have some letters for you."

Eric was a mature man, a major general, a man who commanded hundreds of men, who shouted orders in the field, who never flinched beneath powder or sword. He was, in fact, growing old with the damned war. And yet now he felt his fingers tremor, his palms go damp. "From my wife?"

Washington shook his head. "No, but from France. One from your man, Cassidy. Another from Mr. Franklin."

"Franklin!"

"Mmm. Poor Ben. He's been sent there by Congress to woo the French into assisting our cause. Seventy years old is Ben. And quite the rage of Paris, they are saying. A good choice by Congress, so it seems. The ladies are all charmed by his sayings and his wit and even his spectacles. Even the young queen is impressed by him."

"He is an impressive man," Eric muttered as he ripped open the letter from Cassidy and scanned it quickly. Things were well, the voyage had been smooth, they were living in the shadow of the royal party at Versailles. Everything was wonderful, so it seemed, and yet Cassidy urged him to come. He looked at the letter and realized that it had been written in September. He frowned at Washington.

"The letter went to Virginia before it reached me," Washington said.

Eric nodded, then ripped open the second letter. Worded in the most polite and discreet tones, Benjamin Franklin informed him that he was about to become a father. " 'Seems a pity that the child cannot be born upon American soil as you are so firm and kind and staunch a father of our land, but nevertheless, sir, I thought that the news would delight you and as it seems from her conversation your lady is not disposed to write, I have taken this upon myself . . ."

The letter went on. Eric didn't see the words. He was standing, and he didn't realized it.

All the months, all of the longing, all of the wonder. And now Amanda was going to have a child and she was all the way across the Atlantic Ocean. And Franklin was right. There was no way that the child could be born on American soil. He tried to count, and he couldn't even manage to do that properly. He had last seen her in June. He had seen her in March . . . but no, he would have known by June. What was nine months from June?

"Eric?" Washington inquired.

"She's . . . she's having a child. At last," Eric said, choking on the words.

"At last?" Washington's brows shot up. "My dear fellow, you were married what—two years?"

"Three now," Eric corrected him. "I had thought that we could not, I . . ." His voice trailed away. He knew that no matter how dearly Washington had loved his adopted stepchildren and stepgrandchildren, he had wanted his own child. Washington bore no grudge against other men and loved Martha dearly, yet Eric felt suddenly awkward.

It was the surprise, the shock. He sank back to his chair
and he remembered that he had accused her of being Tarryton's mistress. And he had sent her away in raw fury,
God alone knew what she would feel for him, if she
wouldn't have rejoiced in betraying him in France. No! he
assured himself in anguish. She was not alone. Jacques
Bisset was with her, Jacques who surely knew that no
matter what he had said or done, he loved her. . . .

"God!" he said aloud.

Washington sat back, studying him. "It is winter. I can
foresee no action for some time to come. Perhaps I can
send you with letters for the French to Paris myself. If
. . . if you can find a ship that will sail."

Eric grinned suddenly. "I can find a ship to sail. My
own, George. I shall take the *Lady Jane*. And I will make it
up to you. I will capture a British ship with a multitude of
arms, I swear it."

Washington leaned over his desk. "I will start on the
necessary papers."

"Lady Cameron!"

Amanda was seated in one of the small gardens off the
tapis vert, or "green carpet," the broad walk in the center
of the gardens at the Palace of Versailles. She had gone
there to be alone, but she knew the low, well-modulated
voice very well now, and as was usual, she felt a smile
curve her lip. It was Ben Franklin, and he was huffing a bit
with the exertion of walking. He wasn't a young man, of
course, but he didn't really act like an old man at all. His
eyes were young, she decided, as young as his thoughts
and ideas and dreams.

"I'm here, Mr. Franklin!" she called, and he came
around a newly planted rose bush to meet her.

"Ah, there you are, my dear!"

"Sit—if there is room!" Amanda encouraged him. She
was so very large now, she felt as if she were taking up the
entire garden seat with her bulk. He smiled brightly and
did so.

"How are things going?" she asked him.

"Ah, *pas mal!*" he said, "Not bad, not bad. And yet not so

good either. I think that the French are our friends. Individual counts and barons support me, and I believe that eventually the king and his ministers will fall in for us. I believe the queen is all for me."

"Marie Antoinette? She is quite smitten, sir, I would say!" Amanda teased him. Of course, it was true. The queen was as taken with Benjamin Franklin as all the other ladies seemed to be.

Franklin sighed. "Not that I'm at all sure she even knows what I'm asking for! Alas, they're just children, you see. The king is scarce a boy of twenty-three, and the queen—oh! But then you are barely that yourself, milady! My apologies. It's just that when you reach my age, well . . ."

"There was no offense at all taken, Mr. Franklin. Besides, they say that Louis tries very hard, that he is thoughtful and considerate, but not a very talented ruler as yet. Perhaps he will become so in time. My goodness, I should hope so. This palace itself is so magnificent—and so huge!"

Versailles was huge and beautiful, and under other circumstances, Amanda might have loved it. But she lived with too much bitterness inside of her to truly enjoy the magnificence with which she lived.

She had not believed that Eric should be able to ride away from her so easily—and yet he had. She had watched him from their window when he had ridden, and he had not so much as looked back.

And even then she had thought that he would turn around. That he would come back to her. But he did not. As soon as the necessary repairs had been done to the ship, Cassidy had told her that they would be leaving on the *Good Earth*. She had been delighted to discover that Danielle had recovered fully from her injury at Tarryton's hands, and would accompany her, but she still could not believe that she was being escorted off her own property.

She shivered suddenly. The story of the valiant Nathan Hale had reached France, and she could not forget that had she been a man and captured by some man other than her husband, she might well have swung from a rope herself. Except that she was innocent!

Innocent . . .

She had remembered her innocence during the whole
long ocean voyage. She had remembered it when she had
first started to get sick upon the open sea, and she had
been so wretchedly sick that she had thought it a pity Eric
wasn't there. He would have thought her duly punished if
he could have just seen the green shade of her face. She
didn't normally react so to ships, perhaps it was a just
punishment for trying to save her cousin's ungrateful
throat!

But then, slowly, she had begun to realize that it was not
the sea making her so wretched. It probably took her
longer to discover than it should have, but her mind was
ever active, and she felt as if her heart bled daily. Sometimes she was furious with a raw, scarce-controlled passion; sometimes her anger was cold, something that made
her numb. She swore that she would never forgive Eric,
never. Then she missed him all over again and wondered
if he lived and if he was well. Then she thought that he
deserved to rot for what he had done to her, but then that
thought would flee her mind, and she would pray quickly
that God would not let him die because of her careless
thoughts.

They had nearly reached France by the time she realized, with some definite shock, that she was going to have
a child. Joy filled her. No amount of anger or hatred could
stop the absolute delight that filled her body, heart, and
soul. She had been so afraid that they never would have a
child. Eric had even accused her of trying not to have one.
And now, when all between them seemed severed forever . . .

She was going to have a child. An heir for Cameron
Hall.

Should the hall survive the war. For it was war now. The
colonies were thirteen united states, and it was full-scale
war.

And in the midst of their own personal warfare and battle, a child had at last been conceived. She hugged the
knowledge to herself at first, but by the time they at last
stepped from the *Good Earth* to French soil, Danielle had

guessed her secret. Danielle wanted her to write to Eric immediately, but Amanda could not do so. She was thrilled with the child and determined that she would do nothing to risk the babe's health whatsoever, but the bitterness was alive within her, and she would not write. She would not have him send for the child. He could not have their babe so easily. When he determined to sail for her, then he would find out about the child.

Perhaps there was more, too, she realized, trembling. He had accused her of adultery with Robert. She could not believe that he meant his words, but then she had never seen Eric so angry, so cold, as he had been that last time. She could not forgive him. She swore to herself that she hated him.

But it was, of course, a lie, and she prayed nightly that he had not been killed. News came daily to the French court. Even if it was old by the time that it reached there, Amanda thrived on all that she heard. Virginia, Manhattan, Long Island, New Jersey, Pennsylvania—and Trenton. She heard about them all. General Washington's maneuvers of the last days of December and early January were being characterized as some of the most brilliant in military history. And Eric was always with Washington, so it was always possible to know how he fared. Fine, and well, she was always told. A Virginia horseman to match any, he was usually seen mounted atop his beautiful black horse, Joshua, and always at the forefront of action. He had survived every confrontation.

So far.

It was nearly spring. The first days of March were upon them. Snows would be thawing in Pennsylvania and New York, and it would be time for men to go to war again.

He could die, she thought. He could die without ever knowing that he had a child. And he would have one soon. Any day, perhaps any hour.

"You look cold," Franklin chastised beside her. "You should not be out here, Lady Cameron, and certainly not alone."

"Oh, I'm not alone, Mr. Franklin. A man of your acute vision must have observed that I am never alone! No, sir, my husband's man, Cassidy, is with me now. And if you will note later, sir, there will be a handsome Acadian man near me, and there is my maid, of course, and my sponsor here, the Comte de la Rochelle."

Franklin nodded and patted her hand. "Well, my dear, there was a rumor, you know, that you were sympathetic to the British."

Her eyes widened. A sudden burst of emotion hurtled past her walls of cool defense. "Rumors! Sir, shall I admit all to you now?" He was her friend, she realized. One of the best friends she had ever had. She knew why he was loved. It wasn't for the things he said, though they were charming—it was the way that he listened, the way he really heard what she had said. The elderly Comte de la Rochelle was very kind, and it was in his apartments in the far wing of the palace where she stayed, but it had not been until Ben Franklin arrived that she had felt comfortable. From the start he had sought to meet with her, he had come to her after his appointments with the ministers, and she had discovered in him a new meaning to revolutionary fever. Until the middle of 1775 he had been eager for reconciliation with Britain, but then he had seen that the desire for independence lay deep in the very hearts of the people. "Once the tide reaches the heart, milady, then no man can change that tide!" he had told her. She had believed him, and she quickly came to see through his eyes. By New Year's day she had realized that she was not just a Virginian but an *American*. She might have been a loyal British subject once, but she was an American now. What that truly meant, she knew, she had yet to discover.

"Amanda, admit to me—"

"Well, sir, there was some truth to rumor," Amanda said softly. Agitated, she rose. She stared back at the palace and caught her breath. Versailles. It was more than half a mile long, she had been told, with two enormous side wings. Once it had been the sight of a small hunting lodge, but Louis XIV had planned a very grand palace, and begun work upon it in 1661. He had hired the best architects, sculptors, and landscape gardeners. His successors had added to it, and now the palace boasted hundreds of rooms, marble floors, hand-painted ceilings, and the most beautiful gardens and landscaping that could be imagined. The king and queen and their retainers lived in such splendor and opulence that it was hard to imagine. They were like children, masters of this fairyland.

She looked from the beauty of the palace, rising against the sun, to Mr. Franklin, and she smiled. He was so plain and simple beside it all, his hose a dull mustard, his breeches blue, his surcoat a dark maroon, and his heavy cloak black. A civilian tricorn sat over the bald spot atop his head, and his hair, snowy white and gray, tufted out from either side. His face was wrinkled and jowled and reddened from cold and wind, but within were those eyes of his, soft blue beneath his spectacles, seeing and knowing all. And he was so much more impressive than the men of the court in their silks and satins and ungodly laces. And the women! Some wore their hair teased and knotted a good foot atop their heads. They called much of it Italian fashion—the most outlandish of it. Thus the term "macaroni." It was used in the song that was becoming very popular called "Yankee Doodle." This impressive fellow was far from "macaroni" fashion! Her smile slowly faded. Neither could they ever accuse her husband of being so. He had never even bent to fashion so far as to powder his hair. His shirts were laced, but never ostentatiously so. And when he moved about the estate he usually wore plain wool hose and dark breeches and a shirt that opened at his throat to display the bronze flesh of his throat and chest and the profusion of dark hair that grew short and crisp upon it . . .

"I was not guilty!" she swore suddenly. "Would God, sir, that you at least would believe me! I was free, can you understand? They had blackmailed me with my cousin, but once I knew he was free, they had nothing else to use against me. I gave away nothing!"

"There, there, now!" Franklin was on his feet. He caught her hands and brought her back to the bench, sitting again. "You must be careful. Mustn't upset the babe! Why, I remember my own dear children's birth . . . I've a son who is still with the British, my dear, so trust me, I do understand. Most men understand. This war is a fragile thing! If you say you are innocent, then I believe you."

"That simply?"

"Well, of course. I do believe that I know you rather well."

She started to laugh. "My husband should have known me well."

Franklin sighed. "He is a good man, Lady Cameron. I've known him long and well too, and you must see things as he did. His name is an old and respected one. It was risked, and he believed that it was by your hand. He fights a war, he marches to battle daily. You have mentioned to me that you do not correspond. I implore you, madame, when the babe is born, you must write to him."

She withdrew her hands quickly. Eric could die! He could ride into battle with his musket and his sword, and he could falter and fail. Exhaustion could overtake him, and his great heart could stop. She could not bear it if he were to perish!

But he had exiled her, cast her away. God knew, he was probably planning divorce proceedings this very moment. She had sworn that she would not forgive him. Her heart had grown cold.

But he could die. . . .

The thought was suddenly so painful that she doubled over. She couldn't breathe.

"Lady Cameron?" Franklin said anxiously.

She shook her head. "It's all right. It's all right. It's quite faded now."

He nodded, watching her anxiously still. When she seemed to have recovered, he smiled. "I've a confession of my own, dear. The moment I arrived here, I wrote to your husband."

"What?" She gasped in dismay.

"I had to, my dear. Lady Cameron, I was sent to England last, and while I waited there at the order of my country, my own dear wife departed this world. Life is short, and wisdom ever so hard to gain, and too oft gained to late. Forgive me—"

"Oh!" Amanda interrupted him. The sharp, blinding pain had seized her again. It was not worry, she realized then. She had gone into labor.

She rose, gasping. "Mr. Franklin—"

"It's all right!" he assured her, on her feet. "A first labor takes hours and hours, Amanda. Hours and hours—"

"Oh! But the pains are coming so quickly."

"Well, then maybe this labor will not be hours and hours! Oh, dear, this is not my forte—"

"Lady Cameron!"

She swung around. Both Cassidy and Jacques were hurrying up to her. She smiled. "See," she told Franklin. "I never am alone."

But she was glad that she was not alone, for the next pain doubled her over. She thought that she would fall, but she was scooped up into strong arms. She looked up and she saw Jacques's dear face, and she smiled and touched his cheek. "Thank you," she murmured.

He did not smile, but searched out her eyes. She was glad of his strength, for the palace was so very big, and her chambers were at the far end of it. They left the gardens and traveled long hallways. Finally Jacques burst open a set of molded double doors; they had reached the apartments of the Comte de la Rochelle. The elderly French statesman was sitting before the fire, warming his toes, when they entered.

"My dear—" he began, but he saw Jacques's face and moved quickly instead. "Danielle! The lady's time has come! Be quick, I shall send for the physician!"

Jacques carried her into the beautiful room that had been assigned her. Danielle was already running in before him, sweeping back the fine damask bedcurtains and the spread. Jacques set Amanda down. Suddenly she did not want him to go. She squeezed his hand. He touched her forehead and smiled to her, and in softly spoken French he promised her a beautiful son. Then he left. Danielle urged her to sit up and started tugging on her silk and velvet gown.

"I can help—" Amanda assured her, but the pain attacked her savagely again, and this time, it was so sudden that she could not help but cry out.

"Hold to the bed frame!" Danielle advised her. "Ah, *ma petite*! It will be much worse before it will be better!"

Danielle was so very right. For hours the pain came at short intervals. At first Amanda felt that she could bear it —the result would be her child, the babe she so desperately craved. Someone to hold and to love and to need her.

Then the pain became intense, and so frequent that she began to long for death. She swore, and she cried, and some point she didn't know what she was saying. Exhausted, she drifted to a semisleep in the few minutes between the pains. She dreamed of Eric Cameron, coming toward her in his boots and breeches and open shirt. He had loved her once, she thought. His eyes had danced upon her with silver and blue desire, and his mouth had turned into a sensual curl when he had touched her. He had held her against so much danger, but she hadn't trusted in the strength of his arms. He was speaking to her, accusing her of things.

"You have done something. You have done something to deny me a child." She protested. She promised that she had not. But he accused her anew, the silver lights of laughter and desire gone from his gaze. "Betraying bitch!" But there is a child now! she tried to tell him. He already had the baby; he held it high and away from her. "My son returns with me, my son returns with me—"

A savage pain, just like the thrust of a knife, cut across her lower back and wound around to her front.

"Easy, *ma petite*, easy!" It was Danielle who spoke, Amanda realized dimly.

Amanda screamed, trying to rise to consciousness. Her eyes were wild, her hair was soaked and lay plastered about her head. A cool cloth fell upon her forehead, smoothing back her hair. "No!" she screamed the word. "He cannot have my baby, the lying, treacherous bastard shall not take the baby away—"

"Amanda, if you mean me, my love, I've no intention of taking the babe away. If you'll only be so good as to deliver him to us."

Her eyes flew wide. She had to be dreaming still. He was there, standing above her. It was Eric with the damp sponge, cooling her brow, smoothing back her hair. She stared at him in distress and amazement. He could not be there. He despised her so, and now he was seeing her thus! Wretched and in anguish and so much pain. And though he spoke softly, she thought that there was bitterness in his voice. And coldness, like an arctic frost.

"No," she whispered, staring at him.

"Aye, my love," he retorted, his devil's grin in place, silver and indigo glittering in his gaze. He was nearly dressed as in her dream, wearing ivory hose and navy breeches, his frock coat and surcoat both shed, the laced sleeves of his shirt shoved high upon his muscled arms, his hair neatly queued back from his face.

"Please, don't be!" she hissed, and she did not know if she wanted him gone because she was angry still, or because she was so afraid that she could never attract him again.

His glance moved toward the foot of the bed, and she realized that, of course, they were not alone. She followed his gaze and saw Danielle and the French physician. She swallowed tightly. Again a pain seized, swift and sure and barely a minute from the one before it. She cried out pitifully, unable to hold back. Danielle whispered feverishly to Eric.

"It's over twenty-four hours. I do not see how she bears it."

"It is time now," the French physician said. "She must find the strength to bear down."

Eric's arms came around her. "Go away!" she begged him.

"He has said that you must push, Amanda. I'll help you."

"I do not want your help—"

"But you shall have it! Now do as you are told."

It was not so hard, for an overwhelming desire to do so came to her. Nor would Eric let her quit. When she would have fallen back he pressed her forward, his voice full of command. "Push, madame!"

"I am not among your troops, Major General!" she retorted, and then she was gasping and unable to say more, and they let her fall back at last.

"Come, come! A little Cameron head has nearly entered into the world!"

"Again, Amanda—"

"Eric, please—"

"Push!"

She did so, and that time she was rewarded with the sweetest sense of relief. The child emerged from her body and the physician exclaimed with delight, slapping the tiny form. A lusty cry was heard, and Danielle called out, "A girl! *Une petite jeune fille, une belle petite jeune fille—*"

"Oh!" Amanda gasped. She had been so very happy, so thrilled and excited. But then pain had seized her again, and she was suddenly terrified that she was going to die.

"What is it?" Eric demanded harshly.

"The pain—"

The Frenchman severed the birth cord, Danielle took the squalling baby girl. Eric gripped her hand, staring at her. "You are not going to die, my love. I have not finished with you," he promised her.

She wanted to answer him, but she could not. The urge to push had come upon her again.

"*Alors!* There are two!" The doctor laughed.

"Push!" Eric commanded her again. She could not. She was so exhausted she might well have been dead. He lifted her up, forced her to press forward.

"*Bon! Bon!*" the doctor exclaimed, nodding to Eric. Eric let her fall back, cradling her shoulders. She closed her eyes. She could remember the security of those arms. Once he had held her against the world. And now they were very much strangers. They were enemies to a greater extent than they had ever been. But he was there, holding her. Because he wanted their child. . . .

But she had a daughter, and she was so grateful! The baby was alive and well and—

"A boy, Lord Cameron!" The doctor laughed. "A boy, small, a twin, but all his fingers and toes are there! He will grow! His color is good. He is fine."

A son. She had a daughter and a son. Her eyes closed.

They had said that they were healthy. Twins. Two . . . and both alive and well and with good color. She wanted to see them so badly. She couldn't begin to open her eyes.

"Amanda?"

She heard Eric's voice. She felt his arms, but she could not open her eyes.

"My lord Cameron, you have gotten her through, but she has lost much blood, and the time, you see. I still have work to do with her, and then she must sleep. My lord, Danielle has the girl. If you insist upon helping, take your son."

"My son. Aye, gladly, sir! I will take my son!"

She heard Eric say the words, and then she heard no more.

She must have slept a very long time, and very deeply, for when she awoke she was bathed and clean and wearing a soft white nightgown and her hair was dried and tied back from her face with a long blue ribbon. She awoke hearing a fretful crying. She opened her eyes, a smile on her face as she reached out for her infants.

Danielle was with her, she saw, smiling grandly as she walked over to the huge draped bed with the two bundles. "Your daughter, milady, or your son?" Danielle teased affectionately.

"I don't know!" Amanda laughed, delighted. They were both screaming away. She decided to let them scream for a moment, removing their bundling, checking out the tiny bodies. "Oh, how extraordinary!" She laughed, for her baby daughter had a thatch of bright red hair and the little boy was very dark. Both had bright blue eyes at the moment. She checked them both swiftly, counting fingers and toes. "Oh, they are perfect!"

"A little small, so we must take care. Lord Cameron was anxious to leave, but the size of these two has slowed even him down."

"Leave!" Amanda gasped.

"We're going home," Danielle said.

"We—all of us?"

"Mais oui! What else?"

Amanda exhaled slowly, afraid to speak her fears. No husband would have taken his infants—and not his wife. Not even Eric.

Yet that did not heal the distance between them.

"You must try to feed both. Jeannette Lisbeth—the queen's woman—says that you can hold both. . . ." Danielle came to her and adjusted the babies in her arms and her gowns. Amanda cried out with a little squeal of delight as her twins latched upon her breasts, tugging, creating a glowing sensation within her.

"They are so very small, however shall I manage?" She rested her chin atop one downy head, and touched a little cheek with her finger. "Oh, Danielle! Now I am so afraid. There are so many awful diseases—"

"Shush, and enjoy your children, *ma petite.* God will look after us all!"

Amanda smiled at Danielle's statement. She took delight in the infants, touching them, smiling. But then she stiffened, startled and wary, when the door suddenly opened without a knock. She would have quickly drawn her gown together except that she could not.

Eric had come. He was really there. Tall, elegant this morning in dark brocade and snow-white hose and silver-buckled shoes. She wanted to tell him that she was glad he was alive; glad he had come. But she could not. The breach between them was too great. She had told him that she loved him once, and he had called her a liar. She would not make the mistake again.

And yet his eyes fell instantly to her breasts where the babies feasted noisily. He seemed to drag them back to hers.

"You might have knocked," she told him coolly.

"I might have," he agreed smoothly, "except that a man should not be required to knock upon his wife's door." He glanced at Danielle. "Mam'selle, if you would . . . ?"

"Danielle!" Amanda wailed.

But Danielle was gone. Eric approached the bed. The little girl's mouth had gone slack. Her eyes were closed. Eric reached for her, swathing her in the blanket, setting her with care and skill upon his shoulder. His large bronzed hand looked mammoth against the child.

He glanced her way. "I do believe that they are supposed to burp this way."

Amanda nervously closed her gown, setting her infant son upon her own shoulder, patting the little back. She kept watching Eric, but he paid her little heed, giving his attention to their daughter. He did not look at her when he spoke at last. "I should like to call her Lenore."

"That was—"

"Your mother's name, yes. Does that suit you?"

"Yes," she said softly. "And—our son?"

"Jamie," he said huskily. "A Jamie Cameron began life in a new land. This Jamie Cameron will begin life in a new country."

"The war has not been won," Amanda observed.

His eyes fell upon her coldly. She lifted her chin, not wanting to fight, not knowing how not to do so. "And with what you said to me when we last met, I had doubts you would claim them as your own," she murmured.

She held her breath, awaiting his answer. She so desperately wanted him to disclaim his words, to vow some small word of love to her.

His eyes stayed upon her. "As this is March eleventh, I daresay the timing is quite right since our last—encounter."

Tears stung her eyes. She refused to shed them. "I wish that they were not yours!" she lied softly.

He stiffened, his back to her. "Ah, my dear wife! And you claimed to love me so the last time that we met!" She was silent. He turned to her. He set the baby down carefully in one of the cradles that had been brought and came to stand beside her. She nearly flinched when he reached down to touch her hair. He did not miss her reaction. He picked up his son even though a sound of protest escaped her. "The lad sleeps," he said. With Jamie Cameron set in his cradle, Eric came back to her cradle again.

He reached into his frock coat and produced a small velvet box. He withdrew a ring from it and took her hand. She tugged upon her fingers but he held fast. A second

later a stunning emerald surrounded by diamond chips
was set upon her third finger. "Thank you," he said very
softly, and it was the tone of voice that could set her heart
to shivering, her very soul to trembling. She wanted so
badly to reach out and stroke his face. No matter how
tender his words, she dared not. "I did not mean to be so
crude. I do, however, live sometimes for the day when I
might meet Lord Tarryton once again. You forget, I discovered you once within his arms."

A smile escaped her. "And rescued me from them, if I
recall."

"Yes, but I admit, I cannot forget that you loved him,
and fears have often tormented my dreams. But I thank
you for my children—healthy twins were far more than I
dared dream. I would that they had been born at home—"

"You sent me here."

"Aye, and I would bring you home now. But, Amanda,
you must swear to me that you will no longer betray my
cause."

"I did not betray your cause—"

"I ask you for the future."

She lowered her head, feeling the urge to burst into
tears. He still did not believe her. He had always been
there for her, even in the midst of childbirth! But he did
not believe her, and she knew of no way to heal their
breach.

"I will not betray you, I swear it," she said softly.

His knuckles rested upon her cheek. He opened his
mouth as if to speak. She turned her head aside. "This is a
travesty of a marriage, is it not? When you loved me, I did
not love you. Then I loved you—and you did not love me.
There is nothing now, is there?"

His hand fell and he walked away from the bed. She
heard the door open, and yet he hesitated. "Aye, there is
something," he said. Her eyes rose to his. Cobalt fire, they
fell upon her, and touched her flesh and blood and entered deeply inside of her. "For you are mistaken. I have
loved you since I first laid eyes upon you, milady, and I
have never ceased to love you."

The door closed. She was alone.

XVII ❧

It was several days before Amanda saw Eric again. Although she pondered his words endlessly when she was awake, it seemed that she was often exhausted in those first days. Danielle assured her that producing live, healthy twins was no easy task and that she deserved her rest. And in those days, countless gifts came to her, from the Comte de la Rochelle, from Benjamin Franklin, and even from the young king and queen. Marie Antoinette sent her Flemish lace christening gowns, as beautiful and opulent as the Palace of Versailles. While she was still abed, the twins were taken to be baptized, in an Episcopal ceremony, although the French royal court was devoutly Catholic. Though no one dared say it to Amanda, infant mortality was high, and so the ceremony was quickly arranged. Danielle stood as godmother to both infants, while Amanda was delighted to have Ben Franklin stand as their godfather.

By the end of a week she was feeling much stronger, and though she had been offered a young wet nurse by the court, she was determined to care for both of her babies herself. It was trying but greatly rewarding, and she could not forget for a moment how deeply she had feared that she would never have children.

Now she had two, precious beings who still brought her to awe. She never tired of searching over their little bodies, of counting fingers and toes, of studying their eyes and their hair and their noses and chins, trying to decide just whom they resembled. "I shall show you some of your ancestors!" she promised. "There's a huge gallery with rows and rows of Camerons! You shall see, and then we shall decide!"

They were way too young to smile, but still, she thought that Jamie, especially, watched her with very grave eyes. His father's eyes. They already had a tendency to look cobalt at times, silver at others.

She had her infants . . . and she had Eric. And he had even said that he loved her, that he had always loved her. But could it be enough? He had come for her—but she was certain that he still did not trust her.

And he stayed away from her. He came to see his new son and daughter, she knew, for Danielle always informed her. But he did not wait to see her when she wakened. She didn't know where he slept at night, but there Danielle assured her too. He was across in the comte's room, and the comte was in his eldest son's quarters. And Eric was not often around, Danielle continued, because he had been entrusted by Congress and General Washington to take messages to the French ministers. He also spent hours with Mr. Franklin.

They would leave for home on the first of April. Eric would arrive in time to fight during summer and fall—if the fledgling country survived so long. Sometimes it terrified her that she would be bringing her children home to a land of bloodshed.

The twins were a full two weeks old when she awoke to find Eric in her room, rocking one cradle while seriously observing Lenore. Amanda felt her eyes upon him and he turned to her. A misty shield covered any emotion, but his expression seemed as grave as Jamie's was often wont to be.

"We still leave on the first of April. I hope that is convenient for you."

She nodded, wishing that he had not caught her so unaware. Her hair was tousled, her gown was askew, slipping down from her shoulder. She had wished so badly that she might be more dignified, more perfect, more beautiful. He had said that he loved her. And they were so distant still, strangers who met between the explosions of cannon balls and the clash of steel.

She slipped out of bed and went to him, touching his arm. "Eric, maybe we shouldn't go back."

"What?" He swung around, amazed, staring at her hand where she touched his arm. Her hand fell.

"I was just thinking—maybe we should stay here. In France. We could survive. We would not need so very much—"

"Have you lost your very mind!" he asked her.

She backed away from him, shaking her head. "I am afraid! Look at the strength of the British army. They can keep sending men and more men! They have Hessians and Prussians and all other kinds of mercenaries. The colonies—"

"The United States of America," he corrected her very softly, his jaw twisting.

"We cannot pay our own troops!" she exclaimed. "Eric, if we should lose the war—"

"We?"

"Pardon?"

"You said 'we,' my love. Are you part of that 'we'? Have you changed sides, then?"

She exhaled, mistrustful of the tone of his voice. She felt at such a disadvantage, clad in the sheer silk gown, tousled by the night, barefoot. Eric towered over her in his boots. He was dressed fully in his uniform with his cockaded and plumed hat pulled low over his eyes, his breeches taut about his muscled thighs, his spring cloak emphasizing the breadth of his shoulder. She trembled slightly. He would not come to her now—indeed, he did not seem interested in her—but she wished suddenly and desperately that she could sweep away the time and the anger and the hatred and rush into his arms, just to be held.

She forced a cool and rueful smile to her features. "You have called me a traitor. Well, sir, if I was for the British, then I was not a traitor at any time, unless that time should be now. Am I for the colonies now—excuse me, the United States of America? Yes, I am. And no thanks to you, Lord Cameron. You haven't the gifts of persuasion that Mr. Franklin so amply possesses. I should very much like to see the Americans win. It's just that—"

"That you doubt that they can, is that it?"

She flushed and lowered her head slightly. "I have never known quite what it was to love with the need to protect until these last few days. I am afraid."

Eric was quiet for several seconds. "As far as I know, madame, the British have yet to make war on children. I have to go back. You know that. You've known where I stand, and just how passionately, from the very beginning."

"And you knew where I stood," she reminded him softly.

"I just never thought—" He broke off, shaking his head.

"What!" Amanda demanded heatedly. She knew what. He had never thought that she would take it so far as to betray her home. "I have told you that I did not—"

"Let's not discuss it—"

"If we cannot discuss it, then we've nothing at all to discuss!" she cried.

He stiffened. For a brief moment she thought that his thin control upon his temper would snap, that he would wrench her into his arms, that he would demand her lips as he had been so quick to do in the past. She prayed silently that he would touch her.

He did not. He bowed deeply to her. "I leave you to the care of our children, madame. Remember that you must soon be ready to travel."

* * *

It was not so difficult to leave behind Versailles, no matter how beautiful it was. Amanda had never really entered into the inner circle of the court, but she had made friends, and she would miss them. Most of all, though, she would miss Ben Franklin, who would stay on in France until his mission was completed. He hugged her warmly when the party bundled into the coaches that would take them to the port.

"Ah, I do long for home! But then, my dear, I am too old to be a soldier, so this is how I must serve. God with you and yours in all your endeavors!"

She was going to cry, Amanda thought. Mr. Franklin had offered her a quiet and steady friendship when her world had been awry, and she would always love him for it. She kissed his cheek impulsively and climbed up into the coach with Danielle and the twins. One of the babies was thrust into her arms, and she sat back, listening as Franklin said his good-byes to Eric, giving him the last of his communications homeward to Washington, the Congress, and his daughter.

Amanda heard the crack of the whip, and she realized she was leaving Versailles for good. It hurt to leave Mr. Franklin and the comte, who had been kind, but that was the only pain. A raw excitement was already burning in her heart. She was very eager to go home. The soft whisper of the river already seemed to sound in her blood. She could feel the salt against her face, the heat of the summer's day; she could see the leaves in the autumn, falling with their beautiful and brilliant colors upon the leaves and the water. She could see the stables and the smokehouse and smell Virginia ham. Please God, she thought, let it be there when we return! Let Cameron Hall still stand!

It would stand, she thought. Eric had told her that the British were threatening the north—they had been, at least, away from southern shores.

He did not ride in the carriage with her, but chose to ride a horse alongside. Nor, even during the long journey to reach the water, did he tarry with her long. When they stopped for an evening meal and a bed for the night, he ordered her a room and had food sent to her and Danielle and the twins. It was Jacques who saw to her welfare most often. And each time Jacques approached, he stopped to admire the twins, never touching the pair but watching them with such a poignancy about his eyes that her heart seemed to catch in her throat. Amanda would wonder what tragedy had touched the man's past to cause such a look in the eyes.

By the fifth of April they were upon the open seas, heading for home with a steady wind. Amanda and the twins had been given the captain's cabin. She assumed that Eric had chosen to take the first mate's berth and that the first mate was in with his fellow officers. She felt very well this trip and was eager to walk the decks. Unfortunately, the crew aboard the ship was composed of many of the same men who had discovered her last June with a sword in her hand. While none of them seemed to harbor her any ill will, Amanda still felt awkward around them. Eric was captaining his own ship and, once again, keeping his distance from her. She tried to remind herself that he did not trust her and that she had every right to despise him for his treatment. But again she could not forget that he had said he loved her, and she could not rid herself of the pain of the estrangement. She wondered about him by night. She lay awake and she wondered about his life, the life she had never known, the life of a soldier. She knew that women followed the armies, some for love and some for money, and she wondered how he had spent his time, if he had managed to forget her frequently in the arms of another. She hated the thoughts. They tormented her again and again.

It anguished her, too, that now, when things should be so very fine between them, he drew a greater distance from her daily. He might have claimed that he loved her, but any man who could so thoroughly ignore his wife must have some interest elsewhere. Determined to taunt him, she took to spending her time on deck. Jacques was her friend and would always listen to her, and Frederick, who had accompanied Eric, seemed quite adept with the sea for a printer-turned-soldier. One evening she had managed to gather quite a group about her as she described some of the very outlandish fashions of the French and Italians at Versailles. Then someone started singing:

> "Yankee Doodle went to town,
> A-riding on a pony,
> Stuck a feather in his cap,
> And called it macaroni!"

They were all laughing when Frederick suddenly sobered. Amanda looked past the group of men to see that her husband was standing before them, dark and towering and very silent. In the night his eyes were ebony and condemning and she was glad of it, for she was ready for a fight.

"My love, I hear whimpering from the cabin. Shouldn't you be about the babes?"

"But they sleep, my love, I am quite certain," she returned.

"I say that I have heard crying, and I ask, milady, that you see to it," he said harshly, his eyes narrowing.

The air, the night, seemed charged. This time it seemed that all these men who so loved and admired her husband were on her side. Amanda came to her feet, smiling sweetly. "Please, please, gentlemen, do forgive my husband's horrid lack of manners. I quite often do myself."

With that she swept by Eric, hoping that traces of perfume would haunt his clothing where the silk of her own touched him. She even hoped that she had soured his temper, but he did not follow her. In dismay she realized that the next days followed as the first had done. They were halfway across the ocean, and still, except for an occasional meal with Frederick and Jacques and others in attendance, he did not speak with her all.

The twins were her delight. The sea air seemed to do wonders for them, and when the days were warm, Amanda brought them to the deck. The crew, hardy hands one and all, acted like fools before the babes, clucking, making faces, vying for attention. Amanda, holding Lenore, laughed at one mate's antics and looked up, searching for Eric. She discovered him not far away, his eyes upon her, pensive and dark. She flushed. He did not look away. "Isn't she clever, Eric? I could swear that Lenore smiles already, and it has nothing to do with bubbles in the belly!"

He smiled at last. "Aye, my love. She is clever indeed. Like her mother."

Amanda did not know what the comment meant, and so she turned away.

Soon they were approaching Virginia. Eric often ordered her curtly belowdecks then, for he was wary of British schooners. Frederick told her that they had battled and seized two British warships on their trip to France. "His lordship hoped to catch on to that Lord Tarryton or Sterling, but alas . . ." His voice trailed away as he remembered that Nigel Sterling was her father. "Begging your pardon, my lady, but they did invade Cameron Hall—"

"There is no pardon necessary, Frederick. Two ships! You battled two ships?"

"Aye, lost only three of our crew, one wounded, two dead, and sent them packing down to Charleston with skelcton crcws in place. Lord Cameron promised General Washington that he would take a ship or two, he did, that's how he gained the time to come to France. And he won't be wanting to have any run-ins with the Brits now, not with you and the little lad and lass aboard!"

Amanda thanked him for the information. She knew that they would make Virginia by the next night. That evening when the twins slept she left them in Danielle's care and went atop the deck, seeking out Eric. She saw him at the rail, staring out at the sea and the stars and the night, a tall, rugged silhouette against the velvet patina. Inhaling sharply, she touched her hair, stiffened her spine, and walked softly toward him. She had not quite reached him when he spun around, his hand reaching for his sword. He relaxed when he saw her, and she realized that he was ever ready for a fight now that the war had become a part of his living.

"What is it, Amanda? You should be below. The night is cool, and we are in dangerous waters."

"Virginia is not so dangerous. You have said so yourself —that is why you are allowing me to return."

"Tell me what you want, and get below."

"For one, my lord, I am not one of your servants to be ordered about!"

His lip curled with a trace of amusement. "You are my wife, and still suspected by many to be a traitor, and therefore your position is more precarious than that of any of my servants."

"Then perhaps, Lord Cameron, I will not care to live in your abode!"

"What?"

She shrugged extravagantly. "Sterling Hall still stands, I do believe. I can take my children and go home."

"The devil you will, madame—"

"Lord Cameron!"

Eric's words were interrupted as the lookout shouted down from the crow's nest. "Lord Cameron! Warship off to the left, sir! She's flying England's colors."

"Be damned!" Eric swore, spinning around. "Frederick, the glass! Gunners, to your stations. Can you see her up there, mate? How many guns is she carrying?"

"Six portside, milord!"

"I can take her," Eric muttered. "I don't dare run, she'll follow us home." He spun around, suddenly aware of his wife again. "Get to the cabin, Amanda."

"Eric—"

"For the love of God, will you go? Our children are there!"

She started to speak again, but then closed her mouth and turned quickly. She had barely scampered into the cabin when the roar of a cannon was heard.

"Take Jamie, please!" Amanda said to Danielle. Lenore was already awake and whimpering. Amanda swept her daughter into her arms. Seconds later the ship shivered and trembled.

"We've been hit!" Danielle called.

Amanda hurried to the window, drawing back the small

velvet drapes. A ship was just coming along hard broadside. A cannon boomed again. Amanda gasped. A direct shot had hit the ship that was almost upon them. The force of the explosion and fire sent her flying back. She landed hard, trying to protect Lenore as she fell on the floor.

There were screams and horrible shouts. The British ship was going down, but those crewmen who had survived the blast were coming aboard. Amanda closed her eyes against the clang of steel and the sound of musket shot. She huddled on the bed, holding Lenore tight. How long could it go on, the horrid, horrid war! How many times could Eric fight—and himself survive?

Eventually the sound of battle began to die down. Amanda walked toward the cabin door, trying to hear. There was nothing. She hurried back to Danielle, thrusting Lenore into her arms along with Jamie. "I'll be back."

"Amanda, you come back in here! You were surely told—"

"Danielle, shush, please!"

It didn't matter, Amanda was already out the door. She paused, choking as powder filled her lungs. As she hurried along the deck, she stepped over the bodies of fallen men, redcoats and patriots alike. She rushed on, suddenly horribly frightened. There was so much silence!

When she came around to the helm, she heard the fighting again at last. It was down to one-to-one combat, the British navy men highly visible in their colors. She looked frantically about for Eric. He was engaged with a young sergeant. Suddenly another man came up behind him. Eric swung around in time to avoid the blow to his back, but the second opponent had caught his sword, and the silver rapier went flying down to his feet.

Amanda screamed, then raced forward. "Amanda!" She heard the roar of his voice as he stepped toward her, grasping the helm rail, staring down the steps to her. He didn't seem to care that he could be skewered at any moment, his concern was for her.

She caught his bloodied sword up in her hands and raced toward him. He clutched it from her hands, his eyes meeting hers. Then he thrust her behind him and set to

dueling his opponents once again. He seemed to move on
clouds, agile and able, always a superior swordsman. And
always he kept her behind him, until he leapt forward
suddenly, catching the sergeant with a quick thrust, then
slicing the second man as he rebounded from the first.
With a groan the second man slumped to the ground.

Eric looked from the men to her. He touched her cheek,
wondering. "I told you to go to the cabin."

"I did go to the cabin."

He smiled. "Madame, you were supposed to stay within
it."

"I might have saved your life."

"Indeed, my lady, perhaps you did."

"Lord Cameron!" Frederick called, limping over to
them. "The English ship is sinking, and there are live men
afloat out there."

Eric's eyes remained upon Amanda's. He smiled. "We
must pick them up. They go to the brig, Frederick, but by
all means, we must pick up the living!"

Frederick turned to go about his task. "Will you go back
to the cabin now?" Eric asked her.

She nodded, smiling, and turned around.

That night was so very different from that long-ago June
day when she had been forced to accompany Robert Tarryton. Now she was heartily cheered by all of the ship. The
maids and servants and craftspeople and artisans hurried
down to greet the ship, eager for a glimpse of the Cameron
heir. Eric held the twins up high, one in each arm, and
accepted the congratulations of his servants, slaves, and
dependents. A coach awaited them. Amanda returned to
the house alone—Eric had the business of the British pris-
oners to deal with and more. Her heart caught as they
approached the house, and then she seemed to grow
warm, and tears burned her eyes. She loved the place so
very much! She hoped that it would not be awkward there,
that enough of the people knew her and loved her well
enough to understand that she had not betrayed them.

"My lady!" Richard, too excited to be staid, came running down the steps, eager to snatch away one of the

twins. "Two! Two! Why, we'd no idea. Of course, we'd no idea at all until Lord Cameron sent word. I do declare, milady, but the lad looks like his father did! Just alike. And with a mat of hair upon his head too! But then, who knows, we cannot tell until the wee ones have grown a bit, eh, madame? But you must be weary, come, come along now!"

Amanda smiled, following Richard. When she entered the hallway she saw that Margaret was standing on the stairway, very still and very white. The servant lowered her head and hurried down the steps. "I'll leave, milady. I needed me wages, so I waited here working, but I'll leave—"

"Margaret, you needn't leave. No one need leave. You thought that I had betrayed this hall—I can only swear to you that I did not. If you believe in me, you are welcome to stay."

Margaret was crying. "Thank you. Thank you, milady. May I tell the same to Remy?"

Remy had actually spat at her. Amanda ground her teeth. How could she condemn the servant when her husband still did not believe in her?

"Yes," she said softly. "Remy may stay."

Before Margaret could start thanking her again, Amanda hurried on up the stairs. Richard came along, and Danielle with Lenore. Richard showed her to the nursery—the room that had once been hers had been cleverly converted with a basin and drawers suitable for the blankets and tiny garments of a babe, and a beautiful bassinet with mosquito netting draped about it. "There's two, milady, you needn't fret! There's been twins before, there will be twins again, I daresay! We'll have the second down in no time."

"That's fine. I shall take both babies in with me for a while," Amanda assured Richard.

"Yes, milady. And may I say welcome home. We've missed you, we have!"

She smiled. "Yes, Richard, you may say so. Thank you."

Amanda brought the twins in with her to nurse, and when they had become sated and slept, she called for Danielle. By then both bassinets were ready. The two women set the babes to sleep for their first night in their own home.

When she returned to her own room, she discovered that Richard had sent her a steaming tub, with French soap and huge snowy towels and a silver tray filled with wine and plate of ham swimming in honey and raisin sauce with fresh green beans and summer squash. She smiled with gratitude, then she shivered slightly, remembering how like that last night things seemed.

Still, she sipped the wine and sank into the bath. There had been no such luxury over the nine weeks it had taken them to return. When she finished she stepped out of the tub and wrapped herself in the towel, drying her hair before the fire. Then, with her towel swept around her, she sat at her dressing table and started to brush out her hair.

And it was then that he entered the room. In his boots, breeches, and open-necked shirt, he stepped into the room and closed the door. Amanda turned slowly around to meet his gaze. He strode slowly across the room until he came to her. Then he lowered himself upon one knee before her and touched her shoulders. His hands moved slowly over and around her breasts, and the towel fell away. She caught her breath, wishing that she were not so eager for him. But firelight danced in his eyes, and in her own, and with a poignant ache she realized that it had been a year since he had touched her. She could not protest what she desired with all of her heart, and if things were not perfect between them, she was still his wife. And she was here once again, in the room they shared. No matter what his words, no matter how he fought her, she could see and feel the heat of the desire about him, and instinctively she knew that he had never wanted another woman as he wanted her.

"Perhaps I should go," he told her. "Maybe I've no right to be here, madame."

She swallowed, alarmed at the strength of the sensations that swept through her at the simple soft stroke of his fingers upon her swollen breasts, rolling lightly over

the dusky rose of her nipples, stroking again the under-
flesh.

"I have waited for you," she told him solemnly.

"And I have been the worst fool in the world, and if you
had sent me away, lady, God help me, there is no way that
I could have gone."

He stood and scooped her up into his arms. When he lay
her down upon the bed, he paused and looked over the
length of her. An soft explosion, a curse, a cry, escaped
him, and then he was upon her. He had never touched her
with such care, with such tenderness. His touch stirred
her, his kiss aroused and awoke her, and as his lips and
fingertips and tongue traveled and caressed the length of
her, whispers, then moans, escaped her. He drew her ever
upward, and when she thought that she would cry out and
beg that she could bear no more, he would gently ease her
just slightly downward again, his tongue delving soft and
vulnerable flesh.

And when he came to her she did cry out, shuddering,
holding tight, winding her limbs about him. The need to
be with him was so great, the strength of his body so
shocking, that she nearly whispered all that she felt. She
almost told him that she loved him. But just in time, she
bit back the words, and she cried out her longing instead
and he dove and swept within her, becoming the world,
searing her soul, taking all of her, and bringing everything
of life, and just a little bit of death.

There was no time for them. Perhaps that was the most
bitter fact that she seemed always to have to face. Eric was
gone all the next day, seeing to the estate, the planting, the
horses, the building, the repairs. They did not even have
dinner together, but Amanda waited, and when he came
to her, she welcomed him with her body silken, her arms
eager to close about him. They made love until it was
nearly dawn, holding tight.

In the morning it was time for him to leave again. It was
the middle of June, and Eric had been away from the war
a long time. Virginia was peaceful enough, but the British

offensive was moving in the northern states, and there had already been several battles.

As usual, Amanda stood on the steps, ready to watch Eric ride away. He was upon Joshua, ever the excellent horseman, exceedingly handsome in his uniform with his plumed hat, high boots, his hair still damp. Amanda approached him with the stirrup cup, for it was tradition now, and as he returned the cup to her, she met his eyes with her own wide and grave upon his. "I never did betray this hall, Eric," she told him.

He leaned down to kiss her lips. "Care for them, Amanda. For the twins. And if anything happens to me, fight for this place. With whatever you have. It is their heritage."

He kissed her again. Tears flooded her eyes, and she stepped back. He was riding away to war again, and though he might love her, he still did not trust her. He did not believe her, and he was telling her that if the war was lost, she was to keep Cameron Hall by any means available—including a plea to the British should the master of Cameron Hall be hanged.

She watched the horses ride away. "I do love you," she whispered aloud. But there was no one to hear.

In December she sat upon the rail at the paddocks watching Jacques put the yearlings through their paces. Danielle came running down the pathway from the house, waving her arms frantically. As she leapt off the fence, alarmed, Amanda quickly felt her worried frown slip into an incredulous smile.

Damien was coming close behind Danielle.

Amanda let out a shriek of pure pleasure and raced madly along the dirt path until she pitched hard into her cousin, crying and laughing, shouting his name, crying and laughing all over again. He scooped her up and swung her around and held her close, and at last he set her down.

"My God, how are you here?" she demanded.

"One furlough in how many years?" he teased. Then he sobered. "There aren't many furloughs these days," he said grimly, and her heart thundered hard.

The war was not going well, she thought. "Come on into the house. Look at me, I am a disaster!"

"They say you run one of the finest estates in Virginia," Damien said dryly.

Amanda shrugged, walking up the back steps to the house. "Come into the parlor and have a brandy." He was looking ragged, she thought. His brass buttons were not shining, his boots barely seemed to have soles, and his coat was nearly threadbare. "Damien! I cannot believe it!" she cried, and hugged him all over again.

In the parlor she served him brandy and felt his eyes upon her. Seated casually in a chair before the fire, he lifted his snifter to her. "Amanda, you are thin and lithe and more beautiful than ever. Your features are ever more delicate and refined. You thrive, cousin, even as a matron."

"Matron!"

"Well, you are a wife and mother of two. And I am most eager to see my new relations. God knows, there are few enough of us!"

"The twins will be down soon, Damien. Danielle will bring them when they awake. Tell me, what is happening? How is—how is Eric?"

Damien leaned forward, frowning. "The war? Let's see. A young lad named Alex Hamilton is Washington's secretary now, and doing a damned good job of it. He knows money better than any of those fools in Congress. What else. Ah—we've another young man, a Frenchman. The Marquis de Lafayette. He is a volunteer who rides to death with a smile upon his face—and does wonders for our cause. General Washington is wonderfully impressed with him, and I must admit, so am I. The war, let's see. There have been so many battles! The British meant to split the colonies, you know. Right down the Mohawk Valley. They did not manage that. In April they attacked Danbury— Benedict Arnold held them back. Burgoyne took Ticonderoga in July, but I am very proud to say that he surrendered on the seventeenth of this month. General Arnold again, with some fine help from Morgan's riflemen. We lost the Battle of Hubbardton, we won the Battle of Bennington. The Battle of Brandywine—your husband was magnificent at that one. Riding that giant stallion of his . . . few men are better with a sword. Still, Howe very skillfully turned the American right, forcing Washington back toward Philadelphia. General Howe—with the help of his brother, Admiral Howe—has taken Philadelphia now. This winter, cousin, the British will sit in the splendid homes of Philadelphia. Washington is moving his forces to Valley Forge."

"But Eric—"

"Eric is alive and well," Damien said irritably.

Amanda sat back, surprised. "Damien, you used to be so fond of Eric yourself! What has happened?"

Distraught, Damien rose and stood before the fire, watching the flames. "I did not care for his treatment of you," he said simply.

Amanda sighed, clutching the arms of her chair. "Damien, I was betraying him."

Shocked, Damien turned around. "What?"

She didn't want to distress him further, but she had to tell him the truth. "Not when the British came to destroy the supplies here, someone else is guilty of that, and someone will betray the Virginians again unless Eric does believe me and look elsewhere. But, Damien—" She hesitated just a second and then plunged onward. "Damien, Father used to blackmail me with you."

"Me!"

"They knew all along that you were running arms from western Virginia to Boston and Philadelphia. First he promised to arrest you and see you hanged. He killed your horse, Damien. Don't you remember? In Williamsburg."

"Oh, my God!"

Amanda didn't look at him. "Then you were his prisoner. He promised me that there were all manner of things he could do to you."

"Oh, Amanda!" He came to her, kneeling down, taking her hands into his. "My God, I am so sorry! I did not know! How could you risk so much for me?"

She touched his cheek. "Get up, Damien. I love you, remember? We have always had each other, and besides, it is all over now."

He stood and walked back to the fire, and she realized that he was hesitating. "It isn't really over," he said at last.

"What do you mean?"

"I mean that you should be with your husband this winter."

"But—"

"Martha always comes to stay with George when he settles into his winter quarters. And you—you need to come."

"I haven't been asked," Amanda said stiffly. "I don't think that he believes me yet." She sighed. "I know that he does not completely trust me, no matter how far it seems that we have gone. God knows, I might betray something were I to be there!"

"You need to be there!" Damien persisted.

"Why?"

Damien stuttered and then cleared his throat. "Anne Marie is there."

"Anne Marie Mabry?"

"She has followed her father to war. And she cooks often for Eric. And—"

"And what?" Amanda demanded.

Damien lifted his arms and dropped them. "I don't know. But you need to be there."

She felt as if giant icy fingers gripped her heart and squeezed, and then she felt an awful fury rip through her. How dare he judge her when he . . .

Anne Marie had always cared for Eric. Always. Amanda had known that the night she had first met him.

The cold, and then the heat, settled over her. She tried to breathe deeply. If he meant to have another woman, she told herself, he would do so. She could not walk with him everywhere.

She could not force him to love her.

But she could discover the truth of it, and if he was determined to have Anne Marie, then he would not have her at home waiting eagerly for his return!

"I—I think that I will accompany you to Valley Forge, Damien. When you're ready to go."

He smiled. "That's my darling, daring cousin. What of the babes?"

How could she leave them? Danielle would care for them. They were old enough now to eat food, and though it would hurt her, she would find a wet nurse. They would be well. She would be the one to be empty without them.

"They will be fine here," she assured Damien softly.

He smiled again. "Well then, I am glad that you will ride with me. We should leave within the week. I've some business in Williamsburg . . . and then there's Lady Geneva."

"Lady Geneva?"

"Cousin, even I was destined to fall in love."

"With Geneva!"

"And why not?"

Why not, indeed? Geneva was beautiful, sensual, and perhaps just right for Damien. "No reason. How long has this been going on?"

"Affairs of the heart move slowly in wartime, Mandy. And sometimes quietly. This, as you call it, has been going on for several years now."

Amanda started to laugh. Damien cast her a hard warning glare and she laughed all the harder.

"Amanda—"

"I am delighted, Damien. Absolutely delighted. And a week will be fine. I need time to leave the twins and time to gather supplies to go. I cannot imagine that they are overly endowed with food and blankets for the winter."

"Hardly," Damien said dryly, then smiled. "Laugh away at me, then, cousin, if you will! I shall be eager to see the show once we arrive."

Amanda sobered quickly. He winked her way, taking full advantage of his own turn to be amused. He lifted his brandy glass.

"To the winter at Valley Forge!"

Neither of them was quite aware yet of what those words would mean.

XVIII ❧

Amanda had known that things were going badly. She knew that General Washington had gone to Valley Forge from his defeat at Germantown, and Damien had warned her that the men were in bad shape.

But once Damien had identified himself and they entered into the compound—she, Damien, Geneva, and Jacques Bisset—Amanda was still stunned by the appearance of the men and the encampment.

Snow rose everywhere, piled high, part of the biting cold of the winter. The soldiers' homes were crude log buildings that they had constructed themselves. Smoke billowed from makeshift chimneys, windows were covered with canvas or paper. There didn't seem to be a leaf or a straggling bush left alive anywhere; about the encampment there were only the barren and naked branches of tall trees, skeletal, deathlike.

Yet the camp was not so appalling as the men. As

Damien flicked the reins and the horse dragged the cart onward, they passed hundreds of men. Lined up along the trail, some waved, some saluted, and some just stared. They huddled in frayed blankets, shivering, staying close to one another. Amanda's eyes fell toward the ground and she gasped, despairing to see that many had no shoes, but stood in the snow with their feet bound in rags.

"My God!" she breathed, and tears stung her eyes. "Dear God, but perhaps surrender would be better than this!"

No retreat, no surrender. The words rose in her heart. They had always been there, between her and Eric. And now they seemed appropriate for the ragtag army. They had come this far. Surely they were weighed down heavily with despair.

Damien exhaled behind her. "Washington endures this place day after day while there are those in Congress trying to tear him down. I've never seen a man so willing to suffer with his subordinates, so touched by all that he sees." He flicked the reins again. "There, up ahead, are the command quarters. I see your husband's ensignia. There lies your home, Amanda."

"And what of mine?" Geneva asked sweetly from the rear.

Amanda swung around to grin at her old friend. Geneva had been eager to come. She had sworn that she could cure many a man of whatever ailed him. But looking about the complex, she did not seem so assured.

"My dear lady, I shall see that you have the finest accommodations in the place!" Damien assured her.

"See that you do," Geneva replied sweetly. Amanda could feel the sparks flying between them. She glanced at Jacques and grinned, then lowered her head, still smiling. They were both so strong-willed and determined upon their own way. Perhaps they deserved one another.

Damien pulled in on the reins. As he did so, Amanda saw Eric appear in the doorway of one of the huts. He was striking as he stood there, very tall in the shadows. But even his uniform seemed ragged, his boots were shined but worn, the brass upon his frock coat was heavily tarnished. His face was lean and hard, perhaps more arresting than ever, taut with character, his eyes very blue against the bronze of his features. But they were not welcoming eyes. They did not touch her with warmth, but with reserve.

She had thought to run to him, to find herself swept off her feet. Suddenly she could not run. Her heart was caught in her throat. Eric remained still, and Jacques helped her down from the wagon.

"Lady Cameron!"

Thankfully, Washington had stepped out from around her husband, a petite, rounded woman in a mob cap coming behind him. "Lady Cameron, as your husband seems tongue-tied, I must welcome you to Valley Forge. Martha, have you ever met Eric's wife? I hadn't thought so, well, you must do so now. Lady Cameron—"

"Amanda," she breathed quickly.

Many had speculated that George had married the widow Martha Custis for her money alone—there had been many more attractive and younger women available to him at the time. Amanda realized instantly what Washington had seen in the woman. As the older woman welcomed her with a kiss and hug, Amanda was enveloped by an overwhelming sense of warmth. There was a kindness in her light eyes that was unmistakable. She attracted just like the comforting heat of a fire.

"Damien, you rascal, you disappear and return with two beautiful young ladies!" Washington called. "Lady Geneva, welcome. Good God, Cameron, shouldn't we have them in out of the cold. And you too, Monsieur Bisset. Do come on in. All that we have is yours, however meager that may be!"

"We've brought supplies from Cameron Hall," Amanda said softly. She thought of the meat and grain and coffee and tobacco in the barrels and chests aboard the wagon, and she thought of the thousands of men here. It would hardly make a dent.

"Amanda?"

Eric reached out a hand to her at last, stepping forward. His fingers curled around hers and he drew her close, kissing her coolly upon the cheek. He asked her quickly about the twins and she said that they were well. Then he led her inside, and she instantly stiffened.

Anne Marie was there, standing by a coffeepot that heated over the hearth fire.

"Amanda!" Anne Marie came forward, kissing her swiftly on the cheek. Amanda tried to smile in return. Damien and Geneva and the Washingtons were entering, and it seemed that everyone was talking at once. Anne Marie hugged her.

"So you have been fighting this war with the men, have you?" Amanda asked sweetly.

"I've followed Father from the very beginning," Anne Marie agreed. "I should say, since he decided to cast in with the patriots. I'd no real idea for the longest time just which way we were meant to go."

"This is a horrible place to be," Washington said suddenly, softly. "Horrible. I've eleven thousand men here. Of that number, almost three thousand are without shoes or are half naked, and Congress tells me there is nothing to be given my men, nothing to be done. Ah, ladies, you should not be here."

"Oh, posh!" Mrs. Washington protested. "If I did not see you, Mr. Washington, in your winter quarters, why, then I should have no husband at all."

"I wonder if I do have one at all," Amanda said sweetly. The company about them laughed; Eric did not.

"Well, we've something of a stew to eat tonight," Anne Marie said. "Please, everyone, sit. We'll have something."

Amanda felt acutely uncomfortable, a guest in her husband's living quarters, while Anne Marie was the very comfortable hostess. She held tight to her temper, noting as she sat that a woman's cloak was upon the crude peg by the door and that there seemed to be other signs of constant feminine occupation of the hut, such as the lace dusters on the table sills. The main room consisted of the hearth, a large raw center table, and some poorly crafted chairs. There was a doorway leading to a second room. It was cracked open and Amanda could see a rope bed within it, covered it by a thin green blanket. There were trunks and a desk within the bedroom too, but everything seemed sparse and empty and cold.

She caught Eric's eyes. A trace of amusement flickered across them, as if he thought that she had surveyed her surroundings and found them entirely lacking. As if she were wishing that she had not come.

Well, she was not. Reckless and irritated, she tossed back a stray curl and bent her head to listen to General Washington as he spoke, assuring Damien had they had come from hard times before. "And curious pieces of luck have been ours, as if God does smile upon us now and then. Monsieur Bisset, did you know that we barely reached Trenton? We did so by a play of card, can you imagine? Colonel Johann Rall was playing poker on Christmas Eve, and was so engrossed that when a messenger handed him a warning that we were launching a surprise attack, he merely shoved it into his pocket. The note was discovered only after the attack, when the colonel lay dead."

"One might say," Damien joked, "General, that you were the one holding the full house."

"Ah, yes. But how fickle is life, eh?"

"How fickle indeed," Geneva murmured.

"You see," Mrs. Washington said, rising to ladle out the stew, "God is on our side. We've only to wait and see!"

She was a determined woman, determined to make the night go smoothly. Baron Von Steuben, another volunteer to the American cause, arrived, and was fed, and explained some kind of a military tactic to the men. The hour grew late. Mrs. Washington told Geneva that they had an extra room where she might sleep while other arrangements were being made, and people began to leave. "I guess Jacques and I get the floor out here, eh, Lord Cameron?" Damien asked. There was still that edge to his voice.

"It's the best I have to offer," Eric replied, his tone cool in return.

"I must get back," Anne Marie said.

"I will escort you," Eric told her. He didn't glance toward Amanda as he took his great cloak from the pe

Anne Marie said good-bye to Amanda, then walked out into the cold wind. It buffeted her. Amanda gritted her teeth as she saw Eric reach for the woman instantly, catching her arm.

What went on here? She wanted to be reasonable, and logical, but he spent years calling her a liar and traitor, while he had always had another woman right behind him while he went to war.

And now Jacques and Damien were both in the main room, and unless she chose to cast aside her pride totally and have an argument that would draw them all in, she had no choice but to smile and say good night sweetly and walk into her husband's bedroom. She wanted to throw something—and preferably right at Eric!

She removed the blanket from his bed and sat down by the fire, drawing the blanket around her. Twenty minutes later she heard the door open and then slam closed, and then she heard Eric speaking softly with Jacques. She smiled, hoping that he imagined her eagerly awaiting him. He would find things far different.

But she never knew what he imagined. The door opened and he stood there, pulling off his gloves. His eyes fell upon her with little surprise. Coming in, he closed the door softly and leaned against it.

"So you rode in winter wind all this way to come and sleep upon a cold dirty hearth," he said at last.

She rose to her knees, holding the blanket about her, nudging a log with a crude iron poker. "No, my lord Cameron. I did not come all this way to do so—but rather I arrived here and found it the expedient thing."

He swore impatiently and crossed the floor to her, catching her hands and dragging her to her feet. "What are you talking about?" he demanded harshly.

"Anne Marie," she said flatly.

His lip curled slightly. "Ah."

"Ah! And that is all that you have to say?"

"What can I say? I'm sure that Damien has sliced me to ribbons on that matter, quite competently."

Amanda jerked from his touch. Cold, she swallowed and

forced herself to raise her chin. "You've nothing to say in defense."

"I've much to say. I've never touched her—all right, that's not exactly true. I kissed her once. When I had been told that you had sold out my inheritance and my marriage. And once again, quite innocently, before I left for France." He leaned against the wall, crossing his arms over his chest, watching her. "Of anything else, I am innocent."

"Damien—"

"Damien is ever loyal to you, and he has not forgiven me the first."

Her knees were trembling. She was afraid that she would completely lose her temper, that she would cry out in frustration and anger and pain. She could not tell if he was telling the truth or not, she knew only that they had been apart again and he was not glad to see her. "I don't believe you," she whispered.

"Amanda, my God—" He took a step impatiently toward her. She raised a hand against him and despite herself, her voice was high and close to tears.

"You've never believed me, Eric. Well, this time, my lord, I am afraid that I do not believe you! Don't touch me."

"Amanda—"

"I mean it, Eric!"

He went still, his eyes narrowing. "Am I to be punished then, dear wife? Denied your charms and my rights?"

"My lord Cameron, I'm well aware that your life was far from empty before I entered into it—"

"Regretfully entered into it."

"You had an affair with Geneva!"

He seemed slightly surprised, but shrugged, and she felt ill and jealous and couldn't help but imagine that he was lying. He and Sir Thomas had been partners, and he and Anne Marie . . .

"Amanda, I can hardly be blamed—"

"You had a wicked reputation, Eric!" she reminded him.

He laughed softly. "Amanda, my God, we are talking about years ago—"

"I don't believe you!"

"Well, I will be damned! Amanda, come here!"

"No! I don't want you touching me tonight!" she vowed heatedly.

She heard the grate of his teeth and then he smiled very slowly. "Ah, yes, I am supposed to take care because your cousin and your—because Damien and Jacques sleep outside the doorway. Well, Amanda, don't fool yourself. If I wanted—if I chose, Amanda!—I would seize upon you here and now, and that would be that, and I would not give a damn if the whole of the camp was aware of it."

He took two long steps toward her. A scream nearly tore from her as his hands landed firmly upon her and she was lifted up and tossed upon the narrow bunk. "Oh, you bastard!" she hissed to him.

But he backed away from her then and bowed deeply. "You may have the bed. And you shall have things, milady, just as you wish them. You needn't sleep on the floor. I shall find another place to lay my head!"

With that he slammed out of the room. Amanda watched him, then she turned over and cried softly into the pillow. There would never be a good time for them, she thought. Never more than brief moments when passion drew them together. She could not even grasp at the straws anymore. . . .

She had come here. And she was alone.

Walking out in the cold snow, Eric quickly determined that he had been a fool. When he thought that Damien had sown the seeds of discontent and suspicion so thoroughly over such a rather sad incident, he felt fury fill him. And when she had pulled away from him, as if his touch made her shudder like something that crept and crawled upon the earth, he had known that he had to walk away. Walk away, when he had thought of nothing but lying down beside her, with her naked flesh beneath him. . . .

He groaned aloud and paused in the night, patting the nose of the packhorse that had drawn the cart from Cameron Hall. The horses had been unharnessed, but the crates still remained unpacked. He looked over the wagon and smiled. They were desperate at Valley Forge. They spent the days and nights drilling—and foraging for food. There were so many men to feed. They deserted daily. He did not blame them. He didn't know how many times he had wanted to leave the bitter cold of Pennsylvania and ride back to the Tidewater where winter was ever so much milder. Where his home and children awaited him. Where a well-crafted fire and decent food could be had. Home, to Amanda, to a chance at their marriage.

And now she was here, and like an ass, he had walked away from her. His fingers wound into fists. Damn her! He had spent bitter-cold, lonely nights alone again and again. She had been in his dreams forever and ever, and now . . .

Now he was too proud to go back. "Damn her!" he whispered. And then he sobered. She thought that he had been cold. That he hadn't wanted her, that he had, perhaps, been having an affair with Anne Marie.

She didn't understand. There were many men who still did not trust her. Rumor from Virginia had reached the whole of the army, and Nigel Sterling's daughter was still known as a Tory—whether she had truly changed her coat or not.

And that he did not know if he could believe himself.

He grated his teeth hard and swore out loud, his breath creating a mist upon the night. He wasn't going back. Not until she asked him.

Or not until his slender hold upon sanity did break, and he swept her heedlessly into his arms.

A week later Amanda was working in the huge sickbay, bringing water to the countless men down with smallpox. It was terrifying just to see the men stretched out before her—there were so many men ill, thousands of them.

She wiped her brow, offered a Connecticut rifleman an encouraging smile, and moved on to the next bed. Hands suddenly slipped about her waist and a whisper touched her ear. "Well, cousin, he is not sleeping with the illustrious Anne Marie. Her father came home from his foraging expedition the same night that you arrived, and I know

Thomas Mabry very well. Nothing illicit is taking place in that hut!"

Amanda swung around in dismay. "Damien, I did not ask you—"

"Oh? You're not curious as to where your husband is sleeping?"

"No, I'm not!" Amanda lied.

Damien made a *tsk*ing noise at her. She sighed impatiently, noted that one of her patients was burning up, and hurried back to the barrel to moisten a towel for his forehead. "Damien, I'm busy here."

Damien leaned against a support pole. "Well, the last three days he has been out foraging. And I think that I know where he was before then."

"Oh?"

"But then, you're not interested."

She kicked him as hard as she could in the shin. "Damien—"

"With Von Steuben. Von Steuben is brilliant—I think that he might whip us into a viable fighting force after all. Well, if enough of us live. But Eric knows Indians—and the Brits have half the Mohawk tribes on our tails. So they've much to talk about, you see."

"I see," she said, then she paused, because she knew where her husband was at that moment—standing just inside the doorway, watching her with Damien.

"Ah, Major General Lord Cameron!" Damien said quickly. He saluted sharply and disappeared through the sickbay. Amanda watched him, winding his way through the endless makeshift cots and the various women and doctors who moved about the room. Then she felt a rough hand upon her arm. She swung around once more to find that Eric had come to her, his expression was grim.

"What are you doing in here?"

"Why, I'm trying to help—" she began.

"These men have smallpox!" he reminded her.

She smiled. "I had it. Damien and I both had it as children, and they say that if you survive—" She paused. "What are you doing in here?"

"Trying to get you out."

A man groaned on his pallet. "Lord Cameron! Eh, sir, we're about ready to ride again, eh?"

The man was feverish; his eyes were bleary, but they had touched upon Eric with something like adoration. And Eric patted the man's shoulder, heedless of disease, and assured him with a smile. "No, Roger, we're not ready to ride. Not until spring. But Von Steuben is waiting for you, have no fear. He'll drill you to the ground once you're up and about. I promise you, lad."

The sick man laughed. His eyes rolled, then fell shut. "My God, I think he's died!" Amanda said miserably.

Eric felt the man's heart, then touched his forehead. "No, he's just breathing easy again. Von Steuben may get his hands on the boy yet."

He straightened, staring at Amanda. She wanted to say something to him, anything to bring him back. But words would not come. She couldn't apologize—he owed her the apologies, and he would never see it, and never admit it.

And he was standing in the smallpox ward!

"Get out of here, Eric!"

"Come with me. I want to talk to you."

She sighed and looked around. There were many women in the room. Wives, sisters, daughters—and lovers and whores. The officers' ladies, the poor privates' women, some in velvet and lace, and some in homespun. Tears suddenly stung her eyes, and she realized that in a way, that was what it was all about. The colonies had joined, and the people had joined. If the war was won, it would be a new land indeed, with a new society and new look at life. Here a man could aspire to greatness no matter his birth. A blacksmith could fight alongside the landed gentry. The country would belong to all of them, the wives the sisters, the daughters, the lovers and the whores.

"Amanda?"

"I'm coming." She untied her apron and hurried o the sickbay with Eric. The weather had not improve wind came scurrying furiously about her and s ered. Eric quickly swept his greatcoat about headed her toward the open stables. She felt his her, her heart quickening as she walked.

He drew her into the stable. Not far from them a smithy's fire burned and hammering could be heard as a harness was repaired. Amanda leaned against the rough wooden wall, watching Eric, waiting.

"What?" she demanded.

He smiled. "Do you know where Howe's men are spending their winter?"

She stiffened. "In Philadelphia."

"Mmm. Twenty-eight miles from here. Some of our men were discovered foraging and taken prisoner. God knows, maybe they'll fare better with the Brits than they do here, but most men still count the cost of freedom high."

"Why are you telling me this!" she exclaimed.

"Because someone is getting information through to the British."

She gasped, astounded. She'd barely been away from the place, except to ride out with Damien one afternoon. Her voice was low and trembling with fury when she spoke. "I do not believe that you would dare to accuse me again!"

"Amanda—"

She shoved at his chest as hard as she could, feeling tears well behind her eyes. "Don't! Don't speak to me, don't come near me, don't you throw your foul accusation at me anymore! Damn you!"

She ran away from him, ignoring his voice as he shouted to her to come back. She didn't care who saw them, she didn't care who heard. She was certain that most of the camp knew that he spent his nights away from his wife anyway.

Gasping, she tore back to their hut. Jacques was within, sitting on a bench, cleaning muskets. He looked up sharply when she entered.

"What is it, milady?"

She shook her head. The tears spilled onto her cheeks. "Oh, Jacques! How can he be so blind! I have everything that I can and still . . ."

He rushed to the bench, glad of the arm he set about to comfort her. He had been with her so long. Always there, always there. No matter what the tempest of her life, she felt that she had a defender. He whispered gentle words in French to her, soothing words. Suddenly the door burst open. Eric had followed her home.

And there she was, in Jacques's arms. She wondered if he wouldn't fly into a rage at that and accuse her of more awful things.

But to her amazement, he was absolutely silent. Jacques didn't even pretend to move away from her—he stared at Eric over her head.

And Eric didn't say a word. He closed the door and left.

That night she lay awake in bed, cold despite her flannel gown and the rough blanket and the fire. Her teeth chattered miserably. Suddenly she heard a commotion in the outer room, the door bursting open, voices rising, then falling.

Then there was silence.

And then the door to the bedroom seemed to shatter open upon its hinges. Eric stood in the doorway in his high boots and heavy cloak and plumed hat. She sat up instantly, afraid and wary. He was drunk! she thought. But he was not. "Tell me that you are innocent," he said, his voice low and husky.

"I am innocent," she replied, her eyes wide and challenging and level upon his.

He smiled and strode firmly into the room. She leapt from the bed, backing away to the fire. "Eric! Damn you! Don't you think that you can come swaggering in here—"

"I do not swagger, my love. I stride."

"Well, you cannot stride—"

"Ah, my love, but I can!"

And he could. He was before her, catching her wrist, spinning her into his arms. She protested, crying out, swearing as the best of the soldiers might, and pummeling his chest. He laughed, ignoring her efforts, and swept her up into his arms. Her fight, however, off-balanced him, and they crashed heavily down upon the bed together. "Eric Cameron—"

"Shush up and pay attention, Amanda." She had no choice. His sinewed thigh was cast heavily over her hip and his hands were taut upon her wrists. His words touched her lips, warm, soft, beguiling. The tone of his voice was deep and quiet and richly masculine, reaching deep inside of her. "I believe you. I believe that you are innocent. Now, listen to me, love, and listen this once, for I shall not make a habit of explaining. I am innocent, too, of all charges. I admit, there were times when I would have bedded another woman if I could have for the sheer loneliness of this life. Yet I could not, you see. There is no other woman with a cascade of rich silken hair the color of fire, and no other woman anywhere to charm the soul with the steady gaze of emerald eyes, the velvet caress of her voice. I have never faltered once, Amanda. From the night that I first saw you, I wanted you and no other. It shall never change. No matter what I have believed, I have wanted you. And I have loved you. Now, lady, if you would, cast me out again. Into the snow."

A slow, sensual smile curved lazily into her lips. "If I cast you out, will you go?"

"No."

She sighed extravagantly. "I did not think so."

"So?"

"Let go of my wrists."

"Why?"

"Because I cannot touch you this way."

His hold upon her eased. Her fingers trembled as she rubbed her knuckles against his cheek, then arched high against him, winding her arms about him as she found his lips with her own. She hungered for his kiss, playing with his tongue, bringing it deeper and deeper into her mouth, as if she drew upon other sexual parts of his body, intimating all that she would do. A dry, hoarse sound tore from him, and he returned the kiss aggressively, his lips caressing and consuming hers, his tongue demanding hers hotly within his mouth, his hands feverishly upon her face and within her hair. Then he tore away from her, casting aside his cape and his boots. He all but tore his frock coat away, and stumbled from his breeches to descend heavily upon her again, his hands feverish as they immediately set upon her calves and then her naked thighs, shoving the gown up high on her. She laughed, delighted at his eagerness, but when his lips touched hers again, she was determined to arouse him even as he stirred the most frantic and glorious yearnings within her. She stroked the magnificent muscled breadth of his back, and she brought her hands low against his ribs, and over the tightness of his buttocks. She teased his abdomen with the stroke of her fingers, and then she closed her fingers around his shaft, trembling with sweet pleasure at his cry and mammoth shudder at her evocative touch. She stroked and teased, gently caressed, and brought about a rougher rhythm, and then caressed with the greatest tenderness again. But then she found her fingers entwined with his and the length of his body was thrust between her thighs. His mouth formed over her breast, and all of the heat and hardness was thrust within her, and ecstasy seemed to flourish and grow and to boundless heights.

Snow fell outside; the wind was bitter, and its cry was harsh upon the winter's night. But none of it mattered to her that night. He rose high above her, his face contorted with his passion, his eyes a deep blazing blue upon hers. She did not allow her lashes to flutter, but as the sensations swept through her with chaotic abandon, she moistened her lips and dared to whisper to him again.

"I love you, Eric. I love you."

He fell against her, cradling her head, his fingers and palms upon her hair, her cheeks. His lips found hers and whispered above them, "Say it again."

"I love you." Tears stung her eyes. "I love you, I swear it, with all of my heart, I love you."

He groaned, and he whispered again that he loved her. And when everything exploded between them, he whispered it again, and then he held her in his arms and they both watched the fire, and she told him that she had loved him for a very long time—even when she had hated him—and he laughed, and they made love again, and she didn't think that anything, ever, had been as good.

It was very late when she finally slept.

Somewhere, in the middle of the night, she awoke. Puzzled, she wondered why. The fire still burned. Their doo lay slightly ajar, and the outer room appeared to be empty, despite the shadows. Some noise had disturbed her, she thought. She didn't move. They slept naked and entwined. Her husband's broad shoulders were slightly bared, and she drew the blanket more tightly about him. Then she slept again.

Later, much, much later, she awoke. She had been dreaming, she realized, and she had been soundly asleep. It was late, for the sun was out and almost brightly so, especially for winter. She had slept the morning away, she thought, and she had awakened now only because someone was frantically calling her name.

"Amanda! Amanda, for the love of God, wake up!"

Her eyes focused at last. It was Geneva, her beautiful eyes wide and frightened, her hair tumbling down about her shoulders. "Amanda, come on, wake up. You must come with me right away. Eric has been hurt."

"What!"

Stunned, stricken, Amanda sat up. The covers began to fall and she caught them to hide her nakedness.

"Eric has been hurt. He went out with a foraging party and he was hit by mistake. I think that his leg is broken. Damien is arranging for a conveyance to bring him back. But he wants you. Now. Oh, Amanda, come on!"

"Oh, dear God!" Terrified, Amanda sprang from the bed and hurriedly searched for her clothing. Her trembling caused her trouble as she tried to pull on her hose, but at last she managed. She forced herself to be calm enough to dress. She ignored her hair, letting it fall down her back in tangles.

Hurt . . . hurt. He had been wounded. Men died when they were wounded. Men died when they were wounded because infection and disease spread so rapidly. No! No, God, please, no, after all of their years together they had finally come to really love one another, to trust one an-other, to need one another. She could not lose him now. He had fought in endless battles, and always with courage, and always so selflessly. He could not die.

"Geneva, how bad is he?" she asked anxiously, reaching for her cloak.

"I don't know yet. I just know that he wants you. Come on now, hurry!"

They ran out to the snow. Two horses were waiting. "Where's Damien?" Amanda asked anxiously.

"Getting a wagon. Amanda, let's go. Before it's too—"

"Oh!" Amanda cried out. She wondered if Washington knew, or Frederick, or any other of his close friends or fellow officers. They wouldn't let him die if they knew. They would not let him die, she was certain!

"Geneva, perhaps I should get someone else!"

"Damien is doing that! Amanda, there is no one else about now. We have to hurry!"

"Oh, God, yes!"

She leapt upon the scrawny horse Geneva had brought for her even as Geneva gracefully catapulted upon her own mount. In seconds they were racing through the camp.

"Hey!" someone called. "Wait! Where—"

"We haven't time!" Geneva responded.

She whipped her horse into a mad gallop. Amanda followed suit, and they were quickly beyond the gates and frantically plowing through the snow. Geneva managed to find something of a trail that had been trampled down, and the floundering horses found their footing again. Amanda was glad, for it seemed that they raced forever. The wind whipped her cheeks and the cold was so bitter that she could no longer feel her fingers about the reins, or her toes in the stirrups. Her heart thundered with fear.

Away from the camp, they slowed for a while. "We need to hurry!" Amanda cried then.

"It's far. The horses won't make it. We'll let them rest a bit, then race them again."

And so they plodded along. Anxiety grew and swelled within Amanda's heart. She did not move a foot that she did not pray again, pray for her husband's life.

They began to race again. There seemed to be nothing, nothing before them, just the endless white of the snow-drifts, just the skeletal leaves of the barren trees. The camp even seemed far behind them. Very far. So far that it seemed like a miniature village, a child's toy, and not a place where grown-up men suffered and died.

"Geneva, how far? Where is he? Have we missed him."

"No, no!" Geneva shouted back.

They kept racing. Suddenly, ahead, Amanda saw an embankment of fir trees. Rich and green, they covered the landscape.

"Just ahead!" Geneva called.

"Thank God!" Amanda shouted in reply. She forced her tired horse to draw close beside Geneva's. "There? In the woods?"

Geneva nodded, her lashes falling over her beautiful eyes to form crescents on her cheeks. "Yes, Amanda, in the woods."

The woods . . .

The thicket of green pines suddenly came alive. Horsemen came bounding out from both directions, horsemen wearing the bright red colors of a British cavalry unit.

Amanda drew her horse quickly to a halt, determined to turn back and flee as quickly as possible. "Geneva, the British! We've got to escape! It's the damned redcoats—"

"There is no escape! Look around. We're surrounded."

They were surrounded. There was no direction in which she could escape.

"The British—"

"I know," Geneva said quietly.

Stunned, Amanda stared at her friend. Then she understood. "It's you. You're Highness—I never really was! You called Robert and Father to Cameron Hall, you've been sleeping with my cousin for whatever information you could gain. You—you whore!"

"Tsk, tsk, Lady Cameron!"

Amanda swung her nag of a horse around as a rider approached her. Well clad, well fed, sitting his horse very well, it was Robert Tarryton. "What a horrid thing to say to an old friend!" he taunted Amanda.

"Traitor!" Amanda snapped to Geneva, spitting toward the ground.

"Traitor! Ah, no, milady. Geneva is not the traitor—you

are. You should be frightened. We hang traitors, you know. Ah, but a lovely lady? Maybe not. You're much too useful. You see, my love, with you my prisoner, I just might get your husband at last. And maybe a few more of your illustrious patriots. Eh, love? I might even manage to pick off the entire Continental Army."

"Never. You'll never beat them, Robert. Never."

"They are dying. They are beating themselves."

"No. You don't understand, do you? It isn't guns—it isn't even in battles. The revolution is in the heart of the people, and you can never take the heart, Robert. Not you, not Howe, not Cornwallis, not King George."

"Brave words, Amanda. Let's go. I'm willing to bet that I can nab a victim or two for the hangman. Hurry back, Geneva. It's time now to bring Lord Cameron for his lady."

They had led her here with lies. They would bring Eric out in the same manner.

She couldn't let it happen.

She dug hard into the flanks of her horse, wrenching the reins around. The animal shrieked out and reared up. Amanda slashed the reins about, catching Robert across the face with length of them as he tried to lunge for her. He faltered as leather stips whipped his face and Amanda's horse bolted, then lunged forward.

"Get her!" Tarryton commanded.

She tried. The valiant little horse tried. But ten horsemen were bearing down on her. A red-coated rider suddenly jumped forward. Caught in his arms, she was brought down, down into the snow with the soldier firmly upon her. Flakes were in her mouth and nose and eyes. Coughing, she fought for breath.

Then rough hands were upon her as Robert Tarryton dragged her to her feet. When she stood he slapped her hard. "Bitch!" he accused her with a quiet smile. Then he wrenched her forward to where his own mount waited. He set her swiftly upon it and mounted in a leap behind her.

His whisper was chilling against her. "I'm just wondering, Amanda, whether to settle my score first with your husband—or with you. We do have a score to settle, mi-lady, and I've imagined endless ways of just how it will be settled!"

"He'll kill you!" Amanda promised on a whisper.

Tarryton broke into dry laughter. He lashed his horse's haunches pitilessly. "No, he'll kill you. You've always been a traitor to him. And here's just another occasion of your treachery. Before I hang him, Amanda, love, I will be sure to let him know that you have been very cleverly planning his demise for the longest time!"

XIX ❦

Eric had just returned to the hut after extensive drilling of the troops with Von Steuben when he heard his name called hysterically from outside. That the place seemed very empty and cold without Amanda about added to his feeling of icy anxiety as he hurried to open the door.

Geneva was practically falling from one of the broken-down old nags that had toughly survived the winter. Damien was rushing over from the blacksmith's to catch her as she fell.

"Damien, oh, thank God! And Eric!"

"What's happened?" Damien demanded.

"Bring her in," Eric urged. "Out of the cold."

In seconds Geneva was inside, sipping brandy, a blanket wrapped about her shoulders. "She insisted that we search for food. Amanda. She thought that we could contribute the men by scouring the country ourselves. Then she

. . . Eric, she's alive but I think that her leg is broken. She needs you desperately."

Cold . . . she was lying out in the cold, shivering, hurt, probably in horrid pain. There was a storm coming too. If the snows came on too densely, they might never find her, she might perish in her attempts to prove herself a loyal patriot . . .

"Dear God!" he whispered aloud, and then he was in motion. "Damien, tell Frederick to arrange for a wagon. Geneva, can you tell me where she is? How to reach her? Frederick will need you to guide him, and I must get to her with blankets and brandy. The cold is so very bitter!"

"Of course, of course—" Geneva said, rising.

But then the door swung open. Jacques Bisset stood in the doorway, towering and dark, a mask of fury upon his face as he stared at Geneva.

"The woman is lying," he said flatly.

"What?" Eric demanded sharply.

"The woman is lying."

"How dare you!" Geneva gasped. "Eric! Damien! You are not going to listen this—this—frog servant! And take his word over mine?"

There was something in her tone of voice that Eric didn't like at all. He smiled slowly, leaning back against the wall. "I have known Jacques most of my life, Geneva. He has never lied to me. Jacques, tell me quickly, what is the truth of this?"

"I followed them. Lady Geneva came here and urged Amanda with her. I followed them when they rode out into the snow. I kept my eye upon it all when they were ambushed by a troop of redcoats. It was planned, Lord Cameron. It was a planned kidnapping."

Eric felt as if his heart were catapulting to his gut and there lay bleeding. His mouth dry, he demanded, "Who, Jacques? Who has taken her?"

"Tarryton. Lord Robert Tarryton. She was lured to your ˌde, and now you are being lured to hers. I didn't know ˌ̣at to do! I could not bear to leave her with them, alone ˌ̣he snow, yet I could not help her unless I came back to ˌ you. She is the bait, Lord Cameron. The bait to lure you to your death." He hesitated, staring at Geneva. If eyes could kill, Eric thought, Geneva would have been lying in blood, slain with daggers through the core of her heart.

Damien backed away from the woman. The fire burned low in the little hut, smoke and soot seemed heavy on the air. Then he took a step toward her. She backed away from him, toward the wall.

"It's a lie!" she cried out. "He's lying and I don't know why! I can't begin to understand—"

"I can!" Eric interrupted harshly. He strode past Damien, wrenching Geneva around by the shoulders. "It was you. You were the one to see to it that Nigel Sterling and Robert Tarryton knew about the arms kept at Cameron Hall. It was you."

"No!"

"Yes," Damien said softly. "I told her. I told her while we lay in bed. The bloody whore!" he exclaimed.

Geneva spat at Damien. He cracked her furiously across the cheek with his open palm. Screaming, she cowered on the floor. "Eric, make him stop—"

"What do we do with her, Eric?" Damien asked, his jaw still twisted savagely, his fingers knotting into fists. "God forgive me, and Eric, would that you could forgive me too! The grief that this woman has caused us all with her treachery, and the fool that I was to believe in her!"

Eric caught hold of Geneva's wrists and dragged her back to her feet. "How many men has Tarryton got with him?"

"Twenty thousand," she said defiantly.

He smiled. "Lie like that again, Geneva, and I will give you far greater injury than Damien has managed thus far. In fact . . ."

He paused, smiling at Damien. "Did you ever realize just how vain our dear Lady Geneva is? Her face is her life. Jacques—I know that this will give you great pleasure. Bring the fire poker. We wouldn't be so heathen as to threaten the lady's life—just her beauty."

Geneva's eyes grew wide with disbelief. Damien grabbed her shoulders, turning her toward Jacques. The tall Acadian approached her smiling, the poker in hand, the end of it burning red from its recent thrust into the fire. He drew it closer and closer to her cheek, just below her eyes. She fought Damien's hold furiously. "Eric, you're bluffing! I know that you are bluffing! You will not—" She broke off, screaming, as the heat nearly singed her lashes. "You would not do this!" she cried.

"Well, not usually, no," Eric agreed. "But I love my wife, Geneva, and by heaven and hell, I will have the truth from you now to get her back!"

The poker moved closer. "All right! All right!" Geneva cried out. "They've barely a hundred. General Howe is enjoying his winter in Philadelphia, there are countless balls and teas and he is living quite well. This was Sterling's idea. He wants you—and Robert wants Amanda. They've taken Robert's company and no more. They knew that you would run recklessly to her aid, and they would take whoever accompanied you, a minor coup. Yet a major blow to the Americans and a warning to would-be patriots when the noble Lord Cameron was hanged!"

Eric ignored her biting sarcasm. "What is he planning? Where does he have my wife?"

"There's . . . there's a house. Ten miles from here. It's surrounded by pines. I was supposed to bring you to the pines. The British cavalry were to take you there."

"Jacques, take her to General Washington. He must decide her fate. Damien, call Frederick, have him rouse company A of my Virginia troops. Then come back, and I'll explain my plan."

"Company A!" Geneva laughed. "You're talking about twenty men. They'll all die, you fool."

"Dear Geneva, I did not ask for your opinion! Jacques, for the love of God, get her out of here!"

He wondered if he should have spoken. Jacques wrenched hard on her arm, practically throwing her out into the snow. He heard Geneva exclaim in pain and out-rage, but then she was silent, and he was certain that she ẖared speak no more. She couldn't understand Jacques's ẖsolute fury; she was only aware that the Acadian would ẖ as soon kill her as look at her.

"I caused it, Eric. I caused it all," Damien said, ashamed. "Can you forgive me?"

"I was the one who was blind," Eric said harshly. "I refused to see until it was too late. Let's get Amanda back. That is all that matters."

"They won't hang her, I don't believe that they'll hurt her. Although Tarryton . . ." Damien's voice trailed away. They both knew what Tarryton would do.

"I've always risked the hangman's noose," Eric reminded him. "And she is my life. Without her, not even the future has meaning. Now listen, I think I know how to do this without losing a single man."

To Amanda, the house seemed almost obscenely elegant after the time she'd spent in the wretched hovels at Valley Forge. The fireplace was marble, the ceilings were elegantly molded, and the walls were covered with handsome leather. A rich carpet covered highly polished floorboards, and she sat in a plush wingback chair, a snifter of brandy in her fingers.

Night was coming. Shadows fell upon the snow beyond the windows. Amanda's fingers curved so tightly around her glass that the fragile stem nearly broke.

Robert Tarryton was returning. She heard his footsteps on the floorboards outside the door.

He threw the door open and swaggered in, pausing at the desk to pour himself a shot of whiskey. He smiled pleasantly to her as he took a seat on the edge of it. "I'm so sorry to have neglected you."

Amanda ignored him, staring out the window. How long would it have taken Geneva to have ridden back? How long until Eric came riding for her? Any time now. He would come at any time. And he would be either shot down by the troops surrounding the house, or captured to swing from the rope already tossed over a tree out bac' The rope had been the first torture Robert had u against her. He had dragged her out back and rubb against her cheek, and he had told her what happer man's body functions when the rope tightens a throat.

Then he brought her here, thrust her into the chair, and left her to arrange his murderous trap. She hadn't been alone long. Her father had appeared to offer her brandy. He had assured her that he would listen to delight to every one of her screams when Tarryton returned. "With pleasure, with delight! I had imagined that you would have suffered with Cameron. I intended that you should, but then, like a fool, you fell in love with the bastard. It doesn't matter. You will suffer now."

"Why!" she had demanded furiously. "Why? What in God's name did I ever do to you?"

"You were born, girl. Born of a whore whom I will never forget. This is my revenge. I pray that there is a god, and that there is an afterlife, so that she can look down and see you suffer!"

Then Sterling had left her too. When she had tried to escape through the window, she had discovered it nailed shut. And beyond it walked a sentry, watching her every move.

Now Robert moved across the room, glancing out the window. He ran his hand over the handsome mahogany of the window seat. "They'll have him any minute. They'll have your husband any minute now. I've ordered that he should be brought here first. I want him to see you before he dies."

"You cannot just hang him so! You must have a trial. You—"

"Want to bargain for his life, Amanda?"

She caught her breath, afraid to hear more, desperate to do so. "You haven't got him yet."

"Ah, but I will." He left the window and walked toward her, smiling as she shrank back in the chair. He grabbed hold of her bodice and wrenched it, tearing fabric. She caught his hand, screaming, clawing at his flesh. He drew her up, laughing as her gown gaped open, laughing still as she wildly clawed for his face. Her nails gouged him and laughter left his face. "When I have him, bitch, he's to suffer a long, long time before he dies. I can have set so that he dangles and dangles and slowly death!" He caught hold of her hands, forcing her back toward the fire, nearly snapping her fingers with the force of his hold. When he pressed her against the wall he smiled again. "Nice house, eh? Of course, your Continentals had pretty well stripped it of food and supplies before we came. Seems the owners must have deserted some time ago. You should see the bedroom. There are silk sheets on a huge bed with the softest mattress you've ever touched. You're used to luxury, though. That's why I thought maybe it should be right here. On the floor, against the wall. You shouldn't be taken in luxury like a lover—no, because you turned on me. You teased and taunted and beckoned—and then you turned on me. So I'm going to have you like a whore. Just like a whore. Right here, and right in front of your husband."

She screamed, twisting her face, praying for death as he reached into her torn bodice and wrapped her fingers around her breast. "I'm going to do this right in front of him—"

Tarryton broke off at a knock on the door. He did not take his hands off of Amanda but called sharply, "Come in!"

She tried to fight him again, kicking, twisting, shoving. But then the fight left her, and she went numb with fear and horror.

Two men with hats low upon their brows dragged Eric into the room. His shirt was bloodied, his hat was gone, his frock coat torn from him. He stood before her, tall and defiant, his eyes deadly, his arms locked behind his back by the men who held him.

"Eric! Welcome!" Robert said. "I was just talking with your wife. No, let's be honest here, we're among old friends. I was just enjoying your wife."

Eric swore violently.

"You're going to hang, Cameron. Within seconds. You're going to hang, and I'm going to watch you, and I'm going to make Mandy watch too."

"You're a dead man, Tarryton."

"No, sir. You're a dead man."

"No!" Amanda cried out. She looked from Eric's passionate, hate-filled gaze to Robert. "Don't kill him. I'll do anything. Anything at all. Please—"

"Amanda!" Eric roared.

"I'll trade my life for his, anything!"

"You won't have that opportunity. How much of your wife do you want to see, Cameron? One last glance of at her throat, at her breast? At my hand upon her—"

"You are dead, Tarryton! Now!" Eric thundered.

Eric shook off the arms holding him and slipped a sword from the scabbard of one of the men beside him. When the redcoat raised his head, Amanda gasped. He was no enemy, but Frederick.

Tarryton dropped hold of Amanda, screaming for his guards. Instantly men flooded along the hallways. Something hurtled through the window, rolling upon the floor. It was Damien. He leapt to his feet, sword in his hand, his knees bent, ready for the fight.

Men flooded in. Amanda stood flat against the wall, holding her dress together at the bodice, still stunned as Robert and Eric set to deadly combat before her. They parried with a clash of steel, they backed away, they met as tight as dancers again, steel clenched together in a battle of strength and wills. Robert fell back, tossing a chair into Eric's path. Eric leapt over the obstacle. His fury led him. Coming before Robert, he thrust toward him with a shuddering blow. Robert's sword flew high in the air, landing at Amanda's feet. She knelt down and grabbed it. Eric held the tip of his sword against Robert's throat. "How dearly I would love to run you through! But what a prize you would be for General Washington!"

"Amanda, get their small arms!" Damien called to her suddenly. Damien, Frederick, and the young captain with them had bested the British guards. Two men lay dead, and two stood still and silent while Damien and Frederick held their swords upon them. Amanda ran to do as she had been beckoned. With her back to the empty doorway, she suddenly felt cold steel against her own neck.

"My, my, gentlemen! What a ruckus over naught!" came a pleasant voice.

Nigel. Nigel Sterling. Her father was behind her again,

his arm wrapped about her, his small dagger digging into her throat. Damien looked to Eric, who stared cold and frozen at Sterling.

Robert Tarryton laughed and shoved the sword from his throat, rubbing the sore spot where the tip had dug into his flesh. "Cameron, you will hang! Unless I can find a way to crucify you!"

"But one life to give for your country, eh, Cameron? And one life to give for your wife," Sterling said pleasantly. "No swordsman could take you, Cameron. Seems it was only love and beauty needed to down you all the while. Eh, my dear daughter? Well, perhaps we shouldn't play around here any longer. Lord Cameron must be hanged and quickly, and, my dear daughter, I intend to see that you thoroughly enjoy the spectacle—"

Suddenly Sterling went silent. Amanda could not turn to see behind him, but she heard the strong voice with the deep tenor that spoke next, the voice with the trace of French within it, cool and furious and ruthless. "Take your hands off of her, you filthy pig!"

It was Jacques Bisset.

"I'll kill her. I'll rip open her throat without a thought," Sterling ground out. And he would. Amanda could feel the chill of the steel, closer and closer against her throat, so sharp, so cold, cold like death. . . .

"Pig!" Jacques swore in French. Then, to Amanda's amazement, the grip on her went lax. She stepped forward, desperately rubbing her throat, then crying out as she watched her father fall. His eyes were wide—his arms, at the last, reached out to her. Blood-soaked, he fell against her. Horrified, she moved away. She saw Jacques then, standing behind Sterling's fallen body. Tall and immobile, his dark eyes devoid of emotion. He looked at her. Emotion returned to him. "He had to die."

"Bloody bastard—" Tarryton suddenly roared. He lunged forward, trying to capture Eric's sword. Eric barely flicked his wrist, and then Robert had fallen too. He had thrust himself upon the blade.

"It was your choice to die!" Eric murmured, drawing back his sword. He looked to Amanda, reaching out hand to her with an awkward smile. "We've got to go, we've got to hurry—"

A new thunder of footsteps on the hallway floor alerted everyone to his meaning. The troops from the pines were coming back, trying to ascertain what had happened.

"Amanda! Out the window!" Eric urged her. She ran to him. He caught hold of her waist and lifted her through the shattered pane. He paused upon the windowsill, then together they fell into the deep snow below them, rolling and rolling. She heard Damien behind them, and then Frederick and the captain. "Run!" Eric urged her, dragging her to her feet. "Run!" He held her hand. The snowdrifts were so high! The British were behind them, and he was pulling her onward and onward. Bitter cold assailed her, the snow rose to her waist, and walking, much less running, was nearly impossible.

"Eric!" she screamed, falling. He fell down with her. They had hit an embankment again, and they were rolling and rolling. Tears stung her eyes and fell icily to her cheeks as they ceased to roll at last, as he rose over her, meeting her eyes. She clutched his shoulders, and she returned his anguished stare. "Oh, Eric! There is but one life! And if it is over, dear God, I would have you know, my one life I would gladly give for you—"

"For you," he agreed, smiling, "and this country."

She kissed him fervently. If the British were about to come, she would seize this last sweet taste of his lips.

"One life . . . to spend with you. No matter how brief, no matter how long, it has been a fire of warmth and splendor."

"Amanda, I love you."

"I love you!"

"Amanda, it isn't over."

"What?"

"I've troops waiting in the forest. I wanted the men to follow us. Indeed, my love, we've got to walk again. We've got to reach the men."

"Oh! You made me say all of those things—"

He smiled, tenderly, handsomely. The rogue, the gentleman, his eyes touched her with a love she could not deny. "But weren't they true? But one life, my love, and freely, eagerly, would I give it to you!"

She laughed. She wrapped her arms around him. "Oh, Eric! It was Geneva—"

"I know."

"Poor Damien!"

"He is a rugged lad. He will survive."

"My father is dead."

Eric hesitated, then he stood, dragging her to her feet. Up the ledge, they could hear the clash of steel. A musket exploded in a volley, then several others answered as if in reply. Eric grasped Amanda's hand. "Come on, I'm getting you up on a horse and out of here."

"I'm not leaving without you!" She panted, following him up the snow-covered decline.

"You'll do what—"

He broke off. They had reached the top of the crest just in time to see that it was over. At least twenty of the red-coats lay dead in the snow. Others were disappearing behind the trees, running. Damien was letting loose with a wild Virginia battle cry.

Eric walked out into the snow and surveyed the scene. "The boots, lads. We need their boots for our own. Then, if we can break through the ground, we'll bury the dead. Frederick! Take my lady back to camp, please."

"But, Eric—" she started.

He caught her shoulders and kissed her lips. "Please, Amanda. If you wait, Damien, Jacques, and I will be back as soon as possible. It's time we all had a talk."

Her eyes widened. He was very serious. Her curiosity and wonder were so great that she could not think to argue any longer.

"All right," she agreed. "But you all hurry!"

She turned about, thanking Frederick for his coat as he slipped it around her shoulder and then taking his arm.

"I didn't think that she'd ever leave!" Damien said "Feisty little wench, eh?"

Amanda was about to swirl around to tell her cous what she thought of him, but her husband was answer him already.

"Patriots are like that," Eric said casually.

"Aye, you're right, my lord! Aye, you are right!" Damien agreed. They laughed together. Amanda did not look back. When Frederick set her up atop a horse, he was smiling, and she smiled in return.

The men returned to Valley Forge within a few hours. Amanda sat at the table in the hut and stared at the three of them, Eric, Damien, and Jacques, as they stood before her, something like errant schoolboys.

Eric cleared his voice to speak, but then Jacques stepped forward. "I killed your father, Amanda."

"He meant to kill me, Jacques," she said quietly. "He—he meant it. He always despised me."

Then Jacques went silent. Eric cleared his throat again. "Amanda, Nigel wasn't your father."

"What?" Astonished, she leapt to her feet.

"But—"

Damien slipped an arm about her, coming down upon his haunches by her side as he led her to sit again. "Didn't you ever wonder that a man could be so cold to his own flesh and blood? I had heard the rumors, of course, but—I remember your mother, Amanda. Just vaguely. She was always so kind and so sweet, and so—"

"Giving," Jacques interrupted him. He looked at Amanda, but he seemed to see beyond her, to another time and another place. "She was beautiful and gentle and sweet, and her voice was like a nightingales, and she cared for everyone about her, be they slave or freedman, worker or gentry. She—she bought my indentured time when I arrived from Nova Scotia."

He paused, hesitating a long moment. His dark eyes fluttered over Amanda. "I fell in love with her," he said, his voice cracking. "And she fell in love with me. We meant to slip away to Louisiana, but he caught us. He left me for dead. I was taken in by Lord Cameron's grandfather, and over the years my body healed, but it wasn't until Danielle arrived that I remembered all that my life had been."

Amanda discovered that she couldn't breathe. She tried to form words. "What—what do you mean?"

"Amanda," Eric said, speaking quietly at last. "Jacques is your father."

There was silence. Dead silence, then Jacques started to speak, his French mingling with his English in his eagerness. "I could not tell you, I did not even tell Lord Cameron, I was so afraid that you would be horrified to know that you were not the daughter of a great lord but the child of a common laborer, a man who worked the land. But I saw, *mon Dieu*! I saw what he did to you, and I had vowed that I would kill them. *Mais, ma petite*, not even then did I mean to tell you, but your husband insisted—I am so sorry. I have loved you greatly from afar, and my life has been made rich just to see you, just to be privileged to touch my grandchildren, to live in the shadow cast by the bounty of the hall. . . ."

Amanda felt numb. So very numb! He was watching her with such anguish, and Eric was staring at her, and Damien . . .

She leapt to her feet, throwing her arms around Jacques. With a glad cry, she showered his cheeks with kisses. "My father! *Mon père!* Oh, thank God, thank God! Eric, how could you have known, how could have guessed and not told me!"

"Well, I—"

"You are not so horrified then?" Jacques asked her, his hands trembling as he held her.

"Horrified? Horrified! Oh, no, I am so thrilled and so very proud! My father was not some monster who lived to take revenge upon me because my mother could not bear his touch! He is tall and handsome and brave and wonderful, and he loves me. He loves me! Oh, Eric, isn't that what matters the most?"

Eric, relieved and greatly pleased, leaned back against the mantel, grinning. "Oh, of course, Amanda." It was both wonderful and poignant to watch the tears hovering in her eyes, to see the wonder upon her face. And Jacques. The Acadian who had always been there for her, loving her, never thinking to speak the truth, when the truth might have caused her pain. "Love—and the man," Eric agreed. "We're fighting for a new world here. For rights, where it is the measure of a man that matters, and nothing more. And I would say, Monsieur Bisset—as a man who has known you since he wore knee breeches—that there is no man of finer measure, or greater measure. No man whom I would rather call father-in-law."

Eric reached out for Jacques's hand. Jacques looked from his daughter's red head to the hand outstretched to him. Their hands met. Then Eric cleared his throat and smiled at Damien, who was staring on delightedly. "Maybe we should give them a few minutes."

"Maybe we should."

Neither Jacques nor Amanda noticed as they left. Amanda was crying, tears of joy. "Danielle! Danielle is my aunt! Oh, how delightful. I cannot wait to see her again."

Eric left her alone until very late, and then returned to the hut. The main room was empty, and so Eric hurried on into the bedroom.

Amanda was there, and for a moment he thought that she slept, she was so very still. He walked over to the narrow bed and discovered that her beautiful emerald eyes were open, that they had a dreamlike quality to them. Her lips were slightly parted in a beautiful rose smile and her hair was splayed about her in ripples of sable and fire, sweeping over the bare and naked beauty of her ivory shoulders. He knelt down by her. As her eyes focused on him, her smile broadened.

"Hello," he said.

"Hello," she returned.

"So . . ."

"Oh, Eric!" She wrapped her arms around him and held him close. "Thank you! Thank you for so much! You've not only given me love, but you've given me our beautiful children, and our home, and now you've even given me a father!"

He chuckled softly. "Well, I can't really take credit for all of that—"

"And you've given me a country, Eric. Today I knew it. I knew it so thoroughly! I knew that I would die for you, and then I discovered that I would die for this cause too. I understand everything that meant so much to you, what it was worth fighting for, worth dying for. . . . It's meant to be, Eric! Not a land for titled hogs such as Nigel Sterling, but for men like my real father. Quiet, dignified, determined to wrest the very best from the land. To give to it. Oh, Eric! I cannot tell you how happy I am! You cannot imagine what it was like to wonder how a parent could hate you so fervently! And he's wonderful, isn't he? Jacques is wonderful!"

"Yes, love, he is wonderful."

Her smile faded. "What of Geneva?"

"They'll hold her in Baltimore until they can see to it that she's shipped off to England."

"It was her all along!"

"Well—almost all along," Eric said.

Amanda flushed. "All right, I was guilty, somewhat. But you sent me to France because of her! You—"

"I most humbly beg your forgiveness, my love."

"Really? You?" She smiled. "I cannot imagine you humble at all. Nor begging."

"Well, maybe not."

She wrapped her arms around him. "But the words sounded sweet anyway."

"Would you like to hear more words that sound sweet?"

"Mmm . . ."

He stood up, cast aside his cloak, and quickly stripped down. He ripped away the blanket and she was cold, but then his body settled over hers, and she thought that she had never know such sweet and beautiful warmth. He caught her face between his hands and began kissing her.

"It's over," she whispered between trysts with his lips.

He paused, looking down at her very seriously. "Amanda, it is far from over."

"The war. It seems so very grim, doesn't it? Dark and grim and frightening. But for us, my love, it is over. Our war is over."

Eric smiled. "Aye, love, our war is over. No matter what time and distance should take from us again, we can never really be parted because we have found our peace. Love—and trust."

She smiled. "Love—and trust."

He started to kiss her again. She caught hold of his shoulders and forced his eyes to hers. "Did you really love me from the very beginning?"

"Mmm."

"Liar!"

"Well, I coveted you with all of my being. How is that?"

"You said—"

He twined his fingers with hers, bracing her hands tightly at the sides of her head. "Amanda!" he wailed.

"All right!" She closed her eyes. She felt the pulse of his body naked against hers, the heat, the wonder of muscle and sinew and hard masculinity. She wondered if it was all right to pray, to thank God, in the midst of such sweet splendor.

She opened her eyes. "I do surrender!" she promised him.

"You do?" Silver mischief rode his eyes like clouds dancing in the night. "Then, my love, I gladly conquer all."

"Eric!"

His laugh warmed and roused her, his breath taunted her ear wickedly. "Love, I surrender all that I am, my heart and my soul, this night! Life has been tempest, and will be again, but through any of my rages and storms, my love, you will know: I have surrendered."

She sighed, and she felt his kiss.

Thank you, dear God, for all of it! For giving me Jacques as my father . . .

She felt his hands upon her breast, his fingers stroking her thigh.

Thank you for the twins . . .

His kiss stroked her shoulder, her abdomen. His flesh against hers was so erotic she could scarcely think, scarcely breathe.

Thank you, God, for this man . . .

She gave up. His touch upon her was flagrantly bold and intimate, daring, defying. A Cameron touch.

"Amanda . . ." he whispered her name.

She gave himself entirely over to his touch. "My love, let

the tempest swirl, the rages fly, I care not! Just so long as you love me, that is all I could ever crave."

"And that is all that I shall ever do," he vowed.

And with himself, his warmth, his need, his love, he set forth to prove his words in every way.

Epilogue

CHRISTMAS 1783

There was a soft fall of snow upon the ground, but Amanda had seen the lone rider coming slowly down the path and she had instantly recognized the huge black horse. Knowing the animal, she was certain that the bundled rider had to be her husband.

"He's home!" she called joyously to Danielle. She left the window and went racing past the pictures in the gallery, and then down the long curving staircase, and to the front doors. Richard and Cassidy both went to the hallway to watch her; Jacques, whittling by the fire in the parlor, just smiled.

Amanda ignored the fall of the soft light flakes that fell upon her face and gown, and she ran on. Eric saw her. He reined in on Joshua and slipped down from his mount. H patted the animal on the haunches, and Joshua trotted on his own. He knew the way home to the stables. J Eric could reach home by himself now. Home. God been a long war.

"Eric!"

He started running too. The distance be shortened, and then he could see her face c eled and exquisite, the years had never seemed to cost her anything. Maybe her beauty had always really been in the emotion in her eyes. He could see them. Emerald, dancing, moist with tears, moist with love.

"Amanda!"

They came together. He caught her up high in his arms and twirled her around. Mist rose between as they breathed in the cold. Her hands were icy; she wore no gloves.

"It's done, then?"

He nodded. It had really been done for some time. The fighting had gone on after that awful winter at Valley Forge, but Von Steuben's drilling had changed the army. They had become an awesome force. And though the British had managed to take Charleston, the south had hung on through the efforts of men like Francis Marion, the renowned "Swamp Fox," and through the talents of men like Nathanael Greene and Daniel Morgan. Finally, in '81, the war had returned to Virginian soil.

Benedict Arnold, Washington's once-trusted general, had been heavily involved. Arnold had married a Tory girl named Margaret Shippen when he took command of Philadelphia. Perhaps she had been the one to turn his heart. Maybe he had been disgruntled over his military progress —several times Congress had neglected him when promoting brigadier generals to major generals. No one really knew. But in the end it was discovered that he had communicated with the British for sixteen months. In 1780 he was in command of West Point, and he planned to surrender the fort to the British general Sir Henry Clinton. His treachery was discovered when British major John Andrew was captured carrying a mesage from Arnold about he surrender.

The news had aged Washington, Eric knew. But West ＊ had been saved. They hadn't caught Arnold, though. ad burst in on Peggy, and she had put on what Eric nsidered to be one of the finest performances of lad in a frothy nightgown, she had cried and adness. Washington, ever the gentleman, had ith the distraught female.

Arnold had escaped to New York.

The British Major Andre, Arnold's comrade, liked and respected by both sides, a gallant man to the very last, was hanged by the patriot forces. It was a sad occasion. And as a British officer, Arnold had entered Virginia to burn Richmond. With Phipps he went about further destruction and marched south to join forces with Cornwallis. Lafayette was sent to Richmond, and then Von Steuben was also sent to Virginia. Cornwallis arrived in Petersburg in May to take command of the British forces in Virginia. In a well-planned ambush near Jamestown Ford, Cornwallis caught General Anthony Wayne's brigade by surprise, but the Americans rallied, fought bravely, counterattacked, and then retreated in good order. By August Cornwallis was moving to Yorktown.

It had been a frightening time for both Amanda and Eric as the British moved so close to home. But the British sidestepped Cameron Hall, coming very near, but never touching the property. Eric had ordered Amanda to leave —she had not. She had sent the twins north with Danielle, but she and Jacques had stayed, burying the silver, the plate, and, most important, the portraits in the hall. Eric had managed to arrive just in time to find her dirty-faced, tramping down the last of the soil cover over the cache they had made to the west of the house.

With Washington's consent and approval, Eric joined his forces with the Virginia militia, Washington himself was in New York, conferring with the French general Rochambeau. They knew that the French Admiral de Grasse was in the West Indies. De Grasse offered his services, and Washington knew that if they could concentrate the sea strength with the land force, he could beat Cornwallis. By September the Americans had Yorktown under siege. Amanda had been with Eric at the end. Cornwallis, hoping to receive reinforcements from Clinton, retired to his i̶ ner fortifications, allowing the American siege equipm̶ to bombard him.

Benjamin Franklin's efforts had more than paid ᴏ̶ French had entered the fray in 1778, and at Y̶ Virginia, Franco-American forces stormed two doubts, and new batteries were established. No one would ever forget waiting through that night! The cunning of the operations, the care, the secrecy, the darkness, the hand-to-hand combat!

On October 17 Cornwallis opened negotiations for surrender. Washington gave him two days for written proposals, but it was to be total surrender. No one had forgotten or forgiven how ignominiously the British had forced the Americans from Charleston.

Cornwallis, however, was determined not to surrender to Washington. Pretending illness, he had his second in command turn over his sword. The British and Hessians stacked their arms. Rather aptly, to the tune of the "World Turned Upside Down," with the American flag rising in the breeze, the troops marched by in surrender. Amanda stood beside Eric as it happened, and he knew that they felt the same thing, that their hearts beat in unison.

The United States of America was, at last, a reality. It was all over but the paper signing. It had been hard and brutal and often terrifying, but now the world was theirs.

But the "paper signing" had taken some time. The Treaty of Versailles had come about by the beginning of 1783, but Congress had taken until April 15 to ratify it, and not even then had Eric been able to come home for good.

Only now . . .

He stood back from Amanda and smiled. "The last of the British left New York, and George said his final good-byes to his officers at Fraunces' Tavern on December fourth. There were tears in his eyes. And in mine, Amanda, I am quite certain. In it all, my love, I would say that his courage and determination kept us going when little else did."

Amanda held his cheeks between her hands and kissed him. "He is a hero, an American hero," she agreed. "But then, so are you, my love, and you are home at last! For good, forever!"

He nodded and swept her hungrily into his arms again, fingers threading through the rich length of her hair. It been ten years, he reflected, ten years since that springtime in Boston when the harbor had turned into

a teapot. Ten long years. His own dark head was beginning to turn gray, but Amanda's hair was still a cascade of
flame, as evocative as her smile, as beautiful as her eyes.

It had been some fight to keep her, he reflected. Just as it
had been some fight to earn the independence that was
now theirs. And of course, once the fight was won, there
was still so much to learn. Marriage was like an odyssey in
which they stumbled and learned, and this new country
would be an odyssey, and they would have to stumble and
learn. And yet his wife, looking at him now with her emerald eyes and her tender smile, was all the more precious to
him for the tempests they had endured.

And this great country they had forged would have to
endure tempests too and yet be all the greater for it.

"You're freezing!" he said suddenly, feeling her hands.
He swept his coat from about himself and set it upon her
shoulders.

"Christmas dinner is almost on the table and the hall is
festooned with holly and ribbons," Amanda said. She
smiled.

"Father! Father!"

He looked toward the house. The twins were on the
steps with Danielle and Jacques behind them. Six years
old now, they were dressed for Christmas, young Jamie
handsome in a stylish frock coat, buckled shoes, and fine
knee breeches, and Lenore a picture of her mother, a dazzling redhead already in a beautifully laced gown.

He glanced at Amanda. "They've grown too quickly, and
I've missed so much of it."

She smiled ever more sweetly as the twins came running down the path. He had been home briefly in September, yet they seemed to have grown since then.

"I think," Amanda told him, "that you're going to have
second chance at watching growth."

Lenore and Jamie both pitched into his arms. K
and hugging them, he didn't quite catch her word
scooped up a child in each arm, he stared at her

"What?"

"Well, I haven't the faintest idea of wheth

twins again or not, but by June, my love, you should get your chance to watch a little Cameron grow."

"Really?"

"Really!"

He managed to kiss her exuberantly with the twins between them.

"*Alors!*" Danielle shouted from the porch. "Come in! *Il fait froid!*"

"Run, little ones," Eric told the twins, setting them upon the ground again. He set his arm about Amanda and they walked toward the house.

Dinner was a joyous occasion. And when the twins had been tucked up in bed, it was still a warm and wonderful night, for all of the household had gathered in the parlor, family and servants, and Eric tried to speak lightly of some of what had happened. "Think of it! We've 'cocktails' now! They say the mixture of spirits and sugar and bitters was born in a tavern in 1776, when barmaid Betsy Flannagan gave a tipsy patron a glass with the brew stirred up by a cockfeather! And we've ghost stories galore. They say a buxom young woman named Nancy Coates fell madly in love with Mad Anthony Wayne, and cast herself into the river when she discovered him returning to Fort Ticonderoga with a society girl. They say that Nancy still haunts the fort, that she walks about bedraggled and wet and calls for Anthony by the light of the moon."

Amanda arched a brow to him in disbelief. Then she leaned toward him, whispering softly, "There is a woman here, alive and well, who haunts your hall, calling your name! Eric! Eric! See there? That woman is going up to bed now and shall wait to haunt you, should you come soon enough."

He laughed aloud. Amanda was up, pausing by Jacques, ~sing the top of his head. "Good night, Father, good ~, all!" Gracefully she swept from the parlor.

~l, then!" Eric rose. "I'll say my good nights too. Danielle, Cassidy, Pierre—Richard."

~ stopped him, standing in the doorway. "Lord ~ is good to have you home, sir. Good to have

Eric nodded. "Thank you. Thank you, all of you."

He left the parlor and he started up the stairs, and when he came to the picture gallery, he paused. He looked at all the noble faces staring down at him, and he smiled rather wistfully. "Well, milords, I think that I am home for good. There is still the forging of a country to take place. And I'm not so sure that I'm 'Lord' Cameron anymore. That title came from the estates in England. But I am still Eric Cameron, gentleman of Virginia. I rather like that. I hope that you all understand."

They would, he thought. They had forged the land, and now he was hoping to forge the new country. They didn't seem too distressed as they stared down upon them.

"I really don't know what the future will bring," he continued. "There's going to be so much to do to unite thirteen very different states. Why, Patrick Henry told me that being governor here in Virginia was a nightmare at first, for laws were so difficult to form, and because they must be made so very carefully. And so I wonder at the future. I promise you, though, this hall with survive—"

"Eric. Oh, Eric . . ."

He heard her voice, coming from the bedroom. Soft and sweet and most certainly—haunting. Very haunting. His grin deepened as he looked at the portraits. Particularly at the portrait of his wife. Ever challenging, ever lovely, her sweet smile as haunting as the tone of her voice.

He bowed low to the portraits. "My lords, I'm afraid that the future will have to wait. I, Eric Cameron, gentleman of Virginia, am most earnestly interested in the present!"

And with that he turned about and hurried down the hall, into the bedroom and into her arms. This was the present, and together they had earned their freedom, their peace, and their home . . .

And the splendor of the night together.

Indeed, the future could now wait!